GEEK LOVE

Katherine Dunn

ABACUS

ABACUS

First published in Great Britain by Hamish Hamilton Ltd in 1989
Published in Abacus in 1990 by Sphere Books Ltd
Reprinted 1992, 1993, 1995, 1996, 1997, 1998, 1999, 2001,
2002, 2004, 2005, 2006, 2007

ISBN 978-0-349-10086-9

Papers used by Abacus are natural, recyclable products made from
wood grown in sustainable forests and certified in accordance with
the rules of the Forest Stewardship Council.

Printed in England by Clays Ltd, St Ives plc
Paper supplied by Hellefoss AS, Norway

Abacus
An imprint of
Little, Brown Book Group
Brettenham House
Lancaster Place
London WC2E 7EN

A Member of the Hachette Livre Group of Companies

www.littlebrown.co.uk

For
Eli Malachy Dunn Dapolonia

This thing of darkness I Acknowledge mine.

— *Prospero*, The Tempest, *5.1.275–6*

Contents

BOOK IV **Becoming the Dragon**

BOOK I
Midnight Gardener

1

The Nuclear Family:
His Talk, Her Teeth

When your mama was the geek, my dreamlets,' Papa would say, 'she made the nipping off of noggins such a crystal mystery that the hens themselves yearned toward her, waltzing around her, hypnotized with longing. "Spread your lips, sweet Lil," they'd chuck, "and show us your choppers!"'

This same Crystal Lil, our star-haired mama, sitting snug on the built-in sofa that was Arty's bed at night, would chuckle at the sewing in her lap and shake her head. 'Don't piffle to the children, Al. Those hens ran like whiteheads.'

Nights on the road this would be, between shows and towns in some campground or pull-off, with the other vans and trucks and trailers of Binewski's Carnival Fabulon ranged up around us, safe in our portable village.

After supper, sitting with full bellies in the lamp glow, we Binewskis were supposed to read and study. But if it rained the story mood would sneak up on Papa. The hiss and tick on the metal of our big living van distracted him from his papers. Rain on a show night was catastrophe. Rain on the road meant talk, which, for Papa, was pure pleasure.

'It's a shame and a pity, Lil,' he'd say, 'that these offspring of yours should only know the slumming summer geeks from Yale.'

'Princeton, dear,' Mama would correct him mildly. 'Randall will be a sophomore this fall. I believe he's our first Princeton boy.'

3

We children would sense our story slipping away to trivia. Arty would nudge me and I'd pipe up with, 'Tell about the time when Mama was the geek!' and Arty and Elly and Iphy and Chick would all slide into line with me on the floor between Papa's chair and Mama.

Mama would pretend to be fascinated by her sewing and Papa would tweak his swooping mustache and vibrate his tangled eyebrows, pretending reluctance. 'Welllll ...' he'd begin, 'it was a long time ago ...'

'Before we were born!'

'Before ...' he'd proclaim, waving an arm in his grandest ringmaster style, 'before I even dreamed you, my dreamlets!'

'I was still Lillian Hinchcliff in those days,' mused Mama. 'And when your father spoke to me, which was seldom and reluctantly, he called me "Miss."'

'Miss!' we would giggle. Papa would whisper to us loudly, as though Mama couldn't hear, 'Terrified! I was so smitten I'd stutter when I tried to talk to her. "M-M-M-Miss ..." I'd say.'

We'd giggle helplessly at the idea of Papa, the GREAT TALKER, so flummoxed.

'I, of course, addressed your father as *Mister* Binewski.'

'There I was,' said Papa, 'hosing the old chicken blood and feathers out of the geek pit on the morning of July 3rd and congratulating myself for having good geek posters, telling myself I was going to sell tickets by the bale because the weekend of the Fourth is the hottest time for geeks and I had a fine, brawny geek that year. Enthusiastic about the work, he was. So I'm hosing away, feeling very comfortable and proud of myself, when up trips your mama, looking like angelfood, and tells me my geek has done a flit in the night, folded his rags as you might say, and hailed a taxi for the airport. He leaves a note claiming his pop is very sick and he, the geek, must retire from the pit and take his fangs home to Philadelphia to run the family bank.'

'Brokerage, dear,' corrects Mama.

'And with your mama, Miss Hinchcliff, standing there like three scoops of vanilla I can't even cuss! What am I gonna do? The geek posters are all over town!'

'It was during a war, darlings,' explains Mama. 'I forget

which one precisely. Your father had difficulty getting help at that time or he never would have hired me, even to make costumes, as inexperienced as I was.'

'So I'm standing there fuddled from breathing Miss Hinchcliff's Midnight Marzipan perfume and cross-eyed with figuring. I couldn't climb into the pit myself because I was doing twenty jobs already. I couldn't ask Horst the Cat Man because he was a vegetarian to begin with, and his dentures would disintegrate the first time he hit a chicken neck anyhow. Suddenly your mama pops up for all the world like she was offering me sherry and biscuits. "I'll do it, Mr. Binewski," she says, and I just about sent a present to my laundryman.'

Mama smiled sweetly into her sewing and nodded. 'I was anxious to prove myself useful to the show. I'd been with Binewski's Fabulon only two weeks at the time and I felt very keenly that I was on trial.'

'So I says,' interrupts Papa, '"But, miss, what about your teeth?" Meaning she might break 'em or chip 'em, and she smiles wide, just like she's smiling now, and says, "They're sharp enough, I think!"'

We looked at Mama and her teeth were white and straight, but of course by that time they were all false.

'I looked at her delicate little jaw and I just groaned. "No," I says, "I couldn't ask you to ..." but it did flash into my mind that a blonde and lovely geek with legs — I mean your mama has what we refer to in the trade as LEGS — would do the business no real harm. I'd never heard of a girl geek before and the poster possibilities were glorious. Then I thought again, No ... she couldn't ...'

'What your papa didn't know was that I'd watched the geek several times and of course I'd often helped Minna, our cook at home, when she slaughtered a fowl for the table. I had him. He had no choice but to give me a try.'

'Oh, but I was scared spitless when her first show came up that afternoon! Scared she'd be disgusted and go home to Boston. Scared she'd flub the deal and have the crowd screaming for their money back. Scared she'd get hurt ... A chicken could scratch her or peck an eye out quick as a blink.'

'I was quite nervous myself,' nodded Mama.

'The crowd was good. A hot Saturday that was, and the Fourth of July was the Sunday. I was running like a geeked bird the whole day myself, and just had time to duck behind the pit for one second before I stood up front to lead in the mugs. There she was like a butterfly . . .'

'I wore tatters really, white because it shows the blood so well even in the dark of the pit.'

'But such artful tatters! Such low-necked, slit-to-the-thigh, silky tatters! So I took a deep breath and went out to talk 'em in. And in they went. A lot of soldiers in the crowd. I was still selling tickets when the cheers and whistles started inside and the whooping and stomping on those old wood bleachers drew even more people. I finally grabbed a popcorn kid to sell tickets and went inside to see for myself.'

Papa grinned at Mama and twiddled his mustache.

'I'll never forget,' he chuckled.

'I couldn't growl, you see, or snarl convincingly. So I sang,' explained Mama.

'Happy little German songs! In a high, thin voice!'

'Franz Schubert, my dears.'

'She fluttered around like a dainty bird, and when she caught those ugly squawking hens you couldn't believe she'd actually do anything. When she went right ahead and geeked 'em that whole larruping crowd went bonzo wild. There never was such a snap and twist of the wrist, such a vampire flick of the jaws over a neck or such a champagne approach to the blood. She'd shake her star-white hair and the bitten-off chicken head would skew off into the corner while she dug her rosy little fingernails in and lifted the flopping, jittering carcass like a golden goblet, and sipped! Absolutely sipped at the wriggling guts! She was magnificent, a princess, a Cleopatra, an elfin queen! That was your mama in the geek pit.

'People swarmed her act. We built more bleachers, moved her into the biggest top we had, eleven hundred capacity, and it was always jammed.'

'It was fun.' Lil nodded. 'But I felt that it wasn't my true métier.'

'Yeah.' Papa would half frown, looking down at his hands, quieted suddenly.

Feeling the story mood evaporate, one of us children would coax, 'What made you quit, Mama?'

She would sigh and look up from under her spun-glass eyebrows at Papa and then turn to where we were huddled on the floor in a heap and say softly, 'I had always dreamed of flying. The Antifermos, the Italian trapeze clan, joined the show in Abilene and I begged them to teach me.' Then she wasn't talking to us anymore but to Papa. 'And, Al, you know you would never have got up the nerve to ask for my hand if I hadn't fallen and got so bunged up. Where would we be now if I hadn't?'

Papa nodded, 'Yes, yes, and I made you walk again just fine, didn't I?' But his face went flat and smileless and his eyes went to the poster on the sliding door to their bedroom. It was old silvered paper, expensive, with the lone lush figure of Mama in spangles and smile, high-stepping with arms thrown up so her fingers, in red elbow-length gloves, touched the starry letters arching 'CRYSTAL LIL' above her.

My father's name was Aloysius Binewski. He was raised in a traveling carnival owned by his father and called 'Binewski's Fabulon.' Papa was twenty-four years old when Grandpa died and the carnival fell into his hands. Al carefully bolted the silver urn containing his father's ashes to the hood of the generator truck that powered the midway. The old man had wandered with the show for so long that his dust would have been miserable left behind in some stationary vault.

Times were hard and, through no fault of young Al's, business began to decline. Five years after Grandpa died, the once flourishing carnival was fading.

The show was burdened with an aging lion that repeatedly broke expensive dentures by gnawing the bars of his cage; demands for cost-of-living increases from the fat lady, whose food supply was written into her contract; and the midnight defection of an entire family of animal eroticists, taking their donkey, goat, and Great Dane with them.

The fat lady eventually jumped ship to become a model for a magazine called *Chubby Chaser*. My father was left with a cut-rate, diesel-fueled fire-eater and the prospect of a very long stretch in a trailer park outside of Fort Lauderdale.

Al was a standard-issue Yankee, set on self-determination and independence, but in that crisis his core of genius revealed itself. He decided to breed his own freak show.

My mother, Lillian Hinchcliff, was a water-cool aristocrat from the fastidious side of Boston's Beacon Hill, who had abandoned her heritage and joined the carnival to become an aerialist. Nineteen is late to learn to fly and Lillian fell, smashing her elegant nose and her collarbones. She lost her nerve but not her lust for sawdust and honky-tonk lights. It was this passion that made her an eager partner in Al's scheme. She was willing to chip in on any effort to renew public interest in the show. Then, too, the idea of inherited security was ingrained from her childhood. As she often said, 'What greater gift could you offer your children than an inherent ability to earn a living just by being themselves?'

The resourceful pair began experimenting with illicit and prescription drugs, insecticides, and eventually radioisotopes. My mother developed a complex dependency on various drugs during this process, but she didn't mind. Relying on Papa's ingenuity to keep her supplied, Lily seemed to view her addiction as a minor by-product of their creative collaboration.

Their firstborn was my brother Arturo, usually known as Aqua Boy. His hands and feet were in the form of flippers that sprouted directly from his torso without intervening arms or legs. He was taught to swim in infancy and was displayed nude in a big clear-sided tank like an aquarium. His favorite trick at the ages of three and four was to put his face close to the glass, bulging his eyes out at the audience, opening and closing his mouth like a river bass, and then to turn his back and paddle off, revealing the turd trailing from his muscular little buttocks. Al and Lil laughed about it later, but at the time it caused them great consternation as well as the nuisance of sterilizing the tank more often than usual. As the years passed, Arty donned trunks and became more sophisticated, but it's been said, with some truth, that his attitude never really changed.

My sisters, Electra and Iphigenia, were born when Arturo was two years old and starting to haul in crowds. The girls were

Siamese twins with perfect upper bodies joined at the waist and sharing one set of hips and legs. They usually sat and walked and slept with their long arms around each other. They were, however, able to face directly forward by allowing the shoulder of one to overlap the other. They were always beautiful, slim, and huge-eyed. They studied the piano and began performing piano duets at an early age. Their compositions for four hands were thought by some to have revolutionized the twelve-tone-scale.

I was born three years after my sisters. My father spared no expense in these experiments. My mother had been liberally dosed with cocaine, amphetamines, and arsenic during her ovulation and throughout her pregnancy with me. It was a disappointment when I emerged with such commonplace deformities. My albinism is the regular pink-eyed variety and my hump, though pronounced, is not remarkable in size or shape as humps go. My situation was far too humdrum to be marketable on the same scale as my brother's and sisters'. Still, my parents noted that I had a strong voice and decided I might be an appropriate shill and talker for the business. A bald albino hunchback seemed the right enticement toward the esoteric talents of the rest of the family. The dwarfism, which was very apparent by my third birthday, came as a pleasant surprise to the patient pair and increased my value. From the beginning I slept in the built-in cupboard beneath the sink in the family living van, and had a collection of exotic sunglasses to shield my sensitive eyes.

Despite the expensive radium treatments incorporated in his design, my younger brother, Fortunato, had a close call in being born to apparent normalcy. That drab state so depressed my enterprising parents that they immediately prepared to abandon him on the doorstep of a closed service station as we passed through Green River, Wyoming, late one night. My father had actually parked the van for a quick getaway and had stepped down to help my mother deposit the baby in the cardboard box on some safe part of the pavement. At that precise moment the two-week-old baby stared vaguely at my mother and in a matter of seconds revealed himself as not a failure at all, but in fact my parents' masterwork. It was lucky, so they

named him Fortunato. For one reason and another we always
called him Chick.

'Papa,' said Iphy. 'Yes,' said Elly. They were behind his big
chair, four arms sliding to tangle his neck, two faces framed in
smooth black hair peering at him from either side.

'What are you up to, girlies?' He would laugh and put his
magazine down.

'Tell us how you thought of us,' they demanded.

I leaned on his knee and looked into his good heavy face.
'Please, Papa,' I begged, 'tell us the Rose Garden.'

He would puff and tease and refuse and we would coax.
Finally Arty would be sitting in his lap with Papa's arms around
him and Chick would be in Lily's lap, and I would lean against
Lily's shoulder while Elly and Iphy sat cross-legged on the floor
with their four arms behind them like Gothic struts supporting
their hunched shoulders, and Al would laugh and tell the story.

'It was in Oregon, up in Portland, which they call the Rose
City, though I never got in gear to do anything about it until a
year or so later when we were stuck in Fort Lauderdale.'

He had been restless one day, troubled by business boon-
doggles. He drove up into a park on a hillside and got out for a
walk. 'You could see for miles from up there. And there was a
big rose garden with arbors and trellises and fountains. The
paths were brick and wound in and out.' He sat on a step
leading from one terrace to another and stared listlessly at the
experimental roses. 'It was a test garden, and the colors were
... designed. Striped and layered. One color inside the petal
and another color outside.

'I was mad at Maribelle. She was a pinhead who'd been with
your mother and me for a long while. She was trying to hold me
up for a raise I couldn't afford.'

The roses started him thinking, how the oddity of them was
beautiful and how that oddity was contrived to give them value.
'It just struck me — clear and complete all at once — no long
figuring about it.' He realised that children could be designed.
'And I thought to myself, now *that* would be a rose garden
worthy of a man's interest!'

We children would smile and hug him and he would grin around at us and send the twins for a pot of cocoa from the drink wagon and me for a bag of popcorn because the red-haired girls would just throw it out when they finished closing the concession anyway. And we would all be cozy in the warm booth of the van, eating popcorn and drinking cocoa and feeling like Papa's roses.

2

NOTES FOR NOW
The Joy of the Worm

Now Crystal Lil holds the phone receiver clenched against her long flat tit while she howls up the stairwell, 'Forty-one!,' meaning that the red-haired, zit-skinned, defrocked Benedictine in room Number 41 has another phone call and should come running down the three flights of stairs and take this intruding burden off Lil's confused mind. She puts a patented plastic amplifier against the earpiece when she answers the phone and turns the knob on her hearing aid to high and screams, 'What! What!' into the mouthpiece until she gets a number back. That number she will shriek up the mildewed staircase until someone comes down or she gets tired.

I am never sure how deaf she is. She always hears the ring of the pay phone in the hall but she may pick up its vibration in her slipper heels. She is also blind. Her thick, pink plastic glasses project huge filmy eyes. The blurred red spurts across her whites like a bad egg.

Forty-one rattles down the stairs and grabs the receiver. He is in constant communication with acquaintants on the edge of the clergy, cultivating them in hopes of slinking back into his collar. His anxious muttering into the phone begins as Crystal Lil careens back into her room. She leaves her door open to the hallway.

Her window looks onto the sidewalk in the front of the building. Her television is on with the volume high. She sits on the backless kitchen chair, feels around for the large magnifying glass until she finds it on top of the TV, and then leans close, her nose scant inches from the screen, pumping the lens in and out before her eyes in a constant struggle to focus an image among the dots. When I come through the hall I can see the grey light flickering through the lens onto the eager blindness of her face.

Being called 'Manager' explains, for Crystal Lil, why no bills come to her, why her room is free, and why the small check arrives for her each month. She is adamant in her duties as rent collector and enfeebled watchdog. The phone is part of the deal.

When Crystal Lil howls, 'Twenty-one!', which is my room number, I stop by my door to grab the goat wig from its nail and jam it onto my bald pate before I take the single flight of stairs in a series of one-legged hops that is hard on my knees and ankles but disguises my usual shuffle. I pitch my voice high and loud, an octave into the falsetto. 'Thank you!' I shriek at her gaping mouth. Her gums are knobby and a faintly iridescent green — shiny where the teeth were. I wear the same wig when I go out. I don't trust Lil's blindness or her deafness to disguise me completely. I am, after all, her daughter. She might harbor some decayed hormonal recognition of my rhythms that could penetrate even the wall of refusal her body has thrown up against the world.

When Lil calls, 'Thirty-five!' up the stairwell, I wobble over to the door and stare one-eyed through the hole drilled next to the lock. When 'Thirty-five' comes hurtling down the staircase, I get an instant glimpse of her long legs, sometimes flashing bare through the slits in her startling green kimono. I lean my head against the door and listen to her strong young voice shouting at Lil and then dropping to its normal urgency on the phone. Number Thirty-five is my daughter, Miranda. Miranda is a popular girl, tall and well shaped. She gets phone calls every evening before she leaves for work. Miranda does not try to disguise herself from her grandmother. She believes herself to be an orphan named Barker. And Crystal Lil herself must imagine that Miranda is just one more of the gaudy females who trail their sex like slug slime over the rooms for a month at a time before moving on. Perhaps the fact that Miranda has

lived here in the big apartment for three years has never pene-
trated to Lil. How would she notice that the same 'Thirty-five'
always answered the call? They have no bridge to each other. I
am the only link between them and neither of them knows me.
Miranda, though, has far less reason to remember me than the
old woman does.

This is my selfish pleasure, to watch unseen. It wouldn't give
them pleasure to know me for who I am. It could kill Lily,
bringing back all the rot of the old pain. Or she might hate me
for surviving when all her other treasures have sunk into mold.
As for Miranda, I can't be sure what it would do to her to know
her real mother. I imagine her bright spine cringing and
slumping and staying that way. She makes a gallant orphan.

We are all three Binewskis, though only Lily claims the
name. I am just 'Number Twenty-One' to Crystal Lil. Or
'McGurk, the cripple in Twenty-one.' Miranda is more
colorful. I've heard her whispering to friends as they pass the
door, 'The dwarf in Twenty-one,' or 'The old albino hunchback in Twenty-one.'

I rarely need to speak to either of them. Lil puts the rent
checks in a basket just inside her open door and I reach to get
them. On Thursdays I take out the garbage and Lily thinks
nothing of it.

Miranda says hello in the hall. I nod. Occasionally she tries
to chat me up on the stairs. I am distant and brief and escape as
quickly as possible with my heart pounding like a burglar's.

Lily chose to forget me and I choose not to remind her, but I
am terrified of seeing shame or disgust in my daughter's face. It
would kill me. So I stalk and tend them both secretly, like a
midnight gardener.

Lillian Hinchcliff Binewski — Crystal Lil — is tall and thin.
Her breasts hang in flaps at her waist but her carriage is still
erect. She had the long-faced, thin-nosed stamp of the Protes-
tant aristocrat. She never goes out without a hat, usually a
tweed hiker with the brim pulled so far down over her pink
glasses that she is forced to throw her head up and back to
catch what faint light and movement her eyes are willing to

deal with. Draped with a few dead rodents she could slip unsuspected into cucumber luncheons.

Following Lily is easy. Her long Bostonian body lurches from one touch point to the next at an impressive clip. She is suspicious and fearless and her progress is alarming. She never passes any vertical shape without grabbing it and feeling it to make sure what it is. Telephone poles, stop signs — she runs at them, catches hold as though just saved from falling, gives them an exploratory rub with each hand, and then, tossing her head back, pushes off toward the next upright shadow that smears across her eye. Lily also uses humans this way. I have seen her move through twenty blocks of crowded noontime sidewalks, swinging from one startled pedestrian to another, grabbing one by a shoulder, patting in examination, while stretching out an arm to snatch at the breasts of the next one in her path. When someone takes offense, snaps or swears or pushes her away, she reels only momentarily before the next body presents itself and she hurtles on, using body after body as handholds through the air.

I toddle along behind. Twenty feet between us is complete protection from her noticing. It intrigues me to see people pause and stare after her as she lunges on her desperate way. Some wide-minded type with a text-book under his arm, surprised at his own stifled impulse to backhand her for using him as a trapeze, a little ashamed, gawks in her wake. Then he turns and sees me, humping along and looking directly into his eyes. The double image scares him. My mother, on the street alone, can be written off with the gentle oddities of rambling mumblers, drunks and beggars, but when I come twenty feet behind, there is an ice moment. Even the smug feel it. They go home and tell their wives that the streets of Portland are filled with weirdos. Their dreams weave a bent linkage between the wild old woman and the hunchbacked dwarf. Or they think we are residents of an institutional halfway house, or that the circus is in town.

A few times a week, apparently convinced that she is in Boston, Crystal Lil struggles up the hill to a big house on Vista Avenue. She runs at the wrought-iron fence, galloping her hands along it, searching for something. Then she stands with her mouth hanging open, an elastic strand of spittle bridging her jaws, and waits on the sidewalk in front of the door. Probably she can't actually make out the shape of the dormer windows, but she waves at them. Occasionally she grabs a pedestrian and shouts, 'I was born there! In the Rose Room! Mama gave us tea in the solarium!' When her captive escapes, she lapses into murmuring. She doesn't register that the Georgian brick is now an expensive condominium. She waits for some old dog or servant to wander out and discover her with tears of joy, the prodigal come home after all these years. Maybe she dreams she'll be taken in and cosseted by her own mother, tucked up cozy in a virgin bed. Only the slim professional men go in and out, sidestepping her skillfully. Eventually she wanders back down the hill to her room on Kearney Street.

Crystal Lil, her door propped open, sits in front of the television with a pan in her lap, a brown bag at her feet. She takes long green beans out of the bag and snaps them into inch-long chunks that drop into the pan. I pause on the stairs, marveling at how she came by those green beans.

Lillian in the supermarket, terrified and angry, her long hands running over shelves, knocking down cans, grabbing at last a box and muttering, reaches out to grab an innocent shopper, thrusts the box into the woman's face, shrieking. 'What is this! Tell me what this is!,' until the shopper, in irritated charity, says, 'Cornflakes,' and shakes loose.

Lily in summer, with the street dirt rising into the thickening heat, lifts her window and shoves two grimy geraniums from the inside of the window to the outer sill. Later that afternoon, Crystal Lil rushes down the sidewalk, grabbing every moving human by the collar, caterwauling, 'Thief! Little bastards! Stole my plants! Thief!' And sure enough the pots are gone, only two faint rings left in the dirt on the sill.

* * *

Jingle of keys. High-pitched burbling in the hall. Lillian delivering the mail. She is supposed to leave it on the table in the downstairs hall. Or, at most, slip it under the doors. Sometimes she uses it as an excuse to come into the rooms.

Once Miranda, frenzied on the floor with her lover, did not answer Lil's knock. The two, beneath a sheet in the brick heat of summer, sweating into each other, lay still, hushed themselves, and were shocked when the door opened and Crystal Lil staggered in, touching walls, grabbing tables, making her way to the heaped sheet itself, where it tented in the middle of the floor, patting the edges, barely missing the tangled legs of the lovers, who lay silent, watching her greedy investigation. After making a complete round of the room she found the table again, put the envelopes on it, and groped her way out, closing and locking the door. Miranda told me this when she was trying to befriend me in the hall, trying to talk me into posing for her drawings.

Miranda seems preoccupied with deformity. She has lured the fat man from the corner newsstand up to her rooms several times to model for her. There is no obvious reason for such a fascination in her own life, even if her living does depend on that tiny irregularity of hers. She is strong and straight. Her spine and legs are as long as history. It may be that the impressions of her infancy are caught somehow in the pulp of her eyes, luring her. Or there may be some hooked structure in her cells that twists her toward all that the world calls freakish.

Miranda is hard to follow. Her stride is as long as Crystal Lil's but without the detours and distractions. She is also alert and mine is not an inconspicuous figure. I usually lose her within a few blocks. Either she leaves me choking in the dust or I have to duck and hide from her swiveling face. I've managed to follow her all the way to work twice in the three years she has lived in this building.

One evening, leaving the radio station, where I had worked later than usual, I saw her at an intersection. She was wearing dark green, a cocktail dress and jacket. She wears simple clothes to her classes at the art school so I was struck by the difference. Her makeup was dramatic and her body moved strangely, unfamiliarly in high-heeled sandals with only thin gold chains to keep them on. I followed her without thinking about it. Of course I would lose her but I took pleasure in the eyes of men on her body. She was apparently going to work. I trailed along all the way down to the Glass House Club. She was slower in her high heels. I watched her pick up an envelope from the doorman. She went around to the employees' entrance and I slipped into the club itself.

The ceiling was an enormous mosaic of mirrors. The walls and carpet were dark. Small islands of light from the table lamps fractured and multiplied in the reflections. The room was large and crowded. There were a few women, but mostly men, several hundred, the tables filled, and the aisles between filled with people standing with glasses in their hands.

I stayed at the back of the room, slid onto a chair against the wall, and only stood up for the show.

A very thin girl was first, her skin tight to her bones with as little muscle intruding as I've ever seen on someone who could still sit up. She pranced around in a gauze veil and undid a few beads as the band concentrated on their bass line. The finale of her act was to pull a comb out of her tightly rolled hair and let it fall shimmering pale down her back, give it a shake, and turn around so we could see that it hung down to the floor (whistles). Then she ground her hips around until she faced us and undid the bead that held her G-string in place. Her pubic hair began to unroll in the same way, a crisp version of her head hair (table pounding), until a soft cloud of nearly white hair billowed out from her crotch, waving all the way down to her knees, the crotch hair and head hair blending. I wondered if she had to depilate the rest of her body. The bald man was chanting into the microphone, 'Yes, it's real, folks, give it a tug there, Denise. We'd let you come up on stage and pull the little lady's hair for yourselves, boys, just to verify it's genuine, but state law forbids, and you've got to admit, a few souvenir hunters could put poor Denise out of business.' She swayed in her hips and the long hair flicked from side to side. 'How do you find her in there? I want to know?' and Denise sauntered smiling offstage, more or less to the beat.

Paulette, the pre-transsexual, was beautiful and slender, with perfect breasts. Paulette's act flourished until the removal of her G-string revealed a shriveled penis and scrotum. The boos drowned the bald man's announcement that Paulette would be leaving for Tangier the following month and would return in December as a real girl.

Miranda was last. The band went steamy and grinding. She came out in long white satin. My dove. My eyes hurt for her, a scorch along the nerve string to the brain. The men in front of me stood up, leaning forward, slapping each other's shoulders and sending out the high-pitched long-toned soooooo-eeeeee's of pig callers. I stepped on my own hands getting up onto the table so I could see. Her long arms were lifted, her hair snapped with light. A young blonde in silver at a table just ahead of me glowered at the backs of the men who were with her as they leaned toward the stage. Miranda with the Binewski cheekbones, the Mongol eyes. Wide-mouthed Miranda, the dancer on long legs. The chill wash of joy hit me: my daughter. She was good. Not great, but good. What's bred in the bones, when you have bones, comes through. And they looked at her, watched her, wanted to squirt her full of baby juice.

Electra and Iphigenia were high-powered performers, they wrung your heart, cramped your brain, brought silence on thousands for half an hour at a time. And the crowds that watched Arturo were funneled out of themselves, pumped into the reservoir of his will. Though I am her mother, I knew that Miranda's little act, her clever little strip with its dignity and timing, was paltry compared to the skill and power I had watched in my other loved ones. But it was strange and different to me, watching these people watching her. Because they thought she was pretty, because they thought it would be good to grab her ass and pump jizz into her. Their bodies lifted up, clean and simple to her in the clear, unconscious awareness of each of their cells' sensing that she would grunt out strong young.

She was down to her G-string with the fluffy lace plume on her rump, she had her thumbs hooked in it, looking over her

shoulder at the crowd, she was waving her ass in a slow sema-
phore of invitation. The frowning blonde at the table had her
chin in her hand. The men were hooting and grunting and
watching with smiles. I held my breath, blinked, and she pulled
the plume down, unsnapped the G-string and whipped it off
with a flourish, waving her ass still, her head tipped up and an
unmistakable giggle bubbling out of her as she revealed the
thin, curling tail that jutted out from the end of her spine and
bounced just above her round buttocks.

The second time — the last time — I simply followed Miranda
to work. I walked out the door at Kearney Street fifteen
seconds behind her and tagged her easily enough through a
heavy rain. She never looked out from under her umbrella until
she stamped her boots at the back door of the Glass House. I
went in the front entrance and left my umbrella in a glass
stand. I moved carefully toward one wall and slid along until I
was fairly near the curtained stage at the end of the room.

There was a commotion in front of the stage. A big tuxedoed
man with a glistening bald head was giving orders in a harsh
whisper. I wasn't tall enough to see who he was speaking to.

Suddenly he jumped onto the stage. There was a crash from
the drummer. A cone of light appeared around the bald man.
There were whistles in the crowd, laughter, sporadic hand-
clapping.

'Gentlemen and jokers! Lively ladies!' The bald man stuck
his long-corded microphone between his legs and wiggled its
silver knob. The crowd chuckled. 'The Glass House proudly
presents its Tuesday-night feature! On Stage Topless Auditions! Any member of the audience is welcome to step up to the
stage at this time and try out for a topless position here at the
Glass House — with the Glass House orchestra! Under
authentic conditions! A ten-dollar prize to each and every
contestant! Ladies and gentlemen, step up and test your talent!
... And here they come folks! ...' A scramble of flesh hit the
stage. The crowd cheered, hissed, whistled, laughed. Five
bodies, bare from the waist up, snarled around the bald man
and then tapered out in a line facing the audience. I began to

sweat. A fat woman with her blouse hanging from the waist of her skirt stood nearest to me, blinking at the audience. Her breasts had fallen, thick and long, mixing with the rolls of fat that hung puffily over her belly. Her arms had the same texture and shape as her breasts and belly. She crossed her arms over her chest in an instant of shyness and then let them drop, forgetting.

Two middle-aged men wore matching red plastic jeans with broad leather belts strapping their adjacent legs together. Their thin white arms wrapped around each other's shoulders and matching ostrich plumes curled up out of their thinning hair. Their raddled faces wrinkled unnervingly beneath an expert Oriental makeup, and their bone-riding nipples were enlarged and glowing with red gel.

A fat man in a glitter jockstrap had little eyes flicking in his pillow-creased face, as his booze buddies belched his name in unison from the front tables.

And the startled young girl was blushing beneath her awkward Pan-Cake, her lips drawn lush, her scared eyes outlined in black, her tiny breasts thrust out on her long, prominent ribs. She wore her lewdest panties and a pair of pirate boots, but she wasn't drunk like the rest. She must have thought she was actually auditioning for a job here.

A bear baiting. The band is brassy spunk. The bald master of ceremonies spanks his hands at the edge of the stage and hollers into the mike as the line pumps and jiggles. I lean my chin on the stage itself, watching the wave of flesh reveal a surprise of blurred nipple every third beat as the fat woman throws her shoulders forward to toss her tits out of their usual resting place beside her sagging navel.

The young girl tries to look professional in the confusion of wobbling red thighs and waving ostrich and the fat man's patch of chest hair. Confusion is burning her. She knows she has been taken, and has wandered into the wrong and maybe the worst place.

The noise is suffocating and I have to squint to see in the strange light. Then cold air hits my scalp and a hand is thumping my hump in an investigative way. 'You forgot one!' is the shriek. My wig is dangling high above my head in a wavering hand. My dark glasses are snatched away and the light sears in at me.

The bald man is staring into my eyes as big hands lift me, my own mouth opening though silent and the music beats into my face and the pinching, bruising fingers trap my jerking arms and legs and breath. There is a shout — many-voiced — and the bald man is coming toward me with a smile and the flabby woman is grabbing at my coat and yanking at the buttons and shrieking, 'Little pink eyes!' and the red pants hop toward me, their crotches bobbling at my eye level, the thick buckles that hold them threatening to kneel in my face. My coat is being pulled away, my big blouse, which is cut with deep darts for my hump and hangs flat to my knees in front, tears in an explosion of buttons that ricochet around the stage without sound because there is no room in this big sound for the little sounds of buttons hitting.

They have come to my chest harness now, thick strips of elastic stretched above the hump and below it to hold a solid band across my ragged dugs and their grey nipples. The bald man is talking to me in a confidential way without his microphone and I feel the movement of his lips and the hot wet of his breath in my ear but I cannot hear him as the harness slides off, scraping my hump, raking my ears, blinding me for a second. I kick as they lift me in the air to pull off my elastic-waisted skirt and wave me upward to the yellow spotlight and bring me down with my shoes hitting the stage and my white underskirt riding up over my crouching knees.

I am standing alone in the light and the big bodies have fallen back from me. The college girl, dumbfounded, is still pumping away with her mouth open, her knees and arms still following an odd order to dance, as her mind is pummeled by what I am, and what they have done to me, and wondering if I am in on it. The crowd is standing up and beating the tables. The laughter is fierce and the band is loud, but barely loud enough, as I lift my thin arms and waggle my huge hands and bob to the light, and my knees begin to shift in what my body calls dance, waving my hump at the crowd, the light warming my scalp and burning into my unprotected eyes. My big shoes thump at the ends of my little legs, and I am proud with my arrow tits flapping toward my knees, and the fat lady standing on my coat is staring, with spittle across her cheek, and the fat man with his electric G-string pumping at his invisible crotch and laughing, and the shouts coming up, 'Christ! It's real!' The twisting of my hump feels good against the warm air and the sweat of my bald head runs down into my bald eyes and stings with brightness and the spirit of the waggling hump moves over the stage and catches red pants, hairy bellies, and all, while I stamp on my buttonless blouse, slide on the tangled elastic harness, and open my near-blind eyes wide so they can see that there is true pink there — the raw albino eye in the lashless sockets — and it is good. How proud I am, dancing in the air full of eyes rubbing at me uncovered, unable to look away because of what I am. Those poor hoptoads behind me are silent. I've conquered them. They thought to use and shame me but I win out by nature, because a true freak cannot be made. A true freak must be born.

There wasn't any graceful way to end it. The band stopped, the bald man shouted, 'Let's give 'em a hand, folks.' There was a surge of catcalls. We all scrambled around for our clothes, clutching them to our chests as we hurried down. Of course there was no dressing room. The restroom was on the other side of the club, so we huddled down in front of the stage tugging awkwardly into clothes. I slid my blouse on inside-out, as I discovered later, put on my coat and wig and glasses immediately, and stuffed the chest harness into a pocket.

The bald man was doling out five-dollar bills like stale cookies. He handed two to me. The shame had already started icing up my valves, and those five-dollar bills were the clinchers. It had been a long time since I had blushed, not since Arturo, maybe. But the hot blood scorched me then.

'What's your name? Can we get you to come down regularly for audition nights? That's a lot of potential you've got. We could work up a nice set using you. We'd up the ante a bit, make it twenty bucks for a turn. We do two auditions a night between the regular acts. You could pick up an easy forty.' He was being perfectly pleasant about it. My wig wasn't fitting and

I couldn't make out why. I kept pulling at it until I noticed that it was on backward. I turned it around and made for the door. Sidling through the crowd, I crammed my brain with static to prevent myself from hearing what they were saying. Run hide quick, I thought, scuttling down the street.

I paced and thumped up and down my room all night. I couldn't lie down at all for fear of Arturo and Papa and my own terrible pride.

3

NOTES FOR NOW
Meltdown, Diving into Teacups from the Thirteenth Floor, and Other Stimulating Experiences

Miranda is talking on the phone as I come in from work. She lolls against the wall, one long bare leg jutting out through her green kimono. She has a towel turbaned over her fresh-washed hair and she hangs up the receiver as I close the door behind me.

'Hi. Got time to come up for tea?'

'No. Thank you.'

Miranda is a student at the Art Institute. Her aim is to illustrate medical texts. She wants me to pose for her drawings. I never accept her offers of tea. I proceed toward the stairs while scrabbling to hang on to my books and papers. She purses her mouth elaborately.

With a grip on the banister and one foot on the first step I can't keep from pausing, from looking at her. She drops her lids halfway and eyes me in a deliberately speculative fashion. A small glitch in my gizzard warns me that Arturo used his eyes this way. His eyes were, like hers, long, slanted almond shapes, though of course Arty didn't have the lashes and brows that Miranda does.

Smiling weakly — does she know or is this just her usual

badgering revenge when I refuse her invitations? — I climb the stairs with her eyes following me.

Olympia Binewski, aka Hopalong McGurk, the Radio Story Lady, is hunched over a book in the glass-walled recording booth at Radio KBNK, Portland. The molasses voice that has earned her living for decades pours into the sponge ear of the microphone and is transformed into silent, pulsing waves that radiate over a hundred miles. She is deep in a dramatic rendition of that speculative classic 'Pit Might.'

In the story the mind-souls of three theoretical physicists find themselves reincarnated (after dying hideously during their search for Schrödinger's demon cat) in the bodies of itch mites inhabiting the pubic hair of a particularly obtuse Los Angeles policeman.

McGurk's eyes twitch up from the book regularly to check the engineer on the other side of the soundproof glass. He watches meters and the clock. He signals two minutes left and McGurk storms into the climax. The theme music comes up and McGurk signs off, 'Until tomorrow . . .' Falling back from the microphone, McGurk stretches to ease the ache in her neck and looks through the glass.

Miranda is smiling in the engineer's booth. McGurk drops the book onto the floor instead of into her briefcase. The engineer is propped on the control panel sporting a paralytic grin, his eyes clamped on Miranda's thorax.

Miranda waves and Hoppy McG. nods, forgetting to put any expression on her face.

I, Hoppy-Olympia, the invisible mom, sit frozen, watching as the engineer talks to Miranda. His hands in the air make typing motions and jerk a thumb in my direction. Miranda nods. The engineer turns to me, walking two fingers in the air. They slip away through the door.

The engineer gives Miranda a tour of the station while I type up the royalty credit for that day's program. My skull oozes sweat. A vacancy behind my eyes makes me nauseated. What is wrong? Why is she here? Why would she suddenly appear at the workplace of a neighbor who barely acknowledges her 'Good mornings' in the hall? Could that senile slut of a nun have broken her word after all these years and told the girl the truth?

I'm in the front office buttoning my coat when they come back. I've just remembered reasons she might be in this radio station that have nothing to do with me. She is visiting a friend, applying for a job, or taping an interview as guest stripper on the *Night Train Hour*. It is coincidence, I decide, and I am getting old and batty, thinking the universe revolves around me.

'I'm taking you to lunch,' she chirps at me, as though we did this all the time. I slide into the elevator and lean against the back wall. She follows me, saying, 'Thank you so much,' as the doors snuff out the engineer's anxious grin.

Miranda turns her brights full on me. 'I hope you'll excuse me showing up here. I knew where to find you because I listen to your program. I recognized your voice when I first heard you talking to Looney Lil in the hall. I knocked on your door this morning but you'd already gone. I need to talk to you.'

The phrase ricochets in my skull. 'Need to talk.' All these years of silence. I have intended, and do intend, to dog Miranda until my dying day, but I never meant to talk to her. My heart tries to climb out through my ears. She pinks up — flustered at what must be a mild glare behind my blue lenses.

The elevator gapes in front of us and I dart through the slow legs of the lobby loiterers and into the faster legs of the midday sidewalk. I feel her behind me, threading the crowd after me, shortening her stride to accommodate me, coming up beside me at the corner.

Sucking air noisily, I lean forward to discourage conversation. She is wearing dark green, her heels bouncing impatiently beside me. There is no pleasure in having her so close. What does she want?

'How about the grill at the Via Veneto? They do a lunch buffet. Miss McGurk?'

I can't look at her. I try to civilize my voice. 'I don't eat lunch.'

The light changes, trapping us on an island in the wide street. The cars swarm around us in a sea of stink. She's caught me on this concrete knob and her harpoon is suddenly revealed,

her eyes, her words ripping out of her. 'Look, forget that you
don't know me. There are two things. First, you've got to
model for me.' Her sweet-simp guise is gone. She is green fire
above Binewski cheekbones. She means to convince me. The
heat of her intention has my throat melting. I want to hold her
face in my hands and push her strange hair back from her
Binewski forehead. The faces behind the windshields save me.
A Binewski never disintegrates in front of the ticket holders.

She is burning away at me, talking fast, her eyes demanding.
The anatomy competition is coming up. She had already won
two years in a row. The judges will be reluctant to give it to her
again. She needs something special, something hot ... Art
school. She is talking art school and she is talking to me. These
two facts amaze me.

'The first year I went to LoPrinzi's gym and did a series on a
body builder. Technical, illustrative, and predictable. Last year
I went to the medical school and did a flayed, emaciated
cadaver. Classic and totally predictable. I've got to show more
than a technician's skills this time. I've got to rock them. I've
got to yank their hearts out.'

Her urgency has my stomach cringing, trying to crawl down
my leg. Is this an accident? Is it coincidence that she comes to
me? All this time of silent watching, my secret care. My anonymous arm holding the invisible umbrella. Could she know? Is
this her way of opening me? Slipping in like the knife that
unlocks the oyster? Or does some pulse in her bones, some twist
in her genetic coil, lean toward me in a blind craving? The
light changes.

'Look, there's a bus bench. Come sit a minute.' She sails
past revving machines in the intersection, collapses onto the
bench and waves me up beside her as she yanks a sheaf of
papers from her bag.

'Reduced copies. You don't get the full effect but you can
see that I'm serious.'

The top sheet shows a hip socket, lushly washed, the hard
lines impatient and powerful. The second sheet is exposed
abdominal muscle, fiercely striated. Then come loving portraits
of callused arthritic hands and bunion-twisted feet, a flayed
jaw, a joyous nude of the blobby news vendor from the corner.

He is hunched on a stool, pudgy hands propped on knees like sagging pumpkins, his acorn head thrown back in surprise on what passes for a neck. I don't understand the drawings, or why they move me. I want to cry, loud and wet with the pain of love. The drawings are as mysterious to me as the school report cards that the Reverend Mother mailed dutifully every few months. No Binewski ever made pictures. I never had a report card. But I saved Miranda's, stacked and wrapped with a rubber band in the biggest of the old trunks.

Her long hand taps at the dangling ink scrotum, the nearly invisible penis of the news vendor. 'Characteristic of the fat-storing pattern in males,' she's saying, 'the belly seems to swallow the penis from the roots up, literally shortening it . . .'

'Disgusting!' snaps a voice behind me.

'Fuck off!' yells Miranda. The critic sniffs away toward the corner. Just a passerby. Miranda lays an arm over my hump to protect me. Pointing at the line depicting a rumpled buttock drooping from the stool, she giggles. 'One of my teachers says I draw like a mass murderer. I hate that ditsy crap, though. Inchy little lines like the hesitation cuts on a suicide's wrist.'

I loll in molten idiocy. All this time of not speaking I had figured her for silly, for toad-braincd, because she is so near normal. All the years of watching have taught me nothing, and I laugh. Leaning back against her arm, tipping my head as the fat man's head tips, laughing voicelessly and weak.

She grins at me. 'That one works, doesn't it?'

I'm laughing despite myself. 'You seem such a nice girl, too.'

'Ho!' she barks. 'Don't be deceived. I've got a tail.'

Something in my face stops her. Her face is suddenly careful.

'That's the other thing I want to talk to you about.' She watches me. 'There's a story, naturally a long one. But the first and last is that I was born with a tail, like a lot of people, but I didn't get it nipped off when I was a baby. I still have it. It's not a big tail, less than a foot long. But most people don't have any bone in their tails. Mine is actually an extended spur of my spine. That's why I always wear skirts.'

I am helpless, pinned by her arm and her eyes until she looks away.

'It's going to rain,' she says. The air is heavy and grey. 'Want to go? Come up to my place? I'll give you lunch and draw you and bend your ear and beg advice.'

'O.K., of course.' I scrabble numbly for my briefcase.

She jounces up, arms wheeling against the sky. 'All right.'

I would die to make her smile that way, would whittle my fingers and toes away if only it could make her long Binewski eyes light this way forever. I jump down to the pavement and dive after her through the swirling bodies. Her dark drawings are still in my fist. I stuff them into my briefcase with a pang. Hide them.

Turning the corner into our block Miranda skips once to keep in step. Across the street, high up in the third-story gable of the wood Victorian, a painter leaning off his scaffold to reach the trim watches us, freezing one hand to the wall, his brush hand poised against the blue air.

Am I contaminating her? Polluting my silence? Obliterating my anonymity? Dangling the ax of my identity over her whole idea of herself?

'You turn high RPMs,' she says, double-stepping beside me. 'Slightly more than two to my one. But' — she laughs once, a fox bark against the mist — 'I'm catching on.' My blankness shows and she tosses her shoulders and arms in a classic Binewski apology. 'Strides,' she says.

Our old house, with its front steps propped like elbows on the sidewalk, looks warm for once. The bottom front windows, Lil's, show a yellow glow. The fourth floor front, otherwise known as Number 41, or The Attic, is lit. Its small dusty window shields the Benedictine on his bed in solitary combat with the rule book. Miranda's windows, third floor front, are white above the blank-eyed vacant room below her. My room on the second floor is at the back, invisible. My view is the dust-blind rear of the warehouse that squats across the alley. Just below my window, like an Oriental pond, the flat tar roof of the square garage is filled with water and moss because of blocked drains.

Lil is standing at attention in her doorway as we enter. Her old face tilts back to stare at our shadows. 'Who is it?' she shrieks.

'Thirty-one,' yells Miranda. Then louder, 'Thirty-one!' and Lil steps back to let us pass.

Miranda talks me past my room. I'm ready to panic and quit, dodge in through my door and apologize as I close her out. She is telling me we should go for walks together, that she often has to dance with shorter people and has no trouble adjusting the length of her stride.

It's been three years since I saw her rooms. Before she came from the train station, still smelling of nuns, I cleaned. It took days, sponging the ceilings, the green wallpaper with its huge white roses like fetal aliens. These were her rooms long before she came here. The first time I visited the building with the fastidiously courteous agent, the big front room, twenty by forty feet, with its tall windows in a row, was marked for her. The bedroom was more normal. The windowless bathroom was claustrophobic. The kitchen was familiar, as though it had been surgically transplanted from a trailer house.

I scrubbed windows and woodwork and the endless cupboards built into the walls. I pounded and vacuumed the heavy stuffed furniture. Everything normal for the almost normal girl.

She was so tall, I thought, she wouldn't mind the distance to the ceilings. With such long arms, I thought, she will like the big room to stretch in.

The day she arrived I stayed close to my spyhole all morning. It was nearly noon when she came, thundering with two other students up the stairs and past the door where my eye was fixed to the hole.

'You got the place free. Who cares what it looks like,' came a young voice. The jumbled baggage and bodies clattered upward. My ear flattened to the door, trying to sift out which voice was Miranda's. If she hated the house, the smells, the soggy slump of the neighborhood, what would I do?

She didn't have much. The three carried all she owned up the stairs in that one trip. All the evidence of her eighteen years on the planet. Twenty minutes later they rushed down again, to register for classes at the art school.

Now beside me in the gravy-dark hall she pushes the door away from her, open, a soft white light sweeps out to swallow me. Her shadow blinks across me as she disappears into the light.

The room is gauze-bright from the four tall windows. The light comes through thin white curtains, cool onto grey walls, simple onto the dark gleam of the bare wood floor.

She tosses her purse, drops her sea-green coat, abandons her tall heels in the middle of the empty floor.

'There used to be furniture,' I say in shock. Where does she sit? eat? sleep? I thought I had provided for her.

'It was awful.' She pauses, arms half cocked above her head, pulling at her sweater. She disappears in a wrestling frenzy, reappears breathless, hurling the sweater at a distant empty corner. 'It's all scattered in other rooms in the building.'

The room is bare. Not a stick. Not a single nail protrudes from the grey walls. Only her clothes trail across the black floor like a love romp. Looking rail-thin in the blouse and skirt, she jerks open a white door hiding canvas chairs folded neatly against the back of the closet. A thin-legged folding table. She whips them out and up, furnishing the place. 'Wait till you see my tea cabinet,' she says, slapping the swaying loop of canvas meant to cradle an ass. 'I've been collecting for weeks.' Through another white door to the tiny kitchen stands the old refrigerator, no taller than I am.

'Vine leaves.' She snatches out jars and plastic dishes. 'Artichoke hearts. Do you like olives?'

The kettle is on the stove, blue flame curling its bottom. She reaches, her long body high above me and her ribs sliding under thin cloth, upward. 'Strawberry, jasmine, mint.' Tea boxes rain onto the counter. 'This is all for you.' She is huge. Her heat beats through the inch of air between us. 'I have no idea what you like so I've been on the watch for anything really special. Just in case you ever came to visit. Now I'm going to get you a dressing gown and you can change in the bathroom.'

The dream lasts only an instant, but in it I have fallen into the cat cage and the tigers are sliding by me, brushing their whole hot length against me. But it is this Miranda, moving liquid past me and out into the big room, miraculously whisking her dropped belongings out of sight, pulling out white painted drawers and doors, allowing glimpses of hidden paraphernalia as she skates, chattering about food, again and again to the resurrected table suddenly crowded with ominous delicacies heaped in small bowls.

A final armload slides onto the table, sketch pads, pencils, a sinister-looking camera. Then she takes half a step back and looks at me through half-closed eyes. A flicker of her father's deliberate calculation passes across her face. An ice knife sticks in my chest.

'It's not cold in here, is it?' she asks.

'No.'

'Good.' She moves to the drawers in the wall. 'I'll do some photos first, while you're fresh, and then sketch until you get tired or fed up.' She flips her voice over her shoulder while bent, rummaging to avoid acknowledging my jitter of fear. She is holding me to my promise.

'The photos will make it easier on you. It hurts to hold a pose for a long time.'

She presents me with a green pajama top and, as I grasp it, she swings open the bathroom door, flicks the light switch, saying, 'There are hooks on the door for your clothes ... whoops! There's the kettle boiling.'

In the tall bathroom I stand staring at the door. I can hear her moving on the other side. The pajama top trails on the floor beside me and she is whistling in the kitchen. Suddenly the staggering love bursts away from me like milk from a smashed glass. She is manipulating me. Pushing me around as though I were nothing but a mobile stomach like the news vendor. She fancies she has me under control. Red anger blisters my guts. She doesn't see me at all. She doesn't know who she's dealing with. I am the watcher, the mover, the maker. She is just like her father, casually, carelessly enslaving me with my love. She doesn't know the powers that keep me here. She thinks it's her charm and guile.

'Tea's ready,' she calls.

I answer thinly, 'Coming,' but whirl in a frenzy, shoving the grit of the green pajama into my mouth and biting down to keep from bellowing.

Her drawing is suddenly in front of me, framed and glassed on the grey wall beside the sink. The darkness is ink and the eyes and teeth come out of the dark and the screaming chicken is bulging vainly away, caught as the teeth close tearing into exploding feathers and black blood behind its desperate skull. Drawn with a bullwhip at thirty paces. Quietly, in the white at the bottom, her penciled hand has scrawled 'Geek Love — by M. Barker.'

I take off my clothes. I can't reach the hooks on the door. I drape the clothes over the toilet tank, drop the wig on top, and stand my shoes on the floor beside it. The pajama top hangs to my ankles.

I sit. She draws. Wearing only my blue glasses I am not cold but my skin rises against exposure, rough as a cow's tongue. The cups steam upward into the pale air. Our island is the size of two canvas chairs and a small cluttered table. We are marooned in the breathing bareness of the room. Darkness rolls out around us, seeping into the distant softness of the grey walls. The curtains shift slowly in their own whiteness, as though the light pouring through them has a frail, moving substance.

She is gnawing an olive pit and frowning at the sketch pad in her lap. The wild hair torching out of the edges of her face mesmerizes me. The millions of hairs in a dozen smoldering tones are as alien as her size, the outrageous length of her. My mother, Lillian, is seventy inches high. I am thirty-six inches high.

'How tall are you Miranda?'

She looks up to focus on my chin, frowning, and says, 'Six feet,' mechanically before her eyes twitch back to the paper in front of her.

Watching her work is comfortable. I feel invisible again, as though she had never spoken to me beyond 'Good morning.' She is not interested in my identity. She doesn't notice it. Her eyes flick impatiently at me for a fast fix — a regenerative fusing of the image on her retina, the model she inflicts on the paper. I am merely a utensil, a temporary topic for the eternal discussion between her long eye and her deliberate hand.

Downstairs in the first floor front, Crystal Lil sits sliding the magnifying glass back and forth in search of the focal point.

The walls around her are slathered with the crumpled glitter of the old carny posters. A dozen glossy young Lilys smile, kick, and reach for the curving gold name, 'Crystal Lily,' that arches against midway blue above her. Dressed in white, a paper Lil arches her back against a blue-green sky spangled with stars. Strips of arsenic-green wallpaper peep between the posters.

In my room everything is just as I found it when I moved in. The stuffed furniture molders against the cabbage wallpaper. My real life sits in boxes and suitcases behind cupboard doors. My real bed is not the creaking acre of springs in the corner, but the dark nest of blankets on the floor of the cupboard beneath the kitchen sink.

Miranda rips out the page she has been working on and absently sails it over her shoulder while she eyes a jar bristling with pens. The page settles, belly up on the dark floor, as she begins dashing ink at a fresh sheet of paper.

'What made you,' clearing my throat, 'decide to be an artist?'

Her eyes flick at my feet under frowning brows. 'No, no. A medical illustrator. For textbooks and manuals ...' Her tongue sneaks out at a corner of her mouth as she slaps stroke after vicious stroke onto the defenseless page. 'See, photographs can be confusing. A drawing can be more specific and informative. It gets pretty red in there. Pretty hot and thick. But the bastards claim I'm undisciplined, too flashy....' Whatever she is doing to the innocent sheet has nothing to do with me. She rips it out and drops it, starting immediately on the page beneath.

'There's something I want to talk to you about.' She tries to make it casual.

The bite of fear — 'She knows!' — grabs my chest and then relaxes. No. I've been sitting here bald and naked for an hour. Too late for that.

She stops chewing her thumb and asks, 'Have you ever been to the Glass House?' At my nod she drops the pen, picks up her tame tool, the pencil, and begins work on a fresh sheet of paper.

'Then you know,' eyes on paper, 'that the dancers, all of us, aren't there for our dancing skills or even our looks, but ...'

rubbing her thumb vigorously across the page, 'because we each have something odd. We call them our specialities.

'What the Glass House calls "Exotic Features" are all in the back room. You know. Separate cover charges for private shows and private parties. Blondes with Dobermans. Group acts. They stage requests, too, for fancy prices. There are one-way mirrors in the peeper booths and special insurance policies for domination or S&M. That's where the girls make money. The club too.'

Her mouth screws up tight as she squints at her sketch.

'Well, there's a regular customer. Not frequent but regular. Once a month or so she comes in for one of the specialty shows. Maybe twice a year she'll foot the bill for a request. At first I thought she was a standard S&M dyke. Now I think it's not pain that she's interested in. She's interested in changing people.'

Something in Miranda's tone catches me. A swirl of familiar fear starts in my gut. She feels it too. I see a bewilderment strange to her face.

'The lady's rich. She pays. She likes transvestites if they want to become transsexuals. If they want to go all the way, she'll pay for all treatments and surgery. That's how Paulette could finally afford it. He could have gone on strapping his balls up tight for the rest of his life if it wasn't for her. The Glass House keeps hiring transvestites and she keeps shipping them off to get real. But she watches. That's part of the deal. She goes along and watches the operation. And it isn't just sex changes. She actually prefers other things.'

A cold thought sinks quietly through me. Again? Miranda draws and talks, looking at my elbows, forehead, knees, tits, anywhere but my eyes.

The long-haired blonde, Denise, who unfurled her pubic hair and danced on her head hair, had furnished one of the recent command performances. They stretched her out on a chrome table in one of the back rooms, and gave her local anesthetics while they burned all her hair off. They set the fire and then ducked back into the glassed-in booths to escape the smell as the girl shrieked in fear if not pain, and the master of ceremonies, in a gas mask and flameproof suit, stood by with the fire extinguisher.

'The dame paid Denise's hospital bills and went to visit her all the time. I went to see Denise the day before she got out. She looks bad. The roots were destroyed and the hair will never grow back. There are a lot of scars on her face. She's not allowed to have any plastic surgery. That was in the contract she signed. You wouldn't believe it but Denise is happy. She says Miss Lick, that's the lady's name, paid her so much she'll never have to work again. Denise says there have been others from the Glass House. One redhead with enormous tits who had them amputated and went to college and is a doctor now!'

My daughter is staring at me. Her eyes are looking anxiously at my eyes. The point is coming. I feel it speeding toward me as she searches my face for a reaction. Any reaction.

'The reason I'm droning on with this silly stuff is that Miss Lick came back to the dressing room after the show last Friday night and asked to talk to me. She's gruff and gross and when she isn't being extremely dignified she's being what she calls a "straight shooter." That means the first thing she said to me was, "Look, I'm not going to make a pass at you, so relax." Maybe it's nuts but I liked her. She took me out for a fantastic dinner, though she didn't eat. She drank the whole time. She pumped me for my life story and, being the shy, reserved type, I spilled the works. The poor orphan brought up in the convent school. The mysterious trust fund covering my art-school tuition and the permanent rent on this place. I had a glass of champagne and colored the whole yarn a glorious purple. She was fascinated. And what it comes down to is, she isn't after my ass, she's after my tail.'

'Ah,' I say. My mouth stayed open.

Miranda leans forward, eager. 'Yes. This is the tale of the tail that I threatened you with, and I figure you will understand what I'm talking about.'

The sketch pad lies unmolested across her knee. One long leg hooked over the chair arm, she looks at me. Her hands are still. Her face is just young now, all the cleverness washed away.

'I was ashamed of it. You know, as a kid. The nuns would tell me it was a cross to bear and a punishment for my mother's sins. I want to just tell you the truth, not purple it up this time.

The nuns were good to me. I loved them. In a funny way the fact that the religion never quite took in me has to do with the tail. It's hard to explain. Maybe I don't even understand it yet. My one prayer was that I'd wake up and my tail would be gone. My backside would be smooth like the others.'

My mouth twists wryly. 'You hated it?'

'Sure.'

I sit, coolly naked, examining her racehorse legs and the jut of her calf out of incredibly thin ankles and remembering my first sight of her head, emerging blood-smeared and dark from between my legs. Her small rumpled face jerked to the side with a profile like a turtle.

And later, with Lil beside me, stretching out the tiny folded arms and legs by gently pulling on her hands and feet, and finding nothing. Nothing but that little pigtail coiled over her buttocks. And Lil's voice, not broken or shrill in those days, saying, 'Well, remember Chick. He didn't look like much either. Go ahead and love her. We'll see.'

Months later she was crawling and learning to stand up, and was getting too big to sleep in the cupboard beneath the sink with me. Her father, whose wide mouth and almond eyes are Miranda's now, looked at her one day when she had tripped and fallen and split her lip on the floor of the trailer and was crying and bleeding, and he said, 'Get rid of her.' And I cried and begged and yanked down her diapers to remind him of that tail, pink and charming, and he sneered and said, 'Get rid of her or I'll give her to Mumpo for supper, stuffed and roasted!'

Now, twenty years later, in this huge room, with Lil downstairs watching a TV screen through a magnifying glass, her mind steeped in the amnesiac vapor of her own decay, and Arty's wonderful face gone to worms despite me, I sit here looking at the full, ripe flesh of this almost normal young female and for a single satisfying instant see her on a platter with a well-basted skin crackling to the touch.

'You say you hate your tail.'

'I did. Then I heard about the Glass House, where they weren't interested if you were just pretty and could dance but wanted something spectacular. It was a joke to audition. Or an experiment. A different approach to my tail. But since I've been working there I don't feel the same way about my tail. Now I think, in a way, it's kind of marvelous.' Her eyes are questions. Is it sane to like my tail? she is asking.

I am too old for this roller coaster. This much anger and this much pleasure should not be crowded into two short hours. My liver, or whatever it is that's trying to crowd its way into my left leg, can't take it.

'This must bore you. It must seem pretty silly.'

'No, I'm just resting my eyes. What does she look like, Miss Lick?'

'Mary Lick. She's forty or something, six feet two, maybe two hundred forty pounds. Short sandy hair. I wasn't sure you were an albino until you took off your shades. This is the first time I've seen you without them. You have a fascinating orbital ridge; I'm just going to get a quick sketch. The deal is that Miss Lick has offered to pay me to have my tail amputated. She'll pay all expenses, recovery as well as surgery. She swears the best surgeon. Plus she'll pay me ten thousand dollars in cash. I don't know what to do. Miss Lick isn't what you'd think. She's rough, but when I was telling her about being an orphan she kept saying, "Keerist," and I could tell she was wrapped up in it. When we left the restaurant, which is out of town a ways, she backed out of the parking lot and into a ditch. There we were with the rear wheels stuck in the mud. She sat there staring out the windshield in the dark. She said, "I've been here a hundred times and this never happened. I'm fucked up. But I'm not drunk. It's that convent, your tail." Then she got out to push and I steered and we got back up on the road. She drove me home and I felt right then that I'd give her my tail or anything else she asked for just because she cared.'

My eyes pop open to the sight of Miranda's increasingly familiar frown. 'Did you tell her that?'

'No. She wanted me to think about it. She's going to stop by the Glass House tonight for my answer. She says if I decide to do it I should wait until school ends and I have the summer to recover from the surgery.'

'Very considerate.' The light is the color of dust now as it catches her hair and the side of her cheek. It leaves her dark eyes in shadow.

'Have you talked to your friends at the club?'

'They're all wild about it. They'd jump at it ... but they all hate their specialties. And I'm not sure I do anymore. That's why I wanted to talk to you. You understand living with a specialty. Better than any of us. I don't know how old you are....'

'Thirty-eight,' I say, and her face shows she thought I was older. I was barely seventeen when she was born. But dwarfs age quickly.

'What I'm asking is, am I crazy to have this liking for my tail? Am I just covering up something else? If I turn this chance down I'd probably regret it for the rest of my life. You must have wished a million times to be normal.'

'No.'

'No?'

'I've wished I had two heads. Or that I was invisible. I've wished for a fish's tail instead of legs. I've wished to be more special.'

'Not normal?'

'Never.'

'No shit! That's astounding! Tell me ...'

'I have to leave.' Reaching down for the pajama top, uncramping my legs to climb down to the floor, padding toward the bathroom door.

'Hey, I'm sorry, I've taken most of your afternoon, you must be beat.... You'll come again, won't you? How about tomorrow? I'll work up some of these sketches and be ready for some more-developed stuff tomorrow.'

Alone in my room with the door finally closed I stand gaping blankly at the grimy window. I had no right to pretend surprise. The nun told me when I first took her there. Horst the Cat Man was leaning on the fender of his van at the gate and I was inside in the visitor's room. I sat hugging Miranda, the toddler — not yet a year old — still in roomy diapers. Trying to talk through my tears to this clean-faced nun, who had seemed so warm and reassuring over the phone.

'What do you mean, a tail?' Her eyes cooled instantly. She tugged at the back of Miranda's diaper. 'Is she retarded?' Miranda clouded at the strange touch, looking anxiously at me. When the diaper dropped to her pudgy knees she closed her eyes and opened her mouth and began to cry.

'Just a little tail,' I was saying.

The nurse came in, chipper, with a clipboard full of forms. She held Miranda expertly, dancing her on a chair while I sniffed and scratched at the forms. The nun muttered softly to the nurse. The nurse sang 'The Itsy-Bitsy Spider Climbs Up the Water Spout' and peeked surreptitiously down the back of Miranda's diaper.

We went to the infirmary, where the nurse chattered rhymes as she stripped the oblivious and chortling Miranda. Probing, listening, peering with tiny flashlights, counting digits, and finally tickling the curl in the tail until Miranda laughed out loud and I turned to grey stone.

'It is not simple surgery in her case, but it would make her life much easier,' the nurse was soothing me. 'You must imagine what her life among normal children would be like. She will shower and dress and swim in a group setting where it will be impossible to hide. Children can be very cruel.'

'No,' I snapped. 'She keeps it. You won't touch it.'

They asked me again five years later as I stood watching Miranda through the window of the visitors' room.

'She prays to be rid of it. How can you deny your own child a chance at a happy, normal life?'

I stared in silence as Miranda swooped, shrieking, down the playground slide, searching to see alive in her all the dead love in me. 'She's happy,' I said. 'You've told me so and I see it. She keeps her tail.'

But she hated it.

I crawl into my cupboard, pull the door shut, and lie curled in the dark, thinking about Miss Lick. I've seen hobbies like hers before.

It is dark when I wake up. I stick my head under the cold-water tap for a while. Then I put a sweater on, then my coat, and a wool watch cap on over my wig, and stump out past the TV voice from Lily's door to catch the Number 17 bus for downtown.

Huddled under the sick fluorescent glare of the empty bus, I stare at a cardboard warning tucked into the rack above the windows. It says, 'Don't get too comfortable.'

The doors sigh to let me out on the echoing mall. I head north toward Old Town and the Glass House. I make one stop in a phone booth. There are several Licks in the books but no Mary or M. It's probably a fake name anyway. Nobody who can afford her kind of hobby could afford to have it known.

The neon clock in the window of the tattoo parlor says nine. Two blocks later I am scouting doorways across from the Glass House parking lot. A shut-down leather shop on the corner gives me a view of the parking lot and the side door as well as a long angle on the front entrance. A heap of garbage bags at the front waits for the morning pickup. Five steps lead up to the door. I sit on the top step and watch the lot fill up slowly. The cars spew out cheerful groups and giggling pairs. Mostly men. I count. Sixty going in before one comes out. None of them is Miss Lick.

The cold wraps me. It isn't real rain, just the heavy mist that takes its time soaking through. The clouds hang low, picking up a dull bruise color from the lights of the city. The flesh-toned office tower known as Big Pink haunts the sky above the crabbed three-storey horizon of Old Town. The tower disappears occasionally in a gust of darkness. My legs begin to ache.

Who do I think I am? What in the name of creeping Jesus am I going to do? The only answer is the sneer from the region of my hip sockets. I go on sitting, watching, feeling like a rat's-ass fool.

Two hours later Miss Lick shows up. She's easy to pick out. Six foot two and 240 pounds in a grey business suit. Her high heels are each big enough to bury an Egyptian in. She trots alone across the parking lot, hunched under an umbrella, and slides into the side door of the Glass House. My pulse whips high at the sight of her but drifts back down to a rhythmless funk as the door stays closed.

It's another hour before she steps out into the harsh light of the parking lot. She looks up and decides against opening the umbrella. She lets the door sink back behind her and stands, head up, mouth open, fumbling in her pockets. I get up. My knees are stiff and unreliable. I shake my feet trying to get some juice into my joints. The blood begins its burn back to life as she starts her march across the lot. She is too discreet to leave her car that close to the place. She's on the corner, turning. I trot down the dark side of the street. A small bar is evicting scum, and the drunken banter covers my shuffle briefly. Three blocks from the Glass House the big woman climbs into a sleek, dark machine parked in front of the blood bank. I write the license number on my wrist with a felt-tip pen and feel as though I've conquered Asia.

Miranda won't get off work for another two hours. She'll take a cab home. I stump over to the bus mall, so delirious with relief and cold that I hallucinate Miranda on every corner. Sitting by the glare-blackened window on the Number 17, I rewrite the license number on an old receipt from my purse. The figures on my wrist are already smearing blue from the mist and my sweat.

I go in to work early the next morning. As I climb onto the bus, a small genderless child lurches in its mother's arms, pointing at me and crowing, 'Little Mama!' The woman holding the child goes a sudden hot red and grabs at the tiny hand, shushing. I turn and hop back down the steps and wave the driver on. I walk to the radio station.

By the time I get there I've decided that the license number has nothing to do with Miranda's Miss Lick. How many big women use the side door of the Glass House? I could be tagging lumpily after a convincing middle-aged transvestite. If Lick is a phony name for subterranean use, I could trail an irrelevant specimen for weeks and never know it.

I slide a license trace request into the newsroom, make two fifteen-second commercial spots for Stereo Heaven and Sun River lunchmeat, and then tape the third installment of

Beowulf for the Blind. I wait until after the *Story Hour* to check my message slot, and find the computer printout of the trace. It is Mary T. Lick. She hasn't changed her name for the Glass House. Her address is a tony high-rise condo in the West Hills, just below the Rose Garden.

In the elevator it occurs to me that Miranda might be waiting for me in the lobby, hoping to guile me into another drawing session. I hold my breath as the doors open, but she isn't there.

I cross the bridge over the concrete river of the sunken highway and walk down to the library. Lincoln High School is directly behind the station and the students on their lunch hour crowd the sidewalks. Two shrill-voiced girls argue hideously on the Charles Dickens bench outside the library. I swim through the heavy doors and up the curving white marble stairs to the index files.

Mary T. Lick has a card of her own, just before Thomas R. Lick, her father. They are both buried in microfilm. I go up another two flights to the periodical room and stake out a viewing machine in the most obscure corner. I camp there with a stack of film reels of old newspapers.

There she is, not smiling, in the society columns. A younger Mary Lick is not smiling at the Hunt Club Opera Benefit. Mary Lick is trapped gloomily between two vivacious gargoyles at the City Club. Mary Lick, standing uncomfortably next to the deep V neckline of a Rose Princess, frowns at the crowning of the Rose Festival Queen. A much younger Mary Lick stands glumly, behind a bald and furious-faced man billed in the caption as Thomas R. Lick, at the ribbon cutting for the Thomas R. Lick Swimming Pool at the TAC Club.

The text skates over guest lists, wardrobes, and buffet menus. There is no comment on Mary's wardrobe, which is the same in all cases, a dark featureless business suit.

Thomas R. is referred to variously as the Lickety Split Food king, mogul, or tycoon. The grimmest and most recent photo of Mary Lick shows her staring moodily at a Salvation Army truck loaded with cardboard boxes. '24 Lickety Split Thanksgiving Dinners.' The caption calls Mary 'The

Lickety Split Food Heiress,' suggesting that Thomas R. has passed on to the obituary page, probably with a 'Lick Splits' headline.

There she is. The old man is spread out on the worm buffet and Daughter Mary is dumping hundreds of Lickety Split dinners into socially unacceptable hands. The seven-year-old item comments that this is the first contribution in the history of the Lickety Split Corporation, but says, coyly, that it might 'signify a new role for the company in the future.'

I cram the copies into my bag and chug home. There's a note under my door. A pencil smear from Miranda. 'Come up and let me draw you.'

When I knock, her door explodes inward, her huge frame surrounded by light. 'Finally.' Reaching for me.

'I can't today. I have some work to do.' Her face falls into conventions masking disappointment. My chest lurches.

'But how did it go with that woman, about your tail?'

She flickers for the connection. Not thinking about it.

'Oh, there's no hurry. She says it's fine to wait until the semester ends.'

'To decide?'

'No. To do it. Have it done.'

'You decided.'

'What the hell. It's silly not to.'

Her insolent look. The careless smirk. She is punishing me for being unavailable. I turn away, sick, and feel my way back down the hall.

She calls after me.

'When can you sit for me again? Tomorrow? The afternoon? Miss McGurk?'

I wave and go downstairs to my room and shut the door behind me and lock it.

Pacing and grinding my teeth. Throwing my wig on the floor and stamping. Why does she make me so angry? My rage terrifies me. I am a monster. I would rip her to shreds. I would swing her up by her round pink heels and snap her long body until that bright, hairy head smashed against the wall. Falling on my knees, shaking. Tangling my hands to keep from breaking something. Sudden gratitude for the nuns, realizing that if she had stayed with me all the years of her growing up I would have murdered her — the arrogant, imbecile bitch, my baby, beautiful Miranda.

I end up curled on the floor, blubbering and gasping. No one comes to comfort me. I lie there until I'm bored and embarrassed at having dried snot streaks crackling on my cheeks. I get angry so rarely. Now twice in two days at Miranda.

I take a shower, get into a flannel nightgown, make instant coffee with hot water from the sink, and push the window up so I can see through. The streak of sky visible above the alley is heavy. I sit on the sill drinking death's-head brew and watching the shadow creep higher on the blind wall of the warehouse across the way. I can hear the pigeons fuddling in the eaves. Rain begins to splat a shine over the puddle on the garage roof below me.

Downstairs the phone rings and then stops. Lil's voice comes, shrill up the staircase, 'Forty Wuunnn,' and from far away a door slams and the redheaded defrocked Benedictine beings his desperate avalanche down the stairs. The pipes gurgle. The heat is coming on.

I drag the big old costume trunk out of the closet and open it. The Miranda Box I call it, though there is little enough of her in it. The shallow tray in the top of the trunk holds it all. School photos. The stack of report cards. The bundled letters from Sister T. that came four times a year for sixteen years. Progress reports: 'Miranda is reading two years beyond her grade level. Her disposition is cheerful but marred by stubbornness and a disruptive tendency.' The test scores. The list of inoculations. The chicken pox report. An indignant letter folded around a printed form crawling with the results of a medical examination.

She was fifteen that year and had ran away and hooked up with an occult guitarist moonlighting as a United Parcel delivery driver who hid her in his 'bohemian' — as the report called it — apartment for three weeks until she got bored and strolled back to the school. She was indifferent to repentance, according to the nun, and far from a virgin, according to the doctor. Heavenly Mary had prevented her from getting pregnant or diseased. They threatened to throw her out or to turn her over to the juvenile authorities. In the end my monthly payments increased by 50 percent and she stayed.

Fingering the blistering letter, I remember precisely the hoops my heart went through over the incident. I was terrified for her, but strangely delighted, as though her wildness were a triumph of her genes over indoctrination. I lay the thin sheaf of drawings she gave me on top of the rest, and then lift the tray out and set it aside.

The body of the trunk is crammed with clipping books, thick stacks of paper wrapped in black plastic. Photographs. Sound tapes. A tight roll of posters held by dry and brittle rubber bands.

This fragile, flammable heap is all that's left of my life. It is the history of Miranda's source. She soars and stomps and burns through her days with no notion of the causes that formed her. She imagines herself isolated and unique. She is unaware that she is part of, and the product of, forces assembled before she was born.

She can be flip about her tail. Or she can try. She is ignorant of its meaning and oblivious to its value. But something in her blood aches, warning her.

I slip the topmost poster from the roll. The paper is stiff, wanting to break rather than tear. Carefully spreading it, uncoiling it, sliding plastic-wrapped bundles onto the corners to hold it down, I open it on the musty carpet.

The Binewskis are revealed, dressed in glittering white, enchanted against sea greens and blues, smiling, together still on wide paper. The poster has a fountain format with the whole family spewing upward from Chick, during his brief 'Fortunato — The Strongest Child in the World' period. Papa killed this poster, along with Chick's act, before the public saw either of them. But it is my favorite family portrait. Chick, six years old and golden, is smiling at the bottom, his arms straight up with his parents standing on his hands. The beauteous 'Crystal Lily' in an openly amorous pose, one leg kicking high out of her dance skirt, wrapped in the arms of the handsome 'Ring Master Al,' our Papa, Aloysius, in high boots and chalk jodhpurs — their smiles leaping upward in yellow light toward our stars, our treasures — 'Arturo the Amazing Aqua Boy,' afloat with his flippers spread angelically in hinted liquid in the upper right corner, his bare skull gleaming and haloed. In the left corner, at a cunningly suggested keyboard swirling out of the blue, 'The Magnificent Musical Siamese Twins, Electra and Iphigenia!' Elly and Iphy with their long hair smoothed into black buns, slim white arms entwined, pale faces beaming out in shafts from their violet eyes.

And I am there also. 'Albino Olympia,' viewed from the side to display my hump, bald nobbly head tilted charmingly, curtsying with one arm pointing at the glorious Chick and his miraculous burden. Chick was six and I was twelve but he loomed a full head taller. The arched banner across the top in joyous glitter, 'The Fabulous Binewskis.'

The wallet-sized school picture from Miranda's senior year shows her face the same size as the Binewski poster faces. I slide the photo around, next to Chick, to Arty, to Papa Al. It is Arty she looks like. Those Binewski cheekbones and the Mongol eyes. Would she see it?

BOOK II
Your Dragon — Care, Feedings and Identifying Fewmets

4

Papa's Roses

The Olympia McGurk profile in the personnel computer of Radio KBNK lists my training as 'Elocution and diction, and microphonic presentation as taught by Aloysius Binewski,' which I wrote calmly and confidently into my résumé as though every well-trained voice would recognize the name of the master.

That was Papa, sitting in the back of the tent at the soundboard, wearing headphones and glaring at me as I stood on one foot on the stage with the old ragged microphone waving aimlessly near my mouth. Papa, hollering, '*Boring!*' at my fiftieth delivery of 'Step right this way, folks!' or mimicking cruelly, 'Ya-ta, ya-ta, ya-ta!' if I fell into a repetitive rhythm on 'From the darkest mysteries of science, a revelation of poetic grace.'

'Move your lips, for shit's sake!' howled Papa, or 'Stop with the mouse farts and *project!*

'That's a double-reed instrument! It is called a voice! It is not a comb wrapped in waxed paper! I gave it to you from the love in my guts for your scrawny and unmarketable carcass, so be kind enough to use it properly!'

And me all the while having to pee — coughing into the mike when my throat was tired and raw — eyes stinging and lips and chin crumpling in grief at his anger. The sweet tinkle of Electra on the bass and Iphy on the treble with Mama's voice counting, 'One and two and . . .' as the twins had their piano lession inside the trailer. The gurgle and hum of the pumps that filtered my brother Arty's 'Aqua Boy' tank. And the dim round moon of baby Fortunato's face peering at me from the dark of the risers above Papa.

51

If I finally did it right and got all the way through from 'Step up, friends' to 'A vision of the miraculous extravagance of Nature for the same simple price as an overcooked hotdog' without a single bellow of rage from my beloved papa, then he would swoop me up in huge arms and tuck me onto a shoulder, where I could grab his astounding hair in my fists and ride high through the tent flaps into the light, with Fortunato's golden head chugging along far below, and we would parade the long street of booths with me laughing down at the red-haired girls who sold the candy and at the toothless wheelman and Horst the Cat Man all nodding at Papa's instructions, and hearing, feeling his huge voice rumble out from beneath my legs, 'This little beetle did her lessons just right today.'

It's funny, in a dingy way, that I make my little living by reading. I have to smile because I used to avoid reading. It scared me.

It never bothered Arty. He read constantly — anything — but his favorites were ghost stories and horror tales.

When we were still children I was the one who turned his pages. He'd lie in bed reading late when everyone else was asleep. I lay beside him and held his lamp and turned the pages and watched his eyes move in quick jerks down the print. Reading was never a quiet pastime for Arty. He rocked, grunted, muttered, and exclaimed. He was in one of his toilet phases at that time. 'Sweet rosy-brown arsehole' was his expression of pleasure. 'Shitsucker' was the pejorative.

'Don't you get dreams?' I asked him. 'Don't you get scared reading those at night? They're supposed to scare you.'

'Hey, nit squat! These are written by norms to scare norms. And do you know what the monsters and demons and rancid spirits are? Us, that's what. You and me. We are the things that come to the norms in nightmares. The thing that lurks in the bell tower and bites out the throats of the choirboys — that's you, Oly. And the thing in the closet that makes the babies scream in the dark before it sucks their last breath — that's me. And the rustling in the brush and the strange piping cries that chill the spine on a deserted road at twilight — that's the twins singing practice scales while they look for berries.

'Don't shake your head at me! These books teach me a lot. They don't scare me because they're about me. Turn the page.'

Maybe it's mean to think, but the best time was before Chick was born. Things were simple. Papa would tell us about the hard times and explain that Arty had brought success to the show, and that Elly and Iphy had helped the business and, because he was a kind man, that even Oly had 'done her part.' There was always work but it was good.

Mornings were our time. After lessons and before the stage shows began at 2 P.M. we were free creatures. Papa connected two chunks of tire tread with a nylon web, and attached web straps to fit over Arty's fore and aft fins. With this rubber-tread armor on his chest and belly, Arty could slither almost anywhere.

Papa thought we should be mysteries that the townies couldn't see without paying. But, if we were in the country, we were allowed to ramble as long as we stuck together.

'Get your asses the hell out of that tree!'

The farmer snapped his belt, doubled against itself, the strap wide enough to sting the air all the way up beside us among the Bings. Arty pressed his head back against the trunk and peered down at the man with the belt. He was old and strong and his eyes clicked on me as soon as I moved. I dodged out of sight and the belt snapped again. The leaves quivered above where Elly and Iphy were perched. They'd been bickering about how many cherries they could eat without sharing a bellyache and the runs. It must have been their high voices that drew this old codger. They were silent now, scared as usual.

'Come down now, or by all that crackles I'll be up there after you!' He didn't really sound mad. He'd stopped a ways out from the tree, too smart to come underneath where things might drop on him.

Arty's mouth moved close to my ear. 'You first, then Elly and Iphy. He thinks it's kids.'

I crammed my voice into the top of my mouth and pitched it silly, 'We're coming, mister, don't hurt us!' I took my dark glasses off and poked my head past the edge so he could see my ears sticking out from under my watch cap. I squinted so he couldn't tell the color of my eyes. The farmer's shrewd eyes tightened on me. His mouth quirked into one corner for a spit.

'I'll hurt you in a minute.'

'We've got to help our brother, mister, just a second.'

Arty stretched his neck and clamped his jaw onto the last twig of cherries I held as I began climbing out of the tree crotch. 'Elly,' I called deliberately, 'Iphy, help me get Arty down.' A long leg appeared with a crumpled pink sock and a white sneaker. I peeked at the farmer. He cracked the folded belt against his high rubber boot. He was watching but he'd loosened a bit. The girls' names did that, soft, old-fashioned things. And the 'Don't hurt us' had him disarmed.

'Psst!' Iphy was looking anxiously down at me while Elly maneuvered the descent. Arty muttered softly up at them, 'Oly goes down first. You hand me down to her and then come.'

'We're coming down, mister,' I called, and then slid away from Arty, down the trunk, gripping with toes and fingers in the deep cracks of the bark to slip down the easy slope of the tree on the side away from the brown-faced man with the belt. When I hit the ground I stepped back, bent forward, and rubbed my cap off against the trunk. I was reaching up for Arty when I heard the old bastard grunt. He'd seen my hump and my bald head. The twins were lowering Arty with three hands and hugging the tree with the fourth. Arty's clothes hissed and snagged on the bark as he slid. I caught his hips on my chest and he slid down my belly to the ground. The twins bounced down the trunk, peering from both sides at the farmer. I turned to look at him. His eyes slit into suspicious surprise. Arty started humping toward him quickly. I jumped after. The twins caught up and Elly held my hand as we moved toward the farmer. He fell down on his butt in the grass. His belt rolled out flat beside him. We went past him fast and out of his cherry orchard.

Later in bed I decided Arty was smart. It was the order of our appearance that got the guy. Here he was cracking his belt and chuckling inside about another summer's batch of kids in the cherry trees. He'd be rehearsing the story already, to tell his wife over chicken and biscuits in the kitchen, as he sat with his sleeves still damp from scrubbing and his hat off showing the pale stretch below his hair where the sunburn ended.

'Caught Jethro's grandkids in the Bings today,' he'd say, 'all up one tree, same as their daddy and his sis twenty years ago.' And he and his wife smiling at each other and her pouring the iced coffee and saying she hoped he hadn't scared them too much. But while all this was readying behind his eyes we stepped out and dropped him. First me, twisted under my hump, the watch cap popping its bald shock, and then the 1.88 seconds for him to register the shape of Arturo and the way he moved, and, most important, which direction he was heading. If that had been all he might have taken a pitchfork to us. But then came the night-haired girls, milk-skinned, flower-eyed, and their two long legs in the slumping pink socks. The old man had thirty years of shooing kids from trees yanked out of him. I wondered if he would say anything at all about it to anybody.

Arty's head jerked around and his eyes ripped at me. The shadows of sharp bone and muscle strained at his tight skin. Anger.

'Pick me up. Now. Pick me up.' He was heavy but I hoisted him from the middle until he leaned against me, upright, then crouched and hefted him onto my shoulder. His head and chest faced the rear, his round butt curving into my arms.

'I hate long grass. Hate it.' His voice came into my left ear as we moved slowly through the field. 'You try humping along with your nose in the snakes and cow shit for a block or two.'

Arty always talked to the people. It was a central charm of his act that, though he looked and acted alien, part animal, part myth, he would prop his chin on the lip of the tank to talk 'just like folks.' Only it wasn't quite like folks.

At first, when Arty was tiny, Al was his enthusiastic master of ceremonies. Arty gradually worked his way in and took over the talking entirely. Before too long Al just stood out front and lured the crowd in.

Arty started with explanatory chat about his own physique but soon discovered the power of piffle and vapor. Greeting-card sentiments, intoned pretentiously in the stage-lit waver of the tank by such an intriguing little deviant, packed a surprising wallop.

Arty and Papa experimented. Arty's show changed in small ways — a pink spotlight instead of red — or, occasionally, in big ways. It was always a sit-down show, a bench-and-bleacher act. The tank and Arty were the only focus. For a while Arty made a dry entrance. He came out on the platform above the tank before diving in. Then he decided that folks wanted to think that he lived in the water all the time — maybe even breathed water. After that he always made his first appearance in the water. He used a screen in the water for a while, hiding behind it and swimming out into the brightly visible part of the tank when Papa signaled. Arty got sick of waiting and had a big tube tunnel run up through the tank floor so he could wait dry in the back and make a dramatic swoosh entrance when the lights came up. Arty spewing upward in a burst of luminescent bubbles with a thrumming fanfare of recorded music. It got the crowd going.

Eventually Arty grew bored with the Gilled Illusion of Aqua Boy, and in his Arturan phase enjoyed parading before his throng (at a distance, in a golf cart) on dry land, but he stuck to the submarine identity for a long time.

As he bitterly pointed out, he wasn't extravagant enough looking to hold a crowd for twenty minutes (the length of the show in those early days) by just lolling around and letting them gawk. He had to *do* something. The seal tricks of his infancy soon palled on him. Swimming was useful. The bright tank in the dim tent was a focus. The water and his floating form were soothing, hypnotic. People stared at the tank and his undulating figure as they would at a bright fire. The tank made him exotic but safe. 'They can relax,' Arty theorized, 'because they know I'm not going to jump up into their laps.' (Arty tended to be snide about laps, not having one of his own.)

'It's a fiendish waste to get 'em into a beautiful sucker zone of mind and then not *do* anything with them,' Arty would lament. So he learned to talk. He recited rhymes, quoted the more saccharine philosophers, commented on human nature. The standard approach, and the line Papa always wanted Arty to take, was jokes, comedy, a creaking stand-up patter that would seem unique coming from the Aqua Boy. But Arty wouldn't go for it. 'I don't want those scumbags laughing at me,' he'd snarl. 'I want them amazed at me, maybe scared of me, but I won't let them laugh. No. Oh, a little chuckle because I'm witty, sure. But not a running line.'

Arty's few jokes, the brief crackling relief from a mystic format, were always dry and biting and directed outward, away from himself.

The misty cauldron of the act was a constant. 'They want to be amazed and scared. That's why they're here,' Arty said.

Gradually, inevitably, he discovered the Oracle. 'The guy who asks the question and thinks he hears an answer is the guy who makes an Oracle.' He'd been reading books on Oriental philosophy and was spouting it solemnly over the lip of the tank one day when a pale woman on the bleachers stood up and asked him whether her fifteen-year-old son, who had run away months before, was alive or dead.

Without thinking at all, without missing a beat, he whipped out, 'Weeping at night alone and yearning for you, working like a man in daylight, silently.' She burst out bawling and hollering, 'Bless you, thank you, bless you, thank you,' as she crawled out over a row of knees and left snorking into her hanky.

She must have told her friends because the next two shows were pimpled with shouted questions from the bleachers and Arty's vague, impromptu answers.

He had the redhead who sold the tickets hand out three-by-five cards for people to write questions on. The act took on a distinct odor of palm reading and advice to the love-or-otherwise-lorn. Papa had thousands of 'Ask Aqua Boy' posters printed and slathered up everywhere we went.

I never knew the twins very well. Maybe Arty was right in

claiming I was jealous of them. They were too charming. The whole crew loved them. The norm crowds loved them. In towns we passed through regularly pairs of young girls would come to the show dressed in a single long skirt in imitation of the twins. Arty wasn't delighted with their popularity either, of course. But he had a way of splitting them. To me they were inaccessible. They didn't need me to do anything for them. Iphy was always kind to me. She was kind to everybody. But Elly was careful to keep me in my place. They were self-sufficient. They needed only each other. And Elly, rest her hard and toothy soul, ruled their body.

I remember Lil with a bundle of costumes in one arm and a bag of popping corn in the other as she stood rigid in the sawdust of the midway and lectured me sternly: 'We use the plural form, Olympia, whenever we refer to Electra and Iphigenia. We do not say "Where *is* Elly and Iphy?" We say "Where *are* Elly and Iphy?"'

If you stood facing the twins, Elly was on your left and Iphy on your right. Elly was right-handed and Iphy was left-handed. But Iphy was the right leg and Elly was the left leg. If you pulled Elly's hair, Iphy yelped too. If you kissed Iphy's cheek, Elly smiled. If Elly burnt her hand on the popcorn machine, Iphy cried also and couldn't sleep that night from the pain. They ran and climbed and danced gracefully. They had separate hearts but a meshing bloodstream; separate stomachs but a common intestine. They had one liver and one set of kidneys. They had two brains and a nervous system that was peculiarly connected and unexpectedly separate. Between them they ate a small fraction more than one norm kid their size.

Jonathan Tomaini, the greasy-haired music-school graduate who became their piano teacher when they had gone past Lily, claimed that Iphy was all melody and Elly was rhythm exclusively. They were both sopranos.

Arty speculated that their two brains functioned as right and left lobes of a single brain.

Elly punished Iphy by eating food that disagreed with them. Iphy would sink into depressed silence, eating nothing. Elly's favorite trick was cheese. Iphy hated constipation like cancer. Elly varied the treatment by gorging on chocolate, even though she didn't really like chocolate and it made her chin break out in zits. Pimples were very obvious on her milky skin. Iphy loved chocolate and never ate it for fear of pimples. Elly's eating the stuff never gave Iphy pimples. The punishment was that Iphy had to sleep next to Elly's pimples, had to live within inches of the molten eruptions.

Iphy felt sorry for everybody who wasn't a twin. Elly despised me.

When Chick came along, both twins adored him. He was such a meek little feather that he worshiped them. Lil and Al were just loved. But Arty was different. He was separate. He fascinated Iphy and he terrified Elly. Elly's harshness flared against anyone who might distract Iphy's attention from her. The rest of us were just fantasy opposition. Arty was dangerous. He flirted with Iphy. He toyed with her.

Elly hated him. She acted, sometimes, as though Arty could tear Iphy away from her.

The Binewski family shrine was a fifty-foot trailer with a door at each end and a one-dollar admission price. The sign over the entrance said 'Mutant Mystery' and, in smaller letters, 'A Museum of Nature's Innovative Art.' We called it 'the Chute.' Like everything else in the Fabulon, the Chute grew and changed over the years. But the Chute had started with six clear-glass twenty-gallon jars, and those jars — each lit by hidden yellow beams and equipped with its own explanatory, push-button voice tape — were always the core.

The Chute was Crystal Lil's idea, and she supervised it. She visited the Chute every day before the gates opened and polished the jars lovingly with glass cleaner. Later, when Al wanted to put the stuffed animals in, he had to clear it with Crystal Lil. She insisted on the maze at the entrance so that the six jars remained the climax of the walk through.

The stuffed animals in their lit glass windows were the usual humdrum collection of two-headed calves, six-legged chickens, and the mounted skeleton of a three-tailed cat. The only live exhibit was a trio of featherless hens that Al picked up from the chicken rancher who had bred them to save plucking costs on his fryers. He couldn't sell them because customers were used to the pimply 'chicken skin' of birds that had their feathers yanked. They didn't trust the smooth-skinned look. These three were cheerful, baggy-fleshed creatures with floppy combs and wattles. They lived for two years before Lil found them, heaped dead in a corner of their cage, done in overnight by some microscopic enemy of innovation. Al had them stuffed and they stayed on in the same cage. One bent over, with head extended as though about to peck at the straw that would never again need changing. One stood alert, with its round yellow eye cocked at the passersby and its right foot curled as though in the act of stepping forward. The last sat cozily in a corner with one wing spread and its head tucked underneath, apparently looking for lice.

Lily would take her pills after breakfast and then go over to the Chute with her cleaning gear. She left the dark green floors and walls to the power-vacuum crew but the glass she did herself. Sometimes I would help, sometimes the twins. Mostly Lily did it herself. She would do a quick, decent job on all the glass windows in the maze, but her true purpose was her visit to the 'kids' as she called them. The jars were Al's failures.

'And mine,' Lil would always add. She would spray the big jars and polish them. She would talk softly, all the while, to the things floating in the jars or to whoever was with her. She remembered the drug recipe Al had prescribed for her pregnancy with each one, and reminisced about the births.

There were four who had been born dead: Clifford, Maple, Janus, and the Fist. 'We always say Arty is our firstborn but actually Janus was the first,' Lil would say as she peered into the fluid that filled up the jar, examining the small huddled figure that floated upright inside.

Janus was always my favorite. He had a down of dark hair curling on his tiny scalp and a sweet sleeping face. His other head emerged on a short neck at the base of his spine, equally round and perfect, with matching hair. This rear brother squinted in perpetual surprise at the tiny buttocks under its nose. The four sets of minuscule eyelashes fascinated me and I wondered how the two would have gotten along if Janus had lived. Would they have bickered like Elly and Iphy? They could never have seen each other except sideways in a mirror. Probably the top head would have controlled everything and made his poor little butt-brother miserable.

Lil always fussed over Maple, who looked like a big rumpled sponge. Maple had two eyes but they didn't relate to each other. Lil said Maple had no bones. She and Al had decided Maple was female because they couldn't find a penis. Lil also clucked and sighed over Clifford, who looked like a lasagna pan full of exposed organs with a monkey head attached. The twins and I called Clifford 'the Tray' when Mama wasn't around.

The Fist wasn't full term but it was obvious where the name had come from. 'I only carried the Fist for five months,' Lil said, and that was her excuse for spending a shade less time on his jar.

Apple and Leona were the two who had lived long enough to die outside Lily's belly. Apple was big but dull. She looked like a Tibetan cherub. Her coarse black hair grew close to her rumpled eyes. I myself could dimly remember her sleeping in the top drawer of Lil's big bureau. She never moved anything but her lips, her eyelids, and her bowels. Her eyeballs were still pointing in vaguely different directions. Lil had fed her from a bottle and changed her, washing her limp body three or four times a day. Lil would talk to Apple and rub her and move things in front of her eyes, but there was never any response. Apple grew fat and there was a smell of old urine around her and the drawer. She was two years old when she died. A pillow fell on her face.

Arty always claimed that Al did it. Elly and Iphy would squeal when he said that, and I would shake my head and change the subject, but we never asked Lil and we never brought it up in front of Al.

Leona was the last jar before the exit and had four spotlights focused to pierce the formaldehyde in which she drifted. Lil would linger over the jar and once or twice I saw her cry as she pressed her forehead against the glass and crooned. 'We had such hopes for her,' she would sigh. Leona's jar was labeled 'The Lizard Girl' and she looked the part. Her head was long

from front to back and the forehead was compressed and flattened over small features that collapsed into her long throat
with no chin to disturb the line. She had a big fleshy tail, as
thick as a leg where it sprouted from her spine, but then
tapering into a point. There was a faint greenish sheen to her
skin but I suspected that Arty was right in claiming that Al had
painted it on after Leona died.

'She was only seven months old,' Lil would murmur. 'We
never understood why she died.'

The sign in the jar room was bolted to the wall and had its
own spotlight. It was carefully calligraphed in brown letters on
a cream background. 'HUMAN,' it said. 'BORN OF NORMAL PARENTS.'

'You must always remember that these are your brothers
and sisters,' Lil would lecture. 'You must always take proper
care of them and keep the roughnecks from jouncing the jars
around on the road.'

The twins and I were expected to share responsibility for the
jars if anything happened to Lil. This burden wasn't even
mentioned to Chick or Arty.

Yet it was Arty who discovered that the kids in the jars
floated close to the top when it rained and sank down to the
bottom when the sky was clear. Al never went into the Chute
himself, but he would ask Lil for the weather report every
morning when she came back from her visit.

5

Assassin — Limp-Wristed and Shy

Lillian Hinchcliff Binewski, eight months and two weeks pregnant with the most extravagant experiment in a flamboyant series — Crystal Lil — bored with the bigness of her belly and the smallness of Coos Bay, Oregon, and fed up with the kaput generator that kept the show closed until a new coil could be installed that night, sat (Our Lil) in the foldaway dinette of the thirty-eight-foot Binewski Road King living van and decided to take a small van and drive over to a shopping center to pick up some prestitched silver-sequined stretch material to make matching costumes for the kids. And for herself after her belly deflated, with a bit of white tulle for a tail.

'Arty honey,' she called, and stubbed her cigarette into the last grime of her breakfast wheat germ where it coated the blue bowl. Arturo, the Aqua Boy, was in the shower and toilet room and it took a minute for him to poke the door open. 'Arty honey. We're going in to that big shopping center. Oly, you help him, baby. We'll all go.'

The pink-eyed Olympia, six years old and bouncy, put down a copy of *National Geographic* and climbed up on the side bunk to take Arty's Dunlop belly-tread off its hook. Arturo was murmuring slyly as Lil tore a long pink fingernail while buckling her sandal. 'I can't hear you, Arty. Be sure to pee before we leave.'

'I said,' Arty slithered up to Lil's foot and lay looking at her long, elegant toes, 'do you think it's a good idea for us all to go?'

Lil stepped over him and swung open the outside door. 'Elly-Iphy,' she shrieked. From the big truck stage next door came the ripple of 'Moonlight Sonata' for four hands and an answering shout from Iphigenia. 'Come here, doves!' and the sonata cut off as Lil grabbed the ignition keys from the Buddha ashtray on the bookshelf.

Arty said, 'I don't want the tread. I'll use the chair. It's easier in public.'

On that sunstruck, restless day, Vern Bogner filled the pickup's fuel tank at the first station down from the camp. He had stopped there on his way up to buy kerosene for the lantern. The old man at the pump watched the meter flip over and hollered at Vern, 'You're leaving early! Get your limit already?' Vern stared grimly through the windshield. The bed of the pickup was obviously empty. Snotty old cocksucker. Sometimes you just wanted to go up in the woods and sit by a fire and slip around a few beers in peace.

Vern Bogner had been produce manager at the Seal Bay Supermarket for five years, and assistant for three years before that. As Vern explained in detail years later, it was a time when his whole life had begun to slide. Despite his experience, oranges had always been hard to stack. He had built mounds and pyramids of Floridas and tangerines and big and little inny and outy navels by the million but he had never been plagued by so many rolls and drops and avalanches as in the past few months.

His wife, Emily, didn't like him much lately. And when he came home from work and said 'Hi' to his own kids, they just snorted and went on staring at the TV. Vern was not at all sure what was happening to him, but a decade later he could still describe the moment-to-moment sensations of that morning.

The day was muggy hot and the smell of gas mixed with the beer in his belly and lifted in a bitter scrape to the back of his throat. Emily sneered at him too. 'Oh, Vern's got lots of trophies — stuffed green peppers, lettuce heads.' And laughter. Even this scummy old station jock was noticing, rubbing it in. Vern turned his head just enough to catch a glint on the barrel of the 30.06 where it hung on the window rack. He'd been out with his fifty-dollar license four times this year and hadn't fired a shot.

When he saw the tall sign for the new shopping center, Vern flicked the turn signal. A brand-new supermarket took up one side of the lot. The dime store and hairdresser and the rest were on the other side of the five acres. He liked visiting other super-markets. He'd take a quick tour of the produce section on his way to the beer. A couple of travelers would get him home.

He had parked and was reaching for the keys when he happened to see a van door open all the way across the lot. A long and distinctly female leg stretched out. It ended in a shiny red sandal with a high heel. Vern paused and waited for the other leg. The legs belonged to an enormous belly, thin arms, and a pile of whipped-cream-colored hair.

Then the things crawled out of the van and began milling around the tall pregnant woman. Vern stared as the wheelchair was unfolded and the small lumpy bald thing helped the limb-less worm thing up into it. Then he reached back for the 30.06 and smoothly, still staring, pumped a round into the chamber.

Arty's chair had an extended control arm that he could reach, but I liked pushing him and he liked having me do it. He said it make him feel royal. Elly and Iphy each slung an arm over the other's shoulder and hopped along, grinning at the old woman who had stopped to stare at us with her shopping cart half off the curb. The twins were ahead of Arty and me, and I could just see Lil's head bobbing in front of them.

I had just put my head down to push when I felt the sting on my hump and saw the little rip come into the back of the chair with a muffled cracking sound. Arty jerked in the chair and let out a roar. The twins toppled forward and the arm around Iphy's neck was spilling red. 'Gun!' That was Arty shouting and I was down on my knees getting a breath to cry as he flopped out of the chair and rolled crazily under the tail end of the nearest car. I scrabbled after him, scraping on the hot pave-ment, my hump burning. Lil's voice flipped up in a quick shriek. I bumped my back on the metal and was trying to cry but I could see Elly and Iphy, with their arms wrapped tight around each other, rolling fast and disappearing behind another car. They left a trail of red blotches where the arm touched as they rolled.

A car horn blared suddenly and didn't stop. The flat bleat floated in a solid layer on the air and human voices popped and chittered far away. I could feel Arty's heat against my leg. I dropped flat and cranked my neck around to look at him. He was on his belly. Blood was running out of his short shoulder and smearing across his flipper before it dripped onto the shade-cool tarmac. His lips were sputtering and big fat tears were sheeting out of his lower lids while his eyes whipped back and forth, searching and mean.

My own eyes and nose were running and the burn on my hump was like a big bee sting flaming poison up through my neck and all the way down to my butt. It was interesting to see the tears coming out of Arty's eyes. I had never seen that before. I never thought of him crying. My own shaky breath and the taste of tear snot on my lip were familiar. Easy. Even the burn on my hump was exactly my size. But Arty's way of crying was new to me. His body was crying but his brain wasn't. The eyes above his tears were as sharp as ever. The blood from his shoulder was sliding faster than the clear fluid from his eyes, but to me the tears were more alarming.

The horn stopped and sirens grew up in its place. Voices jumped and barked and Arty and I lay pressed to the shade beneath the brown crust of the car belly until Lil came creeping and sniffling on her knees, peering under all the cars and calling to us. She couldn't talk when she found us. She dragged me out first and I sat quivering on the hot pavement while she reached far under the car for Arty. The hand that she balanced on had smears of bright red, drying fast. She tugged Arty into the light. She hiked him up onto her belly and stood up. I clung with both hands to the end of her blue blouse and we scuttered across the wide lane to the next row of cars. Behind a small red car Elly and Iphy lay flat on their backs with a big grey-uniformed woman kneeling between their heads. The twins were puckered and red from crying. They stared at the arm that the woman was pressing with a white bandage. The woman's flat eyes and tight mouth never changed as she moved, wrapping the thin arm. Behind them, on the curb, sat the old woman who had stopped her shopping cart to watch us. A man in grey was holding her wrist and talking softly to her. He lifted the prongs of a stethoscope to his ears and slid the listening bell into the collar of her dress, but the old woman's eyes were on me, and then on Arty as Lil laid him down.

Lil was saying, 'These too, please. These too, please,' meaning Arty and me, until more grey uniforms came and put big, hot hands on us and tore my shirt from the back. The bee sting on my hump got a breath of clear air and sizzled fresh. I watched another man put fingers on Arty's neck and Arty's wide lips opened with strings of spit webbing the dark inside his mouth and a high whine came out while white squares of gauze were pressed against the blood. Lil sobbed and caught herself and sobbed again, stroking Arty's head as he lay on the pavement with the big hands moving on him.

'I'm older than I thought,' said a thin voice, and the old woman on the curb lay down. The man in uniform crouched over her and her head turned to stare at us as he lifted her arm to a needle.

The ambulance was crowded but Lil wouldn't let them separate us. Elly and Iphy were at the head of the cot with Arty at the other end. I lay on my side on a padded bench and Lil sat next to me with her long cool hand on my head. The grey-uniformed woman moved slowly and carefully. She asked one of the men to stay with her. She didn't want to be alone in the back with us. The doors were open and we were still waiting. I could see through the doors to the other side of the parking lot where the pickup was parked with the driver's door wide open in front of the supermarket. There were four flashing police cars and the soft distant static of radios talking to each other. A grey figure came away from them and jogged quickly toward us. Blond, with a mustache, his uniform starched and neat. He was grinning and shaking his head as he grabbed a wing of the rear doors in each hand.

Lil bent over me, toward him. 'Who is he? Why did he do that?' Her voice was rough.

The young man nodded to the woman in uniform who sat next to Arty but didn't touch him. 'Some loony. Just crazy. He's moaning that he missed.' The young man closed one side of the door. 'Just rocking in the back of the cruiser saying, "How could I miss?"' The last door closed and the scared eyes of the woman in uniform skittered around at each of us. The ambulance began to move.

When they dropped and flopped and the wheelchair flipped over, Vern felt a sudden warm pleasure that slid off into shock as they fell out of sight. The disappointment was a hot, wet bladder bursting in his chest. They were lined up. In line. His old man would have got all of them with that one steel-jacketed shell. The awful, soggy weep of failure shook him.

He was pressing his face to the smooth rifle stock, oiling it with tears, when a state trooper grabbed the barrel and yanked the rifle through the open window and out of his grasp. His cheek was sliced and bruised by the escaping stock. When the door squawked open he whimpered at the big gun looking down at him. The trooper's boots had the same blood-mahogany depth that his father had rubbed into the wood of the 30.06.

He was leaning his forehead against the steel-wired glass that screened him from the front seat. His hands dangled between his knees, the cold cuffs clipped into the ring bolt on the floor of the patrol car. He had fallen into the momentary peace of blankness. His mind was stretched out flat, featureless. A trickle of color and motion at the outer edges of his eyes informed him that the troopers were moving slowly around the car. There were calm, heavy voices and others lighter, thin, and fast. Witnesses, he told himself. The police had arrived so quickly. He was impressed at their efficiency.

Then it occurred to him that a patrol car might have actually been in the parking lot at the very moment when it happened. He thought of a trooper in the aisle of the supermarket, buying cookies to eat in the cruiser. A faint bubble of old resentment rose in him. They were always after sweets. Few people came to his beautiful fruit bins when they were after a treat....

A dull knocking at the window to his right became insistent. He swiveled his eyes reluctantly, pressing his forehead harder against the partition. A shopper. Her long face with incredible peach skin flushed ripe to the dark hairline pursed and spread its peach-crack lips. The teeth, like sweet corn kernels, whitened at him. The window glass vibrated, telling him '... solutely right, right, you were absolutely ... and she was pregnant *again* ... right ... you did the ... decent ... right' before a pair of blue jodhpurs appeared behind the face and the face jerked away and he saw the dimpled arm swing down over the window beside the distended blouse of the beautiful pregnant girl. She grasped what must have been the handles of a baby stroller and disappeared, and he listened to the rattle of the stroller wheels as the baby and the fetus and their peach mother huffed away.

The sadness of his bruised and aching cheek began to penetrate the calm flow of his breathing. Vern cried again and it wasn't long before the snot hung all the way to his wrists and eased the rub of the metal cuffs.

The nurses were not as disgusted as the doctors but even they were giggling at each other and moving jerkily. The policeman with the thick glasses was sitting in an orange plasti-form chair and trying to keep his holster and his belt radio from jabbing him as he wrote down what Lil said. Lil would talk quickly for a few seconds and then fall silent. Her eyes swiveled frantically from one sheet-wrapped table to the next as she tried to watch us all. The young policeman wrote intently on his yellow pad and then distracted Lil from her surveillance with another question.

Elly and Iphy took the longest. Arty and I were both lying on our bellies, each on our own starch-itchy table, watching as the doctor with the long black braid bent over the twins' wounded arm. The doctor muttered at the white-faced nurse, who kept handing over the wrong shiny metal thing. A doctor with bad skin came back and stood between me and Arty. She began feeling me all over, tapping, listening through chilly instruments.

She hated to touch me. I could feel it and my stomach got cold inside. She edged around the table, pushing her fingers into the sides of my hump but avoiding the thick bandage at the crest.

An old doctor went up to Lily and began to talk to her in an earnest way, putting his stethoscope into the pocket of his white coat and pulling it out and putting it back. Elly and Iphy were not chattering. They stared at each other and at the arm between them and at the braid that dipped and swung as the dark face of their doctor squinted at their blood. Arty was watching my pimple-faced doctor. I looked at Arty, checking to see if these goings-on were all right. He licked his lips and squinted. The bandage started on his shoulder and rode up the side of his neck. It was hard for him to turn his head. The sweat was beading out of his scalp. He was staring at the zit-skinned hands on my hump when he yelled, 'Leave her alone! She's all right!' and the doctor's hands leaped away from me.

'There now, steady, little fella.' The big nurse leaned a hesitant, damp-looking hand on Arty's back to hold him down. Arty's face went into a deep bruise color that he hoarded for serious tantrums.

He opened his mouth wide — his eyes bulging furiously at me all the while. 'Lil!' he bellowed. 'Call Papa, Lil! They'll try to keep us! They'll take us and keep us!'

Lil was glaring at the oldest doctor and saying in her proper Boston, 'I certainly could not condone such a thing without consulting their father.'

'Papa!' howled Arturo, and the twins began to cry their syncopated harmonic wail and I slid off my table and was trying to get my teeth to grip in the full, tight flesh beneath the fat pink nurse's buttock to distract them from Arty, and Arty curled back to bite the big pink hand as the long braid of the dark doctor swung like a whip at the sound of the instrument tray emptying its dozen chrome miracles in a fire rain onto the tiled floor.

That was when Papa came in with Horst the Cat Man. Arty shut up and the pink nurse went to wash his hand. The twins lay back down for the taping to be finished. Papa spoke his best South Boston and the doctor gave up and said he wouldn't be responsible.

Horst scooped the twins up. One of their tear-streaked faces peeked over each of his shoulders. Papa picked Arturo up very gently and took my hand. With Lil close behind, Papa led us all through the swinging doors and past the grey-haired lady blinking at the desk and out through the emergency entrance to where the little van was parked.

6

The Lucky One

She is looking. Her fingers skim the red skull, flutter down the crumpled features, twitch in brief visits to the ears, then slide down for a brief grasp of the tiny jaw. Both her hands now spread, touching the tiny arc of the breastbone, clasping the shoulders tenderly. Lifting the two arms to their bent limit, her fingers probe the joints, checking the dimpled knuckles, counting, recounting the small larval fingers, reaching for the thorax, a firm grasp on the concave buttocks that crease into thin legs, and again the searching repeated. Count of the pea-sized toes. Her eyes slide up to the flat, hooded eyes of her husband, my father, the sire and deliverer. He looks away, picks up damp cloths, busies himself with cleanliness. Her eyes and hands return to the faintly squirming infant. She flips him neatly, his chest in her left palm and her right hand now throbbing in terrible anxiety over the tiny padded spine.

'But ...' she begins, turns the babe back to re-examine his front. 'But, Al ...' And the tent of wrinkles appears on her smooth milk forehead, the doubt that I had never seen in her eyes before. Al turns away and then quickly forces himself to come back to her. He puts his hands on her cheeks and strokes softly.

'It's true, Lil. There's nothing. He's just a regular ... regular baby.' And then Lil's face is wet and her breath is bubbling nastily. Al is darting at me where I am holding Arty up in the doorway, and Elly and Iphy are pulling on my arm, and Al says, 'You kids fix some supper for yourselves — get, now —

72

leave your mom to rest.' And Lil's soggy voice is crying, 'I did everything, Al.... I did what you said, Al.... What happened, Al? How could this happen?'

Al liked the snaky backroads in the hills. He drove like a rock, his whole body slumped in a twitchless, nerveless mound. Even his mûstache seemed frozen over his mouth. Only his eyes flicked constantly and his hands moved the wheel just enough and no more. Arturo sat in the big co-pilot's seat, strapped upright, his eyes flickering like Al's. I leaned on Arturo, half dozing in the dark with the color points of the instrument panel warming my eyes.

Lil hung on the support bar behind us. Her pale hair and face caught the red glow of the dash lights. She swayed lightly on the turns.

'It's nearly midnight, Al.' Her voice was a stretched tissue of sound that meant she was not going to cry, that she was deliberately squeezing back the more obvious forms of grief. It was harder to deal with than her crying. Al's hand tugged at a strand of mustache and then returned to the wheel. His eyes never left the road.

'We'll hit Green River in another half hour.... Did you write the note?' His voice was genially matter-of-fact.

Her body swayed behind me and I could smell a heavy wave of sleep and milk and sweat from inside her robe.

'I've been thinking a laundromat,' she said. 'It would be warm. Women go there.'

The new baby had to be left somewhere. Al sent the rest of the show east to Laramie. Green River, he said, was a good town, clean, where a regular boy could grow up well. The plan was to drive through in the night, leave the baby on a doorstep where he would be found quickly, and then head out, leaving no clues to connect him with a carnival hundreds of miles away. A freighter went past going the other direction. Wind shook us from the floorboards up. Al waited until the roar was gone.

'Lil, honey, this is a small town. The laundromat is most likely not open twenty-four hours.'

'I thought we could put him on top of a drier and put in

enough coins to keep it going all night.' Al was patient, driving stolidly.

'We'll find a place that opens early. A snappy-looking business. Owner a local pillar. Not white-collar, though. No insurance or real estate. I don't want him brought up by an office worker.'

Arturo's ribs swelled against me as he inhaled, then his soft voice, 'A gas station, maybe. Sure to be one on the main drag.'

Al took it as though it had come from his own mind. Arty had that knack.

'A gas station would be about right. You bundle him up warm, Lil. They'll open early to catch the mugs going to work.'

Lil was fumbling in the dark.

'I can't find the writing pad,' she called. Her voice had tears high up near the surface now. Al's big hand touched my scalp.

'Help your ma, Oly.'

I found the writing tablet and a pencil in the drawer. Lil had gone back to the bedroom. Iphy and Elly were asleep as I slid by their bunk. I was proud to be up and useful while they slept.

Lil was propped up on the pillows of the big bed. She was pulling on the long red gloves that she used for shows. The baby slept beside her, wrapped tight in the yellow blanket that had covered each of us in turn. Lil's face was flat and wet with pain. I handed her the pad and pencil and climbed up beside her. She sat up and leaned over the tablet. She gripped the pencil between her long red fingers and opened the pad to the blank middle pages. She rubbed the page with her gloved hand, turned it over and rubbed the other side. Then she turned it back and began printing carefully against the sway of the van. Some tears came out while she wrote and she tipped forward so they would fall onto the page.

'Please take care of my baby,' she read aloud as she wrote. Signed, 'Unemployed and unwed.'

She sighed, tore the page out and folded it. She saw me looking at her. She smiled a weak smile. Her glove came out and rubbed my smooth head.

'I signed it that way so the people who find him will think

that is the reason he was left. I said 'unemployed' rather than 'out of work' to give people the idea that his parents weren't illiterate, anyway. Maybe if they think he came from educated people they'll assume he's got good genetic stock. It might give him a better chance.'

I put my nose into the palm of her glove. I liked her for thinking about that. I liked her for grieving over this regular baby. It made me feel important and loved. I thought she would have really cried if she'd had to give me up.

The morning before, while the plans were still forming, Al had checked out the van. Arty crawled underneath and talked to Al while he cranked the wrenches around. I tried to get close enough to hear but couldn't. Later, at the breakfast table, Al told it as though it had occurred to him without outside help.

'We could go into a big supermarket and wait in an aisle until there was no one else in sight and push the cans of beans aside — you know how deep those shelves are — and lay him on the shelf at the back and then stack cans in front of him again and walk away. When he started to cry it would just take them a few minutes to find him.'

Lil was intrigued, of course, but insisted on stowing her babe not behind plebeian beans but behind artichoke hearts, escargots, some comestible expensive and erudite enough to guarantee that the customer who shoved the cans aside and discovered this sweet morsel would have a certain cachet of worldliness and money.

Then Al remembered the surveillance cameras and other security hardware and discarded the idea. But I knew it had come from Arty originally. It smacked of him.

So, we were doing what Al referred to as 'the sensible thing.' The elderly thin flannel blanket and the kid's unremarkable underwear had all been checked for identifying labels, or floating sequins, that might pin the job on us. Even the cardboard box, an ex-cradle for canned pumpkin, had been checked. Al phoned a grocery from a booth in our last pit stop to make sure they had the brand in the area. Standard brown-paper insulation, layered and crumpled for warmth. Nothing so foolish as a newspaper from anywhere along the route.

And the red gloves, the long suede arms reaching past the elbows, with three cunning buttons at the slit wrist to close them and the fingers so supple her nails and knuckles showed through. And the mid-page of the writing pad wiped of finger-prints. These minor dodges my parents performed as auto-matically as the swallowing of spit. The thinking part came in avoiding too much thought, in the spontaneous flare of not scouting ahead — not speeding — and in the care that Al had taken with the van's checkup back there in Whore Meadow, Idaho, where he made sure we would not break down, run out of fuel, or blow a tire before we were well away from the last sight of our own castoff perfection. The Binewskis weren't crooks, but we had a sense of timing.

I was rustling in the drawer next to the sink for tape. Mama wanted tape to fasten the note on the baby. It was dark and I could see Al's head and shoulders against the bright windshield when the van slowed. I grabbed the sink edge to balance as we pulled off into popping gravel. Al doused the lights.

'Oly, is your mama ready?' His voice was close to me.

'Just about, Papa.'

'Tell her to be quick. We don't want to stop for more than one minute and I'm going to make just one pass through town, so we've got to spot the place and decide fast. Tell her.'

I had the roll of tape in my fist. I shut the drawer and headed for the crack of light showing at the edge of the sliding door to Mama's room at the end of the van.

She was sitting on the bed with the baby's cardboard box beside her. She looked up at me as I whispered Papa's message. She nodded and reached out a red-gloved hand for the tape. We were moving again. She tore off tape and neatly plastered the note to the flap of the box. Tears ran quietly down her cheeks. There was a crackle from the paper in the box. The baby was moving slightly. Mama's eyebrows peaked in a tent above her nose as she looked at me through her red eyes.

'He might wake,' she whispered wetly. 'He's been asleep almost three hours. He'll be hungry.' Her voice squeaked out through the whisper. 'Tell Papa we have to wait till I can feed him. Tell him to park somewhere.' A push in her eyes sent me back, feeling my way toward the cockpit, with tears coming out of my own eyes. As I reached for the support bar behind Papa, the van reeled beneath me and we were turning right beneath a streetlight into the purple shadows of a three-island, twelve-pump gas station with its 'CLOSED — open again 6 A.M.' sign large and pale in the window of the office. On the wall of the office, a tire with a clock in its center hung numbly, with one hand drooping to 12:35.

'Papa,' I started to say, as he lurched up from the seat and swung toward me.

'Gangway, Oly,' he snapped as he pushed past me, a wave of heat and cigar smoke and father flesh moving away toward the open door of the bedroom. Arty smiled at me from the passenger seat. He reared his head back, baring his teeth to show me his excitement.

'No, Al!' came Lil's voice from the bedroom.

'Quick, Lil, get a move on!' and I could see Papa bending over the visible corner of the big bed, reaching.

'Al, I've got to feed him! He's awake!'

But Papa was pulling and the cardboard box slid toward him with Mama's long red gloves attached to it.

'Lily, there isn't time!'

A thin, monotonous siren wailed from the box as Al lifted it and the reaching red gloves towed Mama along in her limp robe. Papa came through the door toward us and put the box down on the floor next to the side door as Mama rushed behind him, with the light from the bedroom door shining through her pale hair. Papa opened the side door and peered out, and Mama hit the light switch as she leaned over the box. Her pink robe and red-gloved hands dove toward the wadded papers that filled the box around the baby.

Papa said, 'Hand it to me, Lily,' as he stepped down to the pavement and turned around to see, as Arty saw, and I saw, Lily tilting oddly, her head against the door frame, her robe

spreading open around her, her whipped-cream hair jerking out
in thick snakes that tried to escape from her head in all directions. We heard the ping of hairpins hitting the window, the
floor, the wall, and Mama's gasp and muffled shriek as she
lifted off the floor and floated, lying on the air while her thick-
strapped brassière stretched away from her with an ugly,
ripping sound, and her feet, in pale lavender socks, stretched
wobbling toward the light in the ceiling, and her hair fell in
coils over her face. 'Mama! Lil! Mama!' we all howled, as her
huge blue-veined breasts burst through the brassière and she
dove into the cardboard box, falling with her breasts in the box
as her arms waved and her head lifted against the pull from the
box and her white legs twitched and crawled on the floor
beneath the rucked and flapping robe and one lavender sock
rumpled its way off her foot.

Then Al was on his knees in the doorway, stroking her head
and saying, 'Sweet shit, Lily,' through her soft sobbing. Arty
grunted, his head craned around the back of the seat. His eyes
overran his wide face. I sat on the floor against the cupboard
with my mouth and eyes open, and Elly and Iphy sat up in their
bunk with bewildered eyes and wide befuddled mouths saying,
'Mama,' in a drawn-out complaint. A painful, thin whine came
out of my own nose and only one voice was silent, only one of
all the Binewskis was not adding to the noise, and that was the
paper-padded morsel in the box, who was invisible except for
one tiny hand opening and closing in a tangled strand of Lil's
white hair. The baby was not crying anymore. When, for an
instant, we were all silent together, we could hear the chuckling
smack of his lips at the bruised brown nipple.

It was a minute or two before Lily could sneak an arm into
the box and lift the baby up to her as she collapsed onto the
floor, and sat with her feet mixing with my feet. One fat arm
and the fuzzy knot of head buried in her breast were all that
showed of the baby outside his cone of blanket. Al crawled in
and sat on the floor beside her.

'What happened?' he asked.

She looked at him with her eyes so wide open that the whites
showed all the way around her wobbling blue irises. She
laughed shakily. 'I guess he wanted to nurse.' She looked down

at the little rumpled face and Al stared at a hairpin on the floor in front of him.

The twins, groggy in their bunk, and Arty with his chin propped on the back of his seat, and I, slumped in the corner, sat gawking as Mama's tired face slowly developed a swelling over her right eyebrow where she'd banged her head on the wall when she dove into the box. She shifted slightly to get more comfortable and her robe slid away from her knees. They were scraped raw, with beads of blood swelling out through the pores.

'Are you saying,' Al stretched out a hand and carefully picked up the hairpin, 'that the baby did that? Hoisted you up like that?'

Mama's eyes snapped with anger. 'I told you he was hungry!'

The tiny fist, like a spider on a sand dune, clenched and opened and clenched against Mama's breast. The suckling sound went on.

Papa was staring at that hand. His lower jaw looked oddly soft and slack beneath his mustache. He got slowly up on his knees and picked up two more hairpins. He found another pin on the windowsill and stood up, looking at the hairpins in his hand. Mama concentrated on the small face at her breast. She seemed calm, forgetful of the tears and the ragged, dangling remains of the brassière.

'Well,' Papa cleared his throat, 'we need to think a little bit, Lily. I'm going to drive on up the road. We'll find a rest stop and pull over for the night.' Mama nodded peacably.

The twins went back to sleep and I crawled into my cupboard and Arty humped his way into his bunk and Mama and the baby went back into the bedroom. Al drove in the dark until he came to a pulloff surrounded by high black firs. Arty and I stayed awake for a long time listening to Papa and Mama in their bedroom. Papa cleaned and dressed Mama's knees and put a cold pack on her thick blue eyebrow bruise. He put the sleeping baby into the crib beside their big bed, and they sat watching together and saw the thin flannel blanket curl slowly

up in a twisted bundle and then push toward the headboard of
the crib, where it lay twitching and scrubbing back and forth all
by itself while the baby slept. Arty and I both heard Papa say,
'He moves things. He *moves* things.' We heard Mama start to
cry again softly when Papa said, 'He's a keeper, darling. He's
the finest thing we've done! He's fantastic!'

Things were quiet after that, except for what the dark trees
were doing among themselves outside. 'Poor Arty,' I thought.
'He'll be miserable.'

We stopped ón an edgeless plateau that stretched to nothing on
all sides, making the eye desperate, shriveling the brain to dry
hopelessness between the dreary sheets of sky and ground.
Papa climbed out of the driver's seat, threw back the side door,
and jumped down. Mama was in the bedroom with the door
closed, still sleeping. Elly and Iphy were huddled on their neat
bunk with a puzzle. I was trying to read over Arty's shoulder as
I turned pages for him. None of us looked out the windows. We
all hated the bleak, flat stretches. Papa had left the door
propped open and a rip of wind twisted into the van, mussing
our pages and carrying dust and the rough sting of sage with it.
Papa was out there, walking in the desert.

He'd been silent all morning, and excited. He wouldn't let
any of us sit up front with him. We'd squared away our beds
and the twins put out cold cereal for breakfast and handed a
mug of coffee up to Papa. Arty had been quiet too.

Papa's boots crunched on the gravel outside and his head
came through the open door.

'Step out here, dreamlets,' he said, then disappeared. None
of us wanted to get out into that wind but we went, silently.
Arty came last and just slid down onto the step and lay there
blinking at the grit in the air. The twins leaned on the van and I
stood near them watching Papa. He paced in front of us. Just a
few steps in each direction and then back. The wind thumped
and whacked at his jacket flaps and lifted his black hair against
the grain. He looked away most of the time out over the plain at
the waving stubs of brush and broom. When he glanced at us,
between phrases, his eyes were dangerous. We listened gravely.

'Your mama and I have decided to keep the new baby.'

Each of us, he said, was special and unique and this baby looked like a norm but had something special too. He could move things with his mind.

'Telekinetic,' said Arty flatly.

Yes, telekinetic, Papa said. And he explained that it was a thing he didn't know about, that none of us knew about, and that we'd have to be very careful for a while until we figured out how to deal with it and what it was good for.

'We'll join up with the show by morning and discuss the situation with Horst. Horst is a trainer and training is what we need. Horst can also keep his trap shut. Now here's the important thing.' And he said we were to act as though he were just a norm baby, even with people in the show who we liked and trusted.

'The army will want him,' said Arty.

'Well, they aren't going to get him,' said Papa.

We all had to stick together like troopers, said Papa, and the baby's name was to be Fortunato, which means Lucky.

Though his body did only the normal cherubic things, Fortunato's effect on the environment at the age of three weeks was already far beyond that of a hyperactive and malicious ten-year-old. He had to be confined to the cubicle we called our parents' bedroom. Mama moved everything breakable, shreddable, or toxic out of her room so the baby wouldn't destroy it or himself. Our tidy van became a heaped bunker. Platoons of makeup bottles and boot-polish cans stuffed the cupboards. All the sequined clothing hung over the twins' bunk. Lamps, clocks, and framed photos littered Arty's unmade bed. Papa's medical magazines and books were stacked everywhere. Mama's sewing machine moved under the sink with me. I slept with my knees touching my chin.

Six of us could live comfortably in the thirty-eight-by-ten-foot van only by dint of religious housekeeping. The mess wore us down. We hated it. Obviously training had to begin immediately for this seventh member of the family.

With some well-placed hints from big brother Arturo, my

ingenious father hit upon the expedient of glycerin and black tape for wiring Fortunato's little buttocks to a miniature electric train transformer and a battery pack. Whenever Fortunato broke dishes or pulled hair or lifted Lil in the air and held her against the ceiling, Papa would gently turn on the power. In a matter of days, however, the precocious Chick, as we called him, learned to unplug the transformer and whip Papa's curly pate with the cord.

Deprivation techniques were substituted, Clyde Beatty style, but Fortunato had to sleep in a heavy wire cage during that experiment because, when Lil refused to nurse him, he would simply yank her toward him and reenact his debut performance.

The raw potential of Fortunato's abilities spurred my parents to research. By the time Chick was four months old. Al introduced the behavioral principles of B.F. Skinner and reinforcement theory successfully replaced deprivation.

Mama finally dared to bring him out of the Chick-proof bedroom. It was several weeks more before she could actually step out of the van with the baby in her arms and walk through the camp without his moving every bright-colored thing in sight.

7

Green — as in Arsenic, Tarnished Spoons and Gas-Chamber Doors

The real trouble, as usual, was Arty. He'd always been jealous. He didn't mind me so much because money was the gauge of his envy and I didn't make any.

The twins, however, drove him wild. After every show he would hook his chin over the edge of his tank, spraying me with the overflow, to demand the number of tickets sold at the gate. 'How many?' he'd holler. But it didn't matter — thirty in Oak Grove, three hundred in Phoenix, a thousand in Kansas City. What he really wanted to know was how he had done compared to the twins. If they had as many or more in their audience he was furious.

Sometimes in those days he would flash to the bottom of the tank and sulk, holding his breath for incredible minutes, eyes bulging outside the sockets so they hid the lids entirely.

When I was five and first took over the duty of helping him after his shows, he terrified me with this tactic. He muttered, 'I'll die. I might as well,' and I wailed and hopped in agony as he sank, staring through the glass.

I ran shrieking to Papa. He clapped his cheek and bellowed at me not to humor Arty when he was 'playing prima donna!'

I ran back dithering, chewing my hands in fright, until Arty finally allowed himself to roll slowly over and drift, belly up, toward the surface, where my short arms could reach him with

83

the crook and tow him to the side. I patted and smoothed his
water-swollen scalp and kissed his cheeks and nose and ears,
weeping and begging him not to be dead because I, useless
though I was, loved him. At last he blinked and sighed and let
his breathing become visible and growled for his towel.

All this over a few tickets one way or another when he was
ten years old. I knew he wouldn't take to the Chick.

Nearly dawn. The show was closed down. Lil and Papa were
asleep. The twins were snugged in their bunk snoring.
Fortunato, the Chick, lay silent in his crib with the blanket
twitching around him in his dreams. But at this end of the van
twelve-year-old Arty sat propped against the table looking over
the ticket-count sheets. I crouched on the floor with my back to
the cupboard doors. If he was angry I would pop open one of
the doors and creep inside bawling, shut myself into the blackness and pull my cap down over my eyes so I could cry into the
wool, and pull Lil's old sweaters over me. He shook his head.
The yellow light gleamed on his skull and I began to sniffle a
little. He threw a look at me — sharp — I gulped down my snot
and grinned at him feebly. He turned back to the ticket sheets.
His voice started slow and soft.

'Now, you know very well what I'm seeing here.' He wasn't
looking at me but I nodded, ready to cry. He was looking at the
papers in a sad, doubtful way. His voice dripped regret.
'Nobody expects you to bring in the kind of money that I do.' I
shook my head. That would be absurd. 'Or even,' he pursed his
mouth, 'what the twins manage.' I put my eyes down onto my
knees and sighed, my whole worthless body quivering. 'It isn't
your fault that you're so ordinary. Papa accepts the responsibility for that.' The moment of silence told me that he was
looking at me. I could feel his eyes on my hump.

As I cried he pointed out the discrepancies. When I did the
talking for his show the tickets were 15 to 50 percent less than
when Al did it. We both knew that Al only let me do it when we
were in Podunk burntout towns for a quick stopover and that
the sales were down all through the midway in those places.
Still, there was some ghastly truth in Arty's needling. Some

probing of my guilt that was right no matter how he lied about it.

Then he would threaten me with the 'institution,' which was the place that I would be sent to if I didn't shape up. 'No matter how generous and kind Papa and Lil are — they wouldn't have any choice,' he would say. His sympathy and understanding washed around me with razors caught in the flow. Arty's depiction of the 'institution' scared me more than death or snakes. The institution was a cross between an orphanage and a slaughterhouse. Worst of all, it was run entirely by norms. The word alone would set my chin trembling. I would beg and grieve and he would allow that I deserved another chance.

'We don't *have* to keep new kids,' Arty sneered. 'Sometimes we don't keep 'em and sometimes they don't last.' He was in his mean lecturing mood, twisting his head to look at me over the back of his chair as I pushed him through the grey dawn to visit the dog act. 'You don't know about the ones before you,' he warned. 'The ones that died. Papa and Mama don't talk about them, but I remember.'

'I help Mama with the jars in the Chute.' I grunted, shoving hard to force the chair wheels through the sawdust. Arty snorted and shook his head. 'There were three before me and two more before the twins. There was another one just before you. That's why Papa let her keep you, because the other one died just before. It gets her down. You wouldn't have been a keeper if the other one had lived. She gets low when she loses one and it bothers Papa to see her like that.'

He was trying to make me cry but I didn't care. I was happy to have him talking to me. He'd been cranky and sullen for a long time. He went about his work, did his shows, ate, slept, read books, and didn't talk much except when he was laying weasel trails for Mama and Papa.

'Which one was it? Just before me?'

Arty rolled his eyes and dropped his voice. 'Leona.' He drew it out like a moan, watching me. I ducked my head and pushed his chair. Leona with the alligator tail would definitely have been a keeper. Leona would have had her own show tent and glow-in-the-dark posters in silver and green. Arty mused wistfully, 'Papa was very excited about Leona. He thought about showing her in a tank. He was hoping she'd stay hairless but he could have depilated her if she'd started sprouting. He even thought about putting her in with me. Papa saw the billing as tadpoles. Different stages of tadpoles.'

He was light and airy about it. I stopped pushing and walked around to face him for a minute. He was nodding and blinking, pretending nostalgia for poor Leona.

'That must have scared you, Arty.' I grinned.

A slow smile spread gradually across his rubbery mug. He wriggled his forehead at me, for all the world like Papa dancing his eyebrows. 'Poor Leona. She just went to sleep one night and never woke up. Mama was just about crazy when she found her the next morning.' Arty's round, wide head did its snake dance, turning on his neck in mock grief, and I knew the taut slide of his skin over tendon and meat, and loved the shadow dip of his bones underneath and the wide smooth roll of his lips.

What I felt was fear. Arty saw it in my face and slid into his whipmaster act fast. 'Onward, Jeeves,' he snapped. 'To the dogs!' I scuttled back to push, wading through the sawdust and keeping my butt muscles clenched to avoid filling my pants.

'Is it O.K. if me and Arty play with Skeet?' I asked. The dog reek from the trailer door might have been Mrs. Minuti's breath. She swallowed and tried to focus through her hangover. Her hair was short and spiky with a clot of last night's supper caught above her ear. She pulled her nightgown out from her chest and belched softly. 'Sure,' she nodded. She didn't complain about the hour or the fact that Skeet was her star poodle because we were the boss's kids and dog trainers are easy to come by. She disappeared inside the trailer and Arty stared tensely at the open door. The dog came scratching around the doorway and jumped down beside me, with his long leash trailing up to Mrs Minuti's shaking hand. She gave me the leash and told me not to let him wander loose.

I hooked the leash on a back post of Arty's chair and wheeled him toward a hard-packed grassless stretch behind the booths. The dog bounced along nosing everything, pissing ten times in two minutes.

By the time we got to the clear spot the dog seemed to have calmed down a little. 'You just stay close and be quiet,' Arty told me. I sat down to watch. Arty called the poodle to him and the silly dog put a paw up on Arty's chair and cocked its ears at him, wagging the pompom on the end of its skinny tail.

Arty hadn't explained what he had in mind. I sneered, 'Arty the wildbeast trainer,' to myself. On the other side of the booths the camp was just beginning to wake up. An occasional trailer door slammed. A voice or two sounded faintly. A mechanic turned over one of the ride engines and let it sputter to death.

Arty looked the dog in the eye. The dog sat, obediently alert, directly in front of Arty, watching his face. Arty froze with his eyes open, focused on the dog, but his face sleep-smooth, expressionless. At first the dog was happy as an idiot — short confidential flips of tail against ground, a swiveling of sharp ears, tongue-dripping grin. Gradually the dog lost confidence, licking its chops and closing its mouth, tilting those ears questioningly forward at Arty. An anxious burst of tail rapping. Then Skeet shoved his nose forward, sniffing worriedly at Arty, letting a thin, high whine out through his nose, skootching his ass nervously against the dirt. Arty sat with his fins curled and still, his face thrust slightly forward and down. The poodle didn't dare look away from Arty's face but began to lick his own nose repeatedly, stand up, then sit down fast with his tail under him, letting his ears droop. Finally, whining, ears flattened, head down and wobbling moron eyes wincing at Arty, the dog slid to the side with a yelp as though he'd been kicked.

Arty threw himself against the back of his chair, breathing deeply with his eyes closed. Skeet backed to the end of his leash and did his best to slink out of his collar. Arty sat back up and looked around for the dog.

'Skeet! Come here!' he ordered. The dog bolted to the end of the leash, snapping himself into the air. He flopped onto his back and lay there, belly up, and began to yowl. Arty laughed a little to himself and said we could take him back. 'I can practice my hate thoughts on the norms in the midway, too,' he said.

★ ★ ★

Arty never bad-mouthed Chick openly. Anything that obvious would have shocked Papa and Mama into the blue zone. But I knew. I was the one who did the most for Arty. I spent a lot of time with him and a lot of time thinking about him. I loved him.

Privately I thought that Mama and Papa loved him only because they didn't know him. Iphy loved him because he wanted her to and she couldn't help it. Elly knew him and didn't love him at all. She was afraid of him and hated him because she could see what he was like. I was the only one who knew his dark, bitter meanness and his jagged, rippling jealousy, and his sour yearnings, and still loved him. I also knew how breakable he was. He didn't care if I knew. He didn't care if I loved him. He knew I'd serve him absolutely even if he hurt me. And I was not a rival to him. I didn't have an act of my own. I drew the crowds to him rather than to myself.

I was supposed to listen for Chick. He was asleep on Mama's bed and I was supposed to stay inside and wait for his waking squeak. I would change his diaper and give him some apple juice and play with him until Mama was finished with the twins' piano lesson.

But the sky was blade-blue, the windows were open, and the redheads were spinning tales just outside. I could hear them laughing. They were lying on blankets in the sun, drinking soda and slathering themselves with oil. The whiff of coconut and lanolin came drifting in through the window.

I was supposed to sit inside by myself and read but Peggy's soft voice began a story, and the other redheads quieted to listen. I couldn't make out what she was saying. I went out through the screen door and around the van to flop on the grass beside the blankets. With the window open I thought I'd hear Chick as soon as he woke. I picked and chewed grass stems as Peggy talked.

It was about a very young boy, fourteen or so, and Peggy claimed it was true. He died for love, she said. His family was poor. He was cut out for heavy work and bad pay, but he was a sweet kid, and he loved a cheerleader in his school. She wouldn't even look at him, of course. Her life was different. But then she got sick and the doctors said it was her heart. She would die, they said, unless she could get a new one. The word went around the school that she was waiting for a donor. The boy was terribly sad for a while, but then he told his mother that he was going to die and give his heart to the girl. His mother thought this was just his sweetness talking. He was healthy. But a few days later he dropped dead. Instantly. A brain hemorrhage, they said. Surprisingly, the doctors found that his bits actually were compatible to the cheerleader's, and they transplanted his fresh heart into her. It worked. Now she dances and cheers again with the poor boy's heart.

The redheads were impressed. Vicki said it would be weird to feel your life pumping through this heart that had loved you. Lisa wondered if the cheerleader would be haunted.

'He was probably worth three of her,' said Mollie. 'A heart like that.'

Then from the bedroom of the van just behind me came a single loud slam like a twelve-pound hammer on sheet steel. In the fading echo Chick was screaming.

I was halfway around to the screen before the redheads even started telling me that my baby brother must have fallen out of bed. Peggy and Mollie were up, following me. By raw luck the screen door latched behind me as I whipped through.

Chick was on the bed, purple-faced and howling. I jumped up beside him and pulled him into my arms. He was shaking and gasping between shrieks. He couldn't make so much noise if there was anything stuck in his throat. I felt for his diaper pins. Were they sticking him? Then I saw Arty.

He was crumpled face down on the floor in the narrow crack between the bed and the wall. He wasn't moving.

'Oly, is the baby all right?' Mollie was rattling the screen door. 'Oly?'

Chick subsided to unhappy burbles and hiccups, and I slid him back onto the blanket. 'Arty?' I whispered. No answer. No movement. At the foot of the bed lay a big rumpled pillow with a grey spot of dampness in its creased middle. The pillow had been tidy at the head of the bed the last time I'd peeked in. Chick could have moved it, but Arty's talk about Leona the Lizard Girl hit me again. I knew. Arty had tried to smother the Chick.

I hung over the bedside, reaching to touch him. 'Arty?' His head was heavy, his fins limp.

Mama and Papa mustn't find out. I jumped down, grabbed Arty by the rear fins, and pulled him back down the carpeted ravine to the bedroom door, and out into the living section of the van.

'Oly? Are you O.K., honey?' Peggy was at the screen door. 'Is the baby O.K.?' Mollie called.

Chick was hiccuping in the bedroom. He sobbed occasionally. Arty was very still. I turned his head to the side so I could see his face. His eyes were closed. A big patch on his forehead was beginning to turn blue. I took a deep breath and ran to the door. The redheads stared in at me. 'I think Chick's O.K .... But Arty ...' I lifted the latch and began to cry.

I huddled on Mama's bed with Chick during the uproar, and heard the grownups decide that Arty had climbed up on the kitchen counter and fallen off onto his head. He was still unconscious when Mama rushed him off to Papa's infirmary trailer.

Chick sat up beside me, his fuzzy hair frowzled, and patted my cheeks with his tiny hands. He ran his fingers into my nostrils and mouth until I smiled, painfully. Then he smiled too, with his few teeth all showing in his floppy grin.

Above us on the painted metal wall was a shallow dent the size of a dinner plate.

'Oh, Chick,' I said.

The twins marched in and commandeered the baby. 'If you'd been inside where you were supposed to be,' said Elly, 'this wouldn't have happened.'

'You could have helped Arty get what he was looking for,' said Iphy.

I hugged my knees and stared numbly at them. The rat was awake in my belly.

They took Chick out to the dining booth to play with him and I lay there on Mama's big lavender bed and thought about

Arty coming in through the screen door and finding nobody and humping his way back to the bedroom and seeing Chick asleep on the bed. I saw him push his way carefully up to the pillows and grapple one onto the baby's sleeping face, Arty leaning on it with his whole weight. So Chick woke up and threw Arty just as he'd thrown a toy or a chunk of banana. Without touching him.

Mama stayed at the infirmary with Arty but Papa came back with the news.

'The poor little apple batted awake and says, 'Mama, Papa,' first thing. I whooped and your mama stopped crying. He couldn't remember a thing about it. He's got a concussion and a dog hair of a skull fracture, but praise be, he'll be right in no time.'

Elly shrugged. Iphy clapped her hands. 'I'm so glad.'

I laced my fingers over my pointed chest and closed my eyes, breathing in gratitude that I hadn't got him killed and that he'd been clear-headed enough to 'forget' what had happened.

We fed Chick from a bottle until Mama and Arty came home the next afternoon. He was good about it. But when Mama noticed the dent in the wall a few days later I told her that Chick had thrown his bottle at it once while she was gone. She tsked but didn't scold him. It was too late, she said. 'You have to 'No' him just when he's done it. He wouldn't know why I was fussing at him now.'

Arty lay on his bunk in the middle of everything and we danced to his tune. The twins waited on him and I helped him to the toilet, and Mama spent all her time thinking of delicate things for him to eat. He was happy. He was polite. He smiled and laughed at the jokes we made to amuse him.

He couldn't read for a while. His eyes wobbled and trying to focus gave him headaches. I read to him in my slow, stumbling way and he corrected and scolded and made me go on for hours. By the time he could read for himself again, I could read almost anything, though my pronunciation was still shaky on words I didn't know.

Mama did her duty by Chick but fussed over Arty. For days

Chick barely appeared outside the bedroom. Then Mama brought him out and tucked him in beside Arty 'to watch while Mama makes supper for her beautiful boys,' as she put it. I felt my stomach claw its way into my throat, but Chick snuggled up to Arty happily and played with his fin. Arty blinked for a second and then went along with it.

I secretly swore to make Arty the king of the universe so he wouldn't be jealous of Chick.

Arty's big tent stayed folded on the trucks through a dozen moves. It cut into our take dramatically. Papa tried to keep Arty from knowing how much money we were losing with him out sick. When Papa sat late in the dining booth doing the books, Arty would ask, 'How's it going?' and Papa would sigh and say, 'Fine, boychik. Don't you worry your poor busted noggin about it.' This put Arty into a foul mood for several days. Finally one night, late, he called out from his bunk, 'I guess the show doesn't need me, Papa. You'd do fine with just the twins if I died.' Then Papa went and scooped him up and took him to the table and showed him how the gross had slipped. Arty was happy again and started going over the accounts with Papa.

It was more than a month before he tried going back into the tank at all. His first test trip into the water was a shock. Papa and I leaned on the tank to watch as he flipped down in his usual straight-to-the-bottom flow. He burst through the surface seconds later, gasping. 'It hurts!' he puffed. 'And I can't hold my breath.'

Papa was grim and silent as he carried Arty back to our van. I knew he was wondering what would happen if Arty couldn't dive anymore. That afternoon he got a set of weights and a bench from the storage truck, remnants of an old strongman act. He set up a gym on the stage behind Arty's tank. Arty began working out and was back in the water within the week. Not long afterward, Arturo the Aqua Boy was back in lights and packing them in.

8

Educating the Chick

A carnival in daylight is an unfinished beast, anyway. Rain makes it a ghost. The wheezing music from the empty, motionless rides in a soggy, rained-out afternoon midway always hit my chest with a sweet ache. The colored dance of the lights in the seeping air flashed the puddles in the sawdust with an oily glamour.

I sat on the counter of the Marvelous Marv booth and kicked my feet slowly. No drips came through the green awning but the air was so full of water that it congealed on my face and clothes whenever I moved. I was watching the summer geek boy, a blond Jeff from some college in the far Northeast, as he leaned on the snack-wagon counter across the way and flirted with the red-haired girl running the popcorn machine.

Behind me in the Marv booth, Papa Al and Horst sat facing each other on camp stools with the checkerboard betwen them. Marvelous Marv had the afternoon off and Horst's cats were fussing and coughing at the damp. The cats' voices roared around their big steel trailer but came echoing dimly through the rain.

Al's cigar butt arced out over the counter past my elbow, spitting red as it died in a puddle.

'Long as you're playing with your boots instead of your brains,' drawled Horst, 'why don't we make this next game for my new tiger cub that I'm going to pick up in New Orleans? I win, you buy me that cub for my birthday.'

I could hear Papa's match scraping the stool leg, then the hiss and a silence that produced a reek of green tobacco from his new cigar.

'Hell, Horst. I've already gifted your birthdays for the next ninety years.'

The click of the checkers being laid out for the new game sounded on top of the thin tinkle of the piano from the twins' practice session in the stage tent. I tried to hear Lil's voice counting shrilly over the treble but the rain didn't carry it.

'That baby's birthday is coming up,' said Horst.

'Almost three,' grunted Papa, 'and I'm still boggled. Keep thinking of great things for him to do and then realizing we can't have it. Begin to think maybe this little guy is too much for me to handle.'

'Nice temper that child has,' Horst's careful voice, not pushing. 'Wished I had a cat as willing and sweet as that child. Wants to please.'

'All my kids are sweet and willing! Show me a family of troopers anywhere to beat them!' Al wasn't really angry, just doing his duty by his own. 'But that's not the problem,' he added. 'No,' Horst agreed.

The sound of a checker jumping twice, then a long silence. Jeff, the geek boy, gave up his wooing for the moment and slogged dejectedly away from the popcorn counter. The red-haired girl smiled after him and smiled as she stabbed pointed sticks into a row of apples dipping in caramel. She began humming a song I didn't recognize.

I rolled through the crowd in the midway with my head at the general crotch level. Music and lights blaring, a thousand arms sweating around a thousand waists. Children, fussing and begging and bouncing, hung onto the tall norms. The legs scissored past me, slowing when they approached me. I was just walking through, from one end to the other, trying to feel the instant when the wallet in my blouse front was meddled with. If I felt anything I would stop and throw my hands in the air and Papa, sitting up there on the roof of the power truck with Chick in his lap, would see me and then I'd walk on.

'Fuckin' kee-rist! What happened to you?' asked a knock-kneed drunk tottering in front of me. I grinned at him and swerved around, with a little cramp in my lungs. Arty and the twins couldn't come out in the crowd like this. Once the gates opened and the norms trickled through, my more gifted siblings hid. The crowd won't pay for what they can see free. There were security reasons as well. They were 'more obvious focal points for the Philistine manias of the evilly deranged.' That's how Papa put it.

A small child looked into my face and wanted to stop but his mother dragged him on. Sometimes when I felt the eyes crawling on me from all sides, I got scared thinking someone was looking who wasn't just curious. I knew it was my imagination and I got used to it, learned to shunt it away. But sometimes I held on to it quietly, that feeling that someone behind or beside me in the crowd — some guy leaning on the target booth with a rifle, or some cranky, sweating father spending too much on ride tickets to keep his kids away from him — anybody could be looking at me in the sidelong way that norms use to look at freaks, but thinking of me twitching and biting at the dirt while my guts spilled out of the big escape hatch he'd cut for them. That helpless rasp of death waiting as he hurt me ... a feeling like that is special. Sometimes you hold on to it quietly for a while.

I told Arty about it once. Arty narrowed his long eyelids and said I was flattering myself and there was nothing about me special enough to make anybody want to kill me. Arty was the master deflater, but his reaction convinced me only that *he* didn't want to kill me. Funny how target potential became a status symbol among us.

At the end of the midway in front of the Ghost Coaster the wallet was still sweating in my shirt. I climbed the entry ramp so I could see the top of the generator truck down at the other end. Papa, with his boots dangling over the roof edge, was dancing Chick on his knees. I waved. He didn't see me. I waited, and waved again. There, he looked. His arm shot straight up signaling me to come back. Chick would probably try again while I was on the way. I jumped down and swam back through the crowd and the music.

The wallet was still in my shirt when I got back to the power truck. Horst was leaning on the front bumper watching papa count a wad of greenbacks. I took out the wallet and handed it to Papa. 'Why couldn't he do it?' I asked.

Papa grinned and jiggled his eyebrows at me. 'Ah, my

froglet, you haven't looked inside that wallet!'

I watched as he unfolded it and spread the pocket. Empty. The sheaf of one-dollar bills he'd put there before I started was gone.

'You didn't feel anything?' asked Papa. I shook my head, watching Chick in his coveralls with no shirt and no shoes and his arms and legs wrapped around Grandpa's shiny urn, absorbed in making breath fog on the mirror metal.

Looking back, it strikes me that we never made sensible use of Chick. I remember when Chick was three or so, helping to get him dressed, packing a small bag with extra clothes and his toy bear. Al would take him sometimes for a few days — just the two of them. 'The beauty of it is being so totally inconspicuous,' Al said. 'A guy with a little kid is more innocent than a man with his wife on his arm. A man and his wife can get up to all sorts of shenanigans together, but the world sees a man with a kid and they figure he's good guy and has more important things to tend to than robbery.'

Those were the pickpocket trips. Al would trundle off in his quietest suit with Chick in tow, and take train or plane to 'The Money Crowds.' They went to the big horse tracks, to the summer Olympic games. They spent four magnificently profitable days at the World's Fair and one topnotch night in the parking lot of the world's biggest gambling casino, with the star-spangled crowd at ringside watching Lobo Wainwright lose his world middleweight boxing championship to that consummate ring general, Sesshu Jurystyf.

All they took was cash. Chick would locate a goodly wad and extract it delicately from wallet, purse, clip, or money belt, leaving the victim with the wallet or purse intact and unmoved. The only real problem, according to Papa, was new bills, which tend to be noisy. Evidently a faint crackle is rarely noticed in a big crowd, however, and they soon learned to pick loud moments.

The most dangerous phase was as the cash left its container and drifted away from its original owner. After that Chick snaked the stuff along close to the floor, winding through legs and under chairs and so on. Nobody ever noticed. The money always arrived in a neat bundle, folded flat, and would slither up Al's pant leg and snuggle into a pouch sewn onto Al's garter.

Later Chick could tell the number and denominations of the bills but early on he couldn't count reliably and Al would wait until they got back to their room at night to slip the bulging pouch off and tally the loot. It added up.

Al had an eye for clothes and manner and he enjoyed picking the targets. His argument was that as long as they stuck to cash they were doing no one a deep injury. 'Nobody carries more cash than they can afford to lose,' Al would say, beaming at us over our bedtime cocoa. 'Now, if we messed with their credit cards we might do some damage. But take the cash from a high roller at 8 P.M. and all he does is rethink a single evening out.'

In a good crowd, on a good night, they might take ten or twenty thousand in a few hours. They were careful — a cheap seat high in the balcony — targets separated from each other, unknown to each other, and very rarely discovering their loss until they were away from the place where it happened.

Al came back with great stories and Chick was always glad to be home. He would arrive looking slightly purple under the eyes and eager to sit in laps.

We all hated these special trips of his. Not Mama, of course, but Arty and the twins and I. The show was our world and Papa's world. It had always been world enough. None of us had ever slept in a hotel or eaten in a restaurant or flown in a plane. Papa enjoyed it all too obviously. And we suspected, each of us, blackly and viciously, that Papa preferred his norm kid to us. With Chick he was free to go anywhere. We could live only in the show.

There were a couple of dozen of these trips after Chick turned three. Papa was feeling worldly. He bought three-piece suits and sometimes even wore one of the show lot.

Chick was nearly four on the morning he and Papa left for a mountain-lake resort that had always refused Binewski's Fabulon a permit. We weren't high-class-enough entertainment for that set. There was a big poker tournament in the major hotel there and, in the same weekend, a championship fight. Papa figured to find a lot of cash in the pockets.

We were set up in the semi-suburbs somewhere and the crowds for the midway were steady but not phenomenal.

I stuck close by Arty when Papa was away, and Arty was nastier than usual all day. He spat in my face after his first show because the twins had sold eighty more tickets than he had.

The last show that night went well for him, though, and he was already chinning himself out of the tank when I got there afterward. He'd outdrawn the twins and I was waiting for him to ask about ticket receipts, but he was thinking about something else. I wrapped him in a fresh thick towel and put him in his chair. He had to be tired from the four shows that day but he seemed sharp and eager. 'Get me down to that phone booth on the street.' We went out the rear entrance and down the dark side of the midway behind the booths. Just a few yards away, the simp-twister rides and the games were having their last spasm of jump on a summer night.

'Tim's on the gate,' I told the back of Arty's head. 'He'll come with us.' We weren't supposed to leave the grounds at all but I figured the guard would be persuadable.

'No. We're going out through the delivery gate,' barked Arty. 'Nobody is going to see us, and nobody is going with us.'

The phone booth near the lamppost had a folding door and a phone book hanging in shreds on a chain. I was nervous trying to sidle Arty's chair into the booth and had to pull him back three times before I got the wheels centered. 'Calm down, piss brain.'

'I feel like I've got hair, Arty.'

'That's goose bumps, ass face. You've got the yellows at being out in the big, bad world. Climb up. There's a coin here somewhere.'

The coin was wrapped in a slip of paper.

'The number's on that paper.'

I stood on his chair and examined the phone.

'Hand me down the receiver.'

He tucked it between his ear and his shoulder while I cautiously droped the coin in and began to dial.

'I've never used a phone, Arty. Have you?'
'Pay attention to the numbers.'
Then I heard the ringing start.

A half hour later Arty was scrubbed and pink and stretched out on his belly on the rubbing table. I trickled oil into the flesh rolls on the back of his neck and rubbed it up onto his smooth, round skull and down into the diamond-dented muscles of his shoulders and spine. His eyes were wide, staring at the wall.

'Who were you talking to? What's it about?' I asked.

His fins spread slightly and his shoulders twitched in a shrug that came up through my hands.

'Never mind, anus. Just rub.'

We had recently bought a big new living van. For the first time the twins and Arty each had a small room. Chick slept on a built-in sofa-bunk. The cupboard beneath the sink was bigger than in the old van and Mama had painted the inside a deep hot blue called 'Sinbad.'

I suppose the van was part of the profit from Papa's trips with the Chick, but the show was growing and doing well too. Every town we played seemed to spill out some new act that would appear on our doorstep begging papa for an audition.

The new van came equipped with a maroon leather rubbing table in Arty's room. He insisted on having his walls covered with matching wine-colored cloth. I wondered where he'd got such an idea.

Papa and Chick arrived in a taxi the next day as Mama was fixing lunch. It was a hot Saturday and the midway was going full blast. Papa looked tired and angry. Chick sat in the twins' lap and ate peanut butter and jelly. Papa took only iced tea.

'Now, Al, whatever happened?' Mama pressed.

'Bastardly thing, Lily.' Papa shook his head. 'I don't know what to make of it. We'd checked in and I went to take a look around while Chick napped in the room. Then I take him down to the restaurant and we're just about to order when three of the hotel dicks and an assistant manager jump us and walk us to an office off the lobby and ask for ID. They're very polite and I'm carrying on like the bewildered but cooperative citizen when the head of security slides in. He fixes me with an eye like a mackerel's ass and says, 'We've heard about you, sir. We've heard a great deal.' They check me out of the hotel right then and tell me I am not welcome in any of their nine hundred branches of coo-coo-prick flophouses, ever. How do you like that? They didn't seem to tumble to the Chick at all, but they had me figured for a pickpocket using the kid as a front. I've slipped somewhere, but damned if I know how.'

Arty listened with a concerned wrinkle above his nose but stayed quiet. He didn't need to say a thing.

It was the end of Chick's career as a pickpocket. Papa set himself to 'think again,' as he put it.

It was a while before Papa got back to thinking seriously about Chick. One of the swallowers got an infection from the burns in his mouth and Papa spent weeks in his little trailer workshop improving a burn salve.

The twins had begun writing music and they did a lot of pouting because Papa wouldn't let them play their own songs in their act.

'Classics. That's what people want. Stick to classics,' Papa would say. 'You play something they've never heard before, how should they know whether you're playing well or not?'

Horst bought a new cat just to distract Elly and Iphy from their hurt feelings. It was a scabby leopard cub rescued from some roadside zoo, and Chick and I and the twins all got ringworm from playing with it. Papa had a wonderful time curing the stuff but Arty wouldn't come near any of us. He used the ringworm an an excuse to abandon his new room and to start bunking in the dressing room on the stage behind his tank. He never moved back into the family van. He ate with us once the ringworm was gone, but his real life became private. He spent his time 'backstage' as he called the room behind the tank. Papa put a guard on the place and complained about the added expense.

* * *

Mariposa, the jaw dancer from the variety tent, had been with the Fabulon since I was a baby. She did gymnastics while hanging from her teeth on a twenty-foot pole fastened to the harness of a cantering white horse named Schatzy. Mariposa had a pug nose and a wide grin and Crystal Lil liked her.

When Mariposa stuck her head in through the open van door while we were eating lunch, Mama called to her to come in and join us. The jaw dancer refused, saying she was rehearsing something new. 'But I want you to come and look at my four-o'clock turn, Lily. Tell me what you think.'

Mama and Chick and I slipped into the tent toward the end of the show when the Strauss waltz was introducing Schatzy and Mariposa, and we stood in the aisle between the banks of bleachers. Schatzy was old but proud and light-footed. She arched her neck and hiked her tail into a banner as she lolloped around the ring.

High up near the lights and rigging, Mariposa, in a flame-red costume, stretched and contorted and spun, dangling by her teeth as she and the pole rocked scarily with Schatzy's gait.

I climbed onto a prop box to watch and Mama hoisted Chick up to straddle her hip so he could see. Though we had a clear view when Mariposa fell, we were never sure exactly how it happened.

She started to swing her legs, setting up to slip into a handstand on top of the pole. Either her timing was off by a flicker or else Schatzy broke stride. Suddenly the flame-colored figure was loose and hurtling downward. She flopped onto the back of the still-cantering Schatzy, drilling the horse to the ground.

In the instant's silence of indrawn breath as the crowd prepared its roar, Chick's voice shrieked out. Schatzy's long, proud head screamed hideously into the sawdust.

Mama pushed Chick into my arms and ran for the ring. Papa was already there, crouching over the bodies in his chalk-white jodhpurs. I wanted to see but Chick, beside me on the box, filled my arms and my face with his howling. His mouth hung loose and his closed eyes sheeted clear fluid and his terrible voice went on and on. People were pushing past us to leave the tent, the crowd evacuating the scene. In the noise I didn't even hear the bullet that finished Schatzy, but I knew that it had happened because Chick stopped his siren screech and fell into simple broken sobs. 'It hurts,' he cried. 'It hurts.' I got him down off the box and rushed him, sobbing, through the press of legs and out of the midway to our van.

Mariposa had cracked her pelvis and one ankle but Schatzy's spine snapped irrevocably. I crawled into Chick's bunk with him and held him while he cried. He was still crying when I drifted off for a nap.

That night and all the next day, Chick wouldn't talk. He wouldn't eat. He wouldn't get out of bed or dress or do his chores. He lay curled under his blankets, facing the wall. If Mama turned him over and held his face to talk to him, he started to cry. If Papa picked him up and rocked him, his tears started. When Arty came in and sneered at him, he stared hugely and silently until even Arty was embarrassed and went away.

Two days after Mariposa's fall, Papa decided Chick needed a dose of Binewski's Beneficent Balm and made Mama hold him while the black spoonful was thrust between his teeth. Late the next day, while the rest of us were working in the midway, Chick finally told Mama that he could have held Mariposa up when he knew she was falling. He had let her drop because he was scared Mama would be mad if he moved a person. Mama gave him permission to save anybody from pain or accidents. Chick drank some fruit juice then, and eventually began to eat again. But he would never eat meat after that. No meat at all.

When Chick was five he lived on corn and peanut butter and he understood more English than he could use. He learned fast and his coordination for moving things was much better than his actual physical ability. He couldn't tie his shoes with his hands but he could do all of Horst's fancy sailor knots — from a Turk's head to a monkey's fist — just by looking at the cord.

'My fingers don't do what I want them to,' he told me. He was trying to write 'Love, Chick' on a horrible water-paint picture of a tiger that he'd made for Mama. She always liked it when he did things with his hands. Arturo jeered at him for it.

Arty figured he should use his hands only when there were strangers around. Arty's line was 'You're acting like a fucking norm.' The twins didn't jeer. They doted on Chick, and taught him to read.

It was becoming apparent that Chick himself had only one ambition and that was to help everybody so much that they would love him. That's where my problem began. Chick left me chewing dust in the slave-dog department. He could do everything better than I could and he never made snide remarks. He was a lovely brat.

That winter was a slow time for the show. Business was steady but we all had time to think and doze around. Giving Papa time to think, as Arty put it, was like pumping random rounds into a fireworks factory. The odds favored dramatic results.

Arty was hanging upside down from his exercise bar doing smooth, steady curl-ups.

'Papa and Horst are teaching Chick to gamble,' I announced. Arty did two more curl-ups before he said, 'What games?'

'Roulette and craps.'

Arty grinned at his own navel. He was deep in his workout, covered with fine sweat. He made one final reach upward and grabbed the grip on the bar with his teeth, coiling himself tightly so his shoulder fins could delicately manipulate the buckles that held his hips in the harness. He swung out, let go of the bar, and landed rolling.

He wriggled to the weight bench and, hooking his hip flippers under the straps, leaned back, tensing his belly as the flippers alternated flexing and relaxing to lift the weights on each side. He started to chuckle out loud, watching the weights rise and fall at the end of his blue-veined, white-tendoned flippers.

'We're lucky, you know,' he laughed, 'that Papa has such a small potato brain.' He laughed deliberately, timing his breathing with the lifts. I watched his corrugated belly do its seductive ripple, complicated by the added rhythm of the laugh.

'Papa's a genius,' I said stoutly. This was Binewski doctrine.
'Heh heh heh,' went Arty's belly. There was scorn in his
eyes. It was familiar enough on his wide mug, but not toward
Papa. He was trying to shock me.

'If Papa had discovered fire,' Arty sighed to the beat of his
lifts, 'he'd think it was for sticking in your mouth to amaze a
crowd.... If Papa had invented the wheel ... he'd have laid it
flat ... put a merry-go-round on it ... and figured that was as
far as it went.... If he'd discovered America ... he would have
gone home and forgot about it ... because it didn't have any
hot-dog stands.'

I sat with my hump propped against the back of Arty's big
tank. The clean chlorine smell of the water of the water drifted
in and out of my lungs.

Al figured six to eight weeks was enough to get Chick started as
a bigtime gambler. The two of them spent hours every day with
Horst — our resident encyclopedia of worldliness — and Rudy
the Wheelman. Rudy's experience supposedly encompassed a
stint as a professional contract-bridge player that had ended
when his wobbly ethics were revealed and he was informed
that, if he ever picked up a deck of cards again, he would lose
both his hands. Rudy had taken refuge in the obscurity of the
Wheel Booth and the comfort of his small, cheerful wife. Mrs.
Rudy was dedicated to folding sheets of paper into birds, fish,
giraffes, and other intriguing forms. She could not work the
midway because she modestly refused to dye her mousy hair
red, but she helped around the lot in many ways.

Obviously Chick couldn't crawl into a rental tux and sip his
chocolate milk from highball glasses in the mirror-ceilinged
casinos of the planet. This, like pocket picking, was supposed to
be done long distance. I don't know the procedure. Papa wasn't
secretive about it, he just never went into detail. Papa had a
tiny lapel microphone hooked to a transmitter and Chick had a
receiver so Papa could give him instructions.

Practice time for Chick and Papa was early, just after breakfast, which cut into my voice lesson, or eliminated it. I had a
tape recorder to use when Papa couldn't make it, but I knew

the tapes were piling up in a cigar box in his desk and Papa never got around to listening to them.

Chick knew I was upset, and that Arty was thoroughly pissed. But he couldn't help being happy at all the time Papa spent with him, and he did his best to make it up to us.

He discovered a new way to clean Arty's tank. Instead of watching a pair of brushes and a sterilizer hose go over the drained tank, Chick stood in front of the full tank and took out every cell, probably every molecule, that wasn't supposed to be there. The green on the glass disappeared in broad, straight swaths like wheat in front of a mower. When Chick was finished the tank was so clean it was almost invisible. A round greenish cloud hung above it. Chick blinked at the cloud and it sailed dreamily across the stage toward the open door of the toilet. There was a faint splash and then the toilet flushed.

Arty and I were sitting on the exercise bench to watch because Chick had come chirping about his 'new way!' My mouth hung open as I thought about setting the Chick on my own cleaning chores. Arty looked steadfastly at Chick, whose proud grin began to weaken and slide off into doubt. 'Show-off,' said Arty quietly.

Chick's face crumpled. 'I didn't mean it, Arty. I'm sorry.' Arty dropped to the floor and crawled into his room, thumping the door shut behind him.

For obvious reasons 'show-off' was no insult in our family, but Arty had a way of turning 'sweetheart' into a thumb in the eye.

I sat looking at Chick. I knew what he felt. The huge buoyant air sack of love that filled his body had just exploded and the collapse was devastating. Poor little stupe. He was just a baby. He hunkered down against the tank with the side of his soft face against the cool glass for comfort. He didn't dare look at me for sympathy. He didn't cry. He just crouched there and ached.

I squinted at Arty's door. He had his radio turned up loud. I got up and walked over to the Chick. His eyes swiveled at me in fear. He thought I was going to pinch him or say something nasty. That proved he couldn't really read minds. I put my arms around him. I rubbed my cheek against his curly ear. He slung an arm around my neck. I whispered, 'It's a great way to clean.'

'Truly?' he whispered. I could hear the tears in his throat.

The dumb little fuck was supposed to be so goddamn sensitive, how come he couldn't figure it out? All he had to do to make me like him was *need* me. All he had to do to make Arty like him was drop dead.

Papa and Chick left with great fanfare. We all went along when Horst drove them to the airport. I can't remember where we were except that it was not Atlantic City, because that's where Papa and Chick were going. They were planning to stay for five days — a long trip but Papa wanted to break Chick in to the game slowly and delicately. Chick had heard that there was a swimming pool in their hotel. Chick was sure he was going to learn to swim like Arty. Arty was utterly charmed to hear this, of course.

That night the show closed down peacefully, but when Lil went to give out the tills the next morning she discovered that the entire take from the two days before — around $20,000 — was gone. The alarms had been cut at their source and the safe — a silly, tinny affair anyway — had been popped open like a melon on pavement. Old-fashioned *plastique*, Horst said, and crudely handled.

Horst went out to the airport for Papa and Chick early on the morning of the sixth day. Papa had looked bad the last time he'd come home from picking pockets. This time he looked like death's rectum. He hugged us all fervently, which was awkward because he wouldn't let go of Chick and carried him the whole time. Chick himself was white and still and didn't smile.

Papa collapsed into his big chair with Chick in his lap. We children arranged ouselves discreetly while Mama fussed in the refrigerator and Horst lit his pipe.

'You both look worn to shreds,' Mama was clucking.

Pappa gave a walleyed look around at our waiting faces and I was afraid he was going to send-us out so he could talk to Mama and Horst. The clink of ice cubes distracted him, and then Mama handed him a tall glass of her famous lemonade.

'Al, I want Horst to explain about the safe,' Mama began. Horst actually reached to take the pipe out of his mouth but Papa cut them both off.

'Lily, I gotta tell you. Horst, I got to get this out. I don't know what in creeping Jesus to think.'

Horst waved his pipe, but Mama twisted her hands, anxious. 'Are you ill? Whatever happened?'

'I came within a gnat's ass of losing Chick,' Papa said. 'That's what happened.' Chick whimpered on Papa's chest and got a pat. 'No. I wouldn't really lose you, honey. It's OK.'

I grimaced at Arty but he was hunched over in his sofa-bunk, watching Papa, and didn't notice.

It took a while for Papa to get it all out. He hadn't got it organized as a story yet. At first, he said, they'd taken it slow and easy.

'I didn't lay any bets at all the first night. Just watched and had him practice. Gave wins to the good faces and grief to the apes and assholes. It was fun, sending some poor hack driver on the roll of his life with his skinny wife hanging on his arm in a faint, thinking 'Shoes for Junior.' Then watching their eyes as they stood under the chandelier and I say 'Red 26' into my button and pay off their mortgage, and whisper 'Red 19' and send their baby to college with twenty minutes at the wheel.

'The fat pricks with the diamond teeth are going off in fits. I was there awhile and then all of a sudden we went dead. Scared the crap out of me. Nothing. I turned in to a quiet corner and I'm practically screaming into the mike, but the wheel goes its own merry way. I go running for the elevator thinking the receiver's broke or he's sick or he's been playing with matches. A million things. But the little turd is crapped out in his chair with the receiver buzzing in his lap. Asleep. I got him into his jammies and tucked him into bed and he didn't peep. With the trip and everything he was just burnt out. He'd never done that before. ...'

They had done well for a couple of nights.

'I'm percolating with forty thousand in the kick, and Chick's eating big soft pretzels and floating in the pool every day and learning to paddle a little. Then, by the fourth night, I'm down the strip. This is no shit, Horst, three blocks. Three from the hotel room and the kid's still got it. No problem. I took him there one time only and he had no problems. Not with the crowds or the distance or anything else.

'So I'm leaning on the table doing a quiet gosh-and-golly hick routine over my roll, when this punk in a red sweat suit, carrying a tennis racket, comes up beside me. He's been there awhile, just watching, and I swear I was smooth as glass, Horst. Slicker than snot on a rock. Nobody would guess. Well, this punk in the sweats could have been a boxer to look at him. Broad on top, narrow ass. Skinny legs. He lays a hand on my arm and says, 'You're doing very well tonight, Mr. Binewski.' He's calling me Binewski when I'm traveling as Stephens. A young guy. Clean-looking. Short hair, face like a baby's butt. Blond. You tell me, Horst, what the fuck should I have done? Am I supposed to say, "You must mean some other guy. I'm Stephens"? He's easing me away from the table, his hand on my arm, out to the lobby saying, "Wonderful run you've been having, Mr. Binewski." And I'm thinking it's another house-dick roust. The crew from Tahoe must have fingered me to every hotel on the planet. He says, 'How's your little boy?' Cyanide-sweet, leading me along. Out by the door I finally ask him for bona fides. I say, "Are you with the casino?" He says, "No, I'm with a larger organization." It's not clear, you see, Lily? When the house dicks jumped me before there was nothing mysterious about it.'

'But I don't want to talk tough or panic because the Chick can maybe hear me and get scared. Then the guy asks where Chick is. Taking a nap, I say. This guy says, "Are you sure?"

'I just took off running — out the door, three blocks — left my chips on the table. Had nine heart attacks getting back to the room, but there's Chick, calm in front of some old movie on the TV, eating a cucumber sandwich on wheat, and the receiver in his lap dead and cold.

'I just about died of relief. Give the kid a pat and sit down to look at my transmitter. Finally figure out the thing is dead. Something's wrong or been done to it. I'm diddling with it when Chick looks at me and says, "Those other guys are coming," through his mouthful of sandwich. And I say, like a numbnuts, "What other guys?" And the door opens and three guys come in. Chick ignores them and starts eating the carrot slices off his room-service plate.

'These guys were crazy young. The kind that show up in the spring to hire on and swear they'll stay forever but they speak good English and their teeth are straight and you know they'll go back to college in September but you hire them anyhow, even though they make stupid mistakes and wallop their own feet with the mallets, and every other year or so one of them decides to unionize the ride jocks and tries to go out on strike. But they work hard and they're lively and they keep the redheads sparkling.'

Papa took a deep breath and stopped. Horst grunted encouragingly around his pipe stem, and Mama got up to refill the lemonade glasses. Papa sipped and sighed.

'I was six kinds of jerk-off not to take you with me, Horst. These guys amble through the door looking like college kids and one of them has a handgun that looks like the CO_2 pistols we used to use on the neighborhood cats. He levels this thing at me and I'm sitting there like a geeked capon, my mouth flopped open, and Chick crunching carrots beside me. The one with the gun starts some "Hey, Mr. B." kind of street snot, and one of the others goes into the bathroom and turns the water on in the tub, hard. The third guy takes the transmitter out of my hand and rips the mike cord out of my shirt and walks me over to the wall to splay out so he can feel me down.

'The other guy comes in, the guy in the red sweats from the casino, and Chick turns up the TV volume. I guess he couldn't hear with all the fuss. And I'm still spread out, hands on the wall, looking over my shoulder. The one little asshole has a hand in the small of my back to keep me there and the punk in red nods and goes to the bathroom door and the water quits and he and the guy from in there come out and he nods at Chick.

'This guy in red has a little popgun and he leans on the wall near me while the other fucker picks up Chick, just like that, and I turn around yelling and the other two grab me and slam me against the wall. That's when Chick noticed there was something wrong. He yelped and they covered his mouth. This one bastard loops a belt over my elbows behind my back and cranks it tight, and the other cocksucker crams a pair of my own socks in my mouth while he holds the popgun to my head. They shove me over to the bathroom door and the guy in red gives an order, and the guy holding Chick puts him into the full bathtub, clothes and all. There's a rag tied around Chick's mouth and . . .'

Papa stopped to gulp lemonade and then sop the sweat from his nose and forehead and cheeks. Mama is frozen, staring at him.

'So Chick's up to his neck with his eyes bulging at me over the gag and the guy in red leans close to me and says, "Now, Mr. B., this is just to let you know how very sincere this message is," and he tells me to keep out of the gambling joints. That I'm treading on staked turf and I should go home and be nice. Then the creeping little reptile says, "Now we're going to show you how it could be if you didn't understand us." And he nods and the guy who's clamped onto Chick starts pushing him under. Chick is looking at me and kicking and splashing and I jump, and I don't know what happened. I must have bumped the guy because he fell over the tub and bounced off the wall. Chick went to the bottom and the bastards were clubbing and clawing me.

'Next thing, I'm sitting in the tub yanking Chick out of the water while one fucker leans over me with a wet gun. His two buddies are worried over the guy on the floor, the one who pushed Chick under. He's out cold and there's blood running out of his ears and nose. They haul him out through the door and the one with the gun backs out after them. Last thing he says is, "Take it to heart, Mr. B. Not betting games. Not here. Not anywhere."

'The bastards got my kick, too. Found it in my socks. Didn't even bother with my wallet. They knew I wouldn't call the cops. Chick cried all night.'

Papa closed his eyes and smoothed both big arms around the

now sleeping Chick. Mama's voice was hoarse and puzzled. 'Chick wasn't afraid of them?'

Papa didn't answer. I watched Arty, who was staring at the ceiling in ferocious concentration. I knew it as though I'd been there. Chick had cried not because he was afraid, but because he'd moved the guy and hurt him, cracked him against the wall.

Mama sent us all out so Papa could nap.

It was an iron-grey morning with a low sky. By the time I pulled a sweater over my head, Elly and Iphy had Arty strapped into his chair and were pushing him down the row behind the midway, talking at him. I ran to catch up. Elly was demanding, in a hard voice, 'How did you do that to them, Arty? I know you did it. I want to know how.' Arty wagged his head in denial. Iphy leaned forward, touching Arty's neck gently. 'Arty, the Chick looked terrible. And Papa. Why do you hate the Chick? You mustn't . . .' Elly slapped Iphy's hand back.

Catching up, I grabbed an arm of the chair and trotted along as it trundled down the dirt track. 'It's not Arty's fault,' I protested.

Elly snorted at me, pushing the chair faster. Iphy shook her head mournfully, 'You don't know, Oly.'

'For shit's sake!' Arty snapped. 'Oly, call Papa. Go get Papa!'

'Don't you dare bother Papa now,' Elly drilled at me. I hopped along beside them in dithering bewilderment. Arty stretched his chin toward the chair's motor-control stick, but Elly's hand whipped to his shoulder and yanked him sharply back, holding him. 'Just sit still. We're taking you for a ride.'

'Morning, kids!' hollered the point guard. 'Morning,' chirped Elly. The show was sluggish in stirring this morning. It might rain and the redheads were yawning in their wagons.

'Take me to my stage,' Arty ordered, his eyes flicking at me.

'This way, Elly, Iphy,' I pointed, trotting back a few steps to lead the way. Elly pressed her lips and walked faster in her own direction with Iphy, sadly determined, pushing beside her. When I caught up again they were on the rear ramp of the deserted Mad Mouse roller coaster. Arty twisted in his straps to glare at the twins. 'You stupid shits!' he snarled.

Elly grinned. 'Are you scared, Arty?'

'Elly, don't,' I wailed. 'Iphy, don't let her.'

The wheels of Arty's chair were on the rails that the Mouse cars rode. Elly and Iphy, planting their white sneakers on the ties between the rails, bent their backs and pushed as the chair slid up the tracks, climbing the steep slope.

The Mouse cars hooked onto a chain-driven winch that ground its way up the center of this slope and brought them to the highest dropoff point, where gravity would carry them and their whooping, screaming cargo down through steep-banked turns with the customers' hands glommed sweating onto the safety bars.

'Please, Elly!' I hollered as the damp earth dropped away beneath me. I couldn't stand up on the tracks, but crept upward on all fours, shaking as I stared down past the black oiled chain with its heavy prongs to the flattened grass and mud below. I imagined the twins' sneakers above me, slipping tripping, tangling, and the twins crumpling to the rails and losing their grip on the chair, which — in my slow-motion mind — tipped backward over the big rear wheels, toppling over the sprawling twins and slamming down at the wrong angle so that its aluminium frame with its hogtied cargo went shuddering down the now thirty-five, now forty, now forty-five feet to the clanging smash of the mud.

'Arty?' I yelled, with my fists frozen to the rails.

Elly's hiss sizzled down at me, 'Shut up.'

I crouched and stared up the rails at the broad pumping hips and thin legs straining into their sneakers. They were very close to the top.

'What do you want?' Arty's voice rose sharp and frail in the grey air. The twins stopped pushing, stood leaning against the steep slope. Iphy's voice, pulling air awkwardly from the work, 'You have to leave Chick alone, Arty.' And then Elly's flat tone, 'You have to realize that things can happen to you, too, Arty.'

'Stuff you. Both of you,' he snapped.

'All right.' Elly was pushing again. Iphy leaned into the slope, digging with her toes. The chair creaked on the rails.

'Get me the fuck down!' Arty bellowed. 'You're dead, Elly Binewski. Your ass is fucking meat!' His huge voice floated thin on the air and all I could see was the edges of the wheels beyond the twins' moving legs. They were at the dropoff point.

'It's real, Arty,' Elly was whispering hoarsely. 'Iphy couldn't stop me and you know it.' Then Iphy, contradicting, 'Oh, Arty, we would never really hurt you. Elly loves you. But you have to understand.'

'O.K. I give.' Arty was too quick. Elly knew him. 'Not so easy, brother.'

From my paralyzed station on the rails I saw the Elly half straighten suddenly, erect, beside the hunched figure of Iphy. Her arms flew up, as though saluting a crowd. 'Hang on!' shrieked Iphy, her hunched shoulders disappearing as the wheelchair slipped forward and dangled over the edge of the drop. Only Iphy's long hands held it now.

'No! Uncle! I give!' wailed Arty.

From below and behind us came a horrified bellow, 'Get the hell DOWN from there, you stupid little bastards!' It was the point guard, Papa's Marine, gaping at us from the ground in shock.

Elly's arms flipped down and she hunched beside Iphy, grabbing the back of the wheelchair again. 'It's all right,' hollered Elly. 'We're coming!'

Then one sneakered foot slid, slowly, down a few inches, then the other, moving toward me. I backed down jerkily, so relieved I could have puked, while the guard's huge shoulders below us bobbed back and forth, his arms stretched out to catch us if we should fall, his voice rumbling that our old man would have his ass as well as his job if we dropped off that goddamn girder while he was on duty and he fucking well KNEW that we knew better, until we were all on the ground trundling along in our own sweat, peaceful and relaxed, nodding at the guard. Arty silent and Elly and Iphy smiling sweetly.

Arty made me take him to his stage and unbuckle his straps and leave him alone. He wouldn't talk at all.

I was furious when I came out and saw the twins strolling off to rehearse with their sheet music. I stalked up to Elly and gave her my fiercest glare. 'You tried to kill him.'

Iphy reached toward me, as if to give me a hug, 'Oly, she didn't tickle me or anything. She just let go.' Elly dragged her on, and snapped back at me, 'You're just Arty's dog! He'd kill us all and you'd stand there holding his towel.' They sailed on.

Papa took some of Mama's pills and slept that day and through the night that followed. The show closed at 9 P.M. and the camp shut down by 10. Even with my cupboard door shut I could hear the rattle and gasp of Papa snoring. It seemed pitiful. I couldn't stand hearing it.

I crawled out in my flannel nightgown and went barefoot through the door and down the hard clay ruts past the dim grey vans and trailers. There were lights on in the redheads' windows but I wanted Arty.

The guard at the back steps of his stage truck nodded as I went in. It was warm and humid in the dark. The heated water tank kept the backstage tropical.

Arty hollered, 'Yes,' when I knocked. He was lying on the bed with the maroon satin bedspread, reading. I crawled up beside him.

'Who do you think it was,' I asked, 'the guys who stuck up Papa?'

Arty squinted at me for a second. I was asking but I didn't want to know. Maybe he decided to teach me a lesson.

'Remember last summer's geek?' He pretended to be looking at his book.

'The yellow-haired boy from Dartmouth?'

'George. They were his fraternity brothers at college.'

I nodded. Arty tipped his head so he could scratch his nose with a flipper.

'The guy Chick moved. Was he hurt bad?'

Arty shook his head slightly. 'Fractured skull. He'll be all right. What bothers me is that they got Papa's kick. That means they got paid twice.'

My head did a slow interior waltz and swooped back to the same word. Twice. So it was Arty who stole the money from the safe, or arranged it. Where would he get explosives? Or learn to use them? I stared at him as he lay against the maroon pillow. He had changed without my noticing. He was thicker. His neck was heavily muscled and set solidly into his heavy chest. Beneath the thin, sleeveless shirt his muscle was as defined as ever but larger, bulkier. Even the wrist joints of his flippers seemed strong. Where the three long toes of his hip fins bent to clutch the bedspread, I saw a curling fuzz of hair clouding the top of each knuckle. I stared. It was the only hair I had ever seen on his glass-clean body. I knew then that he'd gone outside and away from me. For the past few months I'd scarcely seen him. All the hours of every day he had been on his own — not just escaping the irritations of Chick and the twins and their rival stardom, but befriending the geek, talking to people I didn't know, talking talk I hadn't heard, making phone calls without me to dial for him.

I complained, 'Taking the money was against the family. Scaring Papa was against the family.'

His eyes stayed closed but his head rolled impatiently on the pillow, 'Not in the long run.'

I couldn't understand that. The angry, weak sounds of Papa's story, the way those tinhorn brats had stampeded him, Papa the Brawl Buster, Al the Boss, the Ringmaster, Papa the Handsomest Man. I felt robbed. My champion was revealed as a scam and I was embarrassed at all the years I'd let myself feel that Papa was any protection at all. It was Arty's fault.

I opened my mouth to blame Arty, to yell. But there was something odd about him. He was curling slowly onto his side, tighter and smaller. His face was stony except for a puckering twitch beside the long, pale ovals of his closed eyes. A tear squeezed out from under one lid and disappeared immediately into the creasing flesh. It was years since I'd seen Arty cry, not since he abandoned tantrums and went over to the cool, hard image he admired. But it might not have been a tear. His eyes opened and stared past me.

'Elly,' he said. 'I'd kill her but the cunt would take Iphy with her out of spite. And Chick! Can't anybody but me see what he is? What he'll do to us? He'll end up smashing this whole family like an egg if we're not careful.' His eyes swiveled at me in a queer begging gesture.

'You're jealous,' I sneered. 'You want to be the only star!'

He threw himself back on the pillow. On any other face his expression would have said despair and resignation. 'Yeah, you too, I know. He's cute. Almost like a norm. And he's innocent. As innocent as an earthquake.

'Papa gave all those solemn orders of secrecy when he was born but it's Papa who brags and puts Chick on jobs outside where people can see him moving things. There's nobody on the lot that *doesn't* know! They come on in Pittsburgh, quit in Tallahassee, and tell all their friends and the lady next to them on the bus. How long, Oly? How long before the Feds are tucking us all behind barbed wire in the interests of national security?' He's leaning over, glaring at me, shouting.

'Oh, Arty.' It came out soft from my throat. Tired. 'You're just making excuses.'

Now he grew angry, rigidly upright, balanced on his hip flippers and quivering. 'Hey! Did you ever think maybe I *deserve* what I get? Hey? Elly is nothing. She couldn't get a job in a B-bar playing that plinka-plinka crap. All she's got is Iphy. Papa gave it to them on a platter.

'Me? You know what they do with people like me? Brick walls, six-bed wards, two diapers a day and a visit from a mothball Santa at Christmas! I've got nothing. The twins are true freaks. Chick is a miracle. Me? I'm just an industrial accident! But I made it into something — me! I have to work and think to do it. And don't forget, I was the first keeper. I'm the oldest, the son, the *Binewski*! This whole show is mine, the whole family. Papa was the oldest and he got the show and Grandpa's ashes. Before me the whole place was falling apart. I'm the one who got us back on the road. When Papa goes it'll be me.

'The twins don't care if I draw a bigger crowd than they do. They don't have to play or dance or sing. They could sit on a bench and wave and they'd still get crowds. They can afford to be easygoing. Nobody's going to upstage them. And Chick! Of course he's amazing. That's my curse. I'm a freak but not *much* of a freak. I'm like you, fucked up without being special. There's nothing unique about me except my brains and the crowd can't see that.

'You know what I hate? Iphy should have been mine. She should have been hooked onto me. Papa fucked up there. We don't need Elly. If I had been twins with Iphy we would have had something. We could have done something. But my time's coming.'

The flame energy of his anger and disgust flickered. He eased back onto the pillow and a peculiar childface replaced his sneer. He was afraid. His shoulder fins reached toward each other but could never touch, never meet. Falling short, they lay like a failed prayer across his chest.

He lay there staring at nothing, tired out by the draining of his own venom. I crawled up behind him and snuggled close, my belly to his back. This was my reward for endurance. He would never ask for my arms around him but times like this he would allow me to warm him, to warm myself against him. I nuzzled into the back of his neck, breathing carefully so as not to irritate him. I felt his fin stroking my arm. When he spoke again I could feel the low vibration of his voice all over my body. 'You know, Oly, I'm surprised. I didn't think Papa would be so easy to beat. Not this soon. It's kind of scary.'

9

How We Fed the Cats

Al, the handsomest man, looks bewildered and groggy over his first cup of coffee. His mustache is sprung and wild to match his sleep-jagged eyebrows as he peers around the table at us, asking, 'What's this I hear about high jinks on the Mouse Rack with the wheelchair? Eh, dreamlets?'

We all grin dutifully and Elly does her 'Oh, Papa!' routine to disarm him while Mama blearily hands around filled breakfast plates, and drags her kimono sleeves through the butter every time she reaches across the table.

I cut Arty's meat slowly while my chest fills with a yearning that would like to spill out through my eyes and nose. It is, I suppose, the common grief of children at having to protect their parents from reality. It is bitter for the young to see what awful innocence adults grow into, that terrible vulnerability that must be sheltered from the rodent mire of childhood.

Can we blame the child for resenting the fantasy of largeness? Big, soft arms and deep voices in the dark saying, 'Tell Papa, tell Mama, and we'll make it right.' The child, screaming for refuge, senses how feeble a shelter the twig hut of grown-up awareness is. They claim strength, these parents, and complete sanctuary. The weeping earth itself knows how desperate is the child's need for exactly that sanctuary. How deep and sticky is the darkness of childhood, how rigid the blades of infant evil, which is unadulterated, unrestrained by the convenient cushions of age and its civilizing anesthesia.

Grownups can deal with scraped knees, dropped ice-cream cones, and lost dollies, but if they suspected the real reasons we cry they would fling us out of their arms in horrified revulsion. Yet we are small and as terrified as we are terrifying in our ferocious appetites.

We need that warm adult stupidity. Even knowing the illusion, we cry and hide in their laps, speaking only of defiled lollipops or lost bears, and getting a lollipop or a toy bear's worth of comfort. We make do with it rather than face alone the cavernous reaches of our skulls for which there is no remedy, no safety, no comfort at all. We survive until, by sheer stamina, we escape into the dim innocence of our own adulthood and its forgetfulness.

The shadow stayed in Chick's eyes, and a dimness, a kind of fog, settled on him. I think he never quite got over having hurt the fat goon. Chick was crazy like that. Something in his chemistry mixed up with the way the family trained him. He got twisted so that he was more afraid of hurting someone else than of being hurt himself, more scared of killing than of dying. In the numb, dumb way that he knew things, Chick understood Papa's disappointment and felt guilty for it.

Papa took to having depressed spells during which he was inclined to sit alone in odd spots with a bottle. High on a two-day binge, he ordered posters for a 'World's Strongest Child' act, but he shelved the idea during the hangover. Sometimes Horst, or the twins or I, would make a suggestion to try to cheer him up.

'What about sports?' I'd ask. 'What if a pole vaulter got just a tiny boost from Chick at the right moment and you happened to have a bet on the guy? What if a ball got a little nudge toward a goal line?'

But Papa would shake his head and pat my hump. 'Oly, my dove, your grandpa told me long ago, and I should have remembered. He used to say, "If you don't mess with the monkey, the monkey won't mess with you."'

Al and Horst were going off on business for the day. Al told Chick to feed the cats and Chick, as usual, bit his tongue, turned pale, and nodded without saying anything.

Chick bit his tongue more than any kid I ever heard of. Sometimes Al had to use fire-eater's salve on the inside of Chick's mouth.

After Al left, Chick slid up to me at the sink where I was doing the breakfast dishes. 'Come with me, Oly, please?' The dishes flew out of the sink in a silent, clatterless flock. They dipped through the rinse water and dried in the air as they jumped, ten at a time, to their places in the cupboard. I laughed and wiped my hands. Arty was holed up with a book and the twins were practicing piano with Lily.

'Sure,' I said, 'but how come? You've fed them lots of times.'

His soft face rumpled lightly in worry. 'I know. But I don't like it.' His eyebrows went up in a peak of resignation. 'I like the cats. It's the meat. I don't like moving it. Just come along, O.K.?'

Horst always parked the cat van near the refrigerator truck where the meat was kept. When he fed the cats himself, Horst would toss a quarter of beef out onto the ground, jump down after it, slam the truck door, wrestle the beef around by its long leg and whack chunks off it with a huge cleaver. Horst fed the cats through the cage doors, but nobody else on the lot felt comfortable doing that. Horst liked telling stories about how unpredictable cats are. I always suspected him of doing it deliberately to keep people from messing with them. If that was his reason it certainly worked.

The sides of the cat van were hinged at the top and could be cranked up like awnings, shading the cages. There was steel mesh outside the bars, and the walls separating the paired Bengals and lions and leopards were inch-thick plates of steel. Al tried to get Horst to put clear plate plastic up instead of bars and the steel screen but Horst said it would ruin the effect. 'People think big cats should be behind bars. And the screen gives them the feeling that they could get their fingers clawed off if they stuck them through. Besides, the cat smell is important too, and if I put plastic up I'd have to air-condition the whole rig.'

When Chick fed the cats he dropped the meat through the ventilator slots in the roof. We stood outside the refrigerator truck and watched the big bolt lift and the door swing open. Chick reached over and took my hand. 'Is this O.K.? I want to hold your hand while I'm moving the meat.' He was looking pinched. 'Sure,' I said. A beef quarter floated off its hook inside the truck and wobbled out. It flopped onto the big chopping block. The cleaver came out of its slot in the truck's tool rack. Chick worked fast. The blade flashed upward five times quickly and six chunks of meat sailed through the air with exposed fat gleaming. The cats were coughing and spitting as the trapdoors over the ventilator slots lifted simultaneously. The chunks dropped through with a single thunk to the floor. Another quarter jumped out on the block and the door shut while the cleaver was rising and falling. Chick was squeezing my hand gently. The cleaver dipped its square tip into the cutting block and stayed there while the chunks lifted, circled like cumbersome crows, and headed slowly for the flaps in the roof.

'You could do it without the cleaver, Chick,' I said.

'Yeah, but I'd feel the meat more. Can you feel it?'

He was taller than I was and he looked down at me with such a serious intensity that I felt a small quiver of fear. 'Feel what?'

He frowned. Words never came all that easily to him. 'Well, how ... dead ... the meat is.'

I stuck my tongue out at the corner of my mouth and squinted at him through my sunglasses. Anybody else in the family except Lily would be pulling something if they talked like that, trying to spook me so they could laugh at me later. Chick was so straight he was simple. He could never really understand the joke when the rest of us were telling whopping lies.

'No,' I said. 'I don't feel anything.' He pursed his mouth and I heard the meat land inside the cages and the snarling of the cats. Chick looked so sad I knew I'd failed him. 'I'm sorry, Chick.'

He swung an arm over my shoulders and leaned his face down against my head. 'It's okay. I just thought you might feel it if I held your hand.'

'Shit,' said a clear voice behind us. We wheeled together as though we were the twins. It was one of the red-haired girls. She shrugged her round shoulders at us through her peacock shirt and laughed nervously. 'I just never get over how you do that, Chick,' and she waved gaily and teetered away on her tall heels.

We watched her go, Chick's arm still around my shoulders, my arm around his waist. For one instant my eye escaped and I could see us as we must have looked to the redhead. Two small figures, one bent and distorted, shielded by cap and glasses, and this slim, golden boy-child, several inches taller, holding the dwarf close while chunks of meat sailed over them in the air. I hugged Chick. His peach sheek rubbed my forehead and nose. I wondered how he did move things and, while that wondering was creeping into my skull, I realised that I had never wondered about it before. Had any of us really wondered? Even Al and Lil? Or had we all been so caught up in the necessity of training him and protecting him and protecting ourselves from him and figuring ways it would be safe to use him and finding out exactly what he could or couldn't do that we never got around to wondering?

'Chick,' I said to his fine yellow hair, 'how do you move stuff?'

His head came up slowly from my shoulder and he looked surprised. Then his face focused. I was thinking how ridiculous never to have asked him. He started to blush. He let go of me and passed his hands over his ears as though he knew I was making fun of him. 'Oh, you know,' he said. The cleaver levered itself out of the chopping block, flew to the sterilizer hose hanging from the refrigerator truck, and danced in the white gush from the nozzle. The hose stopped and the cleaver leaped toward the truck door, which opened just enough to let it in. Then the door closed and I knew the cleaver would be settling into its slot. Chick was bright pink now.

'No, I don't know, Chick. Tell me.'

A small rock by the truck wheel began to spin in place. It flipped over, still spinning, then hopped onto its side and began to roll in a tight circle. The equivalent, probably, of another kid scuffing his shoes or twiddling his own ear in embarrassment. He was my little brother, of course, so I got impatient. 'I'll pinch you, Chick! Tell me how you move stuff!' The rock lay down quietly.

'Well, I don't really. It moves itself. I just let it.' He looked at me anxiously while I chewed on that and found it unsatisfying.

I shook my head. 'Don't get it.'

'Look,' he turned me toward the cats. The side of the van lifted and the prop poles slid into place so I could see the cats in the shade. They were all eating, standing over the meat, wrenching it, or lying with chunks between their paws, fondling it.

'You know the water tank at the back?' said Chick. As I watched, the small taps over the troughs in each cage opened slightly and trickles of water flowed. One of the Bengals leaped at its tap and began batting the stream with its paw. 'Water always wants to move but it can't unless we give it a hole, a pipe to go through. We can make it go any direction.' The tap that the Bengal was playing with suddenly opened wide and a gush of water splatted into the big whiskers. The cat jerked back and then lunged forward, pressing his whole face into the heavy spray, twitching his ears ecstatically. 'If you give it a big hole,' said Chick, 'a lot comes out. If you give it a pinprick you get a slow leak.' He was struggling to make me understand. I watched the tiger play and felt a thickness between my ears. 'I'm just the plumbing that lets it flow through. I can give it a big path or a small one, and I can make it go in any direction.' His anxious eyes needed me to understand. 'But the *wanting* to move is in the thing itself.' We started off toward the big tent.

'Did I help?' I asked.

'Sure,' he said.

Arty, wheedling from the sofa, called, 'Chick, I'll bet there's a lot of that roast beef left over from dinner. I sure would like a sandwich made out of that beef, with mayonnaise and horse-radish. What do you say? Will you make me one?'

Chick, with a comic book under his arm, having worked for hours at other people's jobs and looking now for just an apple and a visit with Superman — this vegetarian Chick, who will eat unfertilized eggs and milk but never (no, please don't make him) fish or fowl or four-legged beasts or anything that notices when it's alive and talks to him about it if he touches it — this

Chick knows Arty is being mean, and will force him to move the meat rather than using his hands and a knife, and says, 'Sure, Arty, white or whole wheat?'

He tries. He gets the plate of beef from the refrigerator and casually grabs a knife from the drawer.

'Chick!' snaps Arty indignantly. 'You're not gonna use a knife, are you?'

Caught, Chick admits, 'I was gonna move the knife.'

But Arty roars, 'Drop all that norm shit! Why did Papa give you that gift if you're going to piss it away like a norm? Move the meat. Move the meat!'

And so precise leaf-thin pages of beef separate themselves from the pink roast and arrange themselves with a swoop of mayo and a flip of horseradish on a dancing pair of homestyle whites, and they all come together on a pretty blue plate that glides out of the dish rack to give them a ride over to where Arty is picking his teeth with a fin and watching.

'There you go,' says Chick.

'Thank you so much,' says Arty, who is perfectly capable of making his own sandwiches if there is nobody around to do it for him. Arty clamps a fin on the sandwich and takes an enormous bite, watching Chick's face as he chews. 'Dullicious!' he mouths around the mess.

'Good. I'm glad.' Chick smiles and steps out of the van and walks around behind the generator truck, where he vomits painfully and tries to think of something besides what the cow said to him as he sliced her.

They were fighting and their door was locked. The thumping woke me. I burst out of my cupboard thinking of elephants or earthquakes. The thin paneling of their cubicle room thonked toward me a fraction of an inch. I could hear them gasping. I ran to their door. The knob wouldn't turn. The early sunlight slanted in through the window over the sink. A huge body slammed against the door on the other side. They'd wake up Al and Lil. I slid Chick's door open and his huge eyes were waiting for me. He was afraid.

'Help me,' I whispered. 'The twins are fighting.'

He rolled out of his blankets and grabbed my arm. His hand was wet.

'Unlock it.'

He looked at the doorknob. It turned. The door opened. They were rolled in a knot on the bed with spider elbows jerking out and in, a flailing leg whacking a heel into a thin, pajama-clad back. Their breathing was short and loud and a hand came out of the mess, pulling a long skein of black hair up into the light of their small window.

'Hold their hands.' I nudged Chick. Two hands spread out against the pillow and a fist landed with a smack and a squeak. 'All the hands! All!' I snapped. Four arms splayed in the air away from the twisted bundle of pajamas. A leg swung back for a kick and then froze.

'Can you hold them?'

Chick nodded, looking at me. His eyes had crusts of sleep in them. Elly's face lifted out of a mass of black hair — a red scratch across her forehead. She drew back on her long neck and shot forward, whooshing out a phtt of air as she spit into the tangled hair beneath her.

There was no hiding from Al and Lil. The scratches and bruises were so visible that the twins couldn't do their act for four days. They were sick and sore. They lay in bed with their faces turned away from each other all that day. Al and Lil were very upset.

'You must never do that again! You must never fight with each other!' The old incantation poured in shocked desperation from the parental mugs. The twins refused to explain what it was about.

Chick was helping me drain sewage tanks that afternoon. We were both glum. We stood and watched the gauge on the pump that emptied our van's tank into the tanker truck. I kept thinking about what they'd looked like when Chick had opened the door. Like a thing that hated itself.

'They always bicker,' I said.

Chick nodded, watching the gauge dial. 'But they were really trying to hurt each other.' Chick's head fell forward, his chin nearly touching his chest. The back of his neck was so thin and golden, and his tawny head was so big above his skinny shoulders. Seeing him hit my lungs like an ice pick through the ribs. He was pretty.

'I wonder what it was about?' I murmured.

Chick sighed. His head wobbled. 'Iphy said his name in her sleep,' he said.

Lil made Ali Baba and Forty Thieves Chicken for dinner. She was rubbing lemon juice over her hands to get rid of the garlic smell while we all sat around the table waiting for the oven bell to sound.

The twins were excited about something, whispering to each other. Al was talking about an old road manager he'd run off the midway twenty years before. The guy had shown up again that day looking for a job.

'Vicious god, Lil! He looked eighty years old! He looked like the grave had spit him back up, disgusted!'

Lil tsked over her lemon-juice hands. Arty watched the twins. Chick and I leaned on Papa from opposite sides, leeching his warmth.

Lily was dishing out the chicken when Iphy finally spoke up.

'We have a new turn for our show!' Iphy glowed. It had to be tricky. Iphy always did the talking if a 'No' was possible. It was hard for anybody to say 'No' to Iphy.

'We do a standing vertical jump onto the piano top and spring off into a synchronized-swim dance number in the air. We fly out over the audience and back while the piano goes on playing the "Corporal Bogwartz Overture"! Doesn't that sound great? We practiced this morning! We'll use pink floods and three pink spots to follow us over the crowd. Do let us, Papa! Chick can handle the whole thing *so* easily. He knows the music already. He learned it in two sessions! It takes exactly one and a half minutes and it'll be our finale. He can just run in during the last five minutes of each show, stand behind the screen, and be finished when we touch the stage for the bow! Please, Papa, Mama? Come and see it after dinner; you'll love it!'

Chick was hiding his face behind Al's arm. Arty's eyes

stayed on Lil's big spoon, lifting out chicken and putting pieces on plates.

Al was laughing. 'What a picture! Wouldn't that flatten 'em? Hey, Crystal Lil! How about these girls? Sharp?'

'Flying,' Lil murmured. 'Mercy.'

Elly was pink with eagerness, her hopeful, fearful eyes fixed on Arty, who said nothing. He rocked slightly in his chair, seemingly interested only in the food that was accumulating on his plate with the help of Lil's spoon.

It never happened, of course. Arty squashed it. If the outside world tumbled to it, or even suspected it was not a trick, we'd drown in power plays for Chick. Stay with the straight path of what we were each gifted with ... Did we think Al hadn't done enough for us, that we had to monkey with his work? Iphy was disappointed but willing to understand. Elly never said anything about it.

We probably looked sweet, the twins and I, in our blue dresses under the shady apple trees, with big bowls in our laps, snapping green beans on a summer afternoon. But the apples on the tree were gnarled and scabby and the twins' glossy hair and my sunbonnet covered worm-gnawed brains.

'Arty wouldn't hurt anybody.' I was lying vigorously as I snapped away at the smooth-skinned beans. 'You're the one, Elly. You're jealous of Arty when he's just trying to take care of family.'

'Oly, you know Chick would be floating in formaldehyde if it looked like he was going to steal any of Arty's thunder by being a big success.' Her hands ripped the beans to pieces, dropping the tips and strings into one bowl and the usable chunks into another. Iphy's hands did the same task lightly, delicately.

I pushed on doggedly through my beans. 'Arty still thinks Chick can be useful.'

'Sure,' Elly sniffed. 'As a workhorse and a slave. Chick can save us a lot of money. It takes ten men five hours to put up the tops that Chick can put up in one hour by himself. And Chick's pay is a pat on the head.'

Iphy sighed, 'You should be kinder.'

Elly muttered at her own fingers. 'I'm just taking care of you and me. That's all I'm thinking about. He hates us. He's selfish.'

'Not selfish! Scared! He's scared all the time, Elly! You know it!' Iphy's hand lifted in fright, demonstrating Arty's terror. I shrugged off goose bumps, thinking, I'm scared too. Because I know Arty. I know him better than either of you do.

'Let him be a preacher. Let him have all those creeps sucking around him. They'll puff him up. But he'd better leave us alone, and Chick too. And you can tell him that, Oly. There, take all these beans to Mama!'

'Be nice, Elly,' I pleaded. 'Just be nice.'

'I'll be nice, she muttered dangerously. 'You'd both let him cut your throats before you'd complain!'

Without any of the family taking much notice, Arty became a church. It happened as gradually as the thickening of his neck or the changing of his voice. From time to time one of us would remember that things hadn't always been that way. It wasn't that Arty *gòt* a church, or created a religion, or even found one. In some peculiar way Arty had always been a church just as an egg is a chicken and an acorn is an oak.

Elly claimed that it was malice on Arty's part. 'He has always had a nasty attitude toward the norms. Iphy and I like them except for the hecklers and drunks. They're good to us. Papa tends the crowds like a flock of geese. They're a lot of work and bit of a nuisance but he loves them because they're his bread and butter. Mama and Chick — and you too, Oly — you three don't even know the crowds are there. You don't have to work them. But Arty hates them. He'd wipe them all out if he could, as easy as torching an ant hill.'

'Truth' was Elly's favorite set of brass knuckles, but she didn't necessarily know the whole elephant. If what she said about Arty was 'true,' it still wasn't the whole truth.

Arty said, 'We have this advantage, that the norms expect us to be wise. Even a rat's-ass dwarf jester got credit for terrible canniness disguised in his tomfoolery. Freaks are like owls, mythed into blinking, bloodless objectivity. The norms figure our contact with their brand of life is shaky. They see us as cut off from temptation and pettiness. Even our hate is grand by their feeble lights. And the more deformed we are, the higher our supposed sanctity.'

The first time I remember him talking like this was the one very rare night when he had an ear infection and couldn't do his act. I stayed with him while the rest of the family worked. He sat on the built-in couch in the family van surrounded by the popcorn he'd spilled, the kernels getting smashed into the upholstery as he bounced around talking and dipping his face into his bowl of popcorn and nipping at hot chocolate through his straw. I laughed because he had butter smeared around his eyes as he pumped this piffle at me.

I was crushed when Arty ousted me from the Oracle. Originally, I had been the one who sorted through the question cards and actually went on stage to press the face of the chosen card against the side of the tank while Arty hovered, bubbling on the other side, to read it and then shot to the surface to give the answer. Then Arty decided he wanted a redhead to do it. He had them parade in a giggling line outside their dorm wearing shorts and bras so he could choose the best figure. he said the crowd would have more respect for him if he was waited on by a good-looking redhead. 'They'll wonder if I'm balling her, decide that I am, and think I must be a hell of a guy if this gorgeous gash puts out for me even though I'm so fucked up. If it's Oly waiting on me, they figure it's just birds of a feather.'

I still took care of him after each show, but for a long time I sulked and ignored the act.

The Aqua Boy changed again. For a while, he answered only generic questions distilled from the scrawled bewilderments and griefs that piled up on the three-by-five cards. Then he stopped answering at all and just told them what he wanted them to hear. Testifying, he called it.

What Arty wanted the crowds to hear was that they were all hormone-driven insects and probably deserved to be miserable but that he, the Aqua Boy, could really feel for them because he was in much better shape. That's what it sounded like to me, but the customers must have been hearing something different because they gobbled it up and seemed to enjoy feeling sorry for themselves. You might figure a mood like that would be bad for the carnival business but it worked the opposite way. The crowd streaming out from Arty's act would plunge deeper into the midway than all the rest, as though cantankerously determined to treat themselves to the joys of junk food and simp twisters to make up for the misery that had just been revealed to them.

Arty thought about the process a lot. Sometimes he'd tell me things, only me, and only because I worshipped him and didn't matter.

'I think I'm getting a notion of how to do this. O.K., a carnival works because people pay to feel amazed and scared. They can nibble around a midway getting amazed here and scared there, or both. And do you know what else? Hope. Hope they'll win a prize, break the jackpot, meet a girl, hit a bull's-eye in front of their buddies. In a carnival you call it luck or chance, but it's the same as hope. Now hope is a good feeling that needs risk to work. How good it is depends on how big the risk is if what you hope doesn't happen. You hope your old auntie croaks and leaves you a carload of shekels, but she might leave them to her cat. You might not hit the target or win the stuffed dog, you might lose your money and look like a fool. You don't get the surge without the risk. Well. Religion works the same way. The only difference is that it's more amazing than even Chick or the twins. And it's a whole lot scarier than the Roll-a-plane or the Screamer, or any simp twister. This scare stuff laps over into the hope department too. The hope you get from religion is a three-ring, all-star hope because the risk is outrageous. Bad! Well, I'm working on it. I've got the amazing part down. And the scary bits are a snap. But I've got to come up with a hope.'

Arty had the advance men make up special flyers to hit certain churches. 'Refuse!' they blared. 'Arturo, the Aqua Boy!' and then a list of our dates and sites. Though Arty never mentioned anything resembling a god, or an outside will, or life after death, church groups started showing up. In the grim blasted regions where the soil had failed or the factories were shut down, whole congregations would drift through the gates, ignoring the lights and sights of the midway, and find their way to Arty's tent. They paid their price and sat numbly in clumps on the bleachers waiting as long as it took for his show to begin. When it was over, they would leave the grounds together, ignoring everything.

'Too poor to play,' Papa said.

'The one buck they've got, I'll get,' said Arty. But it wasn't the money that excited him. It was that those who never would have come to the carnival came just for him.

Mama was dreamily pleased. 'Arty's spreading his wings,' she said, nodding to herself. But his wingspread took in more than the bleachers in his own tent. And all the time he was taking over more and more control of the carnival itself, and becoming more obvious in the orders he gave.

10

Snake Dance — Immaculate

I was eleven years old that year. Chick turned six and the twins were approaching their fourteenth birthday. Arty was sixteen and in a hurry.

He got his own big van with a platform to connect it to the family van. No fuss about it. Papa just shrugged when Arty had him write out the check. The guards lugged the furniture from the dressing room behind Arty's stage, and I arranged it. Mama busied herself moving Chick into Arty's long-abandoned cubicle in the family van.

As Arty got stronger, Al and Lil wilted. Each week they seemed softer and browner at the edges. Lil was scatty and vague more often. You could catch her any hour of the day with her collection of pills and capsules shuttling in and out of the handbag she kept by her. She did her work but she got thinner and her breasts began to droop. Her clothes didn't hang on her in the old smooth way. Her makeup was a little blurry to begin with and tended to slip by lunchtime. Long before closing each night the mascara and rouge would slide into thick smudges. There was something missing in her eyes.

This was the year she decided she had taught the twins all that she was able, and hired the fancy piano man to teach them. Arty claimed that this was the cause of her frail weeping. The twins said it had started after Chick was born and had simply increased.

We didn't ask for Papa's opinion. Al was listless one minute and irritable the next. He'd go out to give orders in the morning and find that Arty had already passed the word for the day.

He'd nag and snap and stand over the crews while work was being done. He took to spending more time with Horst and to showing up half buttoned into his tailcoat and with his mustache unwaxed for his Ringmaster routines. Then Dr. Phyllis appeared.

Al had always fancied himself a healer. His hobby was reading medical journals. He collected first-aid kits and drugs. He was an enthusiastic amateur general practitioner, and as soon as we could afford it — years before Arturism was in swing — he bought a small second-hand trailer and set it up as a little infirmary. His fascination with human mechanics certainly came before and probably sparked his idea for manipulating our breeding, and he did have a knack for it. We thought of it as part of his Yankee spirit. He was enthralled by medicine but furious with doctors for hogging the glory just because they'd managed to get a piece of paper to hang on the wall.

With Al's hobby, the Fabulon had been nearly independent of medical folk. Horst was called in as a consultant on veterinary chores, but Al handled anything human himself. The flame eaters figured him for a genius because he cured the many blisters on their lips and inside their mouths. Over the years he set fractures, relocated joints, diagnosed and treated venereal diseases, and dosed infections from the kidneys to the tonsils.

It was Lil who soothed brows, changed sheets, and read aloud for the sick, but it was Al who did the flashy stuff. He lanced boils with a flair, gave vaccinations, irrigated ears, noses, and rectums with equal zest, and made a grand production of extracting a sliver. He was a masterly stitcher — 'scarless wizardry,' as he himself claimed. His career triumph happened the night an elderly lady collapsed in the front row at her first sight of Arty. Al recognized a heart attack, ripped her purple cotton dress down from the throat and clapped disposable electrodes to her chest within seconds of her tumble to the sawdust. He did it right there in front of Arty's tank with seven or eight hundred people in the bleachers watching. She jolted. Her eyeglasses slid off. She voided her colon rather noisly and was alive again, if not conscious.

It was the custom for the midway folk to appear on Monday mornings at Al's clinic if they had complaints. A lot of people said Al 'should have been a doctor,' and that his talent was wasted in the Fabulon. Al didn't see it that way. 'I've got a captive practice of sixty souls,' he'd say, increasing the numbers as the show's population grew to eighty, a hundred and twenty, a hundred and sixty.

Then Dr. Phyllis arrived. She drove into the lot one morning and parked thirty yards back from the cat wagon, which happened to be the last trailer in line that day.

She sat at the wheel and looked out through the windshield for a while. I saw her because I was stumping around the cat wagon rehearsing a lead-in talk. I kept on, pretending not to notice but taking in the shiny white van with a pair of tangled snakes climbing a staff painted next to the side door. I could barely see the vague pale figure behind the polarized windshield. We'd been on the lot for two days and were all set up, so the crews were taking it easy that morning, sitting on trailer steps talking and drinking coffee.

Horst was shaving beside his living van, using a portable razor while he looked into the rearview mirror on the driver's side. Everybody on the lot saw the van arrive but nobody reacted. For all we knew it was an act that Al had hired and not mentioned.

I was thinking she was a snake dancer because of the vipers on the van. I was morbidly fascinated by snakes. The van door opened, a pair of steps flopped out, and she appeared.

She was dressed in white — the uniform, the shoes, stockings, gloves, and of course the snug cap and the face mask. Only her glasses were neutral, clear, the eyes behind them blurred by their thickness.

She stepped smartly down and strode toward the nearest guard. It was Tim Jenkins, a big mahogany weightlifter who had retired from perpetual corporal status in the Marines and had been taken up by Al while his scalp was still visible under his military haircut. Tim was serious about guard duty and clicked his heels as the short, sturdy white figure approached him.

I'd stopped my pacing and was staring, boggle-eyed, at her. I knew it was a woman because of the broad hips and bulging prow. I was figuring her for a Hindu snake dancer — imagining flame shows with reptiles flickering over her gradually revealed flesh, slipping up her arms under the white sleeves, and so on.

I couldn't hear what she said but Tim nodded and looked at Horst. Horst had been watching everything in his mirror. He flipped his razor through the driver's window onto the seat of his van and strolled over. Tim was making introductions and Horst nodded and stuck out a hand. The figure in white pointedly jammed her gloved hands into the pockets of her white jacket. Horst let his hand drop and settled back a hair on his heels. Horst strolled away with the lady in white, toward the two Binewski vans. I trailed at a distance.

It was a bright, warm morning in Arkansas, I think, or maybe Georgia. The dust was brick red on my shoes as I leaned on the generator truck and looked down, pretending to mind my own affairs. I could have kicked myself for picking that fender to lean on when I realized that the fractured thrum of the generator would keep me from hearing any conversation. The white lady was waiting outside Arty's van. She was carrying a thin vinyl briefcase, white. She stood quite still with no nervous movements. Chick's small face peered from the window of the family van.

Arty came out in his chair. His forehead folded down over his eyes with questions. He doesn't know her, I thought. He didn't send for her. He nodded and said something. She spoke, her hands on the white case. Arty guided his chair down the ramp, and she fell in beside him, going slowly away from the vans, talking. She tucked the case under her arm and jammed her hands in her pockets again.

The case didn't stay where she put it but slid out behind her and floated toward the open door of the family van at an altitude of four feet or so. She whipped around and despite the mask I could tell she was glaring at the flying briefcase. Arty looked over his shoulder, stopped, opened his mouth, and shouted at the van. The case stopped just before it entered the door, turned in midair and zipped back to the white lady at twice the speed it had left her. She reached out a gloved hand, snatched it, and stuck it back under her arm. Arty was talking to her. She nodded. They turned away and, with him rolling and her walking, they paraded up and down and around the lot, talking for a long time.

'I think she's creepy,' said Electra. Iphigenia bobbed her head gravely in agreement and popped a slice of apple into her mouth. Arty ignored them both.

'How is she going to be paid? Percentage? Salary? Only when somebody's sick? Or only as long as everybody is well?' Al slid his eyes nervously, trying to be businesslike. Arty was forced to abandon his soup and his pretense of oblivion. He stared around the table at us and then turned to Papa.

'Don't worry about her money. I'll take care of it. She's got a lot to offer us. She's a stroke of luck for this show. She's not a school hack, at least. She's good at what she does.'

Papa looked guiltily into his soup bowl.

Lily smiled dreamily. 'It will be nice having an educated lady around.'

Al patted her hand. Arty was concentrating on his soup again, crossing his eyes to sight down his straw. Chick sat beside Lil in the back of the dining booth, smiling and watching the peas lift, individually, from his soup, jerk slightly until the drip of broth fell back into the bowl, and then swoop down to rest in a military row on his plate. Chick never did like peas. I caught Iphy's eye. She raised her brows and pursed her mouth. Elly wrinkled her nose at me. We girls agreed, silently, that even if we had bubonic plague, the lady in white wasn't going to lay a finger on us.

Dr. Phyllis cowed Al. After that first day he never questioned her presence, or her credentials. He wouldn't even try to ask where she'd come from or what she'd been doing before she joined us. He dithered and protested that she was a 'lady' and a good medic, and 'By the blistered nipples of the Virgin,' he didn't need to know any more than that. The twins and I shook our heads at how little fight he put up when his private passion was usurped. I nagged him to ask questions because, if he didn't come up with some information, Arty would make me try. It seemed that despite his long conversation with her Arty didn't know much more about her than the rest of us did.

I was putting Arty onto the little elevator platform that ran up the outside of the family van one morning when he cocked a wink at me and said, 'I guess you'll have to get old Doc P. to let you look through her microscope.'

I put a foot on the platform beside him, grabbed the lever, and we went slowly up.

It was a sunny morning. Warm. I don't know where we were — a small valley. All around the camp were deep pastures cut by streams with rough hills beyond. The highway sliced through and ran toward a small town, whose chimneys we could see above the trees. There were songbirds racketing in the scrub oaks on the slopes. The honk of a pheasant drifted up from the long grass. Arty wriggled off the elevator onto the roof. He liked to sunbathe up there when he could. Al had put a low rail around the top of the van so Arty wouldn't fall off, at the same time he installed the elevator.

Arty stuck his toe into the elastic of his trunks and worked them down until they sagged off him. He rolled over and arched his back, tilting his belly to the sun, stretching lushly.

'Yep,' he said, 'Little Oly had better do her stuff on Doc P.'

'Here's your fly swatter.' I put it beside him with the handle close to his head, where he could reach it. Arty was, as he claimed, 'fly Mecca,' and he hated them.

'Don't ignore me, Oly,' he murmured as I rubbed suntan oil on his chest.

'I won't do it. I don't like her.'

'Oly, you like her. You like her a lot. She's a fascinating, intelligent woman and you can learn from her.'

'Right,' I said, capping the bottle.

'Give her an ear to pour into. Nobody does that better than you.' He turned his head to watch me step onto the elevator.

'Don't piss on anybody from up here,' I said. 'Papa got really mad last time.' I lowered myself, looking away from him, looking at the brown creek that eased through the grass behind the van.

★ ★ ★

Three hours later I was hauling Dr. P.'s garbage to the camp
dumpster and cursing her and Arty and myself in a thin blue
vapor of rage that hissed through my nose with every breath.
She had accepted my offer of help coldly and stood over me
while I pumped the hydraulic leveler for her van. She gave me
rigid orders about clipping the weeds and grass all around her
van and then made me go over the whole area with a rake for
litter. Then she introduced me to the garbage. She had very
strict ideas about garbage. Each full bag in the can beside her
van had to be slipped inside another bag and wrapped in a
particular oblong shape and tied with string in a proper square
knot. Three of these small parcels went into one large bag,
which was then wrapped and tied with the small knot. Then the
large parcel could be carried to the camp collection.

She considered it proper that I, or someone more efficient,
should be dispatched by Arty to do her chores. She wasn't at all
grateful.

When I got back to her van the door was closed again. I
hadn't yet managed to get inside. I pushed the door buzzer.
Her voice scratched out of the speaker, 'Yes.'

'I'm finished with the garbage, ma'am.'

'That's all for today, then. Have a bath and pay special
attention to cleaning under your nails. Report back tomorrow
morning.'

A month and several towns later I still hadn't set foot in her
van. I'd filled her fuel and water tanks, emptied her septic
system, gift-wrapped her garbage every day, and in each new
site I'd leveled her van, policed her area for litter, and generally
kissed her cold and pendulous buttocks for nothing.

In the meantime she had taken over Al's precious infirmary
trailer.

The sick call was cut in half. Al kept up his Monday-
morning exams of the family but they were conducted in our
dining booth. He didn't have the old zest for it. He went on
tapping and listening and demanding news of our bowel move-

ments. He still lifted our eyelids and peered into our throats and ears and scowled at our nails and rubbed blue gunk on our teeth and, for those of us with hair, checked for lice and ticks, but he didn't have his old glow of joy in doing it. He was sneaking behind her back.

I found this clipping years later in the private papers of the reporter Norval Sanderson, who joined the show sometime after Dr. P. Norval had resources that we Binewskis lacked. When he wanted info on someone's past, he could tap records and microfilm files from any newspaper in the country.

(UPI) A coed at the University of New York was admitted to St. Theresa's Hospital today after having performed abdominal surgery on herself in her dormitory room.

University authorities revealed that Phyllis Gleaner, 22, a third-year bio-chem major, pressed an alarm buzzer in her dormitory room, which summoned the building's custodian at 4:30 a.m., Tuesday. Responding to the buzzer, custodian Gregory Phelps found the student lying on a sterile table, wrapped in bloody sheets and surrounded by instruments.

'She was weak but conscious,' said Phelps. 'She told me not to touch anything in the room but to call an ambulance. She said the room was sterile and she didn't want me touching anything. She was very strong on that. I could see blood all over and from what I saw in the mirrors around her I didn't want to upset her so I went and called the emergency number.'

Police surgeon Kevin Goran, M.D., examined Gleaner's dorm room after she was removed to the hospital. 'It was a makeshift but functional operating theater,' said Goran. 'She had instruments for fairly major abdominal surgery, and an ingenious arrangement of mirrors, which allowed her to work inside her own abdominal cavity.'

Emergency staff at St. Theresa's reported that Gleaner was conscious and coherent when admitted, but was very fatigued. 'She was not really in shock,' said Dr. Vincent Coraccio, staff surgeon at St. Theresa's. 'What was remarkable was the competence of the work. She'd gone all the way in and was finished, evidently, but she got too tired to close the incision. That's when she called for help. All I had to do was stitch her up. A very tidy job.'

Gleaner administered local anesthetics to herself throughout the surgical procedure. Her statements to the hospital staff indicate that Gleaner believed a remote-control device had been implanted next to her liver by an unnamed undercover organization. Gleaner believed that the device was being used to monitor and direct her activities. She performed the surgery in an effort to rid herself of the device. No such device was found by police in searching Gleaner's dormitory room, nor by the medical staff in treating Gleaner.

The clipping was stapled in Sanderson's notebook. One page of his sprawling hand revealed the rest of his Doc P. research.

In an article appearing two days later, the same reporter revealed that university officials attempting to contact Gleaner's family discovered that the background on file was fictitious. She had not attended the schools that she claimed. Her records were forged and falsified. No relatives or friends could be located in the small Kansas town — Garden City — she claimed as her home. The university was embarrassed, particularly since Gleaner's academic record at that institution was brilliant. Her professors acknowledged that she was a reserved individual and denied any knowledge of her private life. They affirmed that her work had been consistently excellent. Classmates claimed little knowledge of Gleaner. She was aloof from everyone.

Gleaner has consistently refused to make any statement or to answer any questions about her self-surgery or her falsified background. Her only comment, relayed through a nurse's aide, was that the university had no cause for alarm since her tuition and fees had always been paid.

11

Blood, Stumps, and Other Changes

The twins turned fourteen in Burkburnett, Texas, during a Panhandle sandstorm as red as a drinker's eye. Birthdays were the only holidays the Binewskis noticed and we celebrated them with all the gusto we could muster. But that fourteenth for the twins was in a rough spot. Wichita Falls had denied us a permit and the front man — new to the job, and a reptile anyway — was scared to tell Al. We didn't find out until the police met us at the lot and escorted our cavalcade out of town, with Al cursing melodically all the way to our next scheduled stop, which was Burkburnett. Burkburnett hadn't decided whether we could have a permit or not. We put up in the rail-yard next to the slaughterhouse and slept with the whish and thunk of the oil pumps for night music.

There were oil wells everywhere. The soil had been abandoned to dust and lizards, and the backyard of every wind-blistered bungalow in town had thrown over ideas of shade or geraniums in favor of the whiskey promise in the mutter of those green grasshoper pumps. Every pump was set in concrete and snugged in by a barb-topped chain-link fence eight feet high. There were pumps in the parking lot of the twenty-four-hour liquor store. There were three pumps on choice plots surrounded by the artificial turf that covered the Terra Celestial Memorial Gardens boneyard. A dozen ravenous steel insects sucked at the shit-caked loam in the mile-square meat-field of empty pens where the beeves, when there were beeves, milled waiting for the knife. The white board fences of the paddocks were guarding only oil pumps that week. The packing plant was closed down.

Past our corner of the meat yard the town began, or ended, in a blasted heap of storefronts leaning on each other to face a million miles of Texas rushing straight at them over the mindless, moundless plain.

The twins woke up bickering. I could hear Elly's harsh whispers behind the screen. Then Iphy, who never really learned to whisper, 'Not better than you. It's different, Elly. Please. Just for our birthday.' It was the same old quarrel. Iphy wanted to sit next to Arty at breakfast. Elly always insisted that they sit in the left side of the dining booth so that she was between Iphy and Arty, who always sat in his special chair at the end of the booth. Elly hated the giggling that hit Iphy when she sat next to Arty. Arty didn't seem to care. I was the one who helped Arty with his food.

I crawled out of my cupboard and tiptoed into the toilet cubicle. Elly was grumbling. She must have given in. She'd given in on Arty's birthday the year before and sulked the whole day. The pink joy from Iphy's smiles had twisted me up. I looked in the mirror trying to see the fear on my face. It was in my liver and invisible.

Arty would rather have Iphy cut his meat than me. The blinds squeaked open in the twins' room. Their voices came out together. 'A horse!' they said, and then a paired sigh, 'Poor thing!'

They left the van door open and, when I came out, they were standing on the bottom slat of the board fence peering through.

'Many happy,' I said, and hugged their long beautiful legs. Then their hands were pulling me up by the arms and I grabbed at the top rail and peered over. Iphy said, 'Hang on to her,' and Elly's arm clamped under my hump.

'He's sick,' said Iphy, who thought all unfamiliar animals were male. 'She's old,' said Elly, who assumed that all living things were female until proven otherwise.

The horse had been orange once but a grizzle of white had paled its coat. Its white muzzle drooped to the ground on a thin, tired neck. Its ears were loose and hanging. Its eyes were nearly closed. Bones jutted through spine, ribs, sharp cow flanks. The tail was so long that it dragged in the muck.

'The feet!' said the twins. The horse was not sleeping. It moved half a step forward. First a rear hoof and then the opposite forehoof lifted slowly out of the black mud that covered them to the fetlocks. Then the horse stopped, lifting again that rear leg, holding it curled so the hoof was above the mud. The hoof was long and curved forward like a human shoe worn over on the outside. The legs were muddy to the knee and bowed oddly.

The sun leaked up over the edge of the plain. The horse stood in shadow in its tiny pen. 'Its feet are rotten,' muttered Elly. Iphy began to sniff in sympathy.

I could feel the faint thunk in the fenceboards from the pumps far off in the middle of the tight maze of paddocks. The sun's yellow knife slit the air, not yet reaching the ground or even the fences, but just touching the heads of the pumps as they rose and then losing them as they bobbed down into the shadow again. The feeble horse stood sunk into itself. Not an ear twitched. Not an eyelid flickered. An early-morning fly crawled over its hanging lips.

'Happy birthday,' Arty said.

Iphy sat next to Arty at breakfast. Al had gone to the sheriff's office to get the verdict on our permit for Burkburnett. Lil hugged the twins every time she passed them and made elegant little melon salads for breakfast. Elly didn't talk. Iphy mourned for the horse all through the meal.

'I want my chair.' Arty was brisk, up to something. I dragged the chair outside and set it up in front of the door. He clambered into it from the top step and looked around. 'Over by that horse.' And I pushed his chair through the dust to the fence. He leaned forward and peered through the slats. The horse hadn't moved. Arty's face rumpled in disgust. He sank back against the chair and looked at me speculatively. 'Well. Go get the doctor. Bring her here.' I ran.

The doctor's big van was by itself at the end of the line with fifty yards between it and the last trailer. She never parked close to the others. Her blinds were open. The twined snakes painted on the van's side held the intercom in their mouths. I pushed the button. The sun was up now, slanting warm and yellow over my hands. The intercom speaker hissed and then her voice came out calmly. 'Yes.' I delivered the message. 'One moment,' she said. The speaker hissed again and went silent. I climbed down off the step block to wait for her. I didn't like to think of her door opening too close to me.

The air was still and dry with a musty, thick taste. The only familiar smell was the faint tang of fuel from the van. We hadn't opened up yet. We hadn't put our mark on the air. I tried to see past the cluster of vans and trucks and trailers to home — to the place at the other end where our van sat, with Arty out front next to the near-dead horse in its pen. Everything was in the way. I pulled my cap down over my ears and jigged anxiously in the dust. I didn't want to look in the other direction toward the dry slut town with its dark windows shaded against us. I bit my tongue when the door opened. The antiseptic smell slid out first. Then I saw her thick-wedged white shoes with the ankles leaping from them. 'Lead the way, please,' she said. And she stepped down toward me. I scuttled.

Dr. Phyllis should have had a nice voice. It was cool and high and always controlled. She never ran off into the ragged edges of sharp like Lil or Iphy. But it still wasn't pleasant. It was monotonous as a sleep-walker. Her words came out cleanly, nipped off surgically with a slightly heavy breath where an *r* should be. She spoke Lil's old tongue, the long, smooth one from the right side of the hill in Boston. Though, when Lil asked her, Dr. Phyllis said she'd never been there. That talk made Lil want her to stay. Lil thought it would be good to have a woman with the show who spoke that way — as though she and Lil might drink tea in the van and talk about home. But it never happened. I didn't mind Lil liking her. Lil was silly about who she liked. But Arty was different.

The dust puffed up behind me as I ran. I hoped it would settle on her white uniform. I wished she wasn't wearing the mask so she would breathe my dust and cough. But she never came out without the mask over her nose and mouth. The white cap was always pulled down tight over her forehead and completely covered her hair. In between were the big thick spectacles. She was completely protected. She didn't speak to me, and she kept up with me easily, walking fast.

Chick was leaning on the arm of Arty's chair as we came up. The two of them were watching something in the dust.

I heard Arty say, 'Push them together.' Chick's head nodded and a small grey snake rose a foot into the air, suspended from its middle like a shoestring, and then dropped back into the dust.

'They're not paying attention,' said Arty.

'Good morning,' said Dr. Phyllis in her high, perfect voice. The snake and a horned toad rose quickly and flew away together into the desert. Chick hid his head against Arty's chest.

'Doctor!' said Arty. 'Take a look at this horse.'

She walked stiffly past me, her hands folded in front of her crotch. 'I am not,' she said calmly, 'a veterinarian.'

Arty jabbed his chin into Chick's wheat-colored hair. 'Scat!' he snapped. The child jumped away from the chair and turned to run. When he saw me, he reached out his soft hand and ran up to me.

'Let's go see what Mama's putting in the birthday cake,' I said. He smiled and we climbed into the van.

Chick sat on the counter, still except when his mouth opened to receive the gobbets of chocolate frosting that would occasionally lift from the bowl that Lil was dipping from. 'Stop it, Chick,' Lil would murmur. And he would smile sweet chocolate at her, and the curl that dropped in front of her ear would stretch out in a soft caress over her cheek and then spring back. I crouched on the floor with my hump against the cupboard door and watched Arty and Dr. Phyllis through the open door.

Her white skirt was stretched tight over her thick legs and square hips. She was pushing her hands deep into her front pockets and rocking on her wedge heels. She gazed through the fence at the decrepit horse. Arty leaned back in his chair and looked up at her, smiling. I couldn't hear what they said.

A brown blob danced in front of my nose. I opened my mouth. It dipped, circled in the air, and zipped onto my tongue. Frosting.

'Thanks, Chicky,' I mumbled. My cap slid forward onto my nose and then back to its original position. Dr. Phyllis leaned an elbow on the top board of the fence and turned her mask and spectacles toward Arty. She propped a white-gloved hand on her hip and nodded. I licked the last of the frosting out of my teeth and let it trickle down my throat.

'I wonder where the twins are,' said Lil. The cake was beautiful. Lil had cut it into the shape of two hearts that interlocked.

I gave the word to Horst and he went right away. He took a pair of musclemen along to help pull the little trailer. I sat on the step of the cat van, smelling the Bengals and waiting for Papa. There were a few cars moving on the distant street now. A barbershop had its door open and a curtain of red and white fly strips hung limp. The guards were drinking from big Thermoses at the end of the lot. It felt odd to be parked without the gates and the booths and the tops going up around me.

After a while Dr. Phyllis marched by, followed by Horst and the two bullies pulling the covered trailer. She had them park it next to her big van. Then she went inside her van. Horst came to me slowly. He dropped heavily onto the step beside me. 'Horse thieving now!' he said.

'Papa will find its owner and pay for it.' The men were grunting and cussing inside the little trailer. The old horse would not get up.

'I wouldn't feed that critter to an alley cat. Grey meat and little of it.'

One of the young men jumped out and stood at the tailgate to pull. With his hands wrapped in the dung-fouled tail he crouched and crab-walked backward. The pale, gaunt flanks hove into view. The flabby hooves and rear legs fell out onto the ground. The blond man inside the trailer was pushing from the other end. The horse rolled out and lay on the ground. Its head flopped down on the end of the long neck and lay still. The white flapping nostrils flared and dropped. The blond man hopped out of the trailer with a rope hackamore and fitted it onto the limp head. He clipped a rope to the chin ring and ran it to the axle of Dr. Phyllis's van.

The guards were moving slightly, standing up, putting their Thermoses behind their stools. A big man crossed the street and walked across the rutted stubble of the lot. Papa. The two guards walked halfway to the vans with him and then went back to their posts. Papa came on. He looked angry.

Burkburnett had forbidden our opening on Sunday. We'd have to wait until the following day. Al was pissed off. He was cursing the cowardly advance man who had done a bunk the first time he ran into a snag. 'Missing Friday and Saturday in Wichita Falls — and having to open on the slowest day of the week in a town that couldn't buy a week's worth of toilet paper for the crew!'

I told Papa what Arty wanted. Al groused but then went off to look for the owner of the horse.

At lunchtime, Lil realized she hadn't seen the twins since breakfast. She flew into a panic and went jittering around on her high red heels with her hands clutching her own shoulders. She teetered from guard post to guard post questioning the big blank-faced men. 'Ain't seen 'em, ma'am. Couldn't miss 'em if they'd come this way.' And they'd switch their chaws and wobble their eyes anxiously as she skittered away, hoping that the little freaks hadn't slipped by them while they were swapping lies about hot nights in Baton Rouge.

Papa was somewhere talking to a man about a horse and I trailed after Mama piping, 'Maybe so,' and 'Ah, they're all right!' and 'Maybe they're buried in the meat yard, shall I get some shovels?' in my most reassuring way as she burbled through her Mom's-All-Purpose-Adjustable-List-of-Horrors that might have happened whenever a child is out of sight. Lil had got to the finger-twisting stage and all the red-haired girls turned out to look. We opened all the empty boxcars on the rail siding and examined all the padlocks on the big sliding doors to the packing plant and were on our way back through the camp line, stopping at every van, trailer, and truck camper. The whole show was on hold because Papa hadn't given the set-up order yet, and Arty was occupied with something else.

Mama decided the twins were having a nap in their own room and we were on our way to look when I noticed the sky. It was a vague milky sheet. Far off at the dull edge of the plain, a blood-red line lay between the earth and the sky. As I watched, the red thickened to a bar and then a band, climbing the sky.

Arty and Chick were next to Dr. P.'s van at the end of the line. Dr. P. herself, arms cocked to plant her white gloves on her white hips, stood in front of Arty's chair nodding her mummy-wrapped head. Chick looked like he was hiding behind Arty's chair.

The wind was picking up. It riffled Chick's hair and pushed Dr. P.'s skirt flat against her legs. Off to the side the old horse lifted its head on a curved and quivering neck, scrabbling at the earth with its mushy front hooves, trying to get grip enough to heave itself upright.

Horst trotted by me with the two guys who had moved the horse. I started to run. I could see Dr. P. opening her van door and waving for Chick to go in. Chick looked at her but both his hands were fastened to the arm of Arty's chair. Arty's chin was jerking toward the door and the doctor. Arty was telling Chick to go with her.

'We're gonna shove that maggoty goat back into the little trailer!' Horst yelled at me as I passed him. It was too far to Dr. Phyllis's van and I was too slow. Her door closed on Chick and he was inside, alone with her. Arty had the bulb control in his teeth and was wheeling merrily toward me when I grabbed his chair arms.

'What'd you do that for?' I puffed. 'What's she gonna do to Chick? Don't leave him with her!'

'Push me home! He's all right. Come on! Double it! Run!'

I grabbed the chair handles automatically and slogged toward his van, still craning my neck to look back at the blank closed side of Dr. P.'s white van. Horst and his helpers were torturing the decrepit brute back into the trailer. I stopped pushing. 'Arty, what is she doing to Chick?'

His smooth-skinned head bobbed at the side of the chair. 'Milk and cookies. Teaching him to play checkers. Move it! Move it! I have to piss so bad I can taste it.'

I threw myself forward, plodding, watching my feet stir the dust into the wheel ruts and noticing that the odd, thin light from the sky threw no shadows at all.

Mama was frantic. Papa was trying to tell her about the fat, bristly tick of a man who owned the horse and had tried to convince Al it was blood stock and would be a three-year-old in prime fettle as soon as it got some oats in its belly. Mama was whipping over every surface in the van looking for a note. A ransom note from the kidnappers or a farewell note from the runaway twins. 'I left a note in my mother's sugar canister when I ran away,' she muttered. Papa followed her, rambling on about the 'used cayuse peddler' and finally noticed something amiss. Mama turned to him with clenched fists and a flaming face.

'Help me find them!'

'What the . . . ??' Papa snatched at her wrist, turning her arm over, checking the number of injection tracks. I saw them toppling into anger.

'Papa, the twins are missing.'

'Ah, the flabby-gashed mother of god!' howled Papa as he sailed out the door trailing Mama. The wind slung the door wide with a flat whack and rushed into the van. I pushed the door closed behind me and took the two steps to Arty's van. I turned the knob without knocking and slid inside. Silence. Carpet. The clean, rich room dim except for a yellow pool of lamplight where Arty lay calmly on a wine velvet divan with a book. He watched me wrestle his door closed.

'Do you know where they are?'

He shook his head. 'But you can soak some towels and pack

the windows and door frame for me. Help keep the dust out.'
His eyes fell back to his book.

I wet towels in the tub, wrung them out, and punched them
into the window frames. Through each window I could see the
crew moving the vans and trailers, turning them end-on to the
coming wind. There was movement in the windows of some of
the other trailers as other hands tucked wet rags or papers
against the cracks.

'Shall I go get Chick?'

Arty looked at the clock. 'He'll be coming here in a few
minutes. He'll make it before the dust comes down.'

'There he is.' I could see him through the window, holding
hands with a red-haired girl as he ran to keep up with her long
legs. They were ducking their heads, hunching into the wind,
the red-haired girl with her free hand holding her high-rise hair,
which blew up and back around her groping fingers.

'Did you ever wonder,' Arty asked, in his coolly speculative
tone, 'why he doesn't fly? He should be able to.'

I yanked the door open as the pair hustled up the steps.

'Oly dear!' said the red-haired girl. 'Crystal Lil wants you,
honey! Chick found the twins. Come on.' I was staring at
Chick, looking for bruises, psychic scars, electrodes planted
behind his ears. Nothing. He was caught up in the excitement
of the wind.

'Leave him with me!' Arty yelled from the divan. Chick's
eyes sprang eagerly past me, his face opening, pleased. He
trotted in as I pulled the door shut.

The redhead grabbed my hand. Hurrying. The wind pushing
so I felt my weight lifting away from me. The sky was a deep
rust above us and the shouts of the crew around us were
shredded to yelping bits that flipped past like no language at all.
'Where?' I bellowed.

I thought she said, 'The Schultzes!'

We blew past the generator truck, the refrigerator truck. I
saw Horst shoving a wad of wet paper into the ventilator slot of
the cat wagon and then the sand hit us. The red-haired girl
screamed a short, high whistle interrupted by coughing, hers
and mine. It was needles from behind, a million ant bites blistering the back of my neck, burning through my clothes. In

front it was worse. A hot cloud of granulated suffocation filling nose, mouth, and eyes with dry powder that stuck to any moisture. It liked the roof of the mouth, the caves behind the nose, and especially the throat.

The refrigerator truck toppled onto its side behind us. We ran and the wind tried to make us fly.

The ten-toilet men-and-women Schultz was broadside to the wind. The same heaving gust that flattened the redhead and me toppled the Schultz off its trailer. On my belly in the dirt with my face buried in my arms, I felt the crash more than I heard it. Then a hand was pulling me up, and slipping my blouse up to cover my nose and mouth. The redhead rushed me along, her own blouse snugged to her face with the other hand. The fine dust sifted through the cloth but I could breathe a little. The wind ripped up my back, raking my hump, clawing at my bare head. My cap had blown away with my sunglasses. There was no sound — the blank roar of the wind-borne sand was seamless.

Hands hoisted me at the armpits and I fell, free and blind, but landed before I could yelp. Inside. Out of the wind. The redhead had found the door at one end of the Schultz and got me through it. I sat in the dark, painfully blinking sand out of my eyes with tears. The deep boom of the wind beat at the tin wall as I lay against it. A warm body lurched into me, collapsed beside me. A hand felt my head, my hump. The air was soft and thick with floating dust and the sick, sweet tang of chemicals and worse. The redhead's warm voice breathed in my ear, 'I'll bet this crapper hasn't been pumped since Tulsa.'

It wasn't actually a Schultz-brand portable toilet. It was a Merry-Loo in a truck box with five booths on each side, self-contained cold-water supply for washbasins, MEN on the port side, WOMEN to starboard. Papa had picked it up cheap with its own truck trailer. It was built of thin fiberboard and was so light that a car or a small pickup could pull the whole rig.

'Yuck! I'm leaning on a slimy urinal!' The redhead scooted over, pushing me into the corner. My head banged on something hard and I reached to feel pipes and chilly porcelain, dripping. The sink. My eyes were flushing out sand and I began to see well enough to know that it really was dark in there.

'The twins and your mom are on the other side. We're on the men's side. If they're still there ... *Lil! Lily!*' she shouted.

'*Mama!*' I yelled, and then coughed with the red dust rasping deep in my pipes. The murk fuddled me. The room was on its side. The sink above me hung the wrong way. If I turned on the tap, the water wouldn't fall into the basin, it would pour onto my head. We were crouched on a wall with the linoleum floor at our backs. What little light there was came in a brown-gravy mist through the plastic skylight in what was normally the roof but was now the far wall. The sand-heavy wind cast dark, rushing shadows across it. Just beyond the urinal that lay beside us, the booths began. The liquid seeping from the cracks reminded me that all the toilets were lying on their backs.

'They're above us.' The redhead was standing up on shaky denim legs. 'Wow! I'm a little woozy!' Fluid was dripping down from what was serving as the ceiling. 'Look, that wall is popping!'

The tab-and-slot construction of the fiberboard wall was loose at the corner above us, drooping. 'Here, climb up and pull on it.'

She hauled me up by my hands, balancing me as I climbed to her knee, her hip, her back. 'I'm gonna stand up now,' she warned. I stepped onto her shoulders, propping myself against the wall, and tore at the loose flap.

'Mama! Crystal Lil!'

'Hey,' from the dark above us.

'Oly, get out of the way. We'll lower Mama to you. She's hurt. Her chest.' It was Elly up there in the dark. I gave the redhead a few extra bruises sliding down. She caught the long, white legs that slid out of the ceiling. Mama's favorite yellow-flowered skirt was torn, and the blue veins on the backs of her thighs glittered oddly in the dimness. She moaned feebly as she eased downward. 'Mama?' Her arms came last. The twins let go and she fell jerkily into the corner with a yelp.

'A light,' Mama said.

The twins lowered themselves through the hole and dropped beside me. They were sodden and they stank. Their hair and clothes were damp with the blue ooze from the chemical toilets.

'It's all our fault,' Iphy whimpered. 'My fault is what she

means,' said Elly. They crouched over Mama and the redhead leaned over her, gently pushing Mama's shock of white hair back from her forehead. Lil was wandering in her head.

We stretched her out flat under the sink and the redhead tore a scrap off the yellow-flowered skirt to lay over Mama's nose and mouth so she could breathe in the floating dust.

The twins were filthy. 'Nothing broken?' asked the redhead. 'Then sit over there. That smell makes my sinuses ache. Crapper dumped on you, eh?'

'I acts,' Mama announced calmly from the floor. 'Me is acted upon.' We all looked at her.

'Is that grammar?' asked Iphy. Mama laced her fingers together on her belly as though she were napping in her own bed.

'I don't know. It may just be talk.' The redhead picked at a scrape on her elbow. 'I'll go look outside in a minute. It might be letting up.'

The wind was gusting now, taking breathing breaks between attacks. There was a little more light. The twins slumped on the floor against the first booth. Their faces were as blank as uncut pies. Their eyes stayed fixed on Mama.

'Happy birthday!' I grinned. Their mouths crimped painfully.

'Were you in here all morning? Mama was worried.'

The two matching faces nodded slightly. The redhead chuckled and whacked at the knees of her jeans, shedding puffs of dust. 'It's their first time bleeding. They thought they were dying.'

Elly glowered, eyebrows bunching downward. 'We knew what it was.' Iphy's eyes tilted up anxiously in the middle, 'We didn't know it was going to happen to *us*, though. We don't feel good. And it's scary. Elly didn't want to come out but I did. I tried to get her to come out but she wouldn't.'

Elly shook her head impatiently. 'How long do these things last? All night? Or what?'

Lil's voice came from under the rag, 'I would have told you more but I wasn't sure it would happen to you.'

My heart was beating a panic in my ears, 'Mama, will it happen to me?'

Iphy licked at her muddy lips, 'Elly wouldn't come out even when Chick and Mama found us. She wouldn't let me unlock the door. Mama told Chick to unlock the door and bring us out but he wouldn't. Because we didn't want to. But it wasn't both of us. It was Elly. Our legs went to sleep sitting on that toilet.'

'Shut up! Shut up! Shut up!'

'Ah, Elly, loosen up. Don't be so crabby,' groaned the redhead. She patted my head. 'Your mama sent me for you so you could crawl under the door of the booth.'

'I would have kicked you if you'd tried,' snarled Elly.

'For Christ's sake, girl, why make so much of a fuss?' The redhead was exasperated. 'It happens to every female.'

'Yeah? Well, it changes things for us. It throws in a lot of new stuff to think about.'

A truck horn started blaring nearby. Its flat voice, thinned by the wind, repeated itself monotonously. Mama opened her eyes. 'Dear Al is so impatient.'

'He doesn't know where you are.' The redhead stood up. The whites of her eyes were blatant in her dust-clotted face. She reached above me to the knob of the horizontal door and pushed it open. The clogged sand in the sill rained down. A rip of wind circled the room, rubbing grime into our faces.

'All right, ladies, party's over. Everybody out.'

'I'm so glad I had that cake in the refrigerator,' said Crystal Lil. 'We wouldn't have had a bite if I'd left it on the counter.'

We were having the twins' birthday party on Mama's big bed. She lay propped mightily on pillows with Papa's elegant bandage wrappings showing through the front of her kimono and her fresh-washed hair frothing like egg whites above her naked, unpainted face.

We vacuumed for an hour and still the red dust drifted in the air. But now, having showered in relays, wearing clean clothes, we could blink our sore eyes and pick the dry, gritty boogers from our noses in exhausted contentment. Papa, leaning against the pillows next to Mama, winked his scoured red eyes at us. 'You girls look a bit better now. Less like a demon crew and more like hungover angels.'

Arty and Chick, of course, were clear-eyed and boogerless, having spent the storm in Arty's air-conditioned van. We all ate cake and traded long, absurd, and competitively exaggerated accounts of How Terrifyingly Near to Death the Sandstorm Brought Me. Papa's version had him wandering from trailer to van hollering questions against the wind and getting unsatisfactory answers and 'wondering where, by the shriveled scrotum of Saint Elmo, you'd all been blown to.' He took refuge in the generator truck and got the bright notion of sounding the truck's horn, 'like a foghorn, so, if you were wandering in that fiend prairie, you could home in on it.'

'Save a big piece for Horst,' Iphy ordered, 'and one for the redhead who helped us. What was her name?'

'Red.'

'*All* the redheads are "Red," scummy! They have regular names, y'know!'

Arty had soothed and entertained his (newly discovered) little pal during the storm by letting Chick read aloud to him from Arty's ancient greeting-card collection. When the wind shifted and Arty's van considered tipping over, Chick prevented it.

Chick did not have a story. Chick did not eat his cake. His plate sat on his lap as he stared around at each of the fascinating taletellers in turn. He wasn't enjoying himself but he didn't say anything. Only after we'd kissed Mama and Papa goodnight and were drifting off toward our beds, Chick caught up with us in the narrow place beside the twins' door, looking up at them sadly.

'What is it, sweets?' asked Iphy.

'I knew where you were. I should have brought you out, huh?' His eyes were growing in his face like the size of the question. Elly smoothed a hand across his hair.

'No, Chicky, you did just right.'

'If I had got you out like Mama wanted, you would all have been home like me and Arty. Mama wouldn't have got a broken rib. You wouldn't have got scared.'

I let go of his hand and punched him softly on the arm. 'Don't feel guilty about me, I had a great time!' and I sagged off to my warm cupboard, leaving the twins to console him or not.

I was standing on Arty's dresser polishing the big mirrored one-way window to the security booth. He was lolling on his new velvet divan leafing through a torn magazine retrieved from the pile in the redheads' trailer.

'If I were an old-money gent with a career in the family vault,' Arty proposed, 'and heavy but discreet political influence, how would I dress?'

I looked back over my hump to see if he was pulling my leg. He had his nose in the magazine so I answered, 'Quietly.'

'But what's quiet for a man with my build?'

'I don't know.' I climbed down and wiped my footprints off the dresser top. 'A tweed T-shirt? Gabardine bikini trunks? Charcoal silk socks?'

'Socks.' He stretched his bare hip flippers, flexing each of the elongated digits separately. He hated socks. 'But I suppose they'd be warm.' he kept turning pages. 'Oh, Toady. Why were the twins hiding in the latrine?'

So that was it. I dropped my cleaning rag and hopped onto the divan, grabbing his lower flippers.

'I'll tell you if you'll tell me about Chick and Doc P.'

'It's no big deal. She doctors that horse for me, I let her study Chick.'

'Study how?'

'Talk to him. Ask questions. Observe. What about the twins?'

'They started bleeding that morning. It got Elly spooked.'

'Bleeding?'

'Their first time. Do you think I'll bleed too?'

He yawned. 'I'm going to do some work now. You'd better go.'

Chick's legs and sneakers were sticking out, toes down, from under the family van. 'Whatcha doing, Chick?'

'Looking at ants.'

I flopped onto my belly and wormed in beside him, careful not to crack my hump against the van's undercarriage. A school of small ants swarmed on a damp lump in the dirt.

'That looks like cake.'

'It's my piece of the birthday cake. They like it.'

'You were over at Doc P.'s again this morning, weren't you? What's she like?'

His hot pink face flashed at me, smiling. 'She's going to make Frosty the horse well. And she's going to let me help her. She's going to show me how to stop things from hurting. Arty says it's good. But today I just moved her garbage out.'

The twins and I were wiping the jars in the Chute with dust cloths and spray cleaner. I rubbed the big jar hard and peered through at Leona the Lizard Girl floating calmly inside. 'Is Mama sick?' I asked.

'She has to sleep,' said Elly. 'Papa gave her an extra shot so she could sleep. It's good for her ribs.'

They were cleaning both sides of Apple's jar. Iphy kept one hand spread across their wide, flat stomach.

'Does it hurt, Iphy?' I asked.

Elly snorted. 'She keeps thinking about it.'

'Let Oly do the Tray, Elly. I'll throw up if we have to do the Tray.'

'You won't puke. Close your eyes while I do it.'

'You think about the bleeding, too,' Iphy protested.

'Yeah, but I'm not going, "Ooh, what's that? Does it hurt?" every time something rolls over in our belly. I'm thinking what it means for us.'

I was working on Maple's jar by then, spraying and wiping. 'What does it mean?'

Iphy's eyes were closed as Elly examined the Tray's jar for fingermarks and smears. 'What if we can have a baby? Don't you ever think about what's going to happen when we grow up?'

Iphy shook her head, eyes closed. 'Nothing will change.'

'What will change?' I was suddenly scared. Elly was impatient with both of us.

'Stupid! What do you suppose is going to happen when Mama and Papa die?'

Iphy's eyes popped open. 'They're not going to die!'

'Arty will take care of us,' I said, dusting the 'BORN OF NORMAL PARENTS' sign. 'He'll be the boss.' But I was thinking I'd marry Arty and sleep with my arms around him in a big bed and do everything for him.

'Right!' Elly sneered. 'We can depend on Arty!'

Iphy tried to be reassuring. 'I'm going to marry Arty and we'll take care of everybody. . . .'

Elly's spray bottle hit the floor as her right hand closed into a white fist and sailed in a short, tight hook to Iphy's mouth, where it smacked, spreading Iphy's lips and snapping her oval head back on her long-stem neck. Iphy tried to stuff her dust cloth into Elly's mouth and block another punch at the same time. They fell, squealing and thrashing, biting and pulling hair. I stood staring through the green lenses of my huge new sunglasses at the convulsing tangle of twins on the floor. I probably could have stopped them, but I didn't feel like it. I turned and shuffled out of the green-lit jar room and down the narrow corridor, leaving the twins to their mutual assault.

We were still in Burkburnett when Dr. Phyllis did the job on Frosty with Chick to help and Papa joining in for the messy bits. They did it late one night in a smallish tent that reeked of antiseptic. The tent was so brightly lit inside that, from the outside, it glowed like a damaged moon heaving with shadows.

I sat fifty feet away on the hood of the humming generator truck and watched their silhouettes. Chick, a tiny motionless lump at one end of a long dark heap, and the squat, bulging form of Dr. P., standing for long periods in one place with only her head and shoulders moving. Al was busy, the large Papa shadow bending, stooping, rushing from one end of the glow to the other, seeming to pace nervously.

They made the big table from a pair of sawhorses and a steel door from one of the vans. The scarcely breathing heap in the middle was the ancient horse.

While Mama and the twins slept, while all the camp fell dark and the midway lights cooled in their sockets and the night guards shifted and spit and sighed at their scattered posts, I watched, leaning on Grandpa's urn, feeling its cold bite working through my hump to my lungs.

A light filtered through the window of Arty's van but no movement showed on the glass.

It took a long time. The black sky should have ached with cold but there was no wind. The stillness was almost warm, almost comfortable. No frogs, no crickets, no birds sounded. I nodded off and woke with cramped shoulders and a sprung neck.

The rotten edge of the sky was moldering into arsenic green when the light in the tent went out. The grey fabric was suddenly dull and three shoddy figures crept out through the flap and trailed away.

I could hear Papa talking in low tones. As they passed me, Chick reached up to grab Papa's hand, the small boy figure drooping sleepily over stumbling legs.

There are parts of Texas where a fly lives ten thousand years and a man can't die soon enough. Time gets strange there from too much sky, too many miles from crack to crease in the flat surface of the land. Horst theorized that we'd all live longer for 'wintering in these scalped zones.' The redheads moaned that it just seemed longer. As the days and miles went on they stopped moaning and leaned toward long silences. Their faces took on the flat, wind-tracked look of prairie. 'The grave looks good by bedtime,' they said, but the complaints lacked their usual spice and crackle.

We'd holed up near Medicine Mound and were taking fearful advantage of the truckers and riggers and a crowd that had come down 250 miles from the Indian Nation in customized maroon buses with fiddle and accordion bands playing next to the toilets and ice chests full of beer every five seats. The Indians stopped off to stretch their legs and their eyeballs at our facilities on their way to the annual stockholders' meeting of some oil company.

Horst himself was reminiscing about the Texas town called Dime Box and the glories of Old Dime Box, which seemed isolated in his eyes to the broad, strong hips of one Roxanne

Tuxbury (pronounced Tewbury) who ran a motorcycle-repair shop there and was undismayed by the indelible stench of cat in a man's chest hair.

Papa was handing out doses of his most rancid tonic before breakfast. 'The winter sun is kind of green and doesn't have the Go juice. That's why you get so sleepy.' Horst was leaning on the door waiting for his secret spoonful of vile black Binewski's Beneficent Balm.

'Just don't let Dr. Phyllis know,' Papa muttered with every pour from his big bottle of Triple B.

'Roxanne Tuxbury always rides a kick-start cycle,' explained Horst, 'and the thighs on that woman are as long and strong as her laugh, which you can pretty much pick up in Arkansas if the wind is right. She wears a little leather halter three hundred and sixty-five days of every year.'

Papa jammed a big spoonful of Triple B under Horst's mustache and bent his famous Binewski eyebrows. 'Too bad Dime Box isn't on our agenda this year. Maybe you ought to take a little van and hop down there for a week. Catch up with us after you've vented your glands or blown your gasket with Roxanne.'

Horst swallowed hard to keep the Triple B down and glared at Al. 'Leave the cats? If you had the sense to winter decently in Florida it'd give a man a chance to . . .'

The bells started suddenly. Chick and Arty, who'd disappeared early that morning, came rolling up fast and shouting, 'Elly! Iphy! Come out here!'

The twins, bug-eyed and wincing, crawled out of the dinette where we'd been finishing arithmetic lessons and waiting for breakfast. Mama forgot her biscuits and I trailed along. Papa and Horst laughed as we all trooped down along the hard clay track toward Dr. P.'s. Arty had a tape player in his wheelchair playing the taped bells loud. The show folk poked their heads out and strolled along, redheads and roustabouts. The flat grey of the day crept up our backs as we came to the shabby covered trailer parked near Dr. P.'s gleaming white mobile clinic.

Arty's chair stopped and Iphy's hand was caught tight in Arty's shoulder fin as Chick stepped forward. There was a rustle and bump from inside the trailer, and then the frost-coated, candy-orange horse stuck his head out the door and came prancing down the ramp to the ground with his mane braided in blue ribbons and his eyes rolling nervously as he arched his thin neck and crow-hopped in the dust. We all inhaled as we saw the long form of the horse, the Dachshorse, the chopped and channeled Basset Horse perched on starry stockings and realized that all four of the mush-boned feet were gone. The horse had been cut off just below the knees and was dancing his sprightly senile horse dance on stocking-covered, rubber-padded half-leg stumps.

'Ain't that something?!' Papa shouted. The redheads 'wowed' woftly and clapped, and Horst whistled a knife blast through his teeth that flattened the old horse's ears. Arty grinned and bowed in his chair, and Chick watched the old horse steadily. Dr. P. did not appear at all.

We all went close to look and pat the sweating, scared horse, and to examine the sock-covered stumps and admire how his tail was tied up in blue ribbon so it wouldn't drag in the dust. Chick stayed close, holding the halter rope. The twins stroked the quivering coat of the stunned old beast and glanced at each other as Arty told them that, though it was late, this was his birthday present to them.

'Thank you, Arty,' they chorused. Papa was praising Dr. P. and Mama set off running for the home van with a cry of 'Biscuits!' and the group shifted and scattered.

Chick let the halter rope slide through his hands and the horse reached for a surviving clump of grey-green near the trailer wheel and bumped his jaw on the ground because he wasn't used to being so low down. Or that's what I thought. Arty leaned back in his chair and looked worriedly at Iphy. 'Are you glad?'

Elly watched the horse stepping gingerly on his shortened limbs, his huge body balanced precariously. Iphy took a breath and patted Arty's shoulder. 'But is he okay, Arty? Doesn't he hurt?'

Chick interrupted quickly, 'No, he doesn't hurt at all.' And I, leaning on Arty's chair arm, wondered if Chick was doing it all, holding the horse up and making him dance. Elly's face turned toward us and she was old. She had sunk into some dark place behind her eyes, and whatever she was looking at wasn't me or Arty.

'So this is what it's going to be like,' she said. Her voice was as dry as the sand that stretched to the sad edge of the sky.

The twins stayed as far away from Frosty the horse as they could, despite Arty's nagging them to 'visit their pet.' Chick took care of the horse. He would probably have croaked when he first woke up and noticed that his feet were gone if it hadn't been for Chick's literal support. Whether Chick had actually kept the brute's heart pumping against his will I don't know. Every morning Chick spent a few minutes jollying the horse into facing another day.

I can't be sure how much information or help Chick got from Dr. P. What is sure is that the tyke spent time with the doctor every day and he wasn't always taking out her elaborate garbage. All he would say when I grilled him was, 'She's showing me how to stop things from hurting.'

Chick also spent time with Arty. Suddenly Arty's nasty attitude had switched to fond big-brotherhood. He let Chick do a lot of work for him — the brand of charity Arty was most generous in dispensing. Arty also debriefed the kid every time he came away from Dr. Phyllis's van. Chick was Arty's mole in the doc's previously impregnable camp. This was clever, considering that none of the rest of us had even got through her door, but I figured it for dangerous.

'What if she decided to dissect him to see how he works?' I asked. 'What if she decides to make a big reputation by writing papers about him for scientific journals?'

'Naah. She won't,' Arty assured me. 'She wants to keep him to herself. She's teaching him to be a painkiller. She says that old horse would have kicked off right away if she'd dosed it with drugs to knock it out. She told Chick about the pain dingus in the horse's brain, drew pictures, and had him fool around inside until he figured out how it worked. She says Chick put the horse to sleep, kept it unconscious, and sat on the pain dingus so the horse didn't have any shock reaction at all. She thinks Chick will help her be a great surgeon. She's not gonna advertise him. She knows she'd lose him if she did.' Arty paused and thought for a second. He gave me an odd, worried roll of his eyes. 'She might decide to take over the planet or something, but I'm trying to keep a tight rein on that kind of stuff. I think it'll work.'

Arty was busy. It's amazing to me even now how much privacy he had in his own van, how much time he spent seeming to lounge around, and how much he got done by giving orders. He was working. His show was changing. He hired his own advance man — a specialist named Peabody who popped in once a month for an hour and then drove out again in a perpetually gleaming sedan. Peabody wore bank-grey suits and an air of smug humility that clashed with the style of the race-track types who did the job for Al. Every town we hit held a larger crowd waiting docilely for Arty. They weren't always poor. They weren't always old.

News cameras were common enough on the midway. We were often booked as a feature of some local crawdad festival or Miss Artificial Insemination pageant or whatever, that drew coverage for us. But the reporters also started doing more interviews with Arty in his tank.

Whatever he was telling them was what they wanted to hear. We were all running flat out to keep up with the crowds. Papa trucked in a portable chain-link fence to close off Arty's stage exit from the people who wanted to touch him and talk to him after his shows.

Arty got a golf cart to toot back and forth in. Papa's guard crew increased to fifty large men dressed in sky-blue uniforms with spangled Binewski badges and arm patches. They carried discreet, telescoping electro-shock sticks and stun-gas spray canisters.

Arty stopped coming to the family van for meals. Mama cooked his food and I carried it to him on trays.

The midway jingled with profits from Arty's crowd. The twins, the geeks, the swallowers, and every act in the variety tent bubbled daily with cheerful audiences, but they were really just waiting for Arty.

Arty was absorbed. Mama treated it as another one of his growth phases. 'He's always been moody, sensitive,' she said.

Papa strode the line from early to late — 'working harder than I ever have!' — jubilant at the gross and his own roaring of orders and arrangements. But he was fuzzy behind the eyes because he was no longer the actual King Cob of all the Corn. In his dire heart he felt the difference. He wasn't working for himself anymore. He was working for Arty. Everything revolved around Arty, from our routes and sites to the syrup flavors in the soda fountains.

We were all nervy with an unspoken anticipation. We were accelerating toward something and we didn't know what.

BOOK III
Spiral Mirror

12

NOTES FOR NOW
Miss Lick's Home Flicks

The library microfilm spews a stream of nuggets. An announcement of the birth of Mary Malley Lick, eight pounds, nine ounces, at Good Samaritan Hospital. The obituary of Eleanor Malley Lick, dead of cancer when her daughter was eight years old. Mary Lick, an uncomfortable fifteen-year-old in a baggy sweater, pictured as 'A sophomore at Catlin Gabel School, who holds the Oregon State Women's Handgun Marksmanship championship for the second year in a row.' Thomas R. Lick cutting the ribbon for the new trophy and smoking room at the Sauvie Island Gun Club.

Then there are articles about all the Lick enterprises. There are fifty-one plants nationwide and a flagship tucked into a bend in the Willamette just north of the Fremont Bridge. The product is Lickety Split dinners — portable food for airlines and for institutions, from rest homes to schools, jails to asylums. Nineteen full menus with special Kiddie, Diabetic, Kosher, and NMR (No Mastication Required) lines. Everything from three to six courses in plastic trays with an indentation for each item. A subsidiary arm leases microwave ovens to clients for 'on-the-spot warming.'

An item about the failure of a labor strike at the Portland plant mentions that Lick Enterprises employed close to eight thousand workers coast to coast and not one of them belonged to a union. Thomas R. fired all the strikers in Portland and hired fresh help unpolluted by notions of collective bargaining.

A mug shot pictures prim young Mary, with her spanking new degree in Business from the state university, recently named Portland plant manager at the age of twenty-four. The caption explains that despite her age she was 'by no means a novice, having worked in the plant for seven years in various departments ranging from bookkeeping to sanitation.'

In the old man's obituary — cancer — seven years later, Mary is listed as Executive Vice President and sole heir to Lick Enterprises.

The last item is a tentative mention in the also-ran list trailing the four hundred richest individuals in the nation. The dry line beside her name explains that, since all Lick assets are privately held, only estimates of her net worth are available.

I take the copies back to my room and read everything again. There is no mention of relatives, friends, or lovers, no names or faces recur near Mary Lick. Every photo shows her isolated even in a group. Her expression is never quite in sync with the cheer or solemnity of those around her. She is alone.

Just before midnight I go downstairs and listen to Lil breathing. Then I go upstairs and knock on Miranda's door. There is no answer.

After the morning shift at KBNK I hole up in an empty office at the station and spend the afternoon on the phone. I enjoy it. I can never be inconspicuous in person. A hunchback is not agile enough for efficient skulking. But my voice can take me anywhere. I can be a manicured silk receptionist, a bureaucrat of impenetrable authority, or an old college chum named Beth. I can be a pollster doing a survey of management techniques or a reporter for the daily paper doing a feature on how employees view their bosses. Anonymous, of course — no real names used and all businesses disguised.

A dozen phone calls into the day I am thinking grimly about my luck. Mary Lick could have played chess or poker or pool. She might have been intrigued by dim, cozy porno shops with black booths for a spy to hide in. It would have been a snap to get close to her if she were a horticulture type or a dog breeder. But no. Miss Lick is physical. Her secretary exclaims, 'She just couldn't get from one day to the next without her two-mile swim in the evening.'

In my family Arty swam and nobody else did. I never learned. Trudging home it occurs to me that things could be worse. Lick could just as easily have gone in for jet boat races, jumping horses, or sky diving. I can learn to swim.

Miranda's windows are glowing yellow as I come up the street. I go straight upstairs to her door and knock. She laughs and takes me in and shoos out a handsome man named Kevin so she can draw me. I sit naked for hours watching her. She draws and makes tea and draws and talks. We don't mention her tail.

The Athletic Club is only a few blocks from the apartment building where Miss Lick owns and occupies the top floor. The club is in the same style as the apartment building, a massive brick-and-glass temple to the joys of insulation. The word is that Miss Lick's father was instrumental in having the club opened to female membership.

'Of course we have been integrated for more than thirty years,' the information girl told me over the phone. I asked to have the club brochures mailed to me. The pamphlets were glossy productions with color photos of the Oak Trophy Lounge (full-service bar), the saunas, dining room, weight rooms, handball and tennis courts, and the Thomas R. Lick memorial swimming pool. I invested in the six-week introductory membership and spent four afternoons loitering in the five-story parking lot across the street to watch Miss Lick's black sedan enter the brick gateway at 5:30 every evening.

I stand in the middle of the deserted locker room, a ditty bag in one hand and a combination lock in the other, staring at myself in the mirror that covers the door. I look old. I have always looked old. The hump is not a youthful thing and the nakedness of my scalp and my hairless eyelids and brow ridges creak of something ancient. I have stuffed my wig into the ditty bag already, waiting for her. 'Always remember,' my father used to say, 'how much leverage you've got on the norms just in your physical presence.' I examine my wide mouth and pink eyes, and the slope of cheekbones into the tiny leg that serves me for a jaw and wonder if it will work this time when I need it to. After all, Miss Lick is not a norm and for all I know she is immune to the usual tricks.

She comes through the door and it starts — her double-take stare reassures me instantly. She is not immune. There is the standard civilized greeting, ignoring the obvious.

'Perhaps you can tell me which lockers are . . .'

I hesitate and she drops her purse on a bench and nods at a row of cabinets against the wall, 'All those without locks.'

I shuffle, apologetic, catching a sidelong glimpse of my awkward figure moving toward the lockers, my heart bulging wild in my mouth with fear that I've overplayed it.

Her seriousness surprises me — the slow weight of her — the lack of cruelty imprinted on her big wary face. Bubbling won't work on her. I set myself to go straight-faced and slow-voiced — to gauge words carefully and understate everything.

She skins out of her tweeds and into the big blue tank suit. Her thick arms and shoulders roll with padded power. Her hands are short and thick, the nails clipped straight across at the tips of the fingers.

'New member,' she says.

'Yes, I joined for the sake of the pool,' I say, looking at the hooks in the locker as I sling my clothes onto them. 'My doctor wants me to learn to swim.' I can feel her eyes on my hump — on the rolls of my neck climbing up to my bald pate.

'Arthritis?' comes her voice.

'It goes with the turf,' I say lightly.

'So I hear,' she says, and I keep my back turned long enough for her to get a good look at me.

Fourth day at the pool.

'Clever contraption,' says Miss Lick, as she snaps the elastic band of my swimsuit that crosses my hump. Her voice is soft and low, at odds with her bigness and her brusque movement. The showerhead suddenly decides on cold and the water hits my jump and my neck and my whole naked head with a bright chill.

'Special tailoring?' asks Miss Lick. 'Expensive?' I smile up at her. She is vigorously massaging her own arms in the spray from the next nozzle.

'Well, it's orthopaedic,' I say, bobbing out of the cold water to stand dripping on the tiles.

'Ah!' says Miss Lick. 'Right.' She pounds her big solid belly with both fists. She flicks her short hair briskly, and her massive jaw wobbles a run of water down onto her chest. I am pulling the rubber cap down over my scalp, feeling it crumple my forehead into rolls over my nose. It pinches.

Miss Lick slides an identical swim cap onto her head, puffing, going red at the edges where her face bulges out of the cap like a ruptured condom.

'Check your feet!' whispers Miss Lick cheerily, and I crouch against the tile bench and dutifully spread my toes and run my fingers between them. Miss Lick is slamming the fire door open and propping it with a rubber wedge. Out she bounces into the shallow footbath that fills the passage between the shower-room door and the pool door. Miss Lick spends several minutes in this high-chlorine footbath before and after her swim. She is concerned about athlete's foot and other fungoid growths.

Miss Lick has kindly offered to give me swimming lessons to counteract the arthritis that is sinking into all my joints. Miss Lick says that all hunchbacks and dwarfs should swim.

I stand knee-deep in the footbath with my nose on a level with Miss Lick's bouncing buttocks, as she jogs vigorously in place in the warm nose-searing chlorine solution. She is looking through the small screened window in the door to the pool.

'Christ! She's there already!' I splash back a step, startled because Miss Lick's side of our conversation has been pretty spartan up to now. This burst of emotion throws me. Then I recognise it. Success. Miss Lick's jaw shoves forward belligerently and her big hands reach back and grasp her buttocks and begin to knead them nervously through the blue tank suit.

'That old nanny goat haunts me.' She looks back with a wry grin at my inquiring face. 'She swims so bloody-arsed slow! And she never stops. She's always in my lane and I'm forever running over her! I tried coming in on my lunch hour. There she was. I tried running in before I got to work in the morning and she was here. She's here every goddamned hour of the day.'

And look at her! She swims like the dead!' Miss Lick stares out the diamond-shaped window and grabs hard at her butt. I pull my tinted goggles down over my pink eyes and close out some of the sting of the chlorine. Her profile blurs in the green lenses and her muttering goes on.

'This may seem horrible but I've actually considered trapping her in the deep end and holding her under. There have been days when I wouldn't have hesitated if I thought I could get away with it.'

She looks anxiously back at me, her eyes bulging through the fat pads of her cheeks. I nod my head at her pale green face. The light moves on the surface of the footbath and streaks jump in shades of green across her face. 'Oh, I can understand that,' I say, and I grin, nodding.

Miss Lick is doing her third lap of what she refers to as 'butterfly' stroke. She will do seven more 'butterfly' laps before she reverts to 'breast' stroke. She does each lap in one minute, which means that the pool will be swamped with three-foot waves and a pounding roar for seven more minutes. Breast stroke is quiet even for Miss Lick. The very old woman who does her mile-and-a-half each day in this pool is clinging to the tile gutter at the side. She will hang there, waiting, until the butterfly is finished. The other swimmers, the young ones, who can evidently breathe under water, continue with their laps. Miss Lick's enormous shoulders have her whole torso free of the water before she splashes back. Her buttocks show briefly like a barrel going over Niagara. I can loll here on the steps at the shallow end, only my legs in the bath-warm water and watch.

I've taken her on her own hook and I have to be careful. She thinks she's adopted me, that she's doing me a kindness, that she's displaying the magisterial stature of her goodness by spending time with me. I have to watch my ass. She is hideously lonely.

The whiskey looks like transparent wood in my glass. I hold it carefully between my eyes and the firelight so the movement of the red flame casts a grain into the brown liquid. The whiskey that I have already drunk sits warmly in my gut and mouth and penetrates the fog in my skull. The corner of my eye registers Miss Lick's heavy wool socks pointing at the fire over her footstool. I am waiting for my palms to dry, breathing slowly until the clammy seep of my nerves sinks back from the surface of my skin. The whiskey is amazing to me. I wonder why I never realized that I would like it. I wonder why I never tried it before. Liking it so much is dangerous now, and so I hold it and look through it, drinking very slowly.

Miss Lick has the bottle on a tray beside her chair and is being generous with herself here in the fire dark. She cuts the wood herself, takes an ax up to the family parkland in spring and drags a chainsaw into the woods on weekends to clean up the deadfalls from the winter. One whole storage cubicle in the basement of the tasteful brick apartment building is devoted to split cords seasoning in the dry dark with a deep resin odor. She goes down in the elevator with a canvas sling over her shoulder and brings up one night's worth at a time. She kneels on the flat granite paving stone in the hearth and nicks off tidy triangular kindling with a hatchet that looks at home in her hand, ticking the slim sticks off a sixteen-inch chunk that rotates quietly under her other hand.

The chairs are dark, supple leather, as big as rhinos. The drapes are a dark plaid in heavy wool. A plaster bust of Minerva, plainted glossy black, sits on the mantel beneath a rack of shotguns.

'I used to go for birds with my old man,' she says.

She talks slowly. Dry barks of laughter punctuate the sad parts to show that she is not sentimental and is not looking for sympathy. She had just described her father, her house in the woods outside of town, her employees, the old but reliable machinery that poops out 3 ounces of gravy 1.8 ounces of niblet corn, 3 ounces of turkey breast, 3.2 ounces of apple cobbler, each in its proper compartment of the plastic trays. She is considering a massive retooling.

'I'll get more ice,' I say, with the bucket in my hand, shuffling to the kitchen as she pads heavily toward the brown-tiled bathroom. The kitchen is blank. Clean and empty. A torn bag containing two dark chocolate cookies lies abandoned on one white counter. The refrigerator door yaws outward from its emptiness. Nothing but a half bottle of ketchup in the door shelves. The mouth of the bottle is caked with scab, and in the freezer section are solid stacks of frozen dinners in plastic trays — unlabeled.

I reach for the lever on the ice-cube dispenser and she is behind me, her big hand swooping past my head to hoist the bucket from me, tuck it up under the spout. Ice rattles out.

'Are these dinners from your plant?'

'Turkey, dressing, pumpkin custard, whipped spuds, gravy. I don't like cranberries.'

'Thanksgiving dinner.'

'Twenty-six Thanksgivings in here. That's all I eat. Nine hundred calories each. So why am I so big?'

The freezer is sighing out vapor. She slips the door closed and stands staring at the gleaming cold cooking range with its dark oven glass.

'Lately I've been eating popcorn instead. Want some?'

She sits on the footstool in front of the fire, long-handled wire screen basket in her hand. The hard yellow kernels in the basket are sliding and bouncing as she quivers her wrist deliberately. The coals below the big chunks of wood flicker black and red and a soft glare reaches up to the basket. The first kernel of corn hisses and jumps, flowering suddenly into a speck of white, then the birdshot peppering as the rest of the kernels go. She watches carefully.

She has a two-quart steel bowl full of popcorn in her lap — a shaker of brewer's yeast on the tray next to the Irish whiskey. She is slowly scooping up popcorn in a big soup spoon and sliding it into her mouth.

'I use a spoon because the yeast sticks to my fingers,' she says. 'It's gritty.'

I lift my glass, full again, and stare through liquid at the fire.

* * *

She talks. People talk easily to me. They think a bald albino hunchback dwarf can't hide anything. My worst is all out in the open. It makes it necessary for people to tell you about themselves. They begin out of simple courtesy. Just being visible is my biggest confession, so they try to set me at ease by revealing our equality, by dragging out their own less-apparent deformities. That's how it starts. But I am like a stranger on the bus and they get hooked on having a listener. They go too far because I am one listener who is in no position to judge or find fault. They stretch out their dampest secrets because a creature like me has no virtues or morals. If I am 'good' (and they assume that I am), it's obviously for lack of opportunity to be otherwise. And I listen. I listen eagerly, warmly, because I care. They tell me everything eventually.

The popcorn is long gone, the fire is dying, and she had decided to show me her life's work — 'My *real* work,' she says — and I feel quite calm, carrying my glass and following her. We have brought the bottle with us but decided we could dispense with the ice. The room has no windows. We have come in through the only door, which is disguised as a locked closet in the bathroom. Only her key will open it.

She gives me the only chair, solid wood, no cushion. A working chair. The whole room is set up for only one person to move in. It is small and lined with racks holding film disks and video cassettes. The screen fills one whole wall. The rest is a battered desk and a bank of filing cabinets. She plods from rack to control panel, talking calmly. She has dropped the rough cheer of her poolside manner. Her tongue is slightly thick in her mouth but she is, I can tell, herself. Her big somber face is intent. She talks as she works.

'People always assume I'm a lesbian. I'm not. I have no sex at all that I know of. No interest, no inclination. Never have. But it's understandable that I give that impression. It doesn't bother me.'

The screen fills with the image of a woman bent over a

computer panel. She seems unaware of the camera. Her hands move rapidly over the control board. She picks up a pedestal microphone and speaks into it. Her face turns toward the camera eye for the first time. She stares past me. Her face is puckered with scar tissue, one eye nearly obliterated by the alien smoothness. Her mouth is distorted into a pulsing gash on one side of her face. As she turns back to the keyboard I notice that she has no eyebrows or lashes and she is wearing a short, curly brown wig.

'This is Linda,' said Miss Lick. 'I went to school with her. She was pretty. Her family comfortable but not rich. A nice girl. Miss Popularity. She put everything into baton twirling, and dates. She was a cheerleader every year from the seventh grade on. Average student. The boys were all over her. She was the oldest of five. Her brothers and sisters were quite a bit younger. She adored them. When we were sophomores she was a princess for every dance and festival. I wasn't one of her good buddies. Never spoke to her. Then one night in the winter of our sophomore year she was babysitting for the little ones while her parents went out. They were all sitting in front of the fireplace in the family room in their nightgowns. They were roasting marshmallows and telling ghost stories.

'I've thought of this so often, visualized this scene. Linda had long hair all the way to her ass. They had all bathed and she was brushing her hair dry and entertaining the little ones.'

On the screen the woman at the computer reaches for the spewing readout. The machine is vomiting fold after fold of perforated paper, thickly printed. She scans it quickly, folding it in front of her in a mounting pile as it rolls out.

'Linda's hobby was sewing. She'd made all the children's nightgowns and her own as well. She didn't use flame-retardant material. She was young, you know. Not thinking. Her mother didn't ask about it. Never occurred to her.'

The scarred woman on the screen rips the end of the printout from the computer, picks up the stack, and gets up from her chair. She turns her back and limps out of the camera's range.

'Well, to shorten the tale, there was a fire — spark caught in one of the little ones' robes. Up it went. Linda saved the child, caught fire herself in the process — ran outside to keep from lighting up any of the others. Went up like a torch, I understand. Long nightgown, long robe, her hair. She was in the hospital for a long time. Lots of grafts. Amazing how much damage was done.

'She refused a lot of the plastic surgery. Expensive. She felt guilty. Her parents had all those little ones to bring up. She said she'd get it done later when she could earn it herself. Parents tried to persuade her but she was fierce about it. When she came back to school she was as she is now, scarred from stem to stern. Different girl entirely from what she had been. Old pursuits, interests, wiped out entirely. Friends tried to be polite but she made them nervous. Boys all gone west as far as she was concerned. Interesting to see the change. She seemed to have taken in the situation completely while she was still in the hospital. Turned her head around. She studied. All that old energy of hers turned to books. Realized, you see, that she couldn't rely on being cute and catching a man — that the life she'd expected was out of reach. But she didn't give up. She made another life — all brain stuff. I admired her. We got to be friends. Still see her. She's a chemical engineer. Done some innovative research. Won prizes. She's told me time and again that fire was the best thing that could have happened to her.'

The camera sweeps over the lifeless computer room. Another camera takes over. An office. The woman in the wig faces the camera. She is sitting at a desk comparing the printout with another sheet of paper. Her forehead only wrinkles on one side. Then we are in a kitchen. Same woman without her white lab coat. She is wearing a bulky sweater, reaching into an open microwave oven and pulling out a plastic-covered tray like the ones in Miss Lick's freezer.

The tape ends and the screen goes to grey static.

'It's not surprising when you think about the precedents.' Miss Lick is philosophical. 'Crippled painters and whatnot. Remember the Arturans roaming the country years ago?'

My frozen face doesn't alarm her. She rolls on expansively. 'Same thing. People put it down because the whole thing had that weird end, but it wasn't too long after Linda's fork in the road and I saw the connection, all right. I'd have run off and joined up with that particular carnival myself if my old man hadn't needed me in the business. Do you remember Arturo?'

I can feel my head bobbing slowly up and down. I have no sense of what my face is doing. Could I be smiling? Does she know? She flicks a hand at me, inviting a response.

'So what did you think of all that? Arturo.'

My throat and mouth are crackling dry and painful. My voice comes out like a rusty chain. 'I loved him.'

She is delighted. 'Ha! I thought so. Probably had a little itch yourself. Wouldn't have minded tagging along on that comet tail, yourself?'

I feel myself nodding, helplessly.

'You're not in a hurry, are you? I'll drive you home. I want to show you another one.'

My eyes pull away from the blank screen. Miss Lick is at the disk rack. I reach for the bottle on the desk. She is going to show me the whole thing. The brown liquid runs right up to the rim of my glass before I can stop it. I set the bottle back carefully. Two deep breaths. I'm having a little difficulty telling the difference between the whiskey and my fear. Miss Lick's glass is empty. I lift my glass and pour three-quarters of the Irish into her glass.

'Oh, thanks. Now this one ...' She is hiking a big hip onto the desk behind me — reaching for the glass. I turn to watch the new scene.

Cars blur the screen — windows, door handles streak past. Then the focus sets. We are across the street from a standard type-C tenement. Garbage leaning against a rusted scrap of wrought-iron fence, a bunch of kids loitering on the steps of a shoddy building. A man wobbles past on the sidewalk, waving his hands and talking to himself. The lens tightens and closes in on a girl and boy on the bottom step. The girl is leaning back against the railing, arching her breasts up at a pimpled boy with a cigarette in his lips. He is trying to look cool and aloof. The girl has black hair, rooched cunningly into coils by her ears. Her face is a Byzantine dream. She purses her lips and blows a smoke ring into the boy's face. Her eyes slant narrowly in a hot half smile.

'This is Carina. Half black, half Italian. Poor as shit. A

dropout but she tested high in aptitudes. Her father disappeared when she was five. Mother a welfare lush picking up a little extra by peddling ass in the dark to johns too old to care or too drunk to notice what she looks like. Specializes in head since she lost her last teeth. She used to refuse dirt trackers but she had to give in on that a few years before this film was taken. Looks like Carina's headed the same way, doesn't it?'

The back of the chair catches my hump wrong and my legs are going to sleep from dangling over the hard edge of the seat. I swig at my glass and move my feet tentatively to keep the blood flowing. The glass is empty. Miss Lick's huge warmth moves close to me with the bottle, filling it. I drink again. Miss Lick is sitting on the desk, tapping her heels against the side. Her big feet in the thick work socks slide in and out of the corners of my vision. I'm afraid to look at her face.

The camera is in an operating theater. A lone masked figure all in white leans over a sheeted body on the table. The camera zooms toward the face of the figure and then the image skids.

'We'll skip to the pertinent stuff.' Miss Lick is pushing levers on the control box. The image staggers and then blurs past in a fizz of color. I run a hand over my face and wipe the sweat on my skirt. My wig is slipping toward my left eye and I can't seem to straighten it one-handed. The screen settles heavily in a small bright room. Yellow walls. Lace curtains. A shelf of books. A desk. The lens slides down to reveal a bed below the camera. Tidy with cushions, the spread matches the curtains and a dark-haired girl is sitting on it with a portable console beside her. She is dictating into a hand mike, using long fingers to spread the pages of the book on her knees. The girl drops the mike suddenly and flops back against the cushions. She raises the books and reads. Her face is corrugated with deep purple gutter of scar. Her lips are twisted, nostrils distorted. Only her eyes and something in the barely discernible bone beneath the raddled flesh seem familiar. The film scutter berserkly. Miss Lick sighs as she pumps the control lever.

'It was acid. But she was completely anesthetized.' I am looking at the dark wood doors of a large chapel. The doors burst open and girls in graduation gowns rush out, their mortars precarious on soft hair.

'The day she graduated from college. Me still worried. She had my heart wrapped in barbed wire.'

A purple face appears in the excited crowd. The gowned figure comes straight down the steps and reaches up to snatch off the mortarboard. She marches straight toward the camera. The focus wobbles as she nears us.

The next view is a drab office with venetian blinds on the windows. The scar-faced girl is at one of the three desks. She is holding a sheaf of paper in one hand and a microphone in the other.

'She's a translator. An enormous gift for languages. But she worked here for a year before I was able to get the camera in. Intelligence Bureau. Tight security. A slip would have cost her the job.'

'It's Carina,' I said. The glass was against my lower lip and the name dropped into it and broke.

'Yes. She's twenty-six now. Second in command in her office. Fluent in five languages.'

The screen is placid and grey. Miss Lick is sliding the disk back into its file slot. I hold the glass away from me and watch the level of the liquid. It is quivering but not a lot.

'You got the idea from Linda?' I ask it calmly, curiously.

'From what happened to her. Not her idea. My idea. But it only clicked because of the Arturans. Not that I'm a disciple. More of an apostle.'

Miss Lick is firm on this point, shoving all the disks straight with the side of her hand, tapping them into symmetry.

'Carina was my first.' She stops and stares at the wall. I can see her remembering. Doubt and worry form in faint nostalgia between the bulges of her face. 'She was bitter. Stubborn for a long time. Despite the money. Despite clothes and school and private tutors. I did everything I could. I was worried for years.'

'What about the mother? Did she . . .?' I raise my eyebrows at Miss Lick over the glass.

She snorts and nods. 'An annuity. She was delighted. I took the precaution of collecting a little evidence on her in case she ever thought she could use more money. I was lucky. Got an infrared disk of her rolling some poor bastard one night. He died of exposure. It was January!'

'I'm impressed with the camera business. Do you handle all that yourself? Do they really not know they're being taped?'

She nods, a faint flush rising up her heavy jaws.

'Old hobby. There's a lot involved if you want to be unobtrusive. Interesting techniques for surveillance and plants.'

I want to go home and think. She doesn't trust me completely yet. She skipped the operation scene. Didn't want me to see the close-ups of the acid working on Carina's face — the fuming mist of chemical burn rising from the bubbling flesh. She isn't sure I'd understand that, or tolerate her pleasure in the sight.

But I can't leave yet. I have to reassure her that she hasn't made a mistake by revealing herself to me.

'You know that all my life I have been in a position to understand what you are doing.' I look straight at her — pour deep honesty out through my pink eyes. Pitch my voice into the nether regions for her. She is staring at me anxiously. I smile the smile at her, the warm one. She is lumbering toward me, her hands stretched out to me like two naked babies, her great face cracking and melting in relief. She is pumping my hand up and down in the hot smother of her big paws. I feel as though my hand is wrist-deep in a fresh-killed chicken.

'Thanks,' she is muttering. 'Jesus.' She is beaming at me. 'You're the first . . .' She is wagging her head in wonder. 'First time I ever dared show anybody.' I try to balance the glass in my free hand but the whiskey sloshes out over the rim and chills my knees where it falls.

I like Miss Lick. Arty always said that was important.

'Find a way to like them,' he said. 'Like them every minute that you're with them. If you can like them they'll be helpless against you.'

It's easy. She is so big and homely and scared. She blushes. When she dresses after her swim, her hair is too soft to control and sticks up all over her head in rooster tails until she greases it and slicks it down. Her eyes are puffy every morning and she is fragile before she has her coffee at the office. She is honest. She wants to do good. All her efforts are toward good.

Miss Lick's purpose is to liberate women who are liable to be exploited by male hungers. These exploitable women are, in Miss Lick's view, the pretty ones. She feels great pity for them. Linda's transformation gave her the idea. If all these pretty women could shed the traits that made men want them (their prettiness) they they would no longer depend on their own exploitability but would use their talents and intelligence to become powerful. Miss Lock has great faith in the truth of this theory. She herself is an example of what can be accomplished by one unencumbered by natural beauty. So am I.

'You are so lucky,' she said that night. 'What fools might consider a handicap is actually an enormous gift. What you've accomplished with your voice might never have been possible if you'd been normal.'

Miss Lick, like many otherwise sophisticated people, is unduly impressed by anything connected with mass media. She believes my radio programs are major artistic achievements. She is sure I am a great success.

Miss Lick has already liberated a number of young women. She never uses force or coercion. She uses money. Carina was the first and gave her the most trouble. She waited until Carina had her degree and was settled in her job before she tried again.

'I had to be sure I was right. It's not something you can do carelessly.'

Carina has never yet told Miss Lick that it was 'the best thing that ever happened' to her.

'I admit that still bothers me,' says Miss Lick, her forehead rumpled with worry. 'But others have said it. Lots of times. Carina's stubborn. Damned stubborn.'

After Carina, Miss Lick was tentative, cautious for a while.

'I stuck with thyroid treatments for the next three. I was nervous about a more drastic approach.'

The disks flickered over a secretary, a high-school hurdles runner, a young prostitute — and then their incredible incarnations. All three so fat they could barely move.

'Lulu, the ex-hooker, is my accountant. The secretary is my office manager.' Miss Lick shoved her hands deep in her pockets and stared at the last image on the screen. A mound of dark flesh lies on a pillow. Thin hair straggling in greasy tangles suggests that it is a human head. Finally I see the tiny eyes gleaming out of dents in what must be a drooping heap of cheeks.

'This was Vita. She was seventeen when we started. I felt terrible.... It was a failure.... I misjudged. She couldn't take it. Tried to kill herself. Pills. She'd been an athlete and this was the wrong route for her. Absolutely the wrong technique. Acid would have been O.K., but not this. Made me realize I had to tailor the treatments. I've been working on bringing her back. Her body is close, now. But her head is ... And she was sharp.' Miss Lick's clenched fists were still against her belly but all the rest of her shuddered.

'So she says, "Just give me the money and watch my smoke. I don't need the operation." And I told her, hey honey, that's what they all say and maybe you'd get the degree and the job but the first prick who rubbed your nipples the right way you'd go down the chute with all the rest. Those forty-fours of yours are a matched pair of concrete boots and you either ditch them or stay on here loading bread trucks and wait for the janitor to get so anxious to bury his face in your fat sack that he offers to marry you.'

Miss Lick is flushed with the rectitude of her argument. The blonde on the screen is a cantilevered mammary miracle in a red T-shirt and tight pants. She bounces majestically as she reaches for big metal trays of plastic-wrapped wheat bread. The disk skids.

'She's not as smart as I figured. All she's good for is a technician.'

A thin-shouldered lab coat with a greasy ponytail turns toward us holding a pair of test tubes up to the light. A squinting examination of cloudy fluids.

'She spends all day analyzing horse piss from the tracks. Big day if she finds a jump drug in a sample. But hell. She's happy. Makes a good living.'

The lab coat is flat. No chest at all.

★ ★ ★

'Damned good surgeon. Made a mistake and landed in my pocket. He's lucky to be practicing and he knows it lasts just so long as I say so. I pay him well for my little jobs and I cover his ass. He used to balk and squirm about it but he's been sewn up for years. He's got kids, a big house, a country club. Reliable character. Truth is, I think he gets a kick out of it. I watch everything. Used to make me sick but I enjoy it now. An acquired taste but there's a lot of finesse involved.'

She will not show me the sections of the disks that record the actual operations.

'I've got several projects going all the time. Prospects that I'm doing research on. Sometimes after I've decided a girl is right and make the approach, it takes a while for her to come around. I've had a few rejections. A few. I'm careful. Never a whisper about it though. Never any trouble. I just offer. No force at all. Nothing to complain about. Nothing illegal. Right now I'm interested in a kind of progressive procedure. Start out with a superficial thing — long hair, maybe — and use it as a kickoff. Bigger rewards dangled in front to keep them going. . . . Interesting. Still experimental, of course, not sure how it will work out in the long run.'

Miss Lick does not mention the Glass House and neither do I.

My new room is unfamiliar and chilly. I lie on the bed and try to learn the way to the bathroom door. A private bathroom here. It's a much lusher joint than my room in Lil's house. No hazy perambulations down the hall to the shared can in the middle of the night. But the other is home and I miss it. This more respectable front is what Miss Lick expects of Hopalong McGurk, and I hope it will keep her from connecting me with Miranda. I arrive early at the radio station every day to get my mail and prevent any accidents from the staff's trying to reach me at my old address.

For a while I told myself that all I needed to do was interfere with Miss Lick's finances. If she were poor, I thought, she wouldn't be able to go on with her projects. I looked around her corporate structure for ways to sabotage her pocketbook. Nothing. I'm not clever with business. Couldn't understand half of it. All I came up with was an idea about incendiary bombs in each of the factories. But they all work on twenty-four-hour shifts and they're too scattered across the country for me to do it all myself. She's got her capital snugged away in safe paper unconnected with the travel-grub business anyway.

Then, in the pool one day, I saw her watching the children. Pretty schoolkids training for the club team. They were like otters, playing around the stodgy lap swimmers. I was leaning on the steps at the shallow end, resting. Miss Lick came to the wall and stood up instead of doing her usual flip and push-off. She glared at the girls, her eyes burned red with chlorine and hatred. Long legs flashed, smooth, angular faces laughed at each other. Miss Lick's head jutted forward from her big shoulders. Her jaw gripped at an odd angle and began to twitch.

My stomach tried to crawl into my mouth. If she couldn't buy them into disfigurement she'd find another way, and in that minute I realized it was lucky she did have money. I'm resigned since then. I like her. She doesn't usually scare me. But I know what I have to do.

I am driving the golf cart and Miss Lick walks alongside. We are somewhere past the fourth green.

'It's a tax write-off. My girls go down as handicapped. No trouble establishing fake accident reports. Private nursing. I'm a bona fide charitable organization with rehabilitation as my main goal. It's the truth too.'

I am glad that Miss Lick has made a big campaign out of her hobby. It gives me more substantial justification.

If Miranda were the only one she'd ever approached I'd do it anyway — but I would have doubted the propriety of dousing anyone's lights permanently for the sake of Miranda's ridiculous little tail. I'm the only one who sets any real store by that tail. Anybody else would call it great luck to get paid for having the nuisance removed.

Sometimes when we've been drinking I can't help smiling at Miss Lick while I picture myself drilling her through the eye with her pop's target pistol. The irony of my killing her righteously for doing what she considers righteous — and she, remember, never killed anyone — is hilarious to me. I must watch my drinking. I like it too much.

I read nothing but murders lately. Six solid weeks of mystery stories on my program. The puzzles intrigue me — and the methods. Surely the simplest way is the best.

I am terrified of trying and failing. The idea of her looking at me, that great hopelessly rumpled mass of flesh seeing me as a betrayer — knowing that I am responsible — that I deliberately led her on and am now hurting her. That image comes to me horribly in my sleep. I can't bear for her to live on knowing that I would try to do that to her. She'd become a real monster — and my creation. No, it has to be absolutely sure, and quick. Very quick.

Meanwhile the cheap editions of murder pile higher and higher in this temporary room. I must be leaving a mile-wide trail. Hiding my intentions from her will be enough — but it will be obvious to anyone nosing around after the fact. Still, I am not as afraid of being caught as I imagined I would be. I'm only afraid of Miss Lick's knowing, and I'm afraid of failing.

Knowing Miss Lick has made me think about Arty again. Wanting to do it didn't make him evil. Getting away with it is what turned him into a monster.

Of course I will have to apply this rule to myself eventually. And I'm glad I've discovered whiskey.

★ ★ ★

I can't spend much time at Lil's house for now. I go in every Thursday night to deal with the garbage and to arrange my notes with the other papers in the trunk for Miranda. I tell myself that it matters, and that the relics of my life will miss me. Sometimes I believe it.

13

Flesh — Electric on Wheels

The guy was obviously sixty but he looked like he'd never stopped training for some tight and lonesome sport, rock climbing maybe, or breaking his own long-distance record for walking on his hands. He sat on the step of Arty's van with his sleeves rolled nearly above his elbows and a pair of suspenders holding up his shin-length work pants. His shoes were high button-and-lace combos that must have been forty years old and made from hand-lasted baby rhino. They had an odd grey luster about half a century deep in elbow oil. Nice shoes, and he had them planted firmly under him and his elbow dug into his knees and his forearms angled up to a peak where his hands clasped. The muscles cut so solidly away from each other that my first thought was of old wood and roof beams.

He had the good sense not to get up when I walked over to him. He nodded and took off his cap as though he meant to air his brown scalp rather than honor me. 'My name is McGurk ... Zephir McGurk, and I'd like to visit with Arturo ... your brother, I think.'

I started my standard routine. 'Arturo undergoes great strain during his demonstrations and requires rest....'

McGurk flicked his window-cool eyes at me, quirked one corner of his mouth and reached down beside him for an elaborate leather-bound case with brass clamps. 'I think I've got something the Aqua Kid would very much like to see. I'm an electrician and an inventor, miss ... And I've been thinking about your brother for a solid year — ever since the show came through here last March. You let me see him. You won't regret it. And neither will he.'

The case wasn't hiding a bomb or a gun. I was sure of that just looking at the guy. I unlocked the door and took him in. McGurk stood beside the table and examined the fingernails of both his hands in a discreet way. I went to Arty's door and knocked.

Though he insisted on the charade of attempted privacy, Arty liked having people clamoring to see him. He swung up onto his red velvet throne and held his face up for me to wipe his nose.

'Stay in the security room,' he said.

I opened the door for McGurk and introduced him as I slid out. In the security room I checked the gun and took off the safety while I slowly opened the ventilator beneath the one-way glass. McGurk was sitting in the armchair. He was looking coolly at Arty's lower body. After a few seconds McGurk's eyes jumped up to Arty's.

'Have your testicles descended?'

Arty was used to impertinent questions. 'Why do you ask?'

'How can you sit upright without hurting yourself?'

'I have well-developed buttocks and I wear a rigid cup.'

McGurk nodded and put the case on his lap. He used a small key to unlock it.

'I've been thinking about your life and I've designed something that may do you some good.'

'That's kind of you.'

'Not exactly. I just couldn't sleep until I came up with a solution.' The case spread open on his knees and revealed an old-fashioned record player with a chrome bar elbowing out from a spot near the center of the turntable. A soft thick tube drooped from the end of the chrome. McGurk looked at the bed and got up. He set the thing on the bed near the wall and stretched the shining bar toward the center of the bed. The tube drooped toward the maroon satin spread.

'The switch cable is pressure operated.' He pulled a rubber ball away from the side and a chrome-wrapped coil followed it, whirring against the case.

'You can hold it in your teeth and have complete control, one click turns it on.' He pressed and a faint hum pulsed into the room. 'You insert your penis in the tube here ...,' his fingers lifted the flaccid bag until a deep pink mouth showed, 'and a second click adjusts the clamps to a firm grip.' The tube jumped and the mouth took on an O form.

Arty began to chuckle. 'Clever. But are you sure you didn't design this for yourself?'

McGurk's head swung around to look at Arty. A crease of irritation flickered between his eyes. 'You're what? eighteen or nineteen years old?' he said. 'I kept thinking what things would be like for you.' He thumbed a pressure switch in the rubber ball. The turntable began to spin and the chrome arm pulled and thrust, pushed and retreated smoothly, with the bag at the end inflated and Arty stared at the pumping chrome arm and its full tip. McGurk leaned forward and pushed his thumb deep into the mouth. The bag sucked and jumped around the thumb as he watched it. 'You get thirty-three, forty-five, or seventy-eight RPMs on this suction tube.'

Arty licked his lips, sniffed carefully to make sure his nose wasn't running. 'Have you tried it out?' he asked.

McGurk pulled his reddened thumb out of the bag and pressed the control switch. The chrome arm stopped moving.

My tall stool was cutting off blood to my legs and I squirmed and craned my neck. Arty was turned away from me, watching McGurk, who slumped down and sat on the bed. 'I'll show you the lubrication and drainage system, but ...' He hiked at his trousers until both knees were bare, white and hairless. The shoes came up his shins and turned into grey socks. 'But I guess you want my credentials,' McGurk said. He reached up his right pant leg. There was a snap and the shoe toppled over with the plastic shin and knee sticking out of it. A dim gleam came from the dark fold of the empty trouser leg. He slid his hand up the other trouser leg and both legs lay on the floor with steel shining out of the hollow tops of the knees. He pulled his pant legs up his thighs and showed the steel caps on the stumps. There were a groove, a few grip protrusions, and a number of electrical contact points protruding from each unit. He looked up, calmly waiting.

Arty pursed his wide lips and rolled them speculatively. 'Shit,' he said. Then he sent a long arc of saliva at the nearest shoe. It hit the laces and trickled down across the holes.

McGurk went on looking at him but there was a deep crease between his eyes.

'You figured it wrong. The whole thing,' said Arty. He rocked slightly, chuckling. 'You've got yourself a little old disability there, so you took pleasure in feeling sorry for me. Well. You figured wrong.'

McGurk was twisting on the bed, reaching his powerful forearms down for the artificial legs. He straightened and jammed the steel ends onto his stumps with a clang. The gun was sweating in my hands.

'You figured ...' Arty was watching carefully now; his eyes swung once to the mirror above his bureau that hid me and the gun on the other side, '... figured we had a common set of interests. Guess you have a hard time with the ladies. Well, I don't. I've got women mooning around begging to take up my slack.'

McGurk was folding the chrome arm back over the turntable, feeding the control cable back into its hole, carefully closing the case, not paying any attention to Arty. Arty sucked his lower lip in between his teeth and popped it out again. He waved his right flipper vaguely. 'You know you're taking the wrong road on those stumps. You're like a man with a beautiful voice taking a vow of silence. You're working hard to pretend they aren't there and you meet a girl in a bar and don't tell her about those knees until you get to take your pants off. You ought to tan your thighs and walk on them. Wear silver sequin pads and dance on a lit stage where they can see you. All those soft girlies come knocking on your door borrowing sugar in the dead of night and sliming for you. You could have that. Not as much as I get but plenty ... You're just going along with what *they* want you to do. *They* want those things hidden away, disguised, forgotten, because they know how much power those stumps could have.'

McGurk was looking now, listening. I could see his eyes sliding on the console, the velvets, the soft deep carpet. I put the gun on safety and stuck it back on its shelf. I flicked the switch as I went out so the lamp on the bureau in Arty's room would go out and he would know I wasn't covering him. I got a contract and took it to Arty. McGurk was smoking quietly and staring at the walls. Arty was saying, '... a sensible man doesn't have to have the top of his head blown off to know the truth when he sees it.'

McGurk signed on as an electrician. He shook hands with me because he couldn't with Arty. Then he went out to sell everything he owned, say goodbye to the two teenage sons who lived with his ex-wife, and furnish his station wagon for temporary living so he could follow the show.

When the blighted stump horse died, our Chick 'took on something terrible,' as Mama said. I came out of the Chute that morning with my nose burnt from the smell of glass cleaner, and heard 'woo-wooing' of a wet, breathy variety that seemed familiar. They were up on the generator hood by Grandpa's urn. Chick was sprawled out flat with his face buried in his hands and Elly and Iphy patted him gently while they looked off in opposite directions at the sky.

I crawled up to help pat Chick. The twins said he'd found Frosty stiff and flat in his trailer. Talking to the fuzzy blond back of Chick's head and the wet pink fist hiding his face, I said, 'Shooty-pooty, Chick, it isn't your fault. He was old and it was his time and you took such good care of him these past few months. He was probably happier than he'd ever been in his whole life.' But the Chick choked and Elly sniffed and said they'd already told him that but he loved the horse and had to cry. I took offense at her snotty ways and told her Chick loved everything and he was going to be a mess if he cried like that every time a geranium conked out in the redheads' flowerpots or something. But Iphy was dreaming sorrowfully at the low grey sky and Elly was not be to baited. She just sighed, 'Probably,' and went on patting Chick.

I slid down and went off to practice a funeral oration for Frosty. It wasn't too bad, though it was never delivered. Doc P. dissected the horse for educational reasons and then had the roustabouts haul the remains to an incinerator.

Late. The camp dark. Two hours after closing. The family was sleeping and I sat in the kitchen sink looking out through the moon mist at the dark without my glasses. A scraping sound from outside. A step. It was behind me on the other side of the van. I slid to the floor, tiptoed to the door in bare feet, peeped silently through. My breath froze — a movement near Arty's door. A tall figure moving there.

Assassin! I thought. In the instant it took me to get through the door I dreamed a long dream of Arty's gratitude at my courageous self-sacrifice in saving him. I saw myself wrapped in white, propped on pillows. Arty enters, white-faced and shaken.... That was about as far as I'd got by the time I locked my arms around the thighs of the dark shape in Arty's doorway and clamped my teeth into a bulge of buttock. The thigh flailed wildly and started to scream as I growled. Fingernails whacked and clawed at my head and scraped at my arms. Breathless shrieks pumped out of the murderer's throat and vibrated through my teeth in adrenal heroics that lit my skull's interior with an epileptic torch.

The light over the door flashed on and shouts closed over me. In relief at being rescued before I broke, though wondering if I would make such a sympathetic figure to Arty if I wasn't in traction, I released my aching grip. Cloth pulled out of my teeth as big arms lifted and held me against a warm chest and a deep voice cracked, 'Jeez, Miss Oly!'

A piccolo hysteria behind me in the doorway. Then Arty's sympathetic voice, 'Are you O.K.? Come in here and let me look.' My heart turned to steaming oatmeal as I wriggled around to see his dear worried face and the corpse of the terrorist I had foiled.

Arty wasn't talking to me. He was in his chair just inside the door, leaning anxiously to examine a jagged rip in the black satin rump of a tall young norm woman whose sobbing face was hidden by a straight fall of blond hair.

'Killer!' I bellowed, struggling to break out of the blue-sleeved arms of the guard who held me. 'She was breaking into your place, Arty!'

The big chest against my fists rumbled, 'Jeez, Miss Oly!' and Arty's chilly white face snapped an impatient look toward me. His wide lips stretched back over his angry teeth as he whipped

out, 'A guest. An invited guest simply ringing my doorbell!'
Then, gesturing the tall, slim girl inside, he backed his chair
away from the door.

The guard in embarrassment at my rigid body in his arms,
was jabbering, 'Sorry, Arty. I brought the lady to your ramp,
like always, and I'd just got to the other end of the van when
the ruckus started.'

'Take Oly back to her door, Joe. Goodnight.' The door
slammed shut.

'Jeez, Miss Oly,' said my guard. He turned, opened the door
to the family van, put me down just inside, and closed the door
on my ice-struck face. I crawled into my cupboard and tried to
swallow my tongue or hold my breath long enough to die. I
hoped they might give me a half-pint urn and bolt me onto the
hood of the generator truck behind Grandpa.

Chick would come to rest his cheek on my cool metal when
he was sad. Mama would polish me every morning before she
went to the Chute and blink away tears remembering my sweet
smile. Then it occurred to me that they might put me in the
Chute in the biggest jar of all and I'd float naked in formaldehyde and the twins would bicker over who had to shine my jar.
I gave up on dying and went over to blubbering into my blanket
instead — imagining razor-slash scenarios of what Arty was
doing with the norm girl and what an asshole I was. I went on
blubbering until I slept.

I kept the norm girl at Arty's door to myself. Arty wouldn't talk
about it. He liked secrets. Without a good reason, Arty
wouldn't admit the he ate or slept. Information was a marketable commodity to Arty. The guard may have gossiped but he
would try to keep Papa from hearing about it. Private arrangements with Mr. Arty didn't get to Al if a man wanted to keep
his job.

I hung on to it — my embarrassment at being an idiot and
my shame at being a patsy. Idiot for jumping a guest while in
the throes of melodramatic fancy, patsy for being pulped by
pain at Arty's involvement with a girl, and a norm at that.

I crept out of my cupboard and peeped through the slats of

the louvered window in our door. I couldn't see much, but several nights of quivering in my flannel nightie in the dark proved it wasn't an isolated incident.

The girl I'd tackled was a stranger, not part of the show. I heard and saw Arty's door open and blurred figures moving into the light several times before I recognized that it was always a different girl.

I crawled into my blankets smiling, slept well for the first time in days, woke as cheery as a pinhead, went joking and grinning around all day. Arty wasn't having a love affair. He was just 'fucking around,' as the redheads called it. What had been a blowtorch blackening my brain with sick, helpless jealousy was now just useful information. A love affair would have shut me out. This gave me an opening. I could tease Arty in private. Keeping mum to everybody else would be evidence of my discretion and encourage him to have confidence in me. If a trickle of puke still riled my throat at the thought of Arty with the long-limbed norms, it was at least tolerable. I needed all the ammo I could get.

Zephir McGurk was a do-it-yourself electrician from the same independent school of thought that spawned Papa's medical hobby. McGurk made do. He read journals and magazines and catalogues from supply houses to feed his ingenuity, but he was an innovator. Even if a thing had been invented and perfected thirty years before, McGurk was inclined to build his own rather than buy the gimmick from somebody else. McGurk was valuable. His pay was minimal cash and what Arty called the 'overflow' of curious females.

He slept in the back of the old but well-kept safari car. He did his work in the utility trailer that housed the power tools and spare parts. He set up a compact and efficient workshop. If he wasn't in the workshop he was asleep or in Arty's show tent. He never socialized in the midway or dropped in on any other act. Zephir was a focused man. Arty was his apple. Arty was the work he'd been given to do.

'It would be good to have some way to spell out my messages in lights,' Arty might say.

'Maybe,' McGurk would say slowly, his head already tumbling possibilities.

Arty went to visit him in the workshop. This flattered McGurk deeply. If Arty was in an energetic mood he'd have me strap him into one of his treads and would lead the way to the workshop with me trailing. He'd go up the step and climb up on the workbench and talk companionably with McGurk.

Other times he'd stay in his chair and sit outside the door with McGurk perched on the step to talk. McGurk had stowed his prosthetic legs in a trunk. He'd gone over to fancy strap-on pads on his thigh stumps. He wore blue or brown leather for his workaday stumps, but he got a pair made of iridescent green satin, embroidered with silver vines, for wearing in the control booth at the top of the bleachers where he worked the sound-and-light board for Arty's show.

It was McGurk who invented Arty's speaking tube — a plastic form that fitted over Arty's nose and mouth. When Arty tongued the button inside, a rush of air expelled the water from the face mask so Arty could breathe and talk into the mask at the same time. The thing stuck up against the front plate of the tank on a long gooseneck that linked it to a gaudy (but phony) console in the bottom of the tank. It actually hooked into the sound system. Arty talking under water was an astonishing improvement over propping his chin on the top of the tank to rap into the microphone. The crowd loved it.

When McGurk built the button receiver that hid in Arty's ear and let him hear the sound system, the crowd, and messages from McGurk in the control booth, Arty offered the electrician his own van and a good raise. McGurk shook his tidy head and politely turned it all down. 'I've got my routine set,' he said. He went on sleeping in his station wagon.

McGurk cooked for himself. He was a fussy vegetarian. He was roasting carrots in an oven in the workshop the day he came up with what we later called 'The Singing Buttock.' He was peering through the oven window at the sliced carrots in a dish. 'What if,' he asked, 'every board in the bleachers was wired for sound?'

Arty was lolling on top of the workbench looking at a sheet of McGurk's doodles for a new colored-light plan. He rolled back his head and squinted at McGurk's broad shoulders. McGurk with his back to you was an imposing specimen even with his shirt on. The oven pinged and he tooked the dish out with a mitt.

'Why?' Arty wanted to know. McGurk dropped the mitt beside the carrots and leaned his big brown elbows on the work-bench. He had his private knife and fork wheeling through the carrots and whipping quick chunks of steaming root into his mouth. He always ate standing up. Three bites went through methodical milling and swallowing before he finally let his eyes drift up to Arty.

'Sound is physical. I've been watching Miss Oly ...' He nodded to where I perched on his work stool. 'Her ticket talking got me thinking. Sounds is a vibration. It carries through matter. When you hear, it's not just with your ears. A sound actually affects every cell of your body, making it vibrate and pass that vibration to all your other cells. That's why they say a sound if "piercing" or a scream "goes right through you." It does. It actually does.' He stopped with his fork in midair and looked at Arty. Arty was watching him, waiting. Arty didn't say anything. McGurk sighed and took a piece of carrot from the fork and chewed it. I watched it go down his thick-muscled gullet.

'I was thinking,' McGurk said, finally, 'that you use your voice real well. I was thinking, what if your voice wasn't just coming at 'em from the air but was vibrating up from the soles of their feet and through their asses up their spines. I was thinking what it would be like if they *felt* what you had to say because the boards they were standing and sitting on were wired to carry that vibration of your voice.'

Arty's eyes were almost bulging, looking at McGurk. His face was frozen for a long instant and then it folded into a smile and then broke at the mouth and Arty's whole body shook toward his mouth, laughing.

'I love it!' he howled. 'I love it!'

The bleachers are empty and singing around me. Arty is chanting in the boards. I sit on the fifth tier and stare straight

at the tank, at Arty, his mouth and nose in the black cup of the
speaking tube. Wires are taped to my wrists and to the insides
of my knees and to my hump, next to the spine. They lead up to
the control booth, where Zephir McGurk is measuring my
physical responses to the sound that he has wired to feed
through every board in the bleachers.

Arty's body floats straight out from the speaking tube,
glinting mysteriously in the bright green water.

'Peace,' says Arty, and the speakers above the tank lift his
voice to the canvas peak of the tent roof. The bottoms of my
feet say 'Peace,' and the padded bones of my pelvis whisper
'Peace' to my bowels. A shiver passes upward into my stomach,
and my spine feels 'Peace' like fear curling upward to my skull
with my shoulder blades flinching around it.

'As I am!' shouts Arty, and my heart nearly stops with the
shock of the sound in my body.

Arty pulls away from the face cup and wriggles toward the
surface. McGurk is hopping down the steps from the control
booth. He is beside me now. Only slightly taller than me on his
stumps, he is watching the wires as he rips the tape off my skin.

Arty's head appears on the rim of the tank, grinning at us.
His face is pale and doesn't look as though it's connected to his
body, which is golden, with slowly flexing flippers gleaming
through the glass.

'That seemed a lot better!' chirps Arty. 'That flat zone
makes it even more effective!'

'Yes.' McGurk holds the ends of all the wires together in one
hand like the leashes to a pack of dogs. He examines the sheet
of readout graph in his hand. 'Yes. With just the upper and
lower register you can make them dance to whatever tune you
like.'

14

The Pen Pal

It was Earlville, on the Gulf of Mexico. One hundred wind-less, muggy degrees. Mosquitoes drowned in your neck creases. The only industry in town was the federal penitentiary. The midway was jammed and the show tents bulged with sweating, stinking, bad-tempered drawls. It got dark but it didn't cool off.

The fat woman surfaced at Arty's last, hottest show for the day. She was young but her colorless hair was scraggled up into tight separate curls with so much scalp between them that she looked old and balding. She was crying as she stood up on the fifth tier of the bleachers and pushed her clasped hands out toward the tank where Arty was deep in his pitch.

'You, darling,' Arty said, and the feel of 'darling' rose up through her puffy ankles and through every buttock in the bleachers. The crowd sighed. The fat woman sobbed.

'You feel ugly, don't you, sweetheart?' and 'ugly' and 'sweet-heart' thrummed the crowd, and they all gasped and she wasn't the only one nodding.

'You've tried everything, haven't you?' said the bright floating spirit in the tank. 'Everything,' murmured the bones of the people.

'Pills, shots, hypnosis, diets, exercise. Everything. Because you want to be beautiful?'

Arty was building it up now, winding them tight.

'Because you think if you were beautiful, you would be happy?' He had the timing pat. Arty was a master of tone and timing. I leaned on the last steel strut of the bleachers in the aisle and smiled, though I'd seen him do it all my life.

'Because people would love you if you were beautiful? And if people loved you, you would be happy? Is it people loving you that makes you happy?'

Now the pitch drops a full octave into the groin groan. I can feel it even in the support poles. The asses on the seat boards must be halfway to orgasm.

'Or is it people *not* loving you that makes you unhappy? If they don't love you it's because there's something *wrong* with you. If they love you then it must mean you're all right. You poor baby. Poor, poor baby.'

The place was full of poor babies. They all sighed with tender sympathy for themselves. The fat woman's nose ran. She opened her mouth and cried, 'Hoooh! Hoooh! Hoooh!'

Now Arty was gentle and low as a train a mile off in the night.

'You just want to know that you're all right. You just want to feel all right.'

And now he dives into the sneer. Arty's sneer could flay a rhino.

'That's all you need other people's *love* for!'

The crowd is shocked into stillness. Arty grabs their throats while they're down and starts pumping the tempo.

'So, let's get the truth here! You don't want to stop eating! You love to eat! You don't want to be thin! You don't want to be beautiful! You don't want people to love you! All you really want is to know that you're *all right*! That's what can give you peace!

'If I had arms and legs and hair like everybody else, do you think I'd be happy? NO! I would not! Because then I'd worry did somebody love me! I'd have to look outside myself to find out what to think of myself!

'And you! You aren't ever going to look like a fashion queen! Does that mean you have to be miserable all your life? Does it?

'Can you be happy with the movies and the ads and the clothes in the stores and the doctors and the eyes as you walk down the street all telling you there is something *wrong* with you? No. You can't. You cannot be happy. Because, you poor darling baby, you *believe* them.... Now, girl, I want you to look at me and tell me, what do you want?'

Arty expected her to stay tongue-tied and blubbering so he could say the next line. That's the way it always worked. But this fat woman was so used to blubbering that it didn't slow her down. She opened her mouth wide and, though I've never really stopped hating her for it, I have to admit she was just saying what all the rest of the damp, wheezing crowd was thinking. She screamed, 'I want to be like *you* are!'

Arty stopped dead still. His flippers froze and he began to sink slowly with his face pressed into the speaking mask and his eyes close to the glass staring out. There was sobbing in the crowd. Soft voices murmured, 'Yes, yes.' Arty was silent for far too long. Had he had a stroke? Was it a cramp? I started forward, ready to run around behind the tank and up the ladder. then his voice came.

'Yes,' he said. 'Yes, that's what you want.' And I could hear his breath go in, Arty's breath. Arty could control a mike and he never breathed so you could hear it.

'And that's what I want for you.'

He didn't go on with his usual talk. He said that he'd have to think how to give this gift to her. He said they should all come back the next day — though he knew few of them would — because he would have something to say to them.

McGurk didn't know what to do with the lights. He was flickering a rainbow that made Arty almost invisible in the water. Finally Arty himself hit the switch that blacked out the tank.

The crowd started to trickle away as I ran to the back of the tank. Arty was already out on his platform and rolling in his towel.

'Arty, what's wrong?' I whispered as I scrambled up the ladder.

'Not a thing,' he said. His face popped out of the towel and he grinned hugely, excited.

'Let's get over to the shower quick. I want to see Doc P. right away.'

The woman who wanted to be like Arty came back the next

day. The crew had just finished sweeping down the bleachers in Arty's tent and were raking the sawdust. The first show had done as usual and it was an hour until the last show began.

I was next door in the ticket booth of the twins' tent snagging the take out of the till drawer into a bag, and punching in totals. A finger tapped the SOLD OUT sign in the barrel window in front of me.

'All sold out!' I hollered, and locked the cash bag.

'There's a dame in Arty's tent!' It was the crew foreman, shrugging at me. I took the cash bag and went with him.

She was sitting up on the fifth tier, where she'd sat before, but now she was the only one. The heat in the tent was heavy and dead. She had a shopping bag beside her and she looked ready to collapse. Her face was dark red. Her eyes were blood-spatter over yellow. She had a little face set into a big pillow of a head, and her arms and legs stuck out of a dress that would have been loose on a linebacker but looked like cheap upholstery on her. She was just sitting, staring at the unlit tank, listening to the gurgle of the pump that aerated and filtered the water.

I climbed up toward her. She looked at me, got a ripple of fear on her face, and grabbed at her shopping bag.

'Hi,' I said. She clutched her bag and nodded, warily. She expected to be chased. I expected to chase her. 'I work with this show, can I help you?' I stood still at the end of the tier and didn't go any closer. She flapped her jaws and then came out with a tiny shrill voice.

'I'm just waiting for the Aqua Man. I'm going to pay but there wasn't anybody to sell tickets. I'll pay when the ticket booth opens.'

Her eyes ran over me cautiously. I was wearing one of the blue sailor dresses that Lil made for me. The blue matched the lenses of my sunglasses. I wasn't wearing a cap so the woman's eyes spent a lot of time on my bare skull.

'I'll sell you a ticket right now so you won't have to worry about it,' I offered, helpfully. I had a roll of tickets in my pocket, and I needed to make sure she wasn't going to pull an automatic out of her shopping bag and perforate Arty. She fumbled out money.

'You were here yesterday, weren't you?' I asked.

'He spoke to me,' she said, counting out coins. 'He said to come back. He would help me.'

I sat down next to her and watched the heat rash on the insides of her elbows and the backs of her knees and in the folds of her chins as she talked. She had got herself into a terrible jam, she said, and it had made her realize ... She was from Warren, Ohio, and her mother was a schoolteacher but had died last year. She took a photo album out of the shopping bag and showed me a picture of a fat old woman.

'What kind of a jam are you in?' I pushed. If she had strangled her old mother I was going to have her escorted to the gate, heat rash and all.

'It's a man,' she said coyly. I couldn't help looking at her with suspicion. She bubbled into tears right away. I looked at the photo album in her lap. She had drawn pink daisies on the cover. I figured she was the type who would doodle LOVE in big, loopy letters and dot her *i*'s with hearts. Her name was Alma Witherspoon. She was twenty-two riding hard on fifty-five. It seems she was a pen pal. She'd always been a pen pal. Seems she'd got the address of a twenty-to-life bank blaster a year or so before. He was up the road in the Earlville Federal Pen. She'd sent him a photo of one of the cheerleaders in her high school. After her mother died she moved down here so she could send him fresh cakes and cookies.

'We're in love,' she said. It sounded like L♡VE. 'He wants to marry me!' she moaned. 'And the warden has agreed! But I thought we'd do it by telephone and now the warden says I have to go out there and do it in his office and Gregory will see how I really *look!*' So she needed to see the Aqua Man. She didn't know anybody in this town. She had no relatives left to turn to. Her heat rash looked contagious. I gave her a show ticket and got away from her. 'You just wait here for the show. Nobody will bother you.'

I took the cash bag to the safe and went over to help Arty get ready. I told him about Alma Witherspoon while I greased him. He lay on the massage bench and nodded. His eyes were eager. He had a funny half smile the whole time.

'She's probably been spinning whoppers to her pen pals for

years about being beautiful and popular.'

'No relatives? No friends?' he asked.

'So she says.'

'Good,' grinned Arty. He stretched and rolled his back under my kneading fingers.

I was doing my talk in front of the twins' tent. 'Siamese beauties linked in harmonious perpetuity . . .' I always had a great time with 'perpetuity' — it was a word you could play like a flute, rolling it up a full octave and whistling 'Dixie' on that last syllable. The crowd was pretty good and most of them were already inside; the last twenty were shuffling in line for tickets.

That's when I saw Alma Witherspoon go by with two of the redheads who helped out in Arty's tent. The tall women beside her made Alma look even wider. She rolled along with her shopping bags and her purse and her photo album all folded sweatily into different rash-angry creases of her dreary body.

Alma couldn't have made a penny as a pro. She didn't weigh as much as a single leg of 'Eleven Hundred Pound Jocko!' or 'Predrita the Plump!' but she wasn't healthy. Jocko and Pedrita were the proudest people who'd ever worked for the show, according to Papa. Alma Witherspoon had the pride of a squashed possum.

'. . . Twin musicians! Twin miracles!' I rolled on, watching the redheads gently guide the wobbly Alma up the ramp to the shower van parked behind the Games of Chance. She put her foot on the top and heaved lopsidedly upward as the door opened. I could see the startled jerk of Alma's wispy head as she saw the staunch white-clad figure in the doorway. Dr. Phyllis nodded, her white mask flashing glare into her thick glasses. her white glove lifted, beckoning. Alma Witherspoon stepped into the shower.

'There is no shock. There is no danger of infection. Young Fortunato's techniques eliminate that entirely.'

Dr. Phyllis watched Arty as she talked; her eyes swiveled behind her pool-deep lenses, probing for an argument that would change his mind.

Arty was looking through the glass window at the sterile infirmary where Alma Witherspoon lay sleeping, with Chick perched beside her on a three-legged stool. Chick was wrapped in one of Dr. P.'s white coats with the sleeves rolled up. His glowing face was bent toward the pillow. His eyes grazed lovingly over the sodden grey folds of Alma's cheek and chins.

'Did you look at that chart I gave you? The healing rate on that spiral fracture was triple the normal expectancy for a patient that age. . . . Arturo? Are you able to comprehend what I am conveying?' Dr. P.'s thin perfect diction entered the ear in a surgical manner. Arty, who had been absorbed in his view of the lumpy sheets and the doughy mound on the pillow, turned to her calmly.

'Doc, I know you can cut her down all at once. I know it would be more efficient. But I want her to have a lot of chances to change her mind.' He turned to look through the window again. He relaxed against the back of the wheelchair. His face was easy as he looked at the creature asleep in the next room. His mouth looked soft. There was a sleepy pleasure about him, almost peaceful, almost warm. There was, oddly, a look of Chick on Arty's face. Arty was happy. He was deeply happy and it was, in some way I didn't grasp, all because of moldy Alma Witherspoon having had all her toes cut off and then when she'd recovered from that, having begged for the privilege of having her feet and legs nipped away as well.

Dr. P. and Chick kept Alma in the infirmary. Arty went frequently to park his chair in the observation room at one end and sit staring through the glass at her bandaged body lying on the second bed from the end.

Once a week, on Sunday mornings, Arty would flick on the intercom and watch Alma's face through the glass as his voice pumped at her from the speakers. She was always overjoyed to hear him. She called him 'Aqua Man' and said she was fine and when could she have more of herself taken away? 'I can't tell you what it means to me each time they clean a little more away, even a little toe. Once it's gone I feel what a weight of rot it was for me. Oh, Aqua Man, you are so kind to me. I thank the stars in heaven for leading me to you ...' and so on like that. She'd blubber away, a pen pal to the core. Her message was always How soon would they take her feet off? When would they take her hands? Could she, by a special dispensation from His Wateriness, skip the feet and have Doc P. just take off her whole legs one at a time? They were such a burden to her and she was in such a hurry to be like HIM.

Arty didn't talk about it but I could see it meant a lot to him. The whole thing had me fuddled. Why should this Alma make him happy? He'd never been that way about any of his visiting night girls — at least not by the time I brought in his breakfast the next morning. He was working harder than ever, reading more, vomiting nervously before each show — 'To clear my head,' he claimed. He schemed and planned with McGurk for hours every morning, playing with lights and sound. But I'd never seen him smile the smiles he smiled in those days, great soft openings of his face with no biting edges at the eyes.

We were up in Michigan when Alma started testifying. She was down to her nubs by then. Her legs were gone from the hip and her arms ended at the elbow. She looked better. Her front still flopped but she'd been eating Dr. P.'s Vegetarian Nutri-Prescription for months. Her skin had some tone and she'd dropped a few chins along with her limbs. More of her face was visible and her wispy hair seemed to have less expanse to drift away from. She was chipper, and she proved that 'feeling good' about herself, as she called it, didn't make her any less irritating than being pathetic. There was a difference, though. Where she had been wetly repellent she was now obnoxious.

'I should say she might feel good about herself, the great lazy lump,' said Lil. 'Lying up there being fed and waited on. When does my Chick get to play? A child his age needs frolic and silliness, not mooning about spooning green gruel into that blob and worrying over her every minute for fear she might feel a twinge of pain! All my other children had time to play even though they worked every day.'

★ ★ ★

I had nothing to do with Alma. To my recollection I never spoke to her directly after the first time in Arty's tent. But I watched her. To give them both credit, Alma was terrified of Doc P. and said nothing but yes'm and no'm whenever the good doc was around. And Alma worshiped Chick. But Chick was her painkiller so I figured her love for him had the same virtuous weight as an addict's for his drug.

Alma's testimony started in the Michigan factory towns. The redheads would wheel her out onto the stage beside the tank before Arty made his appearance. Alma's twittering bat voice fed down through a button mike on her white robe and McGurk bled a little timbre in before he shot it out through the speakers.

'My name is Alma Witherspoon,' she'd begin, 'and I just want to take one minute to tell you all about a wonderful thing that happened to me. . . .'

The rodent squeak chittered in her chest and her stump arms waved in the white spotlight and the bright green tank gurgled, huge, beside her on the dark stage. The funny thing was that it worked. By the time Arty exploded in a rush of bubbles from the floor of the tank, the folks in the stands were ready for him, dry-mouthed and open. And those certain few in the bleachers, those stone-eyed kettles boiling with secret pain, received her message. Those who had been waiting finally found a place to go.

That's the way it began. It was Alma 'Pen Pal' Witherspoon who actually founded what came to be known as 'Arturism' or the 'Arturan Cult.'

There were just a few converts at first, but Alma took over the process of organizing with a smug zest that made me want to kick her.

She was all humility and worship to Arty — a kind of 'Kiss the Ground on which Your Blessed Brown Balls Drag' smarminess. But with the converts she reigned as a high priestess, prophet, and mega-bitch. She originated the concept of 'Artier

than Thou.' She ordered, organized, and patronized. The
redheads, who had to wait on her and wheel her around in a
replica of Arty's chair, hated her. Soon there were enough of
the 'Admitted' to give Alma a full-time staff. The redheads
went thankfully back to balloon games, popcorn, and ticket
sales.

Not that Arty was ever less than In Charge. Though he
appeared only in his tank and did no trivial fraternizing, he
knew everything. Most likely the whole thing in all its details
was Arty's invention. He gave orders to Alma by intercom.

She sat in her commandeered trailer office chirping earn-
estly into the box on her desk and listening reverently to replies.
Her method of passing orders on to the lesser members was as
snooty as that of any conveyor from on high.

She set Arturism up like a traveling fat farm for nuns.
Though she herself had lucked onto Arty while flat broke, all
who came after paid what she called a 'dowry.' Arty said, in
private, that the scumbags were required to fork over everything they had in the world, and, if it wasn't enough, they could
go home and get their ears pierced or their peckers circumcised
and see what that did for them.

The thing grew. Arty's fans — or the 'Admitted,' as Alma
insisted on calling them — began to trail after the show in cars
and vans and trailers of their own. From a half-dozen simple
characters wandering the midway with white bandages where
fingers or toes had been, there grew a ragtag horde camped
next to the show everyplace we stopped. Within three years the
caravan would string out for a hundred miles behind us when
we moved.

Papa hired more guards and had the Binewski vans wired
for security. After a month of phoning and looking and asking,
Papa bought the biggest tent any of us had ever seen and set it
up around Arty's stage-truck.

Dr. P. got a big new surgery truck with a self-contained
generator. Two of the big trailers were converted to post-opera-
tive recovery wards. Chick was with Dr. Phyllis from early
morning until supper every day. He was getting thinner and he

fell asleep at the table leaning on Mama night after night.

'When does he play?' she would ask, her eyes blinking at the air directly in front of her.

Papa talked to Arty and Arty passed the word to Doc P. Dr. Phyllis didn't like it, but two hours each day, one after breakfast and another before supper, Chick was ordered to play where Mama could see him. She started reading fairy tales to him during the morning hour. In the afternoon he dutifully pushed toy cars around the floor of the family van, making motor noises, so Mama could hear him as she made supper.

Having established the chain of command, having petrified two dozen finger-and-toe novices into doing all the paperwork, Alma shed her left arm to the shoulder. She spent hours crooning to herself on her infirmary bed with the screen drawn around her for privacy. Her voice grew frail and she stopped testifying.

She was replaced immediately. Dozens clamored for a chance to testify at Arty's shows. There were thousands waiting, willing to pay, for the right to see and listen.

I was walking by when Dr. P. walked out of her big new surgery truck and heaved the plastic bag containing Alma's last flabby upper arm into an ice chest for Horst to dispose of. She dusted her white gloves against each other and nodded to me. 'Well, that's finished,' she announced through her mask. 'It took a year and a half. I could have done the whole job in three hours.'

After a while, Alma wasn't around anymore. Arty laughed when I asked about her. 'She's retired,' he said. 'She's gone to the old Arturans' home to rest in peace.' I thought he meant she was dead.

15

Press

As their seventeenth birthday rolled past, the twins were fogged in by some musty hormonal mist. They were goofy, aloof, and up to something. Their bickering graduated from intermittent to constant, but the dignity that they felt appropriate to full-fledged bleeders dictated that the running argument be carried on in whispers.

The twin's piano teacher, whom Lil had hired by mail, was the greasy Jonathan Tomaini, with his one shiny-assed suit and two pairs of slightly mismatched socks. He took frequent opportunities to explain how temporary this 'post' was for him and how thrillingly adventurous it was for a concert performer and graduate of fine New York music academies, such as himself, to doss down on a cot in a trailer shared with twelve sweaty, spitting, cursing, chortling roustabouts who viewed him as one rung lower than last night's beer farts. He gushed at how brilliantly gifted the twins were — 'a privilege to spend this brief hiatus in my career molding and influencing such talent.'

The twins claimed — Elly loudly and Iphy with demure embarrassment — that Tomaini never bathed, only washing his hands up to the wrist and his face and neck as far down as his collar. He was, they said, no fun to share a piano stool with. He had things to teach them, though, and they endured the piano stool for hours every day.

Mama was slipping away from us. Her pill intake was up and her body was changing. Large bones came close to the surface as her woman-softness withered. Her eyes were giving her trouble, the focus softening and shortening. Her walk had changed from a melodic flirt to a gaunt, uncertain lurching with her hands extended in front of her, touching. She rattled in endless detail about our various infancies. She forgot things. She left jobs half done and didn't notice when someone else finished them for her. She cried easily and occasionally without knowing she was doing it. She slept.

Papa had taken to antacid tablets for his stomach. He carried half-consumed rolls in every pocket and chewed them constantly. He dithered for eighteen hours out of every twenty-four trying to lash his small winter crew into dealing with the flush of business brought on by Arty's increasingly specialized popularity. The veins in his forehead threatened a stroke while he supervised the production of the expensive and classy 'Ask Arturo' poster series. He was happy, though. The work rush let him forget that he wasn't the boss anymore.

New people kept cropping up and latching on. We were a road show and we lived with the ebb and trickle of faces who appeared, hired on, stayed for a few thousand miles and then, one day, were gone. We Binewskis kept to ourselves. Only the family stayed the same. Hanging out with the swallower's kids or making friends with the palm reader's daughter always ended in separation and forgetfulness. We were easy with strangers but never close.

Arty's growing flock, however, was different. I dreamed one night that Arty cried them into the world. They came out of his eyes as a green liquid that dripped to the ground making puddles. The puddles thickened and jelled into bodies that got up and hung around Arty.

But Dr. P. and the advance man and McGurk, and later Sanderson and the Bag Man and the nebbishes and simps who mooned and crooned around him, were all there because of Arty, no matter what other pretext they might claim. They all belonged to him.

The occasional television crews, doing thirty-second 'Day at the Carnival' bits for the evening news, took a while to tumble to what was going on in the center tent. An hour after the first broadcast of a breathless on-the-spot reporter describing bandaged stumps in a wheelchair, the newspaper people started popping up.

After a few months reporters drove out to meet us on the road. Squads with cameras and notebooks and tape recorders waited for us on every new site as we tooled in and parked. A few towns canceled our licenses before we even arrived. The indignant slams just made Arty smile. 'Those who want to know,' he shrugged, 'will still get the message.'

It wasn't until one of the redheads brought a copy of *Now* to Arty's door one morning that we realized one of the loiterers in the journalistic pack was from that national news magazine. The guy in the lean tweeds had been puttering around the midway for weeks. The ticket peddlers all knew him because he'd flash his photo ID card and mutter, 'Press,' trying to slip into the shows without paying. 'Press your pants,' the redheads would say — a stock Binewski reply — and he'd laugh and pay up.

The *Now* story demonstrated his intentions clearly. The fur-chested Norval Sanderson, with his cynic's eye, bourbon voice, and discreet tailoring, was with us so he could expose the 'ruthless egotism that was exploiting the nation's psychic undertow.'

'Arturism was founded,' wrote Sanderson, 'on the greed and spite of a transcendental maggot named Arturo Binewski, who used his own genetic defects and the weakness of the unemployed and illiterate to create an insanely self-destructive following that fed his maniacal ego....'

Within days, Arty, the clever boy, had turned the attack to his own purposes by distributing ninety-second tapes to every network proclaiming that he was, indeed, the Transcendental Maggot, and that his power to thrive in the decaying frenzy of the planet was available to all those who were willing to accept it.

Norval Sanderson had covered wars, treaties, executions, and inaugurations for two decades. He was sharp and he lacked awe for anything, from earthquakes to heads of state. He was clever, He spent days lounging coolly in the corners of Arty's life, and he published three explosively controversial interviews with Arty in as many weeks. Arty liked him.

What now remains of Sanderson's old spiral-bound note-books, his collection of news clippings, and the transcripts of his interviews with the people of Binewski's Fabulon is wrapped in black plastic and locked in the trunk in my closet. I take it all out when I want to think back. His fast, meticulous script is fading from black to grey, and the paper is brittle in my hands, but I can still hear his lazy drawl with its built-in needle.

From the notes of Norval Sanderson:

... Suspected earlier that Arturo was being manipulated by someone, probably the father, Al Binewski. I saw Arty as a tool for some functional 'norm' who was raking in the cash from the dowries. Spent three hours with Arty today and completely revised my opinion. Arty is in complete control of the cult, of the carnival of his parents, and apparently of his sisters and brother — though there may be some small spirit of resistance in the twins.

Arty is sporadically self-educated with wide lacunae in his information. National and international politics are outside his experience and reading. Municipal power relationships, however, are familiar tools to him. He has no real grasp of history — seems to have picked up drifts from his reading — but he is a gifted analyst of personality and motivation, and a complete manipulator. His knowledge of science is primitive. He relies on specialists in his staff to provide him with effective lighting, sound technology, etc. He is a skilled speaker on a one-to-one level as well as in the mass-rhetoric situation of his performances. He has a sharp awareness of personal problems in others ... professes no ethic or morality except avoidance of pain. Says his awareness is such that he feels the pain of others and is therefore required to alleviate it by offering the sanctuary of Arturism. Obvious horseshit.

His power seems to come from a combination of techniques and personality traits. He seems to have no sympathy for anyone, but total empathy. He is enormously self-centred, proud, vain, disdainful of all who lack the good fortune to be him. This

is so evident and so oddly convincing (one finds oneself
thinking/agreeing that, yes, Arty is a special person and can't
be judged by normal criteria) that when he turns his interest on
an individual (on me) the object (me) suddenly feels elevated to
his level (as in — yeah, me and Arty are too special and unique
to be judged, etc.).

Just when you feel despicable, and that Arty's disdain is too
great a burden to endure, he offers you the option of becoming his
peer.....

June 14:
Ticket count 11,724 for this show. Bleachers packed to the top of
the tent. Arty in tremendous form — his voice booming through
your very bones:

'I want you to be like I am! I want you to become what I am!
I want you to enjoy the fearlessness that I have! The courage that
I have! And the compassion that I have! The love that I have!
The all-encompassing mercy that I am!'

'The 'yes' sighs up from the crowd like a night wind and I
myself nearly weep at being surrounded by pain. I become
convinced, for an hour, that Arty is not injuring them but is
allowing them to acknowledge the pain in their lives in order to
escape from it. A man who had to be a Certified Public
Accountant on my left — a big self-contained man in a decent
suit and well-groomed beard. The wedding ring glinted on his
fingers as his hands gripped his knees. He didn't shout when the
others did. He was silent, focused on the tank and the venomous
worm in it. During the 'As I am' chorus he was frozen so rigidly
that I glanced at his face. He was biting his lip and staring,
unblinking, at the pale squirming thing down there in the green-
lit water. He didn't move. But when I looked again, a trickle of
blood was still caught in his teeth. There was a rollicking grandmother on my right, wailing and whomping throughout. Her
easy tears didn't touch me at all. It was this thick-wallet with
his gleaming well-kept air who shook me up.

For hours afterward, wandering through the crowds in the
midway, walking in the Admitted encampment, I am swept by
the idea, almost believe that having all my limbs amputated will
actually free me from the furious scourge of my days. The

midway finally shut down at midnight and I recovered a little more sobriety as the lights clicked off. In the dark, at last, I went down the road a half mile to the Roamers Rest Tavern and contemplated my momentary conversion ruefully through the amber lens of Resa Inne's (proprietress) corrupt bourbon. I kept feeling a tremor in my shins and thighs and spine, from the voice of that ruinous tadpole. I kept feeling the heat of solid thighs packed against me in that sweltering hour on the bleachers.

I had another pull at Mother Resa's treacle comfort and remembered the Vesuvius coverage ten years ago. We'd goaded the pilot of the big press chopper into getting us the goods. As we bucketed crazily in the hot drafts around the crater and cleared the lip with a gut-chewing swoop, old Sid Lyman dropped his beloved camera and fell to his knees on the steel deck. Praying. 'Good Old' Sid, who cracked abysmal puns while shooting mass graves in Texas, while clicking away at the mutilated children on Cyprus, and while filming six years' worth of intimate war footage — jungle and desert. There was Sid, helpless as his previous equipment skittered out through the open door of the chopper. All Sid could do, aside from what obviously happened in his trousers, was gibber infant prayers as he stared out into that roaring pit of boiling stone.

What bothers me is my inability to recall whether I laughed at Sid. If I snickered then, over the crater, I've a hunch I'll pay for it. I asked the flatulent Resa for another tug at Aphrodite's bourbon teat and hoped, with absurd urgency, that I'd had the sense to bite my lip over Vesuvius.

This sheaf of news clippings was stapled into Norval's notebook:

NIGHT OF CRIME

AP: Santa Rosa, California

A sudden crime wave broke out in this coastal city last night, with looting of one large supermarket and three smaller grocery stores. All the thefts took place in the three hours between 1 A.M. and 4 A.M., and Police Chief Warren Cosenti reports that foodstuffs were the only items taken.

Spokane, Washington.

Eight suspects were arrested inside McAffrey's Stop and Shop at 114 West

Main by officers answering a burglar alarm from the convenience store at 2:30 A.M. The suspects, five males and three females, were apprehended while loading cardboard boxes with foodstuffs from the shelves. All were unarmed, dressed completely in white, and refused to make any statement to police. One man, evidently a spokesman for the group, handed police officers a note reading, 'We have all taken vows of silence. Do what you will.'

Reports that several, or perhaps all, of the suspects are missing one or more fingers or toes have not yet been confirmed.

Spokane, Washington
    County Coroner Jeff

Johnson affirmed, in a press conference this morning, that all eight of the burglary suspects who committed suicide last Wednesday night in the city detention cells took cyanide.

None of the suicide victims has yet been identified, and neither police nor Johnson will comment on the rumors that all of the victims were missing digits from their hands or feet.

Velva, North Dakota:
    Police responding to a burglar alarm at 3 A.M. Monday found the big plate-glass window of the Velva Coop supermarket shattered and whole shelves emptied of goods in what appears to be ...

This headline was cut from the Hopkins, Minnesota, *Clarion*:

GROCERY WAREHOUSE RANSACKED
Police Suspect Carnival Link

On a handbill circulated among Arturans and carnival staff, Norval Sanderson had underlined this passage:

> ... *To eliminate food shortages arising from the increased number of the Blessed, our Beloved Arturo has established a special kitchen truck and mess tent to serve three wholesome meals per day to each and every one of his followers. Novices who have not yet begun Shedding must obtain meal cards from their group leaders,. Guests and visitors will be charged a nominal fee for meals....*

I laughed when I found this among Norval's notes. I

remember the tizzy we were in when this handbill was written. I suppose we weren't far from Hopkins, Minnesota, because it was the Hopkins cops who were snooping around.

I was helping Lily pin up the hem on a new satin coat for Arty. We were in the kitchen of the van. Lily had her sewing machine on the table in the dining booth and Arty was sitting beside it on the table. I was chalking the hem and Lily had her mouth full of pins when the door jerked open and the twins stormed in with Chick.

'Cops,' they said. The twin's faces had matching looks of thrilled horror. Chick nodded gravely. 'Papa's angry. The cops want to talk to Arty.'

Arty had been stretching up tall for his fitting and he sank back on his hips and got a pin in his rump. 'Rar!' He jerked forward. Elly giggled, Iphy reached for him, and I fell off the bench. The radiophone buzzed and it was Al from the office. Chick was right. Papa was very angry.

That was the first we heard of the marauding that Arty's followers had been up to. It seems they were hungry. A lot of them didn't have any money left after turning everything over to Arty. Trailing around after him they had no way to earn any. But none of us had given any thought to how they would all eat. Some of them had been sneaking meals with the show crew but that infuriated the cooks. The midway staff would beat them up or, at the least, throw them out if they suspected who they were. The cooks had stuck up signs on the mess tent saying, 'Midway Staff ONLY!'

The cops arrested five novices that day and impounded the old school bus that they lived in. Behind its white curtains the bus was stacked with cases of canned goods intended for the good people of Hopkins. The police kept us there for a couple of days before they let us go.

Al hired two more cooks and some kitchen helpers, bought another kitchen truck, and relegated a couple of old tents to the followers for dining halls. He fumed, and Arty too was angry at having to spend the money to feed them all. Norval Sanderson took notes and collected clippings and asked questions.

16

The Fly Roper and the Transcendental Maggot

Norval Sanderson was a curious man. He wanted to know everything. When he had exhausted all the Binewskis for the day, or was bored with the antics of the Admitted, he would stroll into the midway and continue his casually relentless examination of every event, phenomenon, skill, artifact, and personality that caught his eye. He wasn't pushy. He was as patient and flexible as water on rock.

He was fascinated by popcorn machines and by the way cotton candy was spun. He charmed the redheads with his attentive interest in their uncountable chores and their extravagantly fascinating life stories. He was intrigued by the engines of the simp twisters and he plagued the mechanics with his probing about the drive lines and exhaust systems of the machines.

Sanderson engaged the customers in conversation and could discover astounding details about the truckers, lawyers, pea pickers, sea cooks, insurance peddlers, students, and factory workers who happened to be pitching coins at the ring toss or standing in line for the Roll-a-plane as he ambled by.

He never got tired of the midway. He scrupulously rode each of the simp twisters once when he first started haunting the show. After that he only watched them. But the games and the acts, the booths and the vendors didn't get old for him. He turned the game managers into exuberant braggarts by inquiring about the details of their work and expressing amazement at their skills.

Al's old front men told him how to find the district attorney or sheriff or mayor or police captain in each town who could be paid off with the proceeds of one fixed game, as a prophylactic against investigations of the roulette wheel and the baseball toss. They told him how to place posters, how to pry a license out of a reluctant bureaucrat, how to rent a site for a song, and all the comes and tells and scams of their craft.

The novice who handed out Arturan literature in the P.I.P. (Peace, Isolation, Purity) booths could count on being quizzed periodically about the reactions of passersby to each brochure or pamphlet.

The snack-stand vendors reported the flavors of Sno-kone or soda pop in vogue in a given locale and how the fashions varied geographically.

Sanderson watched practice sessions and rehearsals and then went to the shows to see the results. He knew the face and name and temperament of every cat Horst owned. He knew the blade capacity of each sword swallower and the octane rating of every fire eater. He knew the geek boys' favorite philosophers and the brand of lotion that the tumblers rubbed on their aching joints before bed.

Whenever he could, he'd snag Horst or a Binewski to keep him company, to turn on the lights in the Haunted Gold Mine tunnel so he could see the springs and trip wires that triggered the sound tapes and the swooping skeletons or gaping corpses, or to walk him though the Chute describing the nature and origin of each glass-encased specimen. I myself have perched, embarrassed and bored, beside him in the stands of the variety tent, answering his endless questions as he gawked delightedly at Papa's miniature circus, with its single ring and its dog act, jugglers, acrobatic clowns, and aerialists.

In the swallowers' tent he watched gravely from the back and asked questions afterward.

When the Death Tower motorcyclists joined the Fabulon, he stuffed his ears with plastic foam so he could lean over the lip of the huge metal cylinder for hours, watching the riders gun their roaring machines against gravity.

He knew the twins' repertoire by heart and could sing their most difficult and popular tune, 'She Was a Salt-Hearted

Barmaid,' with all its grace notes.

Of course he studied every delicate nuance of Arty's show. He scouted the big tent well before Arty made his appearance for each session. Sanderson watched as the ten thousand places filled with the Admitted of varying status. The limbless lay on their bellies in the sawdust in front of the Holy Tank. The legless were behind them on the first slope of the risers. The bandages got ostentatiously thick further up where the ankle and knee crowd jostled each other. Beyond were the novices, all dressed in white and crushed close on the benches, waving their bandages proudly. Behind and above them in the highest bleachers were the unscathed newcomers, the curious, the scoffers, the occasional reporter, all antsy and jiggling to see Arturo the Aqua Man's life-defying invitation to ultimate sanctity. Sanderson sketched charts of the hierarchy and wrote endlessly in his pocket-shaped notebooks.

But, of all the skims and grifts and skills and wonders of the Fabulon, Norval Sanderson's particular favorite was a fairly new act housed in the smallish tent right next to Arty's huge one. It was the least-spectacular turn the Fabulon had ever offered. Yet, though Sanderson would pump me or any other insider for details about the act and the actor, he didn't want to meet the man himself or question him personally. 'Some mysteries,' he'd drawl, 'I'd like to preserve.' And I never resisted when Sanderson hailed me away from pumping septic tanks or counting tickets to join him in a scholarly viewing of 'Mr. Ford's luscious lariat.' I liked the Fly Roper, too.

His friends called him C. B. Ford. He was pot-bellied and bald and he tucked his pants into bright red, rose-stitched, pointy-toed cowboy boots with three-inch heels. There was a calm twinkle to his humor. He had quick hands and no interest at all in becoming an Arturan and tithing up his body parts. What he wanted, and what Arty gave him was a permanent lease on the number 2 tent in the fairway. 'Your big show and my little show,' he told Arty, 'belong on the same card.'

His gift was his ability to bulldog and hogtie houseflies. He claimed to have learned it in the Shetland Islands, where the girls came thirty lonesome miles over the moors to drink nickel beer and see the flicks at the Coast Guard station. 'But,' he laughed, 'those girls were all set on getting to the States so you had to be careful with 'em. Nothing they'd like better than get knocked up by a Yank and have Papa herd him to the altar like one of their shit-dragging sheep.'

There isn't much life in those dim latitudes, he would claim, but there were plenty of flies. And he learned the nature of flies from an old bosun who'd run away to sea from a meat-packaging plant in Nebraska.

'Now the fly,' and he planted his heels and hooked out the silver tabs on his suspenders, 'is not unlike the helicopter.' At this point his lariat would lift, whirling lazily, and begin to spin above his head in a convincing imitation of a fly's orbit. 'Your mother no doubt told you that you'd catch more flies with honey than with vinegar.... But we all know what flies really like best!' With his free hand he would reach over to the velvet-draped table and lift the domed silver lid off the shallow chafing dish. The candle beneath the dish would flutter slightly and the crowd would titter at the steaming pile of dung on its silver plate.

C. B. Ford was particular about the brand of shit he used. 'Cow flop,' he once told me in confidence, 'does not work well. It draws the flies just fine, but the folks in the audience can't see it. It's too runny and you can't pile it so they can see it from the ground. It's no good to me at all if it's dry enough to stack. Dry I could pile it up like flapjacks halfway to the moon, but the flies don't take much interest in it. Horse shit, of course, draws well if it's just fresh, but it doesn't have enough impact on the crowd. Somehow people accept horse shit. Nearly anybody would tell you that the smell is homey rather than bad. We want that bit of shock that you get with real *shit* shit. I won't work with pig shit. Depends on what they're eating but they can be loose as a cow and even when they're firm that pig smell is too much for me. I hate it. So it comes down to either dog or human.

The rope's loop would hover over the chafing dish excitedly while the cord subsided and C. B. Ford took up his bumpkin professorship. His timing was good and his chatter didn't go over anybody's head. He'd play the rope and talk and it was never long before the flies came. 'There's one now.... That's the advantage of fresh bait,' he'd say. He had a screen cage full of flies — big bluebottles that were slow and easy to work with and easy for the crowd to see and hear. He had one of the boys behind the stage just crack the gate on that cage so the flies would come out in a slow drip. Five or six was all he wanted. and as soon as there were a couple of real flies buzzing that chafing dish, his rope would disappear and he'd get a long-haired girl up from the audience to giggle and assist him.

The first fly was always a big to-do. He'd jump all over the stage swiping wildly at the air, come within a frog hair of splatting his fist into the chafing dish a dozen times, get the girl volunteer to flap her arms to flush the little buzzers his way, and all the while talking his talk about the similarities and differences between Herefords and bluebottles until the audience was half-convinced that he was never going to catch the fly but was laughing anyway and jumpy as a drunk with a glass of milk waiting for him to smack a bare hand into the pile of warm dung.

Then, suddenly, he'd catch the fly and hold it, closed in his fist, up to the microphone so they could hear it buzz. Then he'd blow on his thumb knuckle and shout and shake his fist hard, 'to make the fly dizzy,' and then snap his wrist as he flung the fly down hard onto the table. 'Now he's out for a second, but he's just stunned and we've got to act quickly before he regains consciousness.'

Whirling on the long-haired girl and drawing small stork-shaped scissors, he would lift a strand of her hair, separate a lone thread, and snip it close to her skull before she had time to do more than squeak.

'We'll tie a slipknot here at one end and have this big fella hobbled in a jiffy.'

The slipknot in the hair would slide over one of the stiffly splayed legs of the fly and tighten. With a quick flourish a little fluorescent paper sign was taped to the loose end of the hair. While the first fly was recovering its wits C. B. Ford would catch five more as easily as picking grapes and serve them the same way, assuring his blushing assistant that her hair was so thick and lustrous that she could spare six single threads for the taming of half a dozen wild beasts.

Inside three minutes a flock of confused flies was bobbling drunkenly through the air above the audience, trailing the tiny winking streamers that read 'EAT AT JOE'S' and 'HOME COOKING.'

The crowd would flush out through the flaps in a good humor. Inevitably a group of young men would take it upon themselves to swat the burdened flies out of the air or smash them as they sagged down to rest. Also inevitable was the child who was indignant at having the flies killed and did his best to catch one alive to protect it, to take it home in a popcorn box and revere it for having experienced something altogether extraordinary in fly life.

After two months of following Arty around in a rented van, Norval Sanderson left us and took a leave of absence from his distinguished magazine. He went home to West Point, Georgia, as he explained, to see his aged mother and think. For weeks he combed her long, thin hair each night and sat drinking in the dark on the porch long after she went to bed. When Sanderson came back to the Fabulon, Arty claimed it was the cult that drew him. Lily was convinced that Sanderson was bent on writing Arty's biography, but I had a hunch that the Fly Roper was, in some odd way, part of the pull.

Norval caught up with us again outside Ogallala, Nebraska, and knocked on the door of Arty's van during breakfast. Arty left the straw bobbing in his orange juice to smile at Norval. I went on cutting up his ham.

Norval went to the stove and poured a cup of coffee, lifted it in salute to Arty, and then set it on the counter without sipping it. 'I brought you something.' His ironic rasp was as slow and cool as ever. He reached into the unusual bulge in his tweed jacket and pulled out a green glass pint jar crammed with something. 'A token,' he sneered, 'of my profound respect.' He set the jar on the table beside Arty's plate. The swollen thing inside pressed against the glass. It was thinly covered with short dark hairs. Norval grinned mischievously and loosened his slim lizard-skin belt. The flannel trousers slid down past loose silk shorts to his knees. 'Excusing your presence, Miss Olympia,' he mocked, and his thumbs pushed the elastic waistband down and twitched his starched shirttail aside to show the limp circumcised penis dangling in front of a flat and ornately scarred crotch.

'The stitches are almost completely dissolved now, but I'm still bowlegged,' he complained.

Arty chuckled and nodded. 'Don't think that gives you a head start on any other novice. You still have to go through the finger and toe basics before you'll get any credit for that grandstand play.'

Sanderson hiked his pants back up, shaking his head with mock woe. 'I cut off my balls for the man and this is the thanks I get.'

'We all have to start somewhere,' Arty grinned, as I slipped a forkful of ham between his lips. Sanderson leaned on the stove drinking coffee and regaled us with an urbane description of his search for a surgeon willing to perform the task. 'I ended up with an eighty-year-old veterinarian who was Grand Wheezar of his local KKK congregation. I told him that my mother had just confessed, on her deathbed, that she had gone down with a pecan picker and I was actually sired by an octoroon Catholic communist. The old gentleman agreed to do the job immediately. He pats me on the shoulder and says, "Yer right, son, you'd fry in the eternal oil for passing that much taint on to another generation."'

Arty was still laughing when Sanderson went out to move his van into the Admitted camp. As the door closed Arty hooked a fin at the pint jar and slid it into staring range. He put his nose against the tinted glass, turned the jar for another view, and then sat back with a frown wrinkling his bare scalp.

'Goat? or calf?' He might have been asking the jar. 'Maybe a colt or a big dog?'

I was scraping the plates and shaking my head. 'You're as goofy as he is.'

Arty gave me the look. 'These are not Norval Sanderson's balls.'

That stopped me. I leaned to look at the crammed jar.

Arty tapped at the lid with his fin. 'That network reporter

who was here after the first *Now* story told me about it. Sanderson lost his balls to a landmine in North Africa years ago. Fifteen years ago, maybe.'

'Why didn't you call him on it?' My head was frozen.

'He figures I don't know anything. Probably put iodine or something on old scars to make them look fresh. It's kind of cute. Let's give him some rope and see what he's up to. And you keep your trap shut about it.'

'You like him.'

'He's entertaining.'

Passing himself off as a convert didn't seem to require that Norval develop anything you could rightly call reverence. He still sneered and took notes and interrogated anything with vocal cords. But he also came up with the idea for the Transcendental Maggot booth. Arty laughed and and let him do it. The project earned Sanderson a modest income and kept him close to Arty. The booth was small but it had the place of pride at the pivot point between Arty's tent and the Fly Roper. The notion was simple and surprisingly popular. Sanderson collected amputated parts from Dr. Phyllis and cut them into small chunks in each half-pint jar. His maggot farm was reliable and easy. He'd hang fingerless or toeless hands or feet up on hooks behind his trailer for a few days and pick out the worms as they hatched. He sold a lone maggot with its own lifetime supply of guaranteed sanctified feed for five dollars. The ones that graduated to flyhood before he could sell them went to the Fly Roper's wire cage on a dollar-a-dozen basis.

Whatever his intentions, Sanderson was with us to stay. He switched from tweed to twill. He talked casual business, regularly, with C. B. Ford. It took him two years just to shed four toes — two on each foot — but he conscientiously deposited each toe, as he dropped it, in its own jar with its own worm and sold it for the usual price.

17

Popcorn Pimp

The twins were counting the miniature tomatoes in each other's salads at dinner one night when Papa announced that they were getting their own van, 'like Arty's.' Lily was horrified. They were too young at eighteen to live alone, she protested, even in a T-shape set-up with the family van and Arty's. The swallowers would sneak in and rape them and whatnot. The sword swallowers and the fire eaters were Lil's bogey-men at the time. She got hot thinking of the twins at the mercy of the swallowers.

'When they were tiny morsels, still trying to crawl away from each other and getting tangled, up I said, "Blast the heart that takes them from me!"'

Iphy looked scared, but Elly, cool and slow, said, 'We'll take it. I know this is Arty's idea. He's got something in mind. But we'll take it anyway.'

The twins ordered carpets and walls of sea green, and sky-blue drapes and furniture, and a scintillating emerald bathroom. Their bedroom and its huge bed were dusty rose.

In honour of my fifteenth birthday, Mama moved my clothes and treasures into the twins' old compartment in the family van. I sat there sometimes, but I went on sleeping beneath the kitchen sink because the open expanse of unsheltered bed seemed as wide and flat as Kansas.

The twins showed up in the family van for every meal. 'See, Lily,' Papa said one night as the twins sat on the floor winding

226

Mama's embroidery thread onto cards, 'you'd hardly know they moved.'

'Who moved?" asked mama.

Elly had hold of my sleeve and was giving me her 'or else' look.

'O.K., Oly, I want you to do me a favor.'

Iphy's gentle hand lay on my other sleeve and her voice was desperate, 'I *don't* want you to do it. Oly! Please!'

'What?' I was flustered. Elly held out a white envelope.

'Take this over to the judges' stand at the other end of the park.'

Iphy tried to reach the envelope but it was in Elly's far hand, out of Iphy's reach. 'I won't like you, Elly! I won't speak to you!'

'This is for one of the judges. A man named Deemer,' Elly continued, calmly fending Iphy off while tucking the envelope into my hand and folding my fingers over it. 'He's very tall and he's bald except for brown rim around the back. He's wearing a suit and a name tag. Give him this and then run. Don't say anything to him. Don't wait for an answer.'

Iphy flattened her hands over her face. Her fingernails were nearly white. She wasn't crying. She was hiding. I stood clutching the envelope and staring at Iphy's long, thin fingers covering her whole face and tangling with her dark hair.

I took Elly's envelope on the long walk down the screaming midway and through the barbecue smoke of the picnic grounds beyond, to where rows of folding chairs creaked in the grass under the fat behinds watching the crowning of Miss Dalrymple Dairy or the Catfish Queen or whatever it was.

I saw the guy on the judges' stand next to the stage. He was young to be so bald. He had the quiet look of a storybook schoolteacher. He stood behind three fat ladies and a short man with a big belly who was blatting into a microphone hooked to a pathetic sound system. I circled behind and scraped my arm climbing up through the warped plywood at the back of the stand. The speaker's podium and the wide folks were in front of me. I don't think the crowd could see me. I just touched his damp, pale hand, saw the long face turn down toward me and the eyes widening. Then I jammed the envelope into his hand and scuttled back down to the ground and away as fast as I could.

I saw the thin man once more, for a single minute in the moonlight in the twins' doorway at three the next morning. I was spying on Arty's door when the crack of light from the entry to the twins' van five feet away. I slipped out onto the platform and saw him almost clearly as he stepped out. He was wearing the same suit. He looked tired. The door closed behind him.

I stared without moving, thinking to myself that the envelope had been an invitation and that, wow, when I got my own van there would be norm guys coming to visit me.

I've sometimes wondered if the Binewski view of the world stunted my sympathy muscles. We were a close family. Our contact with norms outside the show was in dashes and flashes — overheard phrases, unconnected to lives. Outsiders weren't very real to me. When I spoke to them it was always with a show motive, like a seal trainer using varying tones to coax or command. I never thought of carrying on a conversation with one of the brutes. Looking back I think the thin man was upset and confused. At the time I wondered if Elly had got her way but had been murdered as a result.

He lowered his head to walk away and saw me. 'You brought the note.' He said it flatly, his voice light and even but unfocused as though he'd just waked up. 'That was strange.' He jerked his head back at the closed door leading to the twins. 'I don't think I was right. I think I did something ... wrong. One of them didn't want it. She cried and scratched at me. The other one ... did.' He shook his head slowly, jabbed his hands into his suit-coat pockets, and lurched down the steps and away, leaving me with the sounds of his shoes fading in the gravel.

I figured he'd killed the twins but my previous experience in nabbing assassins to protect Arty made me cautious. I went looking for the corpse before I gave the alarm. The door was unlocked.

I could hear the shower water rushing but I thought he

might have slit their throats in there so I leaned on the bath-room door and hollered their names. The water turned off and the door popped open. Elly was wrapping a towel around her hair as she snapped, 'What do you want?' Iphy was red-eyed, toweling their crotch.

'That guy just left, I thought . . .'

Iphy lifted her eyes to me like the ghost of a murdered child. 'She just sold our cherry!' she cried. 'And I was *saving* mine!'

'Aah, crap!' growled Elly. I trailed them into the pink bedroom and climbed up on the bed to look at the red streak on the dusty rose sheets while they were rifling a closet for their robe.

'Anyway!' Elly piped between the hanging clothes. 'You keep your toad yap shut about it, Oly!'

'I will! Jeez!'

'And Squeak-brain here is going to button up, too. Right?'

'Elly, stop. Oly can know.'

'You didn't have to tell her.'

They were digging in their own sparsely furnished refriger-ator with me peeping around the door before they got squared away about my not being able to tell because Elly would put red-hot needles in my eyes if I did and Iphy couldn't stop her, and Iphy couldn't tell because she was just as guilty as Elly. Their soft, bitter bickering was almost soothing if you didn't listen to the words. They came up with a jug of pink lemonade and grabbed three paper cups and we all went in and sat on the sea-green carpet in the living area.

'So, was it fun?' I asked. 'Or did it hurt?'

'Sure,' shrugged Elly.

'Awful,' winced Iphy.

'I thought there'd be more blood.'

'I thought he'd stay for a while afterward. You scared him off with your blubbering.'

'You don't sound as if it was really fun.'

'The redheads say it gets better.'

'Do you think he enjoyed it? Wouldn't it be awful if he didn't? Maybe that's why he ran off so soon. It'd be terrible if he gave us all that money and didn't like it.'

'Money?' This last was me. Somehow it hadn't sunk in when

Iphy said Elly had 'sold' their cherry.

'Sure, money.' Elly reached under the sofa and pulled out that same envelope I'd delivered to the judges' stand. He'd come up to talk to them after their show the day before. He'd asked if he could visit them, said he'd drop by after he finished judging the beauty contest.

'Is he a schoolteacher?'

'We don't know what he does. He was polite. Kind of gentle. I thought he'd be good to start with. He didn't seem rich so I just said fifty dollars in the note and that he should come after closing.'

'I didn't mean to hurt his feeling. It's just that I was *saving* mine and he was so heavy on me and it hurt.'

'Iphy, listen. He wouldn't have hugged us anyway. They are never going to want to hug us or cuddle up afterward. They are *always* going to get right out of bed and zip up still wet and go away.'

Iphy looked down at their knees, her slender hand folding a hunk of the bathrobe nervously in a movement so much like Mama's that I stared.

Elly peeped seriously into the envelope. 'Maybe I was dumb about this. A virginity like ours could be worth a lot. Maybe we should have taken bids. Kind of an auction. Maybe we could still do that. We'll get better. We can send out flyers. Put it up in lights, "The Exquisite Convenience of Two Women with One Cunt!"'

'Arty will be mad. Arty will just die.' Iphy pleated at the robe. I saw how pretty she was and I hated her.

'He won't care,' I tossed out. 'He does it himself.'

'Arty?!!?' Their twin voices blended in a harmony of shock.

'For money?'

'Well,' now I was confused, off balance. 'I don't think he makes them pay, but ... I'm not sure. Does he, maybe, pay them?'

'Who?'

'All the girls who come to his door at night in shiny clothes.'

Iphy's face stiffened. Elly hooted, laughing. 'Norm girls?' Iphy's lips didn't move over the words.

'Yeah. All sorts.'

'Arty the preacher!' Elly looked up at the ceiling as she giggled. I decided she wasn't a bad sort. But I knew about the pain in Iphy's gut and was glad and ashamed of being glad. If I couldn't have him, she wouldn't either. That was enough to go on. At least I could work for him and be close to him. Elly wouldn't let Iphy do that. I decided I really liked Elly. Her chin dropped down so she could look at me. 'Do Mama and Papa know?'

'Don't be silly.'

'How long have you known?'

'Months.'

Elly grinned at me. Iphy's face suddenly relaxed into mild questioning. 'Elly, we're never going to do it with anybody old or fat, are we? Let's not.'

Sometimes just looking at Al and Crystal Lil. I wanted to bash their heads with a tire iron. Not to kill them, just to wake them up. Papa strutted and Mama doddered and neither of them had a glimmer of what seemed to me the real world. I suppose I wanted them to save me from my own hurts and from the moldering arsenic ache of jealousy. I wanted back into the child mind where Mama and Papa lived, the old fantasy where they could keep me safe even from my own nastiness.

Sometimes when Mama put her arm around me and kissed my smooth skull and called me her dear dove, I almost puked. If I had ever been a dear dove it was in some dream. I still wonder what she would have done if I had been able to tell her. Maybe she could have helped. Maybe she could have saved us.

I didn't understand what Elly was up to with her whoring but I was glad because it made Iphy dirty. I didn't know what Arty was building with his religious trappings but I was happy that he had lots of work for me to do.

Arty in his tank flashing wildly from glass wall to glass wall with the lights flaming on his gleaming body, light exploding out of the rushing froth of bubbles he beat into being until his whole tank roared with fire — then, suddenly, Arty motionless, floating four feet off the bottom, caught in the soft gold light. Arty talking to the people through the microphones set against the glass. Talking until the people talked back, talking until they cried for him, talking until they called out his name, talking until they roared, stamping in the bleachers.

Arty in his golf cart, waving a flipper at the crowds on the other side of the chain-link fence. Arty working in his van, receiving guests while I hid quietly in the stuffy security room behind one-way glass with a goofy little gun in my hand just in case. Arty surrounded by books, tapping notes with one educated flipper on a humming keyboard. Arty reading, muttering into his phone transmitter, Arty reading all the way from Mesa, Arizona, to Truth or Consequences, New Mexico, without looking up, without noticing that the guy driving his rig was battling a stripped gear box the last few hundred miles because the brakes were gone.

Arty in his shower after the show, grey with the drain of whatever was eating him. Arty lying back against the wall of the shower as I scrubbed him with a brush, his eyes closed, his face smooth and dissatisfied.

Iphy decided that if I delivered the messages to their prospects I'd eventually tell Arty everything. The twins got their own phone hookup. They also recruited their piano teacher, Jonathan Tomaini, who protested that he was a musician! An artist! Not a pimp! He announced solemnly that he would inform Al immediately.

And, surprisingly, it was Iphy who sweetly, soothingly explained that if he ever did such a thing they would be forced to scream rape and point all four of their delicately accusing index fingers at him as the culprit. He quieted immediately and Elly gave him her line. He lay back on the blue sofa in obvious defeat and took in every word.

'You know what the norms really want to ask?' said Elly. 'What they want to know, all of them but never do unless they're drunk or simple, is How do we fuck? That and who, or maybe what. Most of the guys wonder what it would be like to fuck us. So, I figure, why not capitalize on that curiosity? They don't care that I play bass and Iphy plays treble, or whether we both like the same flavor ice cream or any of the other stupid questions they ask. The thing that boggles them and keeps them staring all the way through a sonata in G is musing about our posture in bed.

'Believe me, some of them are willing to pay a nice price to find out. The clincher is that you get ten points of the profit for your efforts. That's a little bonus for your salary, isn't it? Won't that sweeten the smell just a little?'

'Ten percent?' he frowned.

'Ten,' Elly nodded.

'Gross?'

'Profit. But we're not a cheap item. We're setting a minimum of a thousand dollars for two hours with additional fees for any variations on the traditional.'

He couldn't help showing his puzzlement. 'I wouldn't have thought that you needed money. It would appear that you are very comfortably provided for, and your concerts are always well attended.'

Elly smiled. 'At our prices we won't be dealing with a waiting line.'

'They'll be people,' Iphy explained, 'who are truly interested in what we have to offer.'

18

Enter the Bag Man

Arty always had a great skin — smooth and tight — never a zit or a boil. Not so much as a wart. He claimed, and it was probably true, that it was all the hours he spent submerged in the heavily chlorinated water of the tank. 'I don't even have itch mites,' he'd say. The time when Chick and the twins and I all had ringworm from mucking with a leopard cub that Horst had picked up cheap Arty didn't get it and he wouldn't let us touch him until we were clean again.

But there were times over the years when Arty's tank developed an odd, slimy moss that seemed immune to the chlorine. It would start in a tiny patch on the glass behind one of the pumps and spread. It also spread to Arty. I was the one who helped him with his shower after each show. I always soaped him and sponged him but he hated being tickled and he was particularly ticklish directly behind his balls, so that was a spot we often missed. When the galloping green caught on in the tank it caught Arty by the balls and in the shady space behind them. I had to use a scrub brush to get the stuff off him.

I hated to ask Chick for help. It infuriated Arty and made it seem that I wasn't worth anything at all since Chick could do everything better than anybody. But on this night Arty was roaring in the tub-shower and thrashing around threatening to bite me as I tried to scrub his privates. I was about ready to drop the brush and holler when Chick opened the door and stuck his head in. 'Oly ...' he started, but I jumped up and grabbed his hand and pulled him into the bathroom.

'Take the mildew out of Arty's crotch!' I snapped.

234

'There's a man outside that I don't like,' said Chick.

Arty wallowed irritably in the hot spray from the shower and rumbled at us. 'Do this shit-squirting job and then worry about that!'

'It's on the back side of the balls, in the wrinkles, and behind his balls almost all the way to his asshole,' I said.

Chick looked at Arty. A thin trail of green smoke — almost invisible — rose from the tub and hovered above the floor.

'What should I do with it?' asked Chick.

'The toilet,' I said.

'No,' growled Arty. 'It might stay in the works and creep up my ass again.'

'Well ...' said Chick. The smoke condensed into a distinct pea-sized puff and wobbled in the air.

I chuckled. 'Put it in Dr. Phyllis's underwear drawer.'

Chick looked at me. 'Now, Oly ...'

'Take it with you! Get rid of it! Throw it into the middle of the Pacific! I don't care!' Arty flicked the shower tap off with his flipper and lurched up, catching the rim of the tub with his chin. I hoisted him out and started to towel him dry.

Chick leaned back against the door and crossed his arms to look at us seriously. 'The man outside wants to see you, Arty, but I don't think you should.'

Arty rotated his shoulders under the towel. He grunted.

'He writes notes,' said Chick. 'He can't talk and he's lost his face.'

'Yah, yah,' sneered Arty.

'He stayed through both your shows and then went to talk to Horst. Horst says he asked about the twins and Oly and Mama and that he claims to have met you before.

Arty looked to see that I had the bottle of oil and then punched the door open and rolled into his room with the towel wrapped around him. He was climbing onto his massage bench when he said, 'Tell the guy to wait. Bring him in fifteen minutes and then get yourself into the security room and keep an eye on him. How big is he?'

'Big,' said Chick. 'But slow.'

'Oly will stay with me,' said Arty, and he stretched and wriggled his flippers and waited for me to start oiling him.

Chick's face crumpled in sour worry from the chin up but he turned and went out with the compressed pill of mold floating behind him a pup.

Arty was sitting in his big chair, dressed in dark wine velvet and sipping at the straw in his tonic water when Chick brought the man in. He was as tall as Al and very lean. He stopped just inside the door, his one eye fixed on Arty, and dipped his knees in what must have been a bow. His face was covered by a grey cloth that fell from inside his baseball cap and drooped into his open shirt collar. Only his right eye peered out at us.

'Mr. Bogner,' said Arty.

I pushed up a chair for the big man and he moved toward it and folded into it slowly and with great care. I remembered a story about a miser who had a deep dent in the top of his head. The rain had filled it with water and there were goldfish in it. The miser moved very carefully and slept sitting up so as not to spill his private fish preserve.

The masked man balanced a pad of paper on his knee and looked at Arty. I stood close, fiddling with a spray can of Paralyzer. The lamp on the bureau went on and I took half a step back so Chick would have a clear view of the big guy through the mirror.

I flinched when he lurched forward and began scribbling on the pad. He ripped the sheet off and held it out to Arty. I took it and held it for Arty to read. The script was a fast block print, very legible. It said, 'I'm glad to see you again. I shot at you in a parking lot ten years ago.' He was leaning forward, his one eye sweeping its gleam over us both eagerly. His baseball cap was dark blue and the bill was pulled down. The top of his veil was tucked under the left side of the cap so he looked like a game of peekaboo. The veil bulged at his neckline in a bag that seemed to swell and fall back with his noisy breathing. He was literally a Bag Man.

Arty was still and staring, no expression on his smooth, wide face, only his eyes weren't blinking and were wider open than usual. He was holding his breath. I couldn't read the Bag Man's eye. It moved and light came off it, but there was no flesh to crinkle around it and tell me what the eye meant. I got a grip on the Paralyzer and dug my heels into the carpet.

Arty let his breath out. Then he took some in. In a half-joking and familiar tone he said, 'Now, why ever did you do that?'

The Bag Man blinked and bent over his knee, writing fast with his pen scratching and jumping in his big weathered knuckles. He ripped the sheet off and handed it to me and then kept on writing. The paper said, 'Things were slipping on me — oranges at first — then everything. My wife and kids had no respect for me. I started going up to the woods with my old man's 30.06 on weekends but I never did any hunting. Just sat by the fire and cleaned the rifle and had a few beers.'

He didn't remember much of the trial, though he was quite clear on being booked. The photographer and the finger-printing struck him as dull. He felt that he should struggle or shout, cry, anything to make the proceedings important. But he was too tired, and looking into the faces of the uniformed men going about their work made him anxious not to disturb or trouble them. 'Who knows what their wives are like?' he thought. Sitting in the cell alone, he decided that he had done something that couldn't be put right. He lay quietly on his bunk and tried to think. On the second day a man came who claimed to be Emily's lawyer. Emily was filing divorce papers.

The trial was vague and boring. He remembered an old woman, very neatly dressed and sharp-voiced. She was sitting on the chair next to the judges bench and she said, '. . . If you ask me I'd say it was a charitable instinct for mercy. I felt the same way. I'm not one who'd say it was a wrong thing to do.'

Vern was confused about the charges. They tried to convince him that what he had done was wrong and after a while he pretended to believe them. But he knew that he was being punished for his failure. After all, they had been lined up. Absolutely in line, and he — the story of his life — had missed.

He liked the State Hospital. He didn't mind the steel mesh on the windows. He had a room of his own and three sets of green pajamas. He swept his floor every morning, ate the food

on the tray, and had a nap on his neatly made bed. When he
woke up the tray and the broom were gone and his room was
bare and tidy again. He slept a lot and managed to forget nearly
everything.

After a year or so he started thinking again, though he didn't
much want to. What he thought about was children. Teddy and
Brenda had been six years old and five when he last saw them.
First he remembered their voices saying 'Dad.' He dreamed
that his only real name was Dad and the other things that people
called him were either aliases or insults. He remembered seeing
a whistle on the shelf of a variety store and wondering if Teddy
would like it, wondering if he should get one for Brenda too.

Then he dreamed that he was in the open door of a plane
several thousand feet above the earth and he had to jump
holding a baby in his arms. It was his baby. He jumped, pulled
the rip cord on the parachute, and it didn't open. The emergency release didn't work. He was falling fast. The wind tore at
him fiercely. He was gripping the baby as tightly as he could
but the wind pried under his arms, strained at his muscles, and
suddenly the baby was loose, falling beside him, just out of
reach. He flailed and groped in the air, trying to reach it. The
baby was falling just a little bit faster than he was. It was below
him, falling away from him as he fell after it. The earth
screamed up at him. He knew that the baby was going to hit
first and he would see it, would know it for a whole fraction of a
second before he was smashed into a pulp himself. The terrible
millisecond of that grief burst in him and he woke shrieking. He
couldn't get the dream out of his head. He prayed that he
would have the dream again but that this time he would fall
faster and be allowed to die first.

The dream was not to be monkeyed with. It did not come
again and it would not go away.

Emily did not answer his letters. He got a formal letter from
a lawyer 'reminding' him that the divorce had gone through
and that he had been denied all communications with the
children.

That was when he remembered the freaks in the parking lot.
Their strange twisted forms danced viciously in his head. They
were cruel and jeered at him.

He decided that Teddy and Brenda were going to become freaks like that if Emily was allowed to raise them.

About that time Vern's mother visited him and he was required to spend every morning and afternoon in the day room with the other patients. His mother made him think of the old lady at the trial. She never talked about why he was there. She talked about her farm, the dairy that Vern's dad had built up and left to her when he died. She said she could sure use a man around the place. The hired hands were shiftless sneaks. She said Emily never let her see the children.

Vern hated the day room. He wanted to be alone again. Then he decided that he wanted to leave the hospital altogether. He started paying attention to the doctors and nurses.

He was released from the hospital three years and six months after he had entered it. His mother met him in the lobby and walked out with him. She led him to a big car and they got in. She drove him home to the farm where he had grown up. Mrs. Bognor took Vern on a tour of the farm and introduced him to the hands. It was spring and the garden needed a lot of work. While his mother fried chicken, Vern sat at the kitchen table and sketched a plan for the vegetable plot on a scrap of notebook paper.

That was Thursday. The following day was a payday for the hands. Mrs. Bognor stuck to the old ways and paid her men and her bills with cash. Just after midnight Vern got out of bed, put on the tan work clothes his mother had bought for him, packed a brown paper bag with more clothes and shaving gear, and eased out of his room. He slipped past the old lady's door and down the stairs. Vern's father had always kept the cash box in a drawer beneath the flour bin in the kitchen. The key had always hung on a small nail in the door of the hall closet. Vern's mother hadn't changed anything.

He was parked outside the grade school at 8:30 on Friday morning. His mother's car was newish and respectable. Vern pretended to read a newspaper and smiled to himself as he watched the kids straggle into school. A little before nine he began to worry that they might have gone in another door. For a moment he wondered if they might have changed so much that he wouldn't recognize them. Then he saw them. They

were together but arguing about something. Teddy gave
Brenda a push and she stamped her foot and yelled at him.
Vern rolled down his window. His whole body was suddenly
flooded with sweat. His voice shook and came out too soft.
They didn't hear him. Brenda tried to stomp on Teddy's sneakered foot and grab a book from him. Teddy laughed and held
the book up out of reach. Vern found his old voice. He disliked
their bickering. He always had.

'Teddy! Brenda!' The pair, caught in their quarrel, looked
guiltily toward him. He was calm again. He knew them well,
after all.

'Dad?' said Teddy. And Brenda, confused and not remembering, looked at her brother and said, 'Dad?'

Disneyland was fine. They drove straight through two days,
put up in a motel across the street from the enormous amusement park, and then spent three days from breakfast until
bedtime glutting themselves on the wonder of it.

Vern was calm and happy. The kids were in a daze of
ecstasy. They collapsed at night too tired to watch the television in their motel room. After they were asleep Vern would
turn the set on, keeping the volume very low. Crouched close to
the set he would watch the late news, listening carefully for
mention of himself or the children. There was nothing. He
knew the police would be looking whether the news mentioned
it or not. He sat up late watching the kids sleep.

When they climbed into the car on the day after they had
finished with the amusement park they obviously expected to
be taken home. Brenda was bouncing a toy crocodile on a stick.
'Mama will like this. I'm going to give it to her.' Teddy
announced that he would give Mom the photo of himself in the
race car. Vern had sidestepped their questions like a bullfighter
for days. Now he took a slow breath and said he thought they
ought to take a look at the Grand Canyon before they headed
back. Maybe ride some horses down the trails.

They kept talking about their mother. Brenda started to worry about school. Her class had planned a roller-skating trip and she suddenly realized that she had missed it. She came out of a gas station toilet crying pitifully. Vern was convinced that she'd been frightened by a molester and he roared through the door marked WOMEN to find nothing but a little room with cracked plaster, a damp, bitter smell, and a trail of sodden tissue paper on the floor. When he got back to the car Brenda was sobbing in the back seat with Teddy sneering at her and the station attendant, a plump teenager with a red oil rag hanging out of his hip pocket, was staring suspiciously at all of them. Vern handed him money and slammed his way into the driver's seat. He flicked the engine on and whipped around in the seat to stare at Brenda. 'Why are you crying? What happened?'

The child's crumpled face opened. She wailed. She buried her head.

'She misses her friend Lucy,' chortled Teddy.

'Oh, for ...' Vern put the car into gear, ripped out of the station and into the road, just missing a trash can and a flashy new motorcycle parked at the edge of the lot.

She cried for ten miles. When they stopped for lunch, Vern took his first bite of sandwich and chewed twice before he realized he was staring at a huge glossy poster of an armless, legless, creature smiling out of a hairless head. Fish flickered beside the worm thing and the wavering blue background made it appear to be underwater. Silver letters marched across the bottom. 'QUESTIONS?' they glittered. 'ASK AQUA BOY!'

Of course he must have seen those posters before, as well as the red and silver ones of the twins that were scattered all down the coast and in every desert town, but he hadn't recognized them.

Now he saw it, flush in the window of the drive-in burger joint — flaring out at the parking lot with fat girls and little kids trailing past on their way in and out.

He made up his mind right then, changing directions, and drove for two days without sleeping. The kids were silent now, wary. He wasn't talking, couldn't talk. He stopped in Redding and went into a sporting-goods store while they stayed in the car. He came out with a long box, put it into the trunk, and got back into the car and drove on. Teddy and Brenda were very good. They didn't ask questions. They didn't fight. They got out at gas stations to pee and didn't ask for Cokes. They said, 'Chocolate,' or 'With cheese please,' when he looked at them in drive-in grub joints, but they said these things very quietly and humbly.

When they passed the 'WELCOME TO SEAL BAY' sign on the coast road Teddy's voice came drifting up over the back seat. 'Dad . . .' softly. And then, 'Dad.' Vern nodded at him in the rearview mirror. He could see the boy's pale, grimy face in the early-morning light. They were both dirty. Brenda's hair was tangled, hadn't been combed in days. The T-shirts and jeans he had bought them in Anaheim were stained and wrinkled. A tang of puppy smell filled the air around them.

Vern had seen several posters now that he knew what he was looking at.

'Everything's going to be all right, son,' Vern nodded cheerfully at the road. 'I'm going to fix everything.'

'Dad . . . Are you taking us home to Mama?' Teddy's voice was as shaky as a man with a snake on his chest. Brenda's eyes were huge in the rearview mirror and she didn't say anything.

Vern scowled at the road. 'No. She's not good for you.' And then they were on their own street and every house and bush was familiar to Vern except that the Bjorns had painted their house blue and put a greenhouse on their side porch. Vern was talking very fast.

'You're going to stay in the car and I'm going in to fix your mother and then we're going to see the Grand Canyon like I said and you're never coming back here again and you'll stay with me always. Now you stay right in the car.' He pulled into the driveway and Emily's car was in the garage and the curtains weren't opened yet and she had let the grass go and the milk and the paper were on the step and he didn't even hear Teddy's voice saying, 'Dad, what are you going to do? Dad? Dad? Dad?' or Brenda beginning a strange little song of 'No Dad, please Dad, no Dad, please Dad,' because he was slinking out of the car, leaving the door open so Emily wouldn't hear it close and he crept back to the trunk and opened it and was taking the shotgun out of its box and breaking it and shoving in shells from the box of ammo and he didn't even notice the two small bodies beside him, tugging at him, yelping, 'No, Dad, don't hurt her — no, Dad!' and 'Please please no no please please.' He swung his arms once to get clear and then pushed through the door that led from the garage to the kitchen and he saw the plastic cabbage that Emily had stuck in a frame on the kitchen wall as a joke years ago and he was reaching for the knob on the bedroom door and when the door opened Emily was there. She was pulling a pair of pants up her thick legs and her blouse wasn't buttoned yet and she looked up at him with her hair flying around her head and he saw her fear in her heavy face and he saw the fear spot just where her neck joined her body — the deep dent where the life eddied close to the surface and he brought the shotgun up and it reached all the way to her, which made him realize she had been right all those years when she complained that the room was too small, and the tips of the barrels almost rested in the hollow of her throat and he squeezed and one economical barrel went off and a lot of Emily went out through her back onto the unmade bed and all the way across to break the big mirror over the dresser and spray the pale lavender wall with dark splotches.

Vern offered Arty a tattered envelope crammed with news clippings to fill in the gaps. Teddy and Brenda had run screaming to the neighbors, a retired couple who had known the children since they were born. Mrs. Feddig called the police while Mr. Feddig held the hysterical kids in his arms. When Mrs. Feddig got off the phone, she took the kids and her husband slid into his gardening boots and was just opening the door to look out when they all heard another blast, louder this time from the yard next door. Mrs. Feddig had a good grip on Brenda but Teddy got away and was right behind the old man when he poked his head through the shrubs and looked into the Bogner's front yard.

Vern Bogner was wandering around the middle of the

overgrown lawn. He was staggering — gently waving his arms. When he wheeled around Mr. Feddig saw no face at all, just a black and red fountain of jumping, bubbling meat with shreds of what might be bone, and the whole front of the man's tan work clothes was covered with it. Teddy screamed until the police came.

Vern was always a lousy shot. His aim had been a disappointment to his dad in the woods and fields when he was a kid. He'd been just that hair off true when he had the Binewski bambini lined up in his sights. He managed to blow his wife out through her own back by dint of a 12-gauge within two inches of her breastbone, but when the final big shot came due he stuck the second barrel of that same 12-gauge under his chin and managed to blast of 75 percent of his face, including his mouth, nose, larynx, one ear, and one eye, and still miss — MISS, mind you — the vital areas that could have finished him.

Certainly he would have bled to death soon if left to his own devices, but the Seal Bay paramedics had been having a slack season. They were full of enthusiasm and delighted at the chance to use all their shiny equipment. Vern lived.

Vern never did have much sense of humor, and after he'd transformed himself by this clumsy method, into what was known ever after as the 'Bag Man,' he was downright maudlin. He spent a year in the hospital and had a lot of surgery. But there are limits to what even an imaginative plastic surgeon can do.

The 'Bag' moniker originated in the plastic pouches that hung from the ends of various tubes into and out of what was left of his head. Since he had no jaw left, neither upper nor lower, eating, when he finally got off IVs, was a delicate liquid process accomplished with various protein solutions and a squeeze bulb attached to the appropriate tube. Breathing was also tricky, and he dripped and gurgled into one of those plastic bags all the time.

Later, when he was required to keep company with people

other than medical professionals, he wore a kind of heavy grey veil draped from his forehead with only his right eye peeking out. The bottom of the veil was always tucked into his collar and the whole thing was bulgy and lumpy from the tubes and bags inside. He had sight in that right eye and he could hear with his right ear. He couldn't talk or taste or smell. He had a hard time if he caught a cold, and he needed more surgery and constant medical supervision.

The murder trial was brief. He lay on a rolling cot in the courtroom and pled guilty by writing the word on a pad of lined yellow paper. He was sentenced to life.

He spent a while in a screened-off corner of a ward in the State Prison Infirmary and made weekly trips by ambulance to a hospital. Then he got evicted from jail. There were budget cuts and congressmen complaining about how expensive it was to keep the Bag Man. After a lot of heeing and hawing they threw him out.

The Bag Man went back to his mother's dairy farm. He hadn't got over the idea of the children. Teddy and Brenda were living with Emily's parents and he was not allowed to see them. He wrote them long letters full of advice and apple-pie wisdom and complicated descriptions of his garden and what to do for slugs and how marigolds related to bush beans and how that was a lesson in being a man.

Emily's mother picked those letters out of the regular mail with her kitchen tongs and slid them into a big manila envelope. When the envelope was full she sent it to the kids' welfare office and started on another one.

The Bag Man sat next to his mother on the sofa every night and watched the news.

It was 2 A.M. The last stragglers had been herded out of the gates an hour before and the show was bedding down. The midway was dark but all around us there were lights in the trailers and vans. Horst was hosting a card game. The candy girls' barracks was full of redheads coming out of the showers with their hair in towels, ready to put their feet up and smoke a little weed and bitch about the townies and about their men, old, new, used, broken. Al and Lil were winding up the night's count and having a drink together with their legs tangled under the dinette table in their trailer. The twins would be brushing each other's hair and chattering on their bed.

It may seem odd that I have no idea what town we were in, but when the show was alive and functioning — especially at night — it felt like the whole world and it always looked the same no matter where we were. In the daylight we might notice that we were in Coeur d'Alene or Poughkeepsie, but at night all we knew was us.

The Bag Man had scribbled and handed us pages for an hour and a half or so. I stood beside Arty, taking each sheet and holding it up for him to read, reading over his shoulder, then adding the sheet to the pile that grew up on the console table. Arty was silent, waiting, reading patiently. Occasionally the Bag Man would pause while we read a certain page, watching anxiously to see if we understood. When Arty nodded at him he would go back to the furious scribbling. Sometimes the print was so hurried that it was hard to read. Once Arty read the page out lout and asked the Bag Man if that was what it said. The Bag Man gurgled and bobbed gingerly and went on writing. Twice Arty asked questions and the Bag Man answered on paper. I had never seen Arty so patient for so long with one norm. Finally the Bag Man stopped writing and sat back. He watched us read the final page. It said, 'I keep my mother's garden and watch TV.'

Arty edged around in his chair and took a sip from his straw. 'Well,' he said finally, 'what can we do for you?'

The Bag Man hunched forward and wrote. The page said, 'Let me stay with you. Work for you. Take care of you.'

Arty stared at the page for a long time. Then he looked at the Bag Man. 'Take off your veil,' he said. The Bag Man hesitated. His hands jigged hysterically in his lap. Then they rose to his head. He lifted off the cap. The veil was tied on. He pulled at a cord and the veil fell down over the front of his shirt. Arty looked. I looked. It was pretty bad. There were a couple of patches of hair growing on one side of his head. The one live eye swiveled and jerked over us nervously. The rest was raw insides bubbling through plastic. Arty sighed.

'You'll have to learn to type. This handwriting business doesn't cut it. We'll get you a machine.'

'We didn't go to his trial?' I tried to remember but nothing came. The last hard picture I had was the lady at the reception desk staring at us as Al carried us out the door of the emergency ward. Arty slumped against his throne and stared moodily at Chick. Chick was lying flat on the floor watching an almost invisible green thread weave intricate patterns in the air three feet above his nose.

'No,' Arty finally grunted. He straightened and looked at me curiously. 'You must have been asleep when the guy from the prosecutor's office came.'

'I don't remember.'

'We were hightailing it for Yakima. Al cancelled all the shows between Coos Bay — where it happened — and Yakima. He wanted to get far away from the parking lot and everything connected with it. We were still in the thirty-eight footer, remember. No add-on sections in those days. We pulled in at one of the big rest areas, still on the Oregon side, to wait for the caravan to catch up with us. They were strung out for fifty miles, Al was going so fast. Lil was nervous and jumping up to look at all of us every five minutes.'

'This was just before I was born, right?' Chick rolled his eyes toward Arty and the green thread straightened into an arrow.

'A matter of days,' said Arty. 'There were only a half-dozen rigs with us and Al was working the radio on the others, giving out our location, when an official car pulled into the rest area and the guy got out. A tidy beard and a three-piece suit. He took a look at the line and tucked a clipboard under his arm and headed straight for us.

'Al was sitting in the pilot's seat watching him. He just said the one word, "Police," and Lily and I clammed up. The twins were asleep and I guess you were too, Oly. Al got up and let the guy in when he knocked. He sat down but he couldn't get comfortable with me there, across from him in the booth. Al offered him coffee and the guy refused. He stuck to his papers. He was in a hurry to leave. He wanted us to come back and

testify at the trial. Al refused. The guy left. Al started talking
guns and security systems. Not long after Chick was born, the
guard routine started. The whole thing made Al paranoid as
hell. And Lil was dipshit, naturally. I learned a lot from it
myself.'

Arty watched the green thread tie itself in knots in the air
and then slither out into a limp line. 'I thought I told you to get
rid of that bastardly mold,' he muttered.

'I will.' Chick lay quite still and the thread became a small
transparent bubble. 'It's nice stuff, though. Comfortable,
peaceful. I like it.'

19

Witness

From the notes of Norval Sanderson:

*Arturo Establishes the Aristocracy of Conspicuous
Absences and Superfluous Presences:*

*'Consider the bound feet of the Mandarin maiden ... and the
Manchu scholar who jams his hands into lacquered boxes so his
fingernails grow like curling death. Even the Mexican welder
sports one long polished nail on his smallest finger which
declares to the world, "My life allows superfluity. I have this
whole finger to spare, unnecessary to my labor and unscathed by
it."'*

— Arturo Binewski to N.S.

Impressions:

*Fortunato — aka Chick (origin of nickname?), 10-year-old
male child — blond, blue eyes. Totally normal physique of the
tall, thin variety. Withdrawn, introverted. Very shy except with
family. Occasionally referred to as 'Normal Binewski' by
Arturo.*

*The youngest of the Binewski children, Fortunato evidently
serves as chore boy and workhorse for the others. He is generally
depreciated for his lack of abnormality and has been made to feel
dramatically inferior to his 'more gifted' siblings. A reversal of
the position a deformed child occupies in a normal family. The
boy spends most of his time tagging after Dr. Phyllis, the cult*

surgeon. The doctor, being a normally formed person, may provide nonjudgmental affection lacking in the boy's family. The Binewskis and all the show folk in general seem to avoid the subject of Fortunato. He is, perhaps, an embarrassment.

Why Only Red-Haired Women Work in the Midway of Binewski's Fabulon

Note: Male crew members — members of acts, booth tenders, mechanics, etc., are not required to conform to any dress or appearance code. Non-show wives and other female relatives traveling with the show, but not appearing in any way, are not required to meet an appearance code. — ALL female performers and workers directly involved in the Fabulon operation — whether snake dancing or selling popcorn — are required to have red hair of a particular bright, though apparently (or possibly) natural shade. Dyeing hair or wearing a wig of the appropriate shade satisfies the requirements as long as the individual agrees never to appear in public without the wig, etc. The only exceptions are the Binewski females themselves — Crystal Lil, platinum blonde, Siamese twins, Electra and Iphigenia, black hair; Olympia the dwarf, hairless, wears caps of various kinds.

Reasons given by those questioned:

Al Binewski: 'Just a visual consistency, like a uniform. Kind of cheerful look that holds the show together. Customers can tell a show employee by their hair color.'

Crystal Lil: 'Al always had a kindness for that color hair. His mother had red hair. And in a crowd we can pick out our girls easily.'

Olympia: 'They always had red hair. I don't know why.'

Redhead: 'Story I got is that Al, the Boss, has a thing against red *hair and Crystal Lil makes sure he doesn't fool around on her by making every girl on the lot wear this damned torch color. I'm a honey blonde naturally. You can probably tell 'cause of my golden complexion. No blotchy redhead skin on me.'*

'The truth is always an insult or a joke. Lies are generally tastier. We love them. The nature of lies is to please. Truth has no concern for anyone's comfort.'

— *Arturo Binewski to N.S.*

'I get glimpses of the horror of normalcy. Each of these innocents on the street is engulfed by a terror of their own ordinariness. They would do anything to be unique.'

— *Arturo Binewski to N.S.*

Excerpts from transcript of conversation with Lillian Binewski — mother — taping unknown to the subject:

'Of course I remember, Mr. Sanderson. It started with a card from my mother. I forget what holiday it was. Easter, maybe. It was a sweet card with a little poem in it. Arty had been talking to his audience from the beginning but — oh, he must have been six or so — he saw that card and he read it over and looked at me in this wise little way he always had and he pipes up. "The norms will eat this up, Lil." He used to call me Lil like his Papa. And that night in his last show, when he was on the rim of the tank near the end, he smiled so sweetly and came out with this little poem. They loved it. They went wild. Then, of course, nothing would do but I must scour the card racks for him in every town we came to. And he was PARTICULAR! I'll say this for him, he was nearly always right. Knew this crowd.

'Why, there have been times, when I'd slip in at the back during his show and stand watching, that he'd even make ME cry, the clever way he had.

'Wait! The change you're talking about! How could I? It was this ghastly town on the coast. Oregon. Just before Chick was born. It was a terrible thing and I always felt that it must have

scarred the children. A madman shot at us in the town. It was terrifying. You can't imagine what it is to realize that there are people at large whose first reaction to the sight of your children is to reach for a gun. But offstage Arty was withdrawn after that. Quiet. Chick was an infant, too, and we were totally taken up with him. He caused a furor in our lives, that Chick.

'My teeth had been giving me trouble. Chick was three or four months old and we were in Oklahoma. One week we were in the same town with a faith-healing dentist and he was getting our crowds. The midway was just dead until his services were over every evening. Then we'd get the runoff but there wasn't much. The faith-healing dentist was pumping them dry. They just went home and stared at the wall when he was finished with them. Well, the third night in a row of standing around looking at each other over the sawdust had us all pretty peeved. And I'd been having these teeth pains again so I decided to sneak over to this auction barn where Dr. . . . . I forget his name was having his healing service.

'Arty had finished for the night. It was only eight o'clock, but he had about seven people in his tent for the early show and we decided it wasn't worth the gas to run the lights for another set like that. So I took Arty with me in his chair. Of course I took guards. We didn't breathe without guards. They were brothers, big boys who had dropped out of college. I forget their names. But these were nice boys. One of them wanted to geek for us. There was trouble with some women's clubs at about that time over cruelty to chickens. But they were nasty white Leghorns anyway. Stupid things. Now, I'd never give a Plymouth Rock or a nice Rhodie to a geek. I love a nice Rhode Island Red. They are the finest breed of chicken. They have character. We used turkeys for a while, too, and they're even stupider than a Leghorn. Albinos they were, blue and red wattles. Al tried out the turkeys because their size made them easier to see in the pit. And white, naturally. The albinos. They take a spotlight so well, and the blood shows so vividly. Now that I think of it, that boy had already been geeking. That's why he wanted to come along. He'd broken a tooth on one of the turkey necks. The bones are so much bigger than a chicken's you know. He was the younger boy. He'd dropped out of Yale, I think, and got Al to *take him on. Then his older brother came to get him to come back to college. They both stayed on as boys will at that age. Especially the clean, well-bred boys.*

'And they always want to strip down and crawl into the blood and mud in the geek pit and scream around, chasing the birds and tearing them to pieces. You could say, well, that's the quickest route. Any other act would take so much time to learn, and that's true. But those boys just get such a kick out of it, you have to laugh. This boy, what was his name . . .? He was good. He had long blond hair and a beard and he'd bury his face in the guts and then snatch his face up and snarl and chatter his teeth at the crowd with gore dripping from his beard. Oh, he had a style about him. But he'd broken a tooth. Got carried away, I dare say.*

'And poor little Arty had been so downcast since the shooting I thought it would be a treat for Arty and I'd be with him by himself. He always just flowered with individual attention, Arty did.*

'So we set out. One of the boys pushed Arty's chair and I walked on one side and the brother walked on the other side of Arty. We weren't far from the main street. It was a small town but a lot of farms in the area. Actually had sidewalks as I recall. We haven't been back there. I can ask Al what town that was. He'll remember. But you know those small prairie towns. Not much paint on the houses, not much grass in the yards. The wind just blisters it off. But the folks are nice, with soft drawls. It couldn't have been more than a couple of blocks to the auction barn. Summer evenings you know, and most folks were up at the dentist's show. A few stayed out rocking on their porches. I remember the geek boy laughing — we none of us believed in this prayer dentistry — that he hoped it worked because his dad was so sore about him quitting school that he'd cancelled his medical and dental insurance.*

'I always liked the cattle smells, hay and milk and dung. We knew the place by the flies. And there was a crowd.*

'That dentist had ten little boys in a white-voice choir. Very sweet and eerie. Remind me to let you listen to the twins' tapes when they were doing white voice. The transition was hard on them, getting the tremolo after their blood flowed. They're still*

*good but their mature voices just don't have the purity and
control that their white voices did. Arty can still white voice if he
wants to, but Oly never did have a white time. I swear that child
cried for titty in a full-throated contralto. Chick still has a pure
little white voice. Sometimes I pass where he's sitting or hear him
in his shower and I think for a moment that he's still a toddler
and I should go make sure he isn't drinking ammonia or something. Isn't it odd that the girls should lose their white voice and
both the boys can still use it? Sometimes I say to Al, "Why is that
. . . ?"*

'Oh no, Arty didn't sing at the dentist. It was the choir and a
few witnesses. Older folks, big jolly men with guts over their
belts standing up next to the dentist showing big gold smiles. It
seems God doesn't use porcelain or amalgam or fancy plastic. He
fills strictly with gold. And some big old farm women who
should have known better.

'The dentist was down in the auction pit with his microphone. Nice-looking man. White hair and spectacles and a quiet
suit. He had a wonderful voice. We stayed in the aisle in the
back because of Arty's chair, which was good because it gave us
a better view than if we'd been up on the bleachers. The dentist
was asking questions. "Do you believe God can heal?" and the
crowd was nice and they liked him and they said, "Yes," a big
yes. "Do you believe God can heal YOU?" and they said, "Yes."
"Do you believe God can fill teeth?" And when the dentist
asked, "Do you believe God can fill YOUR teeth?" we all said yes
to be courteous. It was fun that it was somebody else's show and
we could just go along like paying customers for once.

'Then everybody was praying wild with their mouths open
and their hands waving. The dentist had a good backup line
that it might not happen at that very moment. It might take a
couple of days or even weeks. Still there were plenty of folks
whooping right away that their big hole was filling up with
gold. They were bouncing around looking in each other's mouths
and blessing Jesus. There was no folderol about getting new
teeth. God was a decent dentist. He'd give you a well-fitted
denture but he couldn't grow you a whole new set.

'We laughed all the way back to our lot but, actually, I never
did have any more tooth pain. Eventually all my teeth went and

*this set of plates does me well. But I never had any pain. Arty
would ask me about it and we'd laugh but he seemed to think
about it. He had Oly letter a little card that he taped on his wall.
The thing read, "The only liars bigger than the quack are the
quack's patients." Arty used to just keep me in stitches. Eleven
years old he was then.'*

Arturo to N.S.:
'Why? You're asking me why? You tell me, Mac! I'm not
really in a position to know. You are. Me, I have suspicions. I
suspect people are suckers for a prick. I suspect folks just naturally go belly-up for a snob. Folks figure if a guy acts like he's
King Tut and everybody else is donkey shit, he must be an aristocrat.'

Arturo to N.S.:
'Consider the whole thing as occupational therapy. Power as
cottage industry for the mad. The shepherd is slave to the sheep.
A gardener is in thrall to his carrots. Only a lunatic would want
to be president. These lunatics are created deliberately by those
who wish to be presided over. You've seen it a thousand times.
We create a leader by locating one in the crowd who is standing
up. This may well be because there are no chairs or because his
knees are fused by arthritis. It doesn't matter. We designate this
victim as a "stand-up guy" by the simple expedient of sitting
down around him.'

ARTURISM: *A quasi-religious cult making no representation of a
god or gods, and having nothing to say about life after death.
The cult represents itself as offering earthly sanctuary from the
aggravations of life. Small chalked graffiti, said to be the work
of the Admitted, are found in many locations after the Binewski
carnival has passed through. The phrase 'Peace, Isolation,
Purity' (or sometimes initials P.I.P.) seems to be the slogan.
Many commercial posters distributed in advance of the show
read, 'Arturo knows, All Pain, All Shame, and the Remedy!'*

A fee, called a dowry, is required for entering the novice
stage. The sum varies depending on the novice's resources but the
minimum seems to be around $5,000. Novices are required to
serve for at least three months and sometimes as long as a year as
workers for the cult. Typists, bookkeepers, and organizers are
given longer work periods than labourers. One of the most
important tasks of the work period is serving and caring for cult
members who have already had major portions of their limbs
amputated.

The Admitted must furnish their own travel and living
arrangements. All that is offered in return for the dowry is free
access to Arturo the Aqua Man's shows, and the surgical amputations performed by the Arturan medical staff. Since the medical
staff travels with the carnival, the Admitted must follow the
carnival.

The camp of the Admitted is separated from the carnival camp
by a portable electric fence and a series of manned sentry posts.

The administration is loosely conducted in a large camper
perched on the back of a pickup truck.

The medical facilities consist of a well-equipped surgery in a
large truck trailer with its own power supply. Two large truck
trailers are equipped with monitoring devices and furnished as
post-op recovery rooms. Each trailer has ten beds. A smaller
eight-bed infirmary trailer is always parked near the doctor's
mobile living van, which houses an examining room.

Only one surgeon on the staff, reportedly aided by a skilled
anesthesiologist. Am currently trying to locate credentials and
licensing for the surgeon, a woman who goes by the name of Dr.
Phyllis.

Most nursing chores, feeding, bathing, linen changes, bedpan
provision, etc., are performed by novices in the order.

'The more people we exclude, the more people will want to
join. That's what exclusive means.'

— Arturo to N.S.

INELIGIBLE FOR ADMISSION	GROUNDS
Convicted Felons	Already freaks
Mentally Deranged or Retarded	Unable to make informed decision
Under Age 21 (later 25)	Unable to make informed decision
Over age 65	Already freaks
Chronically Ill	Already freaks
Congenitally Deformed	Already freaks
Accidentally Mutilated	Already freaks

Also excluded, unconditionally, are any who can't provide minimum dowry.

Judgments of degree of deformity that prevents admission are made by administrative staff. Borderline or ambiguous cases (correctable by cosmetic surgery, etc.) may be appealed by applicant for judgment by Arturo, whose decision is final.

ADMITTED WHO BECOME INELIGIBLE FOR FURTHER PROGRESS:

Mentally impaired	Unable to make informed decision
Chronically ill	Already freak — poor surgical risk
Physically weak, deteriorating	Already freak — poor surgical risk

REST HOMES: Theoretically all the Admitted end up at the Arturan rest homes. Administration claims two in existence with plans for twenty more.

Those who become ineligible for progress are sent there quicker but are pitied for having lost access to P.I.P. Those who complete progress (are reduced to head and torso) go to the rest homes with full honors — living, no doubt, the lives of gold-plated pumpkins: bathed, fed, and wheeled around by servants.

Questions: Check death rate (seems unlikely they'd want a

thirty-year-old to live out the allotted twoscore more while being supported by the organization).
Life expectancy?
Numbers of Admitted vs. applicants?
Recidivism, rates?

Attended Policy Meeting: Arty in his office, listening on intercom to conference in the administrative camper. He interjects an occasional remark — hits a button that lights a red bulb in the conference camper. All talk stops in anticipations of HIS voice. Arty, meanwhile, laughing, mimicking the committee members cruelly, with me as his audience. He is constantly informing me that he takes none of it seriously.

The debate is over glands. Should mammaries and testicles be included in progress? (Should they be amputated?) And if so, at what stage of progress, as a final liberating gesture or as preliminary preparation . . . ?

Different committee members present arguments, pro and con, then Arty decides.

Today's conclusion — glands should be included in progress. Order to be taken under advisement by Arturo — decision to be handed down later.

Case of Admitted # 264: Logan M., thirty-four years old — has tithed smallest fingers on each hand. Personal history: Second son of moderately successful insurance salesman and a nurse, raised in Kansas, town, pop. 850. Midwestern University and Chicago. Master's degree in social work. Six years as welfare case worker, no advancement. Three years as juvenile counselor. Two children. Wife (now living in Grand Rapids with kids) has filed for divorce.

Arturan Administrator Theta Moore says Logan M. was rational when admitted but has slipped during progress.

Logan M. lives in a seven-year-old Chevrolet sedan, leases wheelchair. Appears daily at 9 A.M. in show camp with big plastic bag full of day-old bread, used and discarded burger buns, pie crusts, etc. He goes to the cat wagon, parks in front of the screen, and spends an hour or more watching the tigers, leopards, and lions. He scatters the pastry leavings on the ground in front of the cat cage.

Logan M. no longer communicates verbally except to sing — in a cracked falsetto — 'Up to the Land of Kitties!' repeatedly.

CASE DISPOSITION: *Arturo says Logan M. will go to the Missouri Arturan rest home (Camp # 2 near Independence) and will be denied further progress because, Arty says, 'He's off his nut.'*

Conscious decision making is a requisite for progress.

Arturo Binewski, in conversation with N. Sanderson:
'... *if they hang around in groups and avoid outsiders it's not my doing. People generally stick with those who agree with them, anyway.*

'... *Isolation is a standard cult technique but I don't use it. It's standard procedure to get the poor buggers in a low moment, hustle them off to the boonies, and surround them with a strong-arm/soft-spiel combo. How could I do that? I'm a traveling show! Do I seal them into trains and add cars as I make converts? Colonies or communes or reservations are expensive and hard to manage. I've got a weird civil service-style bureaucracy taking hold as it is, and it's a pain in the ass. I don't mind being lord of all I survey but I don't want to have to work at it. It just wouldn't be practical.*

'*As it is, I don't need all that crap. For what I've go to say, the more exposure the folks have to the outside world, the better. Feed 'em newspapers, TV, world reports. Tell 'em about terrorist attacks, mass murders, disease, divorce, crooked politicians, pollution, war and rumours of war! Then go ahead and tell 'em that only fools and half-wits join my outfit. The first half of the news cancels out that particular message. Let the relatives and lovers loose on 'em. All they can stand. Because it's the world that drives them to me. You news guys are my allies. Those soggy wives and cheating husbands and nagging, nutso parents are my best friends.*

'*Didn't you, yourself, turn your back on the whole caboodle? Say the hell with it, and walk away? Truth is, I don't need tricks*

*and traps and brainwashing because I'm giving the poor sorry
sonsabitches what they crave more than air.*

'*See, there's a difference between advertisin' and prosely-
tisin', Norval honey. All I have to do is let 'em know I'm here
and what I stock — corrective surgery! and cheap at the price!*'

Arturo Binewski, in conversation with N. Sanderson:
'... *No. No children. My minimum age limit is twenty-one
and I'm thinking about raising it to twenty-five very soon. Once
in a while we get some maniac who wants his nine-year-old son
or his four-year-old daughter enrolled. No indeed. Not my meat.*

'*Figure it this way. You will anyhow. You been hanging
around politics long enough. I was brought up in a country that
claims you're innocent until you're proven guilty. We protect
children because they have not yet proven themselves to be
hamstrung shitholes. Granted, the odds are lousy that they'll
turn out any other way but it's been known to happen. Isn't that
how you figure it? Seeing how you think I'm punishing all these
folks anyway?*

'*But here, I'll tell you another way to look at it too, just for
fun. I figure a kid doesn't choose. They don't know enough to
choose between chocolate and strawberry, much less between life
and limblessness. Say, just for argument's sake, that I'm really
serious in my own mind about what I offer. Just say I really
think this is a sanctuary. Well, the whole deal depends on
choice. I want people who know what life has to offer and
choose to turn their backs on it. I want no virgins unless they're
sixty years old. I want no peach-cheeked babes who may be
down tonight but will have a whole new attitude after their
morning bowel movement. I want the losers who know they're
losers. I want those who have a choice of tortures and pick me.*

'*I counted up the converts two nights ago and we've got a
Fully Blessed roll of 750 in three years and another 5,000 who
have worked past their first ten digits. You got to figure there's
something going on here. We've got something the folks want.*'

20

The Fix Unfixed

Dr. Phyllis had been working all morning. Arty had given out promotion certificates like cookies all week long. The novices were singing in the hospital trailers, where they watched over the ones who had been promoted that day. Arty was sunbathing on the roof of our van and I sat beside him watching the gentle stir of the midway waking. The awnings were pumped out. The lights all went on at once. The redheads were everywhere, starting the popcorn machines, blowing up balloons at the helium tank, leaning into the greasy vitals of the Mongoose & Cobra ride to make sure the music was synchronized with the lashing of the chairs that the norms would jounce in. The gates were open and the first townies were gawking in at the booths.

On the other side of us, the show camp spread. A line of delicate laundry tossed transparent frills from one of the trailers that housed the redheads.

Far down at the end, where the Arturan camp began, was Doc P.'s white van near the infirmary. All morning there had been a line at the infirmary door as the promoted waited, with their certificates of advancement rubber-stamped in blue ink, for their turn with the Doc. The line was finally gone.

Arty saw her before I did and made a flapping fart-sound of his lips. He was on his belly with his head lifted. I swiveled to look along his line of sight. Dr. Phyllis was marching toward us. She had a straight alley ahead of her and her eyes were fixed on us. Arty ducked his head and lay flat. I watched the cloth of her mask suck in and out against her mouth as she strode along.

'She knows you're up here,' I muttered spitefully. Arty rested one cheek on his blanket and glared at me. She was beside the van now.

Arty sighed. 'Send the elevator for her.'

I scuttled for the small platform and stood on it. 'Coming, doctor!' I called. I waved at Arty as I pushed the descent button.

I hopped off into the dust and Doc P. stepped onto the platform. I tried to look up her white uniform skirt as she went up. I couldn't see past the murk at her knees. Her voice started before the platform stopped.

'Arturo, it's crucial that you reconsider this totally inefficient method! Do you know how many individual digits I did today? Forty-seven!'

I went off for a stroll. There was a clear division between the Fubulon camp and the followers. The show rigs were all tight, tidy, and workable. The followers had strange outfits: pup tents, pickups with campers, tiny trailers that folded out into tents on wheels, several station wagons with bedding and bandages in back, decrepit cars, a converted ice-cream wagon, a bread truck, a pair of ancient Harley-Davidson motorcycles with sidecars. One of the sidecars was shaped like a wooden shoe and the other like a submarine. They belonged to a pair of hard-nosed old thugs, who slept in their sidecars and insisted on having the tattooed skin peeled off their arms and legs as they were removed. They tanned the tattoos and kept them in scrapbooks in their saddlebags. Arty said privately that they would never have joined if they hadn't been old and afflicted with the chickenshits about riding hard in groups. They stuck together and helped each other, scaring off the fawning novices who wanted to suck up to them. Arty was bitter because they were more loyal to each other than to him and because they'd spent a wad on having their cycles converted to tongue-and-jaw controls before they showed up asking for salvation. He was suspicious of them for thinking that far ahead.

I was leaning on a dusty car listening to the soft song from the hospital trailers when the door of the infirmary opened and Norval Sanderson stepped down with a bundle wrapped in a plastic garbage bag. He closed the door behind him and was sauntering coolly away when Horst appeared from behind another van. The big cat man's eyes squinted as he saw Sanderson. 'Well, I swan there, Norval,' hollered Horst. Sanderson eased to a halt and turned graciously. 'Looks,' said Horst in a companionable tone, 'like you've got yourself a tidy-sized chunk of something!'

'Horst, my fine fellow!' cried Sanderson, his fastidiously creased shirt and trousers emphasizing the delicate demonstration of pleased surprise. 'I was just thinking of looking you up for a soothing session over the checkerboard!' Sanderson lifted a pint bottle of bourbon from a rear pocket and offered it. Horst walked all the way around Sanderson slowly, eyeing the plastic-wrapped bundle. Then he stopped beside the reporter and took the bottle. Sanderson was calm and genial.

'Checkers, hunh?' said Horst, unscrewing the cap.

'Outdoors, perhaps,' said Sanderson, 'where can I sit upwind of you.'

Horst slanted a blue glance at Sanderson and tilted the bottle to his lips. 'Aah,' he sighed, and handed the bottle back. 'Now it seems to me that there's some question as to who sits upwind.' Sanderson tipped the bottle, courteously neglecting to wipe the neck on his sleeve. 'By my thinking,' mused Horst, 'a poacher outstinks a cat man any day, and if you've got anything less than a whole thigh in that bundle, I'm a pig's ass.'

Sanderson raised his eyebrows in mock surprise above the angled bottle. He swallowed and looked solemnly over Horst's lanky frame.

'It is an offense, sir,' said Sanderson, 'to justice, to reason, and to the tender female who brought you forth and nurtured you to your present stature, to even consider that you might bear any resemblance to a porcine posterior.' Sanderson nodded gravely at the bottle, shifted the bundle under his arm and took another swig.

'That's my opinion,' said Horst. 'But look here, I thought we had an understanding that you could make do with the bony bits. You get all the fingers and toes anyway.'

Sanderson's shoulders lifted in helpless resignation. 'You have me at a loss. What can I say? Laziness, my dear Horst, will be my downfall.'

They strolled out of earshot as Sanderson handed Horst the bottle and the bundle. Horst tucked one under his arm and the other against his teeth as they disappeared behind a van.

This was their standing argument. Horst wanted the big chunks for his cats. Sanderson had promised to leave the arms and legs and be content with the hands and feet, which were more plentiful anyway. Sanderson hung the bits up on the outside of his van for his maggot crop. It was, he claimed, easier to whack a big chunk on a single hook than to painstakingly string up a shish kebab of small pieces. Horst would carefully explain that hands and feet were useless to him. 'Nothing's surer than my cats would choke on all those little bones. But they'll collect worms just fine.'

Sanderson countered with mild reminiscences of domestic cats stripping fish spines.

Sitting in the dark next to our van on a summer night with the midway roar muted a little way off, Mama was almost invisible in her folding chair. Her hair caught the glow and sometimes a scratch of light hit her long legs as she shifted, folding one leg over the other. It was the after-supper lull, with the chores done and the last shows of the night causing the big tents to glow and billow with the crowd's breath.

I had ushered in Arty's crowd, collected the tickets from the booth, and could sit, waiting for the tent walls to spangle in the rainbow finale of Arty's act. That was my cue to run for the stage exit and help him out of the tank. Mama, after all her years as duenna to the twins' act, had semi-retired. The redheads helped the twins with costumes. Jonathon Tomaini supervised the props. Mama sat outdoors in good weather, crossing and recrossing her legs.

Beside Mama, in my own folding chair, with my feet sticking straight out in front of me, I thought about my innards. Just a few months before I'd had no idea whether my reproductive equipment worked. There was no evidence. But that week I had become a fully-fledged bleeder and was still absorbed by the first change in myself that I had ever noticed. The click and buzz of my synapses kept making the same connection. If you can change, you can also end. Death had always been a theory to me. Now I knew. The terror hurt good and I nursed it and played it like a loose tooth.

'No mosquitoes,' murmured Mama. 'A blessing.'

'A creep!' The shout was from Elly somewhere in the dark.

'Creep! Creep! Creep!'

'Please, just leave us alone,' pleaded Iphy. 'We're quite all right alone.'

'Stay away from us! Don't follow us! Don't wait for us! We don't need your help and we don't want it!' The twins came fast around the end of the van and headed for the low deck that joined the three Binewski units. Behind them, shuffling steadily, wheezing and gurgling, came the stooped figure of the Bag Man.

'Mama, tell him to leave us alone!' The twins swooped past us to their door. The light spilled out of their trailer in a wedge and then disappeared as they slammed inside. The Bag Man's big shadow stopped in front of Mama, hauling in noisy wet air and bobbing in place. The veiled head bent toward the twins' van.

Mama tipped back to look up at the dim hulk. Her hand slipped out to touch my arm. 'Does he understand English?' she whispered. I grunted and she leaned back. Her silver-cloud head nodding slowly in the murk. The Bag Man took in a bale of air and let it out in what might have been a sigh. He lurched over to the deck and sat down with a grunt. He looked ready for a long wait.

Beyond the dark backs of the booths the Ferris wheel started turning. Its flashing bulbs threw a pulse of light over Mama's face. She stared at the wheel.

'That Bag Man,' she murmured. 'He seems so familiar. I'll remember soon.'

Arty laid down the law on the Bag Man. No one but Arty himself and I were to know that the Bag Man was the shootist from that long-ago parking-lot incident. Chick knew the Bag Man was scary, but Chick was resigned to being scared as well as uninformed. As far as anyone else knew, the Bag Man was just another one of Arty's followers.

I was not amazed. It seemed unremarkable that if you failed to murder someone you should become that person's guardian slave. The Bag Man worshipped Arty. Arty did not worship the Bag Man but he made an effort to keep the big lump busy and feeling useful.

I wasn't jealous of the Bag Man even though he took over some of my chores and magnified them. I had been the usual guard in the security room while Arty entertained. The Bag Man set up his residence there. Where I had fidgeted, cramped, sweating resentfully onto the idiot gun, the Bag Man sat on a flimsy cot staring rapidly through the mirror glass hour after hour. As long as Arty was in the room. When Arty went out, the Bag Man trailed after him, looming and snorking like some asthmatic mastiff hypnotized by his master's scent. He waited behind the tank during Arty's show. He lumbered after Arty's electric cart on the way to and from the stage. Where Arty went, there was the Bag Man. When he wasn't looming he dusted and vacuumed, took out trash, emptied waste tanks, and left the more intimate service to me.

I still served Arty's food, took care of his clothes, acted as masseuse and towel brigade for the shows. Arty could give orders to the Bag Man but he could talk to me.

One day in late spring Arty had tried interrogating me: 'What are the twins up to? Why are they so stuck-up lately?'

Arty lay on the rubbing bench, eyes folded to slits watching my face as I pummeled lotion into his ribs and belly.

'I don't know. Maybe they figure you're busy.' I avoided his eyes, concentrating on the rope of muscle above his pelvis.

'I am busy. Are they taking advantage?'

'Don't ask me. I'm busy, too. Roll over.'

He flopped onto his belly and I poured lotion down the deep ditch of spine between his banks of muscle.

'Their gates have been good this year.'

'Not like yours. You're breaking three-ring records every week.'

'They're getting the slops and doing good business. Have they changed their act?'

'Iphy says they're dancing less, and they do play one of their own songs.'

'What are they up to?' His head is cranked up to glare at me.

'Don't twist like that! You'll tighten up on that side!' I could feel the Bag Man's eyes on me from behind the mirror. I started work on Arty's neck and he let the subject drop.

He could have made me tell if he'd pushed. Instead, he sicced the Bag Man on the twins.

'There are more weirdos around all the time,' Arty explained. 'They need their own guard in addition to the general security. Beautiful girls like that. You don't know what might happen.'

The following day the Bag Man had knocked at the door of the twins' domain and handed Elly a small slip of paper torn from his notebook. Iphy leaned to read it:

Arturo the Aqua Man loves you and has sent me to protect you. I will be your guard.

Elly's mouth set thinly. Iphy tried to smile at the Bag Man. 'That's very kind, but . . .'

'Arty means to kill me entirely,' snapped Elly. 'Go away. Tell Arty we don't want you or anyone else guarding us.' Elly closed the door as Iphy called out, 'But it's a kind thought!'

After that the Bag Man followed them everywhere. Elly glared at me accusingly when we met. As Arty's ally I was suspect. One thing about Elly, you were for her or against her. She didn't recognize neutral zones. I sat on the hood of the generator truck polishing Grandpa and wondering what would happen when Arty found out about their paying visitors.

Elly was crying. Iphy looked barely conscious, like a beaten fighter absorbed in the consolations of shock. They were sprawled on the rosy bed, drenched in pink light. Their intricate separateness and unity seemed luxurious in the satin sheets. The nightie was short and sheer and their big, four-armed robe hung in clownish embarrassment, covering the tall mirror on the wall.

Elly grimaced and shook Iphy. 'We'll run away. There are other shows. We'll just go!'

Iphy's eyes opened calmly and I had an uncomfortable feeling that we had been wrong, that Iphy was the strong one. Her placid face quirked at the mouth.

'Don't be stupid. You're panicked. We don't know how to drive. We're too noticeable to sneak.'

'We could go to Mama's sisters in Boston! We could hide in a freight car!' Elly's desperation pumped her from fear to anger.

Iphy backed off gingerly. 'Take a breath, Elly.'

The Bag Man had been following the twins for weeks. This had disrupted their once- or twice-a-month visits from connoisseurs of sexual novelty. But Jonathon Tomaini, who had felt himself defiled by pimping, urged them to take on one special client despite the risk. He had become addicted to his percentage of the profits.

'This is not *just* the state governor, believe me. The man's fortune is legendary. When I realized who he was — I mean, he came to three shows on three consecutive days. The man is utterly fascinated. In LOVE. I knew his face but couldn't place him. He understood *immediately* when I approached him. A gentleman. A man of refined sensibility. He did everything to spare me the humiliation of specific explanations. He made the offer himself, without urging. Ten thousand! Don't tell me it's not worth a little effort on our part!'

It was sheer cantankerous defiance in Elly that made her accept. She wasn't interested in the money or the millionaire. She just hated having Arty cramp her style.

It took me days to figure out what happened that night. The twins had planned carefully. They went to bed early for a solid week to lull the Bag Man into complacence. On the fateful night they turned out the lights at the usual time and waited.

Tomaini was supposed to distract the Bag Man by taking him to the bachelor quarters for a beer and a long talk.

'Get him to tell his story,' Elly ordered. 'He writes so slowly it will take hours. Get him drunk.'

The distinguished visitor arrived at the appointed time, was welcomed, and was settling into some serious exploration.

'He'd had his shower and we'd got him onto the bed and

were just getting really friendly when the door broke open,' explained Iphy. 'I was facing the mirror. I saw the whole thing in the mirror. That's why I threw our robe over it.'

'How was I to know he couldn't hold his liquor?' asked Tomaini. The truth was that Tomaini couldn't hold his beer. Instead of getting the Bag Man to tell his story, Tomaini dwelt on his own favorite subject, himself. The Bag Man recounted the whole episode to Arty. I found a few of the crumbled sheets from his note pad in the trash.

One read: 'He said he could do very special hand jobs because of his piano training. I thought he was going to offer to give me one of these special hand jobs so I got up to leave. He started to cry. He said even if he was ugly he wasn't a freak. Something made me suspicious.'

Another sheet of the notepaper had been torn in two. I pieced it together and read: 'The key worked. I heard sounds behind the bedroom door. A man's voice. I went in. They were on the bed. He was kneeling. Elly was sucking his cock while Iphy licked and kissed his ass. His hands were twisted in their hair.'

I must have known, even then, what my time would be like. I saved these scraps from the Bag Man's hand. I have them still, brown and fragile on the table beside me. Their value to me doesn't come from the blighted hole who scratched the words, it is that they describe mysterious acts by my people. I wonder, for example, if the twins' piano training had given them the Tomaini brand of dexterity with hand jobs? Could a non-musician learn it? Could I?

Children stumble through these most critical acts with no real help from the elders who are so anxious to teach them everything else. We were given rules and taboos for the toilet, the sneeze, the eating of an artichoke. Papa taught us all a particular brush stroke for cleaning our teeth, a special angle for the pen in our hand, the exact words for greeting elders, with fine-tuned distinctions for male, female, show folk, customers, or tradesmen. The twins and Arty were taught to design an act, whether it lasted three minutes or thirty, to tease, coax, and startle a crowd, to build to a crescendo and then disappear in the instant of climax. From what I have come to understand of life, this show skill, this talk-'em, sock-'em, knock-'em-flat information, is as close as we got to that ultimate mystery. I throw death aside. Death is not mysterious. We all understand death far too well and spend chunks of life resisting, ignoring, or explaining away that knowledge.

But this real mystery I have never touched, never scratched. I've seen the tigers with their jaws wide, their fangs buried in each other's throats, and their shadowed hides sizzling, tip to tip. I've seen the young norms tangled and gasping in the shadows between booths. I suspect that, even if I had begun as a norm, the saw-toothed yearning that whirls in me would bend me and spin me colorless, shrink me, scorch every hair from my body, and all invisibly so only my red eyes would blink out glimpses of the furnace thing inside. In fact, I smelled the stench of longing so clearly in the streets that I'm surprised there are not hundreds exactly like me on every corner.

The ten-thousand-dollar john was a prime norm with only a little sag as evidence of his age. His face was wind-dried and his chest had begun the droop that had not yet reached his belly.

He made a speech from the shower, a short, cheerful speech about himself. He'd been poor and he'd made money, he said, he'd changed laws in his time, and killed men and fathered children. He'd seen five million people lining up to punch his name onto a ballot, he'd seen regiments turn and halt and fire because he nodded. 'And I figured I'd come to the end of being amazed. Run out of it, like you'd run out of sugar. But when I saw you lovely girls I thought to myself, maybe there's more to life yet.'

'He said that,' explained Iphy in quiet pleasure, 'as though he were really happy to be here with us. He's the first we ever had who wasn't ashamed and afraid of himself.'

When the Bag Man burst in, Iphy screamed at the mirror. Elly almost vomited on the ten-thou cock and the john leaped clear and snatched at his pants with his eyes alive. He had a gun in those pants, fortunately, and he held it on the wobbling, arm-waving, snorking Bag Man. The Bag Man was horrified. The john was fast with his trousers, and steady with his gun. He shook his head as he circled to the door. 'You don't need shakedowns or badger games, ladies. You could do very well on your own.'

Then he was gone and the Bag Man bent over the foot of the bed and raised his fists and pounded again and again in gurgling voicelessness on the pink and flopping sheets. Elly and Iphy cringed on the pillows at the other end. They heard the car start and the crackling gravel as it rolled away.

The car in the gravel awoke me. It was too close to the vans. I peeked out as the Bag Man began his hammering on Arty's door. The twins' van gaped open with that bright spill into the blackness that always means disaster. I ran in and saw them. Elly was crying. Iphy looked numb. What scared them, what had unstrung Elly, was not knowing what Arty would do.

When Tomaini was doused awake with ice cubes down his shirt front, he talked. He stood, clinging to the back of the visitor's chair in Arty's big room. He gabbled at the floor, the ceiling, the walls, his eyes shifting mightily to avoid the stone-grog form of Arturo, and the menace of the Bag Man at the door.

'I'm a mess! A mess!' yelped Tomaini, his special hands twitching and jumping at his collar, at his buttons, at the stiff strands of his hair.

'How long? Why, months! For many months! Well, since they ... well, I forget how long ... I'm in such a state! They coerced me. They threatened to tell Mr. Binewski that I ... forced myself on them! I was trapped! They were ruthless. Oh, they seem so sweet! Everyone thinks Iphigenia is ... You all do! Miss River-of-Light Iphigenia!'

I watched from behind the mirror in the airless reek from the Bag Man's medicated sheets and saw Arty's face move at last, a small twitch to thaw his lips before trying to speak. He tipped his head at the Bag Man.

'Get his clothes. Some money.' Arty's face closed back up as Tomaini babbled on and the Bag Man flipped open his note-book for a quick scribble. He passed the page to the console table and Arty glanced at it. No more expression on his face than on a grape. Arty nodded.

'The relentless pressure! Like living at the bottom of the sea,' Tomaini was saying as the Bag Man took his elbow and led him gently to the door. 'It's actually a relief that it's over.'

When the twitter lost itself in the distance, Arty was still sitting motionless. I slid off the stool and hit the button that shut off the lamp on his bureau. By the time I got to him his tears were falling. He made no sound at all as I lifted him down from his throne and dragged him over to the bed. He lurched up and rolled onto his belly with his face away from me. I crawled up beside him and patted him but I felt miles away.

'Go.' His voice came, muffled by the coverlet. 'If Chick and the folks are awake tell them everything's O.K. and I'll explain later.'

I went by the console on my way out. The Bag Man's note read: 'Let me break his hands. I'll be careful.'

Mama and Papa were snoring. Chick was sitting up in his bed staring at me when I eased his door open. I put my fingers to my lips. He nodded and I leaned close to him. 'Did you dream?'

He shook his head and touched my arm. 'Want me to stop you hurting?'

'Nah!' I jerked away from him. 'I mean,' I whispered, 'I don't hurt. I don't feel anything.'

'That's weird,' he muttered. He rolled over onto his pillow. His kid face, with a jelly stain on his ear, yawned. 'Seems like there are a lot of people hurting. Seems like I should put them to sleep.' His hands scrabbled at the sheet. He slept.

'Is my face clean? No boogers?' Arty tipped his head back so I could look up his nose. 'Okay. All right.' His eyes were swollen and as red as mine. 'Arty, let me put some ice on your eyes.'

'I want to go now.' He was halfway across the room, humping fast to the door, waiting for me to open it. He brushed past my knee to the platform, turning to the twin's entrance.

'Don't knock. Go in.'

He led the way across the deserted living area, his reach-and-pull locomotion soundless on the carpet. He lunged upright and shouldered the bedroom door open.

Elly glared out of bruised eyes and sneered, 'If it isn't His Holy Armlessness! What an honor!' The twins were sitting up against their bed pillows with their hair wild. The breakfast tray I'd brought was untouched on the table. Iphy looked stern but Elly looked like a mad bat, teeth bared as she peered out from under her eyebrows. Iphy sounded tired and bored. 'What do you want, Arty?'

He leaned there, propped against the door jamb, looking at them. I figured he'd have a set speech ready to flay them with. He'd stare for a while until they were off balance and then spray them with icy words. But when he finally opened his mouth it was the private, alone-in-the-dark Arty who spoke in a thin, scared voice. 'How come?' he asked. 'How come you did that?'

The twins, wide-eyed and wary, were startled too. They had expected 'God' Arty. This feeble and betrayed mortal was a shock. Iphy frowned. Elly's teeth parted but no sound came out.

'I mean,' Arty's forehead folded in peaks of bewilderment, 'you didn't have to do that.' Seeing him like this I was scared. Had the blood exploded in his head? Had his temper triggered some spasm of the brain that changed him? Our fanged armadillo was suddenly peeled, shell-less.

Elly took a breath and got back on her high horse. 'You don't run us, Arty.'

'Oh, hey!' His voice high and ragged.

'We don't worship your ass, Arty. Not at all.'

'Is that it? Iphy, tell me. Did she do it to keep you away from me?' He leaned forward, his flippers slipping on the door frame. A blue vein beat like an angry worm above his ear.

Iphy's shoulders, held tight and high near her neck, relaxed. 'No,' she said. 'I wanted to.'

Arty was back in his van by the time I caught up with him. He swung up into his throne and hit a button on the console with his flipper. He shooed me out. Said he wanted to talk to the Bag Man. I knew when he looked at me that this was our regular Arty, ready to kick ass by remote control.

'*Arty!*'

It was a duet shriek that made me drop Lily's favorite cup onto the counter, cracking off the handle.

The twins were standing in their open doorway with mouths open and arms spread. 'Arty!' they screamed.

The Bag Man's face swam up from the room behind them. His hands closed on Elly's shoulder and Iphy's arm. Iphy looked straight at me with disgust smeared across her face, as the Bag Man pulled them inside.

I followed and saw the twins collapse onto the sofa and the Bag Man standing in front of them writing busily on his notepad. He must have already been there for a while. Slips of paper were strewn on the sofa and on the low table in front of it.

'Arty's in the surgery watching Dr. Phyllis.' I bent to pick up some scraps of paper from the carpet. 'I will be very good to you,' scrawled the Bag Man's hand.

'Oly,' Iphy's tired voice made me look up at her. 'Oly, would you please go get Arty?' The Bag Man bent toward her, handing her his most recent note.

'What's going on?'

'He gave us to the Bag Man,' tittered Elly. 'We're supposed to marry the Bag Man to keep us out of trouble.'

I looked at the wad of notes in my hand. I saw, 'Arty loves you. He knows that I love you.'

'Creepy, hunh?' asked Elly. She grinned at me, and suddenly the twins were giggling hysterically, holding each other's arms, rocking on the sofa. Their two long, lovely feet pointed straight out and tapped the floor in hilarity.

They didn't care how the Bag Man felt, standing there with his bulging veil fluttering around his one blinking eye. They laughed at him, at the idea of him.

Looking at him, I was afraid. When he turned toward me I yelped. His big warm hand clenched softly on the back of my neck and he raised me until my toes barely touched the floor. A high whine pulled out of my throat as he carried me to the door, put me firmly outside, and shut it behind me.

I found Arty in the dark little five-seat theater above the surgery. His silhouette showed against the hot light pouring up out of the glass circle in the floor. I leaned beside him, feeling his coolness as I let my hand brush his bony flippers. He stared, with his chin propped on the rail, down into the surgery. Directly below, a long-haired woman with a white plastic tube mask over her mouth and nose stared up at us. What she saw was a mirror in the ceiling, intensifying the light from the lamps that surrounded it. The woman lay on a white table and was covered to the neck by a white sheet. Next to her head, the small figure of Chick sat, swathed in white, a mask over his nose and mouth, a cap pulled so far down over his hair that it bent his ears out. He wore surgical gloves and was slowly trickling his white plastic fingers through her long brown hair. At the other end of the table was Doc P. in white, hugely fore-shortened, her arms heavy in white sleeves that moved in delib-erate twitches as she worked. The woman on the table stared serenely at us without seeing.

'She's not asleep,' I muttered at Arty's ear.

'She chose not to. He can stop the pain without putting them to sleep. He says most of them like to sleep because knowing and seeing are painful.' Arty stuck his lower lip out and slid it along the railing. 'It kind of goes along with what I'm always spouting, doesn't it?'

'The Bag Man says you gave him the twins.'

Arty's eyes swiveled at me. 'Just to fuck.'

'The Bag Man says "marry."'

'He'd call it that.'

Below us the long-haired woman's eyes turned away from us, her head tilting slightly to look into Chick's masked face. Doc P. was bobbing vigorously at the other end, grabbing tools from the hands of the Admitted nurse, who stood just outside the charmed circle, invisible to us except for the delicate jugglery of glinting tools. Arty watched intently. The climax was evidently approaching.

'A toe?'

'Whole foot.'

With a sweep of her arm, Doc P. flung a messy something toward the bucket on the floor, and accelerated her twiddling of the winking tools.

Arty's eyes focused on the woman's face. Chick's gloved hand rested on her cheek, a small hand. She smiled at Chick.

The smile crept slowly from her eyes, its crease sliding under his stubby fingers.

'Does Chick know we're up here? Can he tell?'

'Don't know. Never asked. Probably.' Arty let go of the railing and flopped into the plush chair behind him. His eyes closed tiredly.

'Arty?'

'Hnnh?'

'It was dumb.'

'Mmm?'

'You shouldn't have done that to the twins, Arty. I know you're sore, but it was stupid. Throwing out the come with the scum, like Papa says.'

His eyes stayed close and a seedling smile sprouted around his mouth. 'Elly will shit bricks to Mars.'

'So will Iphy. Maybe worse.'

'Not Iphy. Iphy can like anybody. That's why she's so powerful. It's easy to fuck up in reading Iphy. Most people don't read her right at all.'

I leaned on the railing, watching him. His eyes were closed again. I tried to think about Iphy being strong.

'But you're right.' He screwed his mouth into the shape of a belly button and then let it fall back. 'It was stupid. Because you know who is going to puke strychnine over it? Me.'

'Yeah,' I said. The light pool was deserted now. Only the long, empty table lay below us. Arty was grinning at me. A floppy bean-shaped smile with eye crinkles to complete the effect. 'How old are you, Toady? Sixteen?' I nodded. My heart was beating at my lungs.

'You bleeding yet? You need a boyfriend? I don't want you running me through this same grinder, you know.'

I could feel the hot pleasure pumping into my face and couldn't keep myself from grinning back at him.

'Nah, I'm your girl, Arty, even with the warts on your ass.'

We giggled and he leaned forward toward me. I caught him in my arms, his chest warm against me, his shoulder blades sliding in my hands. He rubbed his head against my cheek as I squeezed him. 'You always did have shit for brains,' he chuckled. I felt the convulsion of his chest against me with his laugh. 'Think you can still carry me, little sis? Those stairs bruise my ass going down.'

'Oho! That's your trick, is it? Butter me up?'

I propped him and turned around so he could flop onto my hump, clinging to my shoulders with his flippers.

'Don't dig your chin in; that hurts!'

'Your hump is bony! Take it easy!'

I carried him down the narrow stairs to the back of the surgery van, where he'd left his chair and his entourage.

Miz Zegg was waiting with her hands on the push bar of Arty's empty chair. A couple of the administrative novices were hovering with her and they all started to twitter when they saw Arty. Miz Z. came scuttling at me, flapping her hands and nattering, 'Let me help you, Role Model Arturo!' but I spun around and grabbed the chair arms so it wouldn't jump away as I leaned back and spilled Arty into the seat. The novices squeaked and grabbed their long white nightshirts at seeing Arty treated so roughly.

'Don't call me Role Model!' he snapped. 'It's disgusting!'

Miz Z., the latest of Alma Witherspoon's successors to command the administrative office, took a step back and hid her hands in her big sleeves. Arty winked at me and said he'd see me after the show. I gaped in surprise.

'Aren't you coming back to see the twins? They really want you!'

'No.' He shook his head, smiling at me. 'I'm not going to lay eyes on them for as long as I can manage.'

'Arty! You rectum!'

Miz Z. hustled her novices off a few yards so they wouldn't be subjected to the interfamilial indecencies that the Great One allowed to his siblings. Miz Z. didn't know it, but she was going to wait a long time for her turn to get her toes nibbled off. She'd taught business-machine classes in high schools for years and Arty liked the way she ran the office. Arty reached for his chair controls to follow them but I grabbed his ear and glared at him.

'They sent me to get you. What am I gonna tell them?' He blinked and looked back up the narrow staircase leading to the small room on top of the surgery truck.

'Well, I figure the Bag Man is still sort of unpredictable. Why don't you tell them not to struggle too much, not to fight him. I wouldn't want them to get hurt.' He rolled away from me, and the three office ghosties scurried after him. He was off to another meeting, or a visit to the post-op wards, or an interview with some pipsqueak reporter.

I couldn't stand to go back to the twins. The idea of looking at them and telling them 'no hope' made me sweat. I trotted through the morning cool. The sun wasn't high enough yet to fill the shadows between the lines of vans and trailers.

Mama was at the dinette table in our van, deep in one of her assembly-line projects. Twenty-six blue-spangled aprons and matching headbands for the redheads. Glittering cloth ran between her long white hands to its fate under the chattering needle of her sewing machine. I patted her elbow as I came in and she stretched her neck down, offering her cheek automatically for a kiss. A solitary blue sequin was imbedded in the makeup goo next to her nose. I kissed her and picked off the sequin.

'Those twins don't eat breakfast anymore?' she asked. 'They worried about fat? I hardly see them.' The needle gobbled at the cloth and Lil's voice murmured on as I went back toward the big bedroom at the end. The sliding door was half open but the window shades were drawn and the room was heavy with half-filtered heat and the suffocating weight of tobacco. I went for the shelf on Papa's side of the bed. Two books slid aside and I latched onto Papa's blunderbuss pistol. I looked at the safety catch and then stuck the thing into my skirt top, letting my blouse fall loosely over it. The barrel dug me in one spot and the butt gouged me in another. The metal was heavy yet surprisingly warm. I went out pass Mama but she didn't look up.

The twins were rehearsing. I could tell because the Bag Man

was standing at the back steps of their stage truck. As I walked toward him I decided Arty had sicced the Bag Man on the twins just to get the big lump off his own back. The Bag Man started bending and bowing at me while I was still a ways off. I raised a hand and nodded and went up the steps and through the door.

The twins were alone. Another hour before the redheads showed up for fanny-kick practice. Dance, they called it. I saw the dark, gleaming heads bent over the matching sheen of the baby grand. At least they were staying calm enough to comb their hair and do their work.

'The whole cadenza should be written. I don't want any two-bit piano player fucking with improvisation in the middle of my work.' That was Elly.

'All we have to do is place it at the beginning of the move-ment so that it's clearly an integral part.' That was Iphy.

'I'd rather put rude remarks on the score. Here's Oly!'

They both looked up from the music paper, which was spread out on the rack in front of them, and stared past me, eyes flickering anxiously.

'Where's Arty?'

I went close to them, one hand reaching to touch Elly's arm, my eyes glued to Iphy's face. I couldn't look away from her.

When she saw what was in my face her eyes began to die. Their violet deepened to night purple, dull black.

'He's not coming.'

Elly's hand clipped hard to my wrist. 'Did you tell him? What'd he say?'

I wanted to be a street sweeper working nights in Rio, or maybe a florist in Quebec.

'He said the Bag Man is dangerous. Don't struggle. Don't fight him. Arty said he wouldn't want you to get hurt.'

They didn't need to look at each other. They looked at me. Their four hands wandered into a complicated knot in their lap.

'Shall I go to Papa? Maybe Horst? Let me get them.'

The twins were quiet for identical moments like one girl at a mirror. When they spoke it was with the echoing, simultaneous voice that came to them in their rare moments of unity: 'Try, but it won't help.' I nodded, digging under my blouse. 'You remember how this works?'

I set the chunky gun on the shining wood of the piano. It lay there, quiet and nasty. They stared at it. I left before they moved again.

Papa was in the refrigerator truck counting cases of ice-cream sandwiches. I hollered at him that the twins wanted him and he handed his clipboard to one of the lunks who was loading the case. He came down off the truck with an arthritic creak that drowned out my fantasy of him rescuing anybody. I told him where the twins were and went off to visit Grandpa for a while.

Chick was asleep on the hood of the generator truck. His face was in the small green pool of shade cast by Grandpa's urn. The rest of his knobby little body sprawled flat on his belly with his coveralls rucked up to his knees and his socks rumpled down over his sneakers. The skin on his smooth calves looked angry. He must have been asleep there for a while. I pulled his pant legs down to keep the sun off him. He twitched and his baby mouth smacked slightly at the air. The surgical sessions tired him out. The tinkle of music started on the midway. I could hear the whir of a simp twister starting up.

'Chick.'

His eyes opened and his lips closed but the rest of him didn't move.

'Chick, you've got to help the twins.'

He blinked and sat up.

'Did you know Arty gave them to the Bag Man?'

He nodded, stretching and scratching.

I slid over to where I could lean on the urn. 'Wow!' Grandpa was too hot to touch.

Chick licked his lips. 'Arty says the twins are getting married.'

'They don't want to, Chick. They hate the Bag Man. Arty's just doing it to punish them for something. He's got no right to give them to anybody.'

'He gave me to Doc P.' Chick was calm, stating a fact.

'Not the same. You're just with her for a little while to learn stuff.' He didn't answer. 'I sent Papa over to see the twins but he won't be able to do anything. Not when it's Arty's idea.'

'No.' Chick lay down with his sweating face in the tiny pool of shade next to me. The metal hood was burning me through my clothes. A little wind came by and touched my ears.

'Is it nice wearing sunglasses all the time? Is everything green?' He was blinking, getting ready to yawn.

'Chick! Chicky! You could sleep in the twins' van on that pretty sofa. Listen! If anybody tried to hurt them you could stop him. Chick!' His eyes popped open, a puzzled crease came into his forehead.

'Oly, I can't. Arty doesn't want me to. Arty already said I wasn't to do anything. It's like when Mensa Mindy, the Horse with the High I.Q., was scared of the fire hoop and Papa said I mustn't help her. Whatever this is, it's like that for the twins.'

The patient, solid explanation drove me, sliding on my belly, down the fender to the ground. He didn't call after me. I looked back once but he was curled up there on the hot metal with his face in the shade of Grandpa's urn, sleeping.

Papa shook hands with the Bag Man. 'You're going to be joining the family!'

The Bag Man grunted and gurgled and milked Papa's hand with enthusiasm.

'Fine! Fine!' Papa chanted, trying to pull his hand away and looking around for help. 'My little girls in there? I'll just go speak to them! There! Excuse me! Thank you! Splendid to have you aboard! Talk soon!' and Papa escaped into the stage truck.

Iphy and Elly, listening frozen at the keyboard, shared a drooping weight of resignation in their common gut. 'We knew it was no use,' Iphy explained later.

'Ah, there you are, doves! My sweet birds! I just met your betrothed outside! Unusual fella!'

He was too loud, too fast. He flung his arms around them and squeezed them together, planting kisses on their pale matching foreheads. Iphy clutched his hands and spoke softly.

'Papa, please! Don't let Arty do this! Help us!'

'There, dreamlet! Of course I'll help! Nothing but the finest!

'We'll look at the calendar! Shut the whole shebang down for a day! Have a fabulous wedding!'

'Papa, listen! No. No. We don't want to marry him! We hate him! We're afraid of him! Arty is trying to force us — to punish us! Papa, don't let him do it!'

Now Papa, imprisoned in the four white arms, was wriggling to escape.

'Oh, my sweetlings! You're mistaken! Your brother talked the whole thing over with me early this morning. He means the best for you. Given it a lot of thought! This Bag Man — Vern, is it? Don't know him, myself. Seen him tagging after your brother, of course. Arty swears by him! Solid as Gibraltar! Loves you dearly! Do right by you! Natural fears, girlish hesitation! Even your mother! Thought of doing a bunk on our wedding day! Where would I be? I ask you!'

He was a large, determined man with many years of experience in slipper maneuvers. They couldn't hold him. He was still talking fast in the bombastic shorthand of the huckster as he sidled toward the exit.

'Papa,' they chorused, 'help us!'

'Adore! Adore you, my butterflies! Your mother will be so proud!' and he was gone.

The twins sat back down on the piano bench. Iphy, who told me this later, says they were both thinking about the gun.

'We didn't really expect any help from Papa. But we'd stuck that gun into the storage space in the piano bench. You know how the top lifts up? We were sitting on that gun and the idea of it seemed to crawl up inside us like a snake between our legs.'

I hid, sulking in my cupboard under the sink with Mama's sewing machine gabbling a few feet away. Mama was not alarmed at my hiding in there with the door shut. She was glad of the company and talked fitfully to her hands, needing no answers. She was mainly preoccupied with lunch and the way the meal symbolized the breakdown of the family.

'Nobody shows up. They wander in three hours late, sniffling and expecting ... But I am not running a short-order house.... That Chick is ill and I know it and Al and all his pills and potions can claim to heaven that there's nothing wrong but you cannot fool a mother about her own ... drifting ... caught up in alien currents leading mercy knows where.... Next thing we'll get a telephone call and never even notice they left.'

I was going over the list of possibilities. I wondered about Horst or a few of the old wheelmen, or even the redheads. Papa's cronies, Horst included, would never interfere with Binewski's business. If I went to the redheads they might do something. I fantasized marching legions of angry women in high heels and bulging blouses. Then I imagined Papa standing in the dust of the midway with his arms crossed on his chest watching them come toward him and waiting for the exact moment to bellow, 'You're all shit-canned! Pick up your checks!'

What made me really sick was that I didn't want the twins to be rescued. I was glad Arty was mad at them, delighted that he didn't want to see them, cock-a-hoop delirious at the thought of them utterly out of the running for Arty's attention. Big, festering chunks of my heart glowed with a dank cave light of celebration at their lovely talented lives trapped by the Bag Man.

The Twin Club girls who collected the Elly and Iphy posters, autographs, and photos, the duos of vapor-skulled gigglers who showed up in souvenir twin shirts and homemade twin shirts, what would the twin fans think of their glamorous idols being humped by the tube-faced Bag Man? Gross! Gawwwd!

But I hated myself for that gloating. The pleasure terrified me. What if I were really a monster? What if they were really miserable and I didn't do my best to help? What kind of thing would that make me?

'One-thirty, dove!' called Mama. I crawled out of the cupboard and went off to the dressing room to grease Arty for the two o'clock show.

'He must have shut down all the alarms and had Arty give the high sign to the guards. Elly grabbed the gun when we heard the outside door. We sat there in bed waiting for the bedroom door to open. She was ready to use it, but he knocked.

'It was a shy knock ... three gentle taps ... and then the door opened slowly and he peered around it. He waved hello. I felt sorry for him. He seemed so shy. Elly waved the pistol and hollered that she'd shoot. But he just came in slowly, kind of bobbing and bowing apologetically with every step. He sat down at the foot of the bed with his veil puffing in and out and his one sad eye peeping at us. He took out his note pad. There was a message ready on the first sheet. He tore it off and handed it to me. It said, "I love you. Please let me be tender to you."

'While I was reading it he was writing another. The new note said, "If you would rather kill me, it will be O.K." Elly looked at the note and drew a bead on his head. His hands came up and opened his shirt at the throat. He pulled it open and patted his bare chest. The veil came untucked and I could see the plastic bag that hung there and a section of hose hanging down. Elly sat with her elbows propped on our knee, both hands aiming the pistol. She waited a long time. The Bag Man was very still, waiting. Finally she just dropped the gun and looked at me. She said, "I wish he hadn't knocked. I could have done it if he'd just opened the door without knocking." It was a lot worse for Elly than it was for me. She isn't used to doing things that aren't her idea.'

Arty heard the shot and was clambering into his chair when I roared in.

'Mama's in there! With the twins! She just went in!'

'Quick! Push me! It's faster!'

Rushing, terrified, I jammed a wheel on the door and nearly pitched Arty out on his head. The cry came, high and thin. The twins were screaming as we leaped through their living room and rushed the bedroom door.

Mama stood calmly beside the big bed. The soft pink light from the gauze lamps made her look lovely. Her face was bright and tender. Her hair drooped charmingly. Her robe and fluffy high-heeled slippers were oddly tidy; the sash of the robe, for example, was tied in a neat bow.

The twins were hunched in one corner of the bed. Iphy was blinking dazedly at Mama and wincing as Elly heaved her private sector of their guts out onto the carpet.

The Bag Man lay dead and pantsless on the filth-smeared bed. His long naked legs looked bony and floppy at the same time.

'Mama,' Arty said. She turned and nodded at us.

'I finally remembered where I'd see him before.' She looked down at the dark gun in her hands. 'Oly, dear, this looks like your Papa's gun. Would you be so kind as to check the shelf next to my bed? And would you ask ... Oh, here's Al now.'

I'd been asleep when I heard the creaking. Peeking out of my cupboard I saw Mama, white hair glowing in the moonlight, passing through the twins' unguarded door. I was pulling on a robe to follow her when I heard the shot. I jumped to get Arty.

From the files of Norval Sanderson:

Crystal Lil's story, as told to investigating officers (transcribed from tape):

'I couldn't sleep. The moon affects me. I was sitting up in bed, looking out through the small window on my side. Al has always insisted that I sleep on the inside, and he sleeps nearest the door in every bed we've ever shared. It's his protective instinct. He feels that if an intruder were to come through the door he, Al, you know, could defend me. But I had lifted a corner of the curtain so I could look out.

'The moon throws a new and sometimes more attractive perspective on familiar objects, I'm sure you know. But that was how I happened to see this person approach the steps up to the platform. He strode past the window fairly close and the silver light of the moon on his shoulders let me really examine his gait. Gait and carriage, I always tell the children, are such powerful indicators of character. Suddenly I recalled where I had seen this man before, with his stooping head crouched down on his bent neck.

'I thank the merciful stars I was in time. My poor girls. But there, they'll be all right. Quite a miracle that the gun had fallen

*to the floor where it caught my eye. The Bag Man must have
stolen it. Imagine threatening those helpless girls. I meant to
strike him in the heart, but it was an awkward angle with him
on top of the girls, naked below and his shirt unbuttoned so it
flopped and I couldn't tell where to aim, exactly. I had to shoot
from the side or risk the bullet piercing him and going on to
injure the twins. Al always loaded a soft slug, though, for
stopping power. Al was right as usual.'*

Papa hunched over his hands as though his chest was ready to
explode.

'Son, Arty, did you know that this was the guy who tried to
kill you all? Did you know this was the guy from Coos Bay?'

Arty, grey-faced even under the warm gold light of his
reading lamp, shook his head. 'Of course not, Papa. We're very
lucky Mama remembered him.'

'Sweet, frosted globes of the virgin,' breathed Al. 'Imagine
him haunting us all these years. I'll go batso thinking. All that
time. All those chances. Me and my half-assed security.'

Arty leaned against his chair arm, head drooping in fatigue.
'Well, Mama was just in time.'

Elly's face, twisted by revulsion: 'But she *wasn't* in time! He
came when she pulled the trigger. He spurted like a cockroach
oozing eggs as it dies!'

Iphy, calmly: 'Normally we use a spermicide in our diaph-
ragm, but we weren't ready for him and he wouldn't let us put
it in.'

The police wore green wool uniforms. They came in large
groups. The ones who were not actually taking notes, photographs, or fingerprints, or asking questions, took the opportunity to stroll the colorless midway at dawn. When two
patrolmen discovered the redheads' dorm trailers, three more
cops sailed in to question these 'important corroborative
witnesses,' who happened to be making large pots of coffee

while wearing various interpretations of the nightie, negligee, shortie pajamas, and so on.

The coroner drove away in the back of the ambulance with the medical examiner and the Bag Man's body. The officer in charge of the investigation was a heavy, deliberate man with more cheek than neck, and small, steady eyes. He spent a long time with Crystal Lil in the sea-green/sky-blue living room of the twins' van. Lil sat, ladylike and calm on the sofa, while the plainclothes officer leaned over his knees on the chair in front of her, listening, nodding, taking notes on a small spiral-bound pad. Speaking very little, checking his cassette recorder occasionally.

When a uniformed kid came in to hand him a typed sheet, the big man read it slowly, folded it carefully, and tucked the thin paper into his breast pocket.

'Mrs. Binewski ...'

'Lily, please, Lieutenant.'

'Thank you, Lily. We've just received confirmation from Oregon. The fingerprints match those of Vern Bogner, who was convicted of attempting to murder you and your children almost ten years ago. My report will say that Bogner was killed while attempting felonious assault, specifically rape. No charges will be brought. Oregon's been looking for this guy for eighteen months. He left his mother's custody and didn't report to his caseworker.'

'Is this Utah?' Lil asked. 'Are we in Utah?'

'No, ma'am, Nebraska.'

'Why, I could have sworn Utah to look at your troops. So tidy. So disciplined. I would have thought Utah, with their boots polished just so. You must be very proud.'

21

On the Lam

Papa, old in his chair, and Mama, crocheting and dreaming with her eyes open, as we all pretended that this was a night of children and stories like the old days. Only Arty was missing, off alone in his van. The twins held Chick, who was reading aloud to them, and I sat on the floor with my hump warm against Papa's bony leg.

'"What makes you look so white?" said Files-on-Parade.

' "I'm dreadin' what I've got to watch," the Color-Sergeant said.'

Chick's voice, sharp as glass in its chanting, stopped abruptly as he sprang off the twins' lap and whirled around to look at them.

'Did a pin stick you?' The twins' surprised faces opened. Chick shook his head, frowning.

'Ah, the boy's tired of hanging Danny Deever. Too glum!' growled Papa. 'Let him cremate Sam McGee instead. Come, boychik, begin, "There are strange things done!" and give it a roll this time! Breathe from your crotch up!'

But Chick wouldn't recite and he wouldn't crawl up on the twins' lap anymore but came and sat by me while Papa boomed through Sam McGee and we all did north-wind noises, dog-team yappings, and the ghostly voice saying, 'Close that door!'

Papa tottered off to bed soon afterward and Mama went in for her shower. That's when the twins pounced on Chick. He blushed and stammered. He hadn't meant to hurt their feelings.

'But why did you look like that?'

'I just didn't know you had that little guy in there with you. It surprised me. Then I didn't want to lean on him. I thought it might hurt him.'

The matching faces were as grey as old meat. 'What little guy?'

'That one, asleep there,' and Chick pointed. Which is how the twins discovered that they were pregnant for sure.

'We're not going to sit waiting in that fucking infirmary tent with all those slimy norms drooling at us!' So Elly said. Iphy pointed out that Doc P. refused to see them otherwise, and they had no choice.

'Come with us. Oly. Stay with us when she examines us. We're scared of her.'

So we sat on folding chairs against the sunlit canvas wall and listened to the flies buzzing high up around the center pole, and to the twittering of the dozen or so amputees who were waiting in wheelchairs (if they were past the foot stage) or on folding chairs if they were still working on fingers and toes. Chick came and sat beside me with an exotic-bird coloring book and a handful of coloring pens, whiling away his free hour by filling in the eyes on the peacock's tail with slow, painstaking blue. 'Doc P. says this is good for my hands,' Chick explained. None of Arty's followers spoke to us but they all looked at us out of the corners of their eyes. I sat counting the fading yellow grass blades dying beneath the chairs.

When Doc P.'s nurse finally led us up the steps to the examining room of the clinic, Doc P. was not pleased to see us.

'If Chick says you're pregnant and you've missed your period, there's no use wasting my time. You're pregnant. Anyway, I'm a surgeon, not an obstetrician. Your father is the one you should talk to. He's got experience in this field.'

The twins leaned on the examining table, looking humble. She didn't ask them to sit down. She sat, thick and puffy white, masked and gloved, behind her white metal desk, doing spider-mirror pushups with her fingers touching. I was afraid and the twins were afraid. Doc P. was not our turf at all.

'What they wanted,' I croaked, 'was to get rid of it.' The

twins nodded on alternate beats. Doc P. rose up slowly, her white masked face pushed forward, her thick glass lenses winking intently.

'Presumably these talented singers can speak. You have tongues?'

I glanced at the twins, half-expecting them to shove their tongues out in dutiful demonstration.

'Rid of it? Rid of it?' Doc P. crooned.

The twins nodded in miserable syncopation.

'And Papa wouldn't like? Papa wouldn't do it? No. Papa would want you to hatch the monster, wouldn't he? It's been years since poor old Al has had a baby to play with, hasn't it?'

The seeping acid in Dr. Phyllis's tone wore at my bones, peeling my teeth. I tugged at Elly's hand, wanting to leave, but they were staring at her as she sat back down and clasped her hands on the desk in front of her.

'No. I could nip it out of you in five minutes and no harm done. Don't think I couldn't. But I'm not going to, and I'll tell you why. I have a contract with your Arturo, and young Arturo does not wish it. He is looking forward to being an uncle. It's not for me to deny Arturo this pleasure. And it's not for you to defy him. Drink milk. Eat greens. Your abdominal muscles are strong. It will be months before you show. And one last bit of healthful advice. Whatever you've been doing to make Arturo angry, stop it.'

We slogged out past the blank-eyed patients waiting to have their stumps examined.

'It's odd,' Iphy said as we went towards the Chute, 'that's the first time we've ever spoken to her.'

'You never said a word,' I pointed out.

'We've never had anything to do with her or Arty's crowd. Don't they make you feel strange? They're always around, underfoot. That slum camp stretches for acres, but we don't really know what they're doing or why. Should we find out? Are you going to vomit? Elly?'

And Elly did, in the dust between the refrigerator truck and the cat wagon.

* * *

'I was going home for lunch,' said Chick, 'when the twins went boo from behind the cat wagon. I didn't know they were there. They got mixed up with the cats in my head. Elly said I would pick that little guy out of their belly. Iphy too. They wanted me to. I felt kind of surprised thinking maybe I could help them, do something for them, not just moving furniture. Then I felt around, reached in to see what it was like inside, see if I could do it. I try not to go inside people. Sometimes it happens by accident, like sitting on their lap that little guy came out at me! That's what I do for Doc P. and I try not to do it the rest of the time. But the little guy is there, all right. I told them I couldn't do anything to the little guy, that you'd told me specially not to, not to do anything to get the little guy out of them. Iphy went away into herself but Elly scared me.'

'How?' asked Arty. 'Did she yell? Or think hate thoughts? She didn't hit you, did she?'

'No. She pushed OUT, like a thing that won't die.'

'Did you ever get any lunch? No? Those girls in the office made pie. Cut me a slice too. And let's see if you can tell whether I want banana cream or chocolate.'

'Arty, I can't do that.'

'Try.'

'You know I can't.'

From the files of Norval Sanderson:

Chaos rules — midway shut down for the first time in years — Arturo in a genuine frenzy — sweating heavily at the radio transmitter in his van — speaking calmly while his whole body twitches, jerks and writhes in his chair. His shorts and a green velvet shirt, sodden black with sweat, the vinyl of his seat smeared with sweat, Arty's bald pate dripping sweat into his eyes. Little Oly stands by with an endless supply of tissues to mop his face, wipe his eyes. She runs errands. His voice stays clear, unhurried, precise as it goes out over the transmitter.

Big Binewski pops in and out with his mustache tangled — the mother's collapsed in bed with a redhead in attendance — the youngest, Chick, is out with the posse — Arty, at the radio, is in direct contact with fifteen vehicles full of Binewski guards and other show employees — all looking for the twins, Electra and Iphigenia, who have run away from home.

Oly, the faithful watchdog, insists that the twins have been abducted. Oly keeps trying to shoo me out of the van, away from Arty, but I see enough. For example — Arty is sending the posse to clinics and doctors — the addresses found for him by Oly, who leafs through a stack of local phone books that may cover three states. Oly is getting testy at not being able to get rid of me and Arty evidently doesn't care. I decide to let her shoo me. This looks like an all-day session.

Finally she nods me off to the door as though to give me a private word. Turns out she is changing tactics — wants me to go check on Crystal Lil, see if the old broad is still alive, and then — Oly the cool one — would I just drop in on the Admitted Office and see that the Arturans stay calm in the face of this unexpected interruption of routine? Arty is saying, 'Chick, are you hearing me? What about the nurse practitioner service I gave you? . . . Should be within a mile of where you are now . . . ' with the voice of men discussing mild weather.

Standing on the step, I look down at Oly — teasing her that I may change my mind and come back in after all. 'Tell me, Oly, why is Arty so upset? I've never seen him like this!' She shrugs her hump and twists her frog mouth into a pained grin, 'Family. The Binewskis are big on family.'

I stroll over to the redheads' dormitory trailers. They are deserted except for buxom Bella, with a chaw in her jaw, perched in an open door so she can spit at the next trailer while painting her toenails.

Bella snorts at the twins' absence — explains that they've gone off with Rita (the redhead) and Rita's sweetie, McFee, in McFee's elderly pickup. The twins are knocked up, explains Bella, 'probably by that pus sack, the Big Man' — and the girls are looking to get 'scraped out' (searching for an abortion) despite 'His Armlessness, His Almighty Leglessness' having forbid it.

**** *Redheads reading magazines in the Binewski van say*

Crystal Lil is asleep on pills.

**** *The Arturan office queen, Miz Z., unperturbed, has her battalion of campers contemplating their stumps and meditating on P.I.P. (Peace, Isolation, Purity) — generally lollygagging in the sun and oblivious of the situation on the other side of the fence. As long as lunch and supper happen, they won't notice.*

**** *Randy J. — a Binewski guard and ex-Marine who was driving the van when the twins were located. Randy says it was an OB-Gyn office — Chick spotted the pickup and the Rita redhead smoking a cigarette out front. The vigilantes busted in. . . .*

'They were up on the table on their hands and knees, bare ass sticking up in the air kind of pitiful with the nurse getting 'em ready. See us, they about go to the moon, jump down screaming, try to break out the window. I scared they'd hurt themselves, catch hell from the boss. But, Jesus, that little bugger, Chick, steps through and looks at 'em, down they go to sleep in a pile on the floor. We just sort through for arms and legs, tote 'em out to the van and the nurse and the doc dithering behind us. Rita and McFee gone. Jumped in that beat-up old Dodge and gone. Know they're in up to their ass, see?

'Them twins sleep sweet in the back all the way here. That boy Chick did something. Some hypnotism, maybe. Tell you, it scared the shit outa me. You shoulda seen it!'

Which I assume, means that the twins fainted. They're locked in their trailer under guard now as we move on.

Arty is laid up. He's staying in his trailer van. He's got a bandage across one ear and on the cheek on the same side, and a thick dressing on his neck just below that ear. A thin scratch on his chest is visible — just the end of it — at the edge of his shirt collar. He is NOT explaining the damage. He's moody — an anger that alternates with what I suspect is grief. All very controlled, of course. He discusses philosophy. Talks Arturism. Nothing personal allowed.

Oly, his maid of all work, is running constantly between Arty's van and the twins.

The twins are jailed in their van, incommunicado.

The redheads say (buxom Bella, jouncing Jennifer, and Vicki) that Arty went into the twins' van just as they were coming around — waking up from their capture at the doctor's office.

'His Armlessness, the Mighty Fin, was gonna read 'em the riot act. He's all high and mighty and they flipped out on him.'

'Just Elly. She went for him. Tried to bite out his jugular. Iphy couldn't stop her. That Elly's a rocket to Reno when she's rolling.'

'He's in there alone, see. Just the pinky, Oly, to wheel his chair. Oly screams for the guard and jumps on Elly, trying to pull her off. You catch her without her sunglasses you'll see. Oly's got a doozy of a shiner.'

'A week off is what they're saying. First time this show's been closed down that long in more than eighteen years. I can use it. Fine by me.'

Caught Chick crushing ants today in the dust. Shocked me. He's very gentle, usually. I've seen him watch his feet not to step on a bug. Feels terrible if he kills one by accident. I went out to check on the fly farm and heard a muffled thumping around back. There was Chick, dancing and stamping on a small anthill. His face red, eyes glaring, respiration fast. When he saw me he stopped, stood still, looked down at the ground around his feet and burst out bawling. Scrawny ten-year-old kid, wailing like his heart was boiling out through his ears.

I picked him up and took him over to the water tank. Dabbed my hanky under the tap and washed his face and waited for the storm to ease. He leaned on my knee and tried to get a grip on himself. Touched my own crusty heart, I admit. Brave little bastard. Finally started asking questions but got little out of him.

Total gist: He tries 'to be good and help but it seems like everything turns out wrong' and he's 'no good to anybody and ends up hurting instead of helping people.' Pretty heavy load for a tyke.

I beat the bush, working around some of the wild stories they tell about him in the midway. He got embarrassed. Clammed up. At last he says, 'They can't figure out why all the other kids are special and I'm not. They make stuff up, crazy stuff, so I'll seem special too.'

Maybe this crew is getting to me. Maybe I sat too close to too many big explosions and the miniature ruptures in my brain are spreading over to dementia pugilistica. Maybe it's just me being contrary.

The hell of it is, Chick's explanation was a replica of what I've been telling myself all along. But, when he told me precisely that, I didn't believe a word of it. What the hell does he do with that fat spider Doc P.? How come a ten-year-old kid runs the anesthetic for every operation? Some of the stump folks claim it's just air coming through the mask and that the real painkiller is Chick himself. How many times have I heard people claim that their pain disappears the instant Chick comes near them? I've had no discomfort during my surgery but I never noticed anything about Chick. He's just there. I'll pay closer attention next time.

Here I am trying to make a case for healing powers or mental fingers or some such hog wallop. The kid's a colorless little drudge with an inferiority complex at not being a freak like his brother and sisters. He overcompensates with an idiot sensitivity halfway to martyrdom. The perfect patsy. Anything to please. Christ knows, anybody with Arty for a brother is in deep water trying to preserve his self-esteem.

So — the kid says he thinks when he dies all the creatures he has ever hurt will be waiting for him, looking at him, still hurting from the hurt he laid on them. . . . Says he was walking along 'just now' and stepped on a lone ant before he noticed it. 'Failed again as usual' seems to be his feeling. So he flips off the rails and goes beserk on the anthill.

Ike Thiebault, the guard, sits on a folding yellow plastic deck chair next to the door of the twins' van. He nods peaceably at everyone entering or leaving the Binewski van or Arty's van. The portable 'porch' or platform on which Ike sits has steps at one end, a ramp for Arty's chair on the side, and is supposed to have a reticuled flex tunnel over it to keep out the weather. The Binewskis never get around to setting up the tunnel.

Today — 10 A.M. or so — Jouncing Jenny, the redhead who complains about having to color her 'honey-blond' hair, comes up the step with an armload of magazines and catalogues.

'Ike, honey, these are for the twins. I got to deliver 'em,' she says. Ike, who is halfway through a self-help book promising him a method for making money in his spare time, stands up, embarrassed.

'Nobody goes in, Jenny. That's my orders.'

'These are catalogues that just got here in the mail bag. It's just clothes and knickknacks. No harm. The twins want 'em to shop from.' Jenny is rolling her bare golden shoulder at Ike and being gently provocative. Ike is far from immune but locked into his duty.

'Only ones can go in or out is Miss Oly and Mr. Arty. That's my orders.'

'Well, Ike, you take 'em in. It don't matter. The girls want them catalogues. Ordered 'em six weeks ago. You take 'em in.'

'Jenny, you'll think I'm a fool but I can't. I can't go in myself.'

'You can't knock on the door and stand outside and hand in a few catalogues?' Jenny's eyebrows, plucked to whispers, are expressing delicate but scornful disbelief. Ike takes offense.

'Listen, you knock on Arty's door and ask him.'

Jenny backs down immediately. 'I'll just leave 'em here, Ike. If Miss Oly goes in you ask her kindly would she take these catalogues to her sisters.'

2 P.M. Midway swinging noisily in background.

Crystal Lil trips eagerly out of the door of the Big B van with a hunk of sea-green cloth in her hands. Lil has recently gone over to 'sensible walking shoes' as part of her 'Grandma' image but she hasn't adjusted to the low heels and still tends to tiptoe. This is the first time I've seen her wear her spectacles out of the van. She looks energetic and cheery and has, no doubt, just popped an upper or two. She reaches to knock on the twins' door and poor Ike, the guard, hauls himself out of his deck chair stuttering.

'Beg your pardon, ma'am . . .' and the rest I can't hear. It's

obvious he won't let her in to see the twins. She's incredulous. He's embarrassed. It's one thing to turn away a redhead and another thing entirely to refuse the Boss Mom. Her body stiffens as his message becomes real to her. She is suddenly very old, three hundred years' worth of iron-spined Bostonian motherhood. He withers, shuffling, unable to look at her, apparently referring her to Arty. She marches to Arty's door with the blue-green cloth trailing, revealing its form as it flaps behind her — a two-necked, four-armed maternity dress, its hem pitched sketchily in place, its seams unfinished. Arty's door stays closed. No answer. Lil bunches the dress in her fists and lurches back to her own van. Her hair strikes me as grey today, rather than white.

22

Nose Spites Face, Lip Disappears

Arty ordered the twins' tent broken down. Zephir McGurk set to figuring how to use the materials to enlarge Arty's tent. The twins' stage truck remained, closed up for travel. The big piano gathered dust.

Crystal Lil was upset. Papa spent hours trying to calm her. She said the twins had been 'closed down'. He used the word 'sabbatical'.

'They'll have their hands full with the baby.' He'd say, 'Remember how tired you got? They're strong enough, but, Lily, they're beginning to show. They can't be on stage with a bulging belly. We'd have riots in the tents. Investigations.'

'Al, they're not yet nineteen years old. If they stop working now, they'll drift. They shouldn't be idle. And why can't I see them? They need me.'

'It's an adjustment period for them. Settling to the idea of motherhood.'

'Sounds like something Arty would say.'

The security booth looking into Arty's big room was my responsibility again. The cot had been moved out and only the tall stool and the gun occupied the bare cubicle. I could still smell the medicine and sweat and the faint reek of decay that the Bag Man had left behind. I arranged myself on the stool and stared through the one-way glass into Arty's big room. Gradually my legs, in fact my whole ass, went to sleep. Numb and useless. But I was lucky. It was spewing rain outside and

Arty's cuddler for the evening was sitting on the propane tank under his window holding a soggy hunk of newspaper over her hair. By the time he let her in she would look like a smeared possum rather than the tight-bunned little cunt notcher she was. I forget her name. They were all Didi or Lisa or Suki in those days. He'd pick them out of the norm screamers at the gate when he came through after his show. They'd be jumping and howling for a look at him as he came out the back of the stage truck in his golf cart. He'd lean back, grin lots of teeth around the control bulb in his mouth, and drive past the chain-link fence to let them see him. If he stopped the cart I, or one of the security guards, would get his instructions.

'The one in the pink halter top,' he'd say. Or, 'They're all cows in this town. Where are we again?'

'Great Falls,' I'd say.

'Well, get me that rhino in the sequined jump suit and the ostrich in the red skirt.'

I'd stump over to the fence as he drove off to his van.

'Me?' they'd squeal when I waved for them to come up to the fence.

'Me?'

I'd leave them to wait, either in the 'green room,' as Arty called McGurk's station wagon, or on the propane tank outside Arty's window. It was the only chore for Arty that I preferred letting someone else do.

This particular Lulu was stuck in a filthy January rainstorm for three hours by my reckoning, because Arty was in conference with his chief technical advisor, Doc Phyllis.

'What I'd really like ...' Arty was wallowing on his satin bedspread, wearing only cotton briefs. His fins plucked and smoothed the satin. He rolled the bare skin of his head against the slick, warm fabric and arched his back, digging his shoulder blades into the softness.

'Do tell,' murmured Doc Phyllis. She lounged in her chair, one white-stockinged leg and her squeegee shoe flopped over the arm. Her glasses glittered between her white cap and her surgical mask. She had a straight shot at Arty and was probably dissecting his hip and shoulder joints in her head.

'I'm curious about the possibility of separating the twins,' Arty said. Dr. Phyllis grunted.

'Can't be done. I told you that years ago.'

Arty yawned, wiggling. 'Well, I thought you'd be keeping up with new techniques and developments.'

Doc P. was not to be goaded. 'Nothing to do with technique. It's the way they're built.'

Arty flipped over on his belly and looked straight at her. 'What if I was willing to sacrifice one twin to keep the other?'

'Which one?' inquired Dr. Phyllis sweetly.

Arty smiled. 'It doesn't matter.'

Miz Z. was leaving as I came into Arty's place a few days later. She waved a folder at me by way of hello and I caught the words 'Dime Box' on the fly. Arty was in his crisp young executive mode but I asked him about it when she was gone.

'You remember Roxanne? The motorcycle mechanic in Dime Box?'

'Horst's leather-tit girl with the laugh?'

'She's managing the P.I.P. home in Texas. Nine acres outside of Old Dime Box. It's only been open to guests for three months but it's already getting popular.'

Doc P. and Chick were on their way over so I went into the security room. I arranged myself on the stool and tried breathing through my mouth to dilute the medicinal smell.

Doc P. was sitting so straight that her plump white spine never touched the back of the dark padded visitor's chair. Chick was lolling on the carpet with one shoe untied and both socks crumpled down. A small pencil stood on its pointed tip on his bent knee. The pencil rocked steadily like a metronome, broke rhythm for a tiny jig, and then lapsed into a four-four waltz in the space of a thumbnail on his denim-covered knee.

Arty leaned forward against his desk and examined Chick thoughtfully. Arty in his grey vest, Arty in his white collared shirt and black silk tie. Arty with his slim fin bones touching the gleaming wood of the desk. Arty with his pure round skull clearly visible beneath the skin and a blue vein ticking above his ear. He spoke tenderly to Chick.

'Dr. Phyllis tells me that you aren't happy about my plan for the twins.'

Chick's eyes flicked briefly away from the dancing pencil to Arty's face, then back to the pencil. Arty lowered his own eyes.

'Tell me about it, Chick.'

Doc P., with her white-gloved hands asleep in her big lap, blinked calmly at the wall behind Arty and sat very straight in her chair. The pencil fell off Chick's knee to the carpet. Chick sat up and hugged his knees.

'Not good. Not good, Arty. You know.'

Arty's face was hot and still with knowing.

'If you do that,' Chick stared, amazed, as though he had just discovered a wonder, 'I'm not even going to like you, Arty!'

What amazed Chick was no surprise to Arty. Not being liked was familiar ground and all his usual contrivances went into gear. His face slid smoothly into a cartoon of sympathy.

'Why, Chicken Licken, my boy, that's O.K. That's quite all right. Of course your little sensitivities are offended. You can't help being a norm, and I sympathize. But it doesn't matter at all. No, it doesn't matter whether you like me or not, my Chick. Because I like YOU!'

After Chick and Doc P. left I asked Arty what the hell he was letting Doc P. do to the twins anyway. He answered in an offhand, easy way that she was just going to 'get rid of the parasite.' I assumed he meant an abortion and that it was killing the baby that bothered Chick.

I told him about Chick feeling the baby reach out. Arty leaned back in his chair and gave me a dose of silence. When I remember it now I think he was laughing inside as he watched me argue in a half-assed and maybe halfhearted way on the wrong track entirely.

'Go away, Oly,' he said. He turned to the pile of papers on his desk with an exhausted look designed to put me lower than slug slime. It made me mad.

'Are you swallowing your own line of shit, Arty Binewski? Aren't you forgetting that you're just a two-bit freak with a gimmick?'

'Get out,' he ripped back at me.

I went.

★ ★ ★

Chick explained sadly that he could not talk to me about the plan for the twins. Could not and would not. 'You can make me cry,' he said, 'but you can't make me talk about that.' Ashamed, I left him alone.

Arty wouldn't let me in for a solid week. Miz Z. or one of her apprentices would come to the door and tell me, 'Arturo does not wish to see you.'

The guards wouldn't let me see the twins during that time. When I brought their meals, Ike or Mike, or whoever was perched in front of the twins' door, would take the tray from me and give me the dirty tray from the last meal. The notes that I slipped under the plates, and once actually into a turkey sandwich, were methodically searched for and found before my eyes — handed back to me without a word. One of the Arturan ladies was inside with the twins. The guard would knock and the ghostie would open the door and trade trays.

Finally I wrote 'Uncle' on a piece of paper and gave it to the novice who answered Arty's door. She came back and told me to go in and make sure the twins were eating and not flushing their food.

Arty let me do chores again. He didn't talk to me, though. He was completely taken up with his ass-sucking followers. I didn't try to push him. It struck me hard that he didn't need me, that he could shut me out permanently and completely and never miss me. He had all those others dancing for him. For me there was only Arty.

He didn't need us.

I watched that message sink deeper and deeper into the twins. Elly had always known it but it was news to Iphy. Not that they talked to me. They didn't.

I tried to warn them at first. 'Listen,' I begged, 'he's planning an abortion.'

They looked at me. Elly barked. A harsh mock of a laugh. 'Fat chance,' she said. That was the last she spoke to me.

I was the enemy, or as close to the enemy as they were able

to get for the time. They were silent when I was there. Elly never spoke. Iphy said 'please' and 'thank you' when I brought food and did the cleaning for them. They never ate in front of me. They were getting very thin. Their eyes had a bludgeoned depth, burrowing into purple caverns in their faces. They didn't dress. They wouldn't bathe. I didn't tell Arty. I didn't want to bring more trouble on them. As far as I could tell, all they did was to sit up against the pillows in their big bed all day. They didn't read or practice or study. But I saw knowledge grow in Iphy's face and harden in Elly's. They knew more than I did.

I never thought about how wide the twins would be, lying side by side. A regular stretcher would leave their heads and shoulders dangling off the sides. Doc P. sent four novices to take a rear door off a van.

We were strapping them onto the door when Elly opened her eyes and looked at me. A fearful question pushed her dark eyebrows high. Her pupil contracted in the purple iris but her lids were heavy and sank, pulling her grooved forehead smooth as they closed. Doc P. bent over to touch Elly's throat with a gloved hand.

'I wonder,' I piped nervously, 'if this is the same door you did that horse on.'

Doc P.'s white-wrapped head swiveled toward me like a turret gun.

'You remember that horse with the rotten feet?'

She nodded at the novices. With one white-robed man at each corner of the door, they moved forward. They had to tip the door onto its side to get it out through the door. The twins hung slack, hair trailing, as they left the van.

Arty was outside, waiting in his chair with a guard beside him in the dark.

'Wait. Put the light on them.'

A flashlight clicked a cool white cone into the blackness. Arty leaned forward to look at the sleeping twins.

'What's wrong?' His voice was harsh. 'They look terrible! They're sick!'

'What did you expect?' snapped Doc P. 'They've been locked inside for months!'

'But their hair. They could bathe.' He sounded shrill and fragile. The novices looked at him anxiously.

'Arty.' I touched his shoulder and his face turned away from the sprawled sleepers. The light went out and then reappeared further on. Doc P. led the jostling novices down the ramp. Arty's chair followed them and I went along.

We waited outside while they tipped the twins again to slide them through the surgery door. Doc P. stepped down for a last word.

'I'd like to state again that I consider this an improper hour for work of this type. I prefer to work at nine or ten A.M. These predawn hours find the vitality of most patients at its lowest.'

'Yeah, well, I wish you hadn't cold-cocked them!' Arty's voice was ragged.

'Sedatives.'

'Get on with it.'

The door closed behind her and Arty's chair began to roll in the dark.

'They'll take a while to scrub up and get ready,' he muttered, 'but I want to get up in place so I can watch the preparations.'

'Ah, Arty!' I groaned, hobbling behind. 'We can't watch! Not this!' I was still thinking abortion. 'I can't watch.'

But he'd rammed his chair wheel into the truck bumper and was clambering up onto the first step of the narrow stairs that led to the little theater above the surgery.

'You don't have to. I do.' He hurried upward.

I went away and paced round and round the home vans, wishing for Mama and Papa, who were snoring in deep counterpoint. I could hear them through the closed windows. I'd slipped the same drops into their bedtime cocoa as I'd put into the twins' milk glasses.

From the personal journal of Norval Sanderson:

Lovable Dr. Phyllis is quite undismayed at having bungled

Electra's lobotomy. Having reduced that bright creature to a permanent state resembling the liquid droop of a decayed zucchini, the good doctor is inspired rather than chagrined.

Dr. Phyllis has a voice like the breeze of Antartica but it is a young voice — younger than her body, perhaps from being used so little and so carefully. Now she is talking more often, to more people. She's become a glacial evangelist in her new cause. I see her stalking the Arturan office staff, lecturing stiffly to the novices, delivering admonitions to the more elevated.

Her message is succinct and pithy: Lobotomy is the ultimate shortcut to P.I.P. Arturo, she claims, is torturing his followers with prolonged, expensive, gradual amputations. He is denying, to those who have striven to emulate his ideal, the efficient, painless, virtually instantaneous access to Peace, Isolation, and Purity that it is in her power to bestow. Why wait? asks Doc P. Why itch in places you've no longer got? Cut once! Cut deep! Cut where it counts!

And I'm damned if she isn't kicking up quite a ruckus. The novices are mumbling bewilderedly. The elevated are waving their stumps and asking belligerent questions. Doc P. is fomenting radical schism in the Arturan Church.

Arty has a revolution to contend with and where is he? Mooning over his lost love — not Elly, but Iphigenia. He's subtle about it. He only inquires half a dozen times a day about her health and whereabouts. The binoculars set to swivel on the tripod in his window are, he claims, for keeping an eye on the flock. Never would he use them to watch the pale Iphy in her painful progress down the row toward the Chute with her swollen belly pulling her forward while she struggles to balance the flabby monster that sprouts from her waist. She sticks one arm straight out for balance and drags that unreliable leg on the other side.

General opinion about Arty varies, from those who see him as a profound humanitarian to those who view him as a ruthless reptile. I myself have held most of the opinions in this spectrum at one time or another. Watching Arty pine for Iphy, however, I come to see him as just a regular Joe — jealous, bitter, possessive, competitive, in a constant frenzy to disguise his lack of self-esteem, drowning in deadly love, and utterly unable to prevent himself from gorging on the coals of hell in his search for revenge.

The estimable Zephir McGurk informs me, in his laconic way over checkers (a game at which his plodding methodical integrity reveals itself unassailable), that Arty had him design a bugging system that tapped the twins' van into a recording device in Arty's console. He can hear every word, every move.

I find this depressing. The idea of Arty sitting and listening to hour after hour of footsteps, pages turning, toilet flushing, comb running through hair. Elly's conversation had been reduced to the syllable mmmmmm *and Iphy is not in the mood for song. Her piano is covered with dust (according to McGurk) and Arty is listening to her file her nails.*

Doc P. is frustrated by the inefficiency of Arty's method. I mentioned Arty's theory of acclimatization and continually renewed commitment. 'One respects,' I said, 'Arturo's desire for complete understanding on the part of the Admitted. Each elevation being a voluntary step, a considered step, allows those with hesitations to back out at any time.'

But she started up on how many hours she'd spent already just taking off my four toes, and she would be hours in surgery on those remaining, and that would bring me only to the first level of elevation, while, if she were allowed to be efficient, she could take me 'all the way there inside a single hour on the table.'

Her face became quite damp with her effusions, and her final outburst fogged her glasses. 'Now he wants to add on lobotomy at the end! He's talking about sending for all the completions — bringing them back from the rest home a few at a time so I can do yet another job on them! I'm spending eight to ten hours every day in surgery. I'm getting an allergic reaction to my gloves — unless it's the soap. My hands are scaling and my knuckles are swelling.'

I knew better than to suggest hiring another surgeon to help her.

She says Iphy is enjoying a fairly normal pregnancy but may be carrying twins. I asked about Chick, who looks terrible lately. She says he's depressed and she's dosing him with B complex, zinc, and jumping jacks. 'Exercise is the ultimate panacea . . . Oxidation of impurity and so on,' says she.

I talked to Chick in back of the cat wagon this morning. An old tire lay flat in the dust and he was bouncing on it, his bare feet planted on opposite sides, his hands on top of his head, his coveralls flying loose on his thin frame. The coverall straps lay on his bare shoulders, emphasizing the skinniness of a neck the size of my wrist. He was polite as always but thinking of something else. His face turned up to me had a starved, ancient look. He said he was 'waiting for Iphy.' No, he didn't have to work today because Doc was having meetings and giving speeches. (This is the first word I heard of Doc's Surgical Strike.)

I wanted to question him about some of the 'Chick stories' going around but Iphy sagged up, lugging the drooling Elly. Chick hopped off the tire, said 'So long' and ran off to her. He threw an arm around her, tucked his shoulder under Elly's armpit to help support her dead weight. They strolled off, the three. Two? Or do we count the ballooning belly and call it four?

I saw Arty's squad marching down the camp so I went through the fence to catch up. The way he leans forward gives an illusion of speed as the chair hums and groans over the dry ruts and dead grass in the Arturan encampment. His solemn novices don't dare touch the chair unless he asks them to.

He stopped at the open door of a dusty sedan with white rags draped out of the windows to dry. Inside, on the back seat, lay an elevated male with his arms ending in white-wrapped bulges at the elbow and one leg ending at the knee. The plush upholstery of the car lifts a puff of dust every time the man shifts slightly in the seat.

Arty nodded in at the shadowed face. 'Do you have what you need?'

The stump man wriggled, surprised, craning his neck, 'Arturo, sir?' His eyes showed their whites in the dimness.

Arty's scalp was bright in the sunlight. 'Are you well treated? Do you need anything?'

'Well, that boy that's s'posed to help me . . . not meaning to

whine but he's always gone. Yesterday, I couldn't hep it, I wet myself, and by the time he showed up, damned if I didn't have a diaper rash.'

Arty chuckled, nodding. 'Sounds like you need a replacement. What's that boy's name?'

'Jason. But he's a good boy. Just young.'

Arty swiveled in his chair and eyed his entourage. A dozen backs straightened and a dozen faces tried to look bright and eager.

'Who'll serve this elevated man?' Arty asked. The hands shot up — all five fingers spread to show their service status.

'Miss Elizabeth,' Arty nodded. The woman stepped forward, her white dress bunching over her thickening body. Her hair bunned on top of her head. Thirty-five. Something burnt out of her soft face.

'As you hope to be served?' Arty asked.

'In my turn,' breathed the fingerful, toeful Miss E.

'When that Jason boy shows, send him to me.'

Miss E. detached herself from the group, climbed into the front seat of the sedan, and started sorting through a paper bag full of clothes for clean and dirty.

The elevated man, flat on the back seat, waved his stump arms and strained his neck in the shade of his washed bandages hanging on the windows. 'As you are!' shouted the elevated man. Arty nodded and his chair turned and moved on.

Doing his rounds, he calls this. It's a recent development, probably triggered by the Doc and her agitating. I followed him from tent to van to pickup trucks with mosquito nets and sleeping bags in back.

He scolded, sympathized, made peace, moved people from one job to another, from one campsite to a more peaceful spot. He talked to the cooks in the big mess tent to make sure a vegetarian menu was available for those who wanted it. He sent runners from his platoon of disciples to give orders or deliver messages. He spent a good three hours rolling around among the chinless ninnies, the whiners, the leeches, the simps, and the good people in his congregation. He ended up back at his own trailer looking very tired and young. I shoved his chair up the ramp to the deck and opened his door for him.

'So you have a strike on your hands,' I said. He smiled going
in and I followed him. He rolled straight to the desk and started
pushing through papers. 'I've got one rebel on my flippers,' he
grinned, 'but I always knew she'd turn one day. I'm not all that
put out.'

'She's got you over a barrel if she won't cut anymore.'

Arty looked at me with a flat smile. 'I'm not such a fool as
that. I've had her training her own replacement for years.'

Iphy braided Elly's hair so she wouldn't drool on it. Iphy with
hands like angel wings, combing and polishing the long
gleaming strands while Elly lay against her. Elly's head
drooping forward on the too long, too thin neck, her face
blinking emptily at the sofa cushions.

Iphy would wind the long braids into coiled black shells and
pin them over Elly's ears and then do her own. Then Iphy
would turn the blank, soggy face toward her and sponge it carefully, brushing the eyebrows smooth and propping the lower
jaw closed with one hand so that, for an instant, it looked like
Elly. Until Iphy let go and the face fell down again.

Horst drove us to the meadow and parked the small van in the
dust-white grass. Mama helped Iphy out and I handed around
the plastic pails.

'You twins always have flying fingers,' Mama was chattering. 'Flying fingers, but Oly and I will do our part as best
we're able.'

Horst leaned against the bumper with a stick in case we saw
a snake, but he was soon asleep in the sun like one of his cats.

Mama stood against the dust-covered blackberry banks,
reaching high into the rasping tangles of the thorns and
humming. Iphy's fingers were not flying. With the arm
supporting Elly she held the bucket against their swollen belly
and reached out with her other hand, dutifully nipping off the
warm, dark berries and ignoring the ragged red lines scratched
on her arms and their legs by the thorns. She was careful with
Elly, holding her away from the bush, staggering awkwardly,

catching their bare ankles in the vines, working slowly. I
plodded along, picking and getting scraped.

The sun pounded down and the dust drifted up, and after a
while Mama's thin scat voice was far off. Iphy called to me: 'I
need to sit down.'

She was hanging on to a thick, drooping stalk of vine when I
got to her. I took the bucket and tucked myself under Elly. The
lolling blank face rocked against my head as Iphy slowly
turned. We made our way out of the brambles.

'On the grass would be fine,' Iphy said. But I steered her
around past Horst to the narrow shade beside the van. She sank
down and pulled Elly's head over to lie on her shoulder.

'I'll just rest a little. Standing up in the sun . . .'

Horst was wide awake, blinking and tapping his stick in the
dust, pretending he'd never been asleep. I went back to find
Mama.

Later, at the sink in our van, Mama rinsed the blue stain and
the odd spiders, caterpillars, and stems from the bucket.

'Not what we usually start with, but we can go again
tomorrow. And this will set up nicely in about six, eight jars.'

The berries were beginning to simmer in the big pot on the
back burner. Mama pushed her dark wooden spoon into the
foaming berries and circled the wall of the pot slowly.

I leaned my hot arms on the table and said, 'Iphy better not
go tomorrow. She got tired today.' I was smelling the berries
and Mama's sweat, and watching the flex of the blue veins
behind her knees.

'Does them good. The twins always loved picking berries,
even more than eating them. Though Elly likes her jam.'

'Elly doesn't like anything anymore.'

The knees stiffened and I looked up. The spoon was motionless. Mama stared at the pot.

'Mama, Elly isn't there anymore. Iphy's changed. Everything's changed. This whole berry business, cooking big meals
that nobody comes for, birthday cakes for Arty. It's dumb
Mama. Stop pretending. There isn't any family anymore,
Mama.'

Then she cracked me with the big spoon. It smacked wet and hard across my ear, and the purple-black juice sprayed across the table. She stared at me, terrified, her mouth and eyes gaping with fear. I stared gaping at her. I broke and ran.

I went to the generator truck and climbed up to sit by Grandpa. That's the only time Mama ever hit me and I knew I deserved it. I also knew that Mama was too far gone to understand why I deserved it. She'd swung that spoon in a tigerish reflex at blasphemy. But I believed that Arty had turned his back on us, that the twins were broken, that the Chick was lost, that Papa was weak and scared, that Mama was spinning fog, and that I was an adolescent crone sitting in the ruins, watching the beams crumble, and warming myself in the smoke from the funeral pyre. That was how I felt, and I wanted company. I hated Mama for refusing to see enough to be miserable with me. Maybe, too, enough of my child heart was still with me to think that if she would only open her eyes she could fix it all back up like a busted toy.

A redhead went tripping by, red heels stabbing the dust. She looked at me. Her mouth opened to say something, but then she looked away and minced on.

I decided I would go down to where the swallowers were parked and talk to the Human Pin-Cushion. I'd been watching him for weeks. I was nursing this fantasy that maybe he would like to run away with me and join up with some other show, some simp-twister, spook-house show that wintered in Florida and took life easy. I could talk them in for the Pin Kid and do his cooking and his costumes, and run the light-and-sound board for his act. A young Pin-Cushion, just striking out on his own, could do worse than have me for a partner. And, if I worked hard, he'd let me sleep with my arms and legs wrapped around him all night. The Pin Kid seemed to like me too. He laughed at my jokes and actually came looking for me once when I was rubbing Arty down.

You'd think dwarfs and midgets would have drifted through the Fabulon all my life. It was actually, though accidentally, very rare for me to see anyone like me. We'd had the usual monkey girls and alligator guys and an endless migrating herd of fat folks and giants.

Mama often said that fat folks went out of style because every tenth ass on the street now was wider than the one in the tent. Folks could see it free on any block. Giants were also out of work owing, according to Mama, to basketball and the drugs they fed to babies to make them tall enough to play the game.

'It goes in streaks. But some things never go out of fashion.' Hunger artists, fat folks, giants, and the dog acts come and go but *real* freaks never lose their appeal.

It so happened that the Pin Kid who had joined up with our current pack of swallowers was a hunchback. He had regular arms and legs and a great torch of red hair. He was fragile as a glass swan, fine-skinned with freckles, brown eyes, and a clear, honest face. His name was Vinnie Sweeney. He was only twenty years old and he'd been working for years with other acts, trying to save enough money to get his own tent and trailer.

From the journal of Norval Sanderson:

> *Lily is winking conspiratorially at me. She proceeds to dust and polish the lids and jars on the counter. The maggots appreciate it, no doubt. An old line comes to me: 'Lovely you are, and kind to the tender young of ravening lions.'*
>
> *She took a walk with Iphy today, she says. She seems to be ignoring the existence of what remains of Elly — doesn't mention her at all. Is completely taken up with 'my grandchild,' and its current protuberant form.*
>
> *'I swan!' says Lily, making me think of times past when she must have, in fact, swanned. Crystal Lil 'swans to goodness' that Iphy's child is twins and wouldn't it be a miracle and a blessing if it was Siamese twins? She (Lily) says Iphy is far too big for a six-month pregnancy. Iphy says the only thing she wants is to see Arty. Lil asks if I will speak to Arty about it. 'The boy's so busy I don't see him myself except across the camp or if I should peep in at showtime and catch his act.'*

23

The Generalissimo's Big Gun

From the files of Norval Sanderson:

(Iphigenia, pregnant, hugging the lobotomized Elly on the sofa in the twins' van — conversation with N.S.)

'Oly has a boyfriend? Oly and the Pin Kid? How could she have time for that? She's always with Arty.

'I almost had a boyfriend once. Elly would have let me. She thought it was O.K. She shut down when I talked to him. Whenever he came around, she'd cut her voltage way back and stay quiet. She wanted me to go ahead and love him.

'He was just a geek. He was clean between his shows. Laundry, hospital corners on the sheets when he made his bunk up. He was a poor boy, he said, so he knew how to take care of himself. I thought how good it would be ... like you'd be proud to clean and cook for a man who knew how to clean and cook. It would feel right taking care of a man who could take care of himself.

'But he was a norm. At first I thought he was pretty even though he was a norm. But it grows on you. After a while it was his being such a norm that got to me, touched me ... I don't know. Like colors or a spring tree against that kind of blue sky that pulls your heart out through your eyes. Pretty things will swarm you like that, like your heart was a hive of electric bees. He was like that, the geek boy. He made normal seem beautiful to me. And Elly said it was O.K. She wanted me to. So I did. I saw him and was happy. Then I wanted to talk to him and she

let me. Then I couldn't be happy unless I was near him, unless he was talking to me.

'*He laughed a lot and told silly jokes and was going away to college in the fall. He had such a wonderful time being the geek. And he had long, perfect teeth. The redheads called him a darling.*

'*He started paying attention to me. He would come and find us and talk to me. Not to Elly but to me. He'd bring his lunch in a bag and sit by us. He'd wait outside in the morning and walk us to practice. But he talked just to me. He told me things about himself. Sweet, sad things. And Elly damped herself way down.*

'*And a terrible thing happened. He seemed to forget about her. He forgot she was part of me. That was what we'd meant to happen. Elly was glad. She'd crow in bed at night. He touched me. He'd put his hand on my hair, gently. He took my hand. I saw it in his eyes, so I stopped it. Elly was mad. She bit me on the inside of my arm until we both cried. But she wanted to get me away from Arty. She didn't care about the boy at all. She wanted me to love somebody else than Arty. You know Elly. She figured I was going to love somebody whether she liked it or not and she decided she could handle anybody but Arty. Arty is too much for her.*

'*She was mad when I stopped. I couldn't help it. It was a thing that cracked and spilled in my head. Elly understood but she was mad. I know better now. I'll never let it happen again.*

'*He started to love me, you see? He was so pure, like that leaf against the sky. I don't mean he was naïve or innocent or a virgin or even a virtuous boy, though he was nice, but that he was purely, from tip to toe, from nose to tail, absolutely what he was. That was normal with a big N. That was what I loved. But when the look in his eye changed, I realized, if there's one thing a healthy, beautiful, utterly normal boy does not do, it's fall in love with half a pair of Siamese twins.*

'*That's how I learned. It's O.K. for me to love a norm like that. But if he comes to loving me it's because I've twisted him and changed him. If he loves me he's corrupted. I can't love him anymore. I won't pretend it didn't hurt.*'

★ ★ ★

(Arty — conversation with N.S.)

'There are those whose own vulgar normality is so apparent and stultifying that they strive to escape it. They affect flamboyant behavior and claim originality according to the fashionable eccentricities of their time. They claim brains or talent or indifference to mores in desperate attempts to deny their own mediocrity. These are frequently artists and performers, adventurers and wide-life devotees.

'Then there are those who feel their own strangeness and are terrified by it. They struggle toward normalcy. They suffer to exactly that degree that they are unable to appear normal to others, or to convince themselves that their aberration does not exist. These are true freaks, who appear, almost always, conventional and dull.'

(Arturo in response to critics)

'It's interesting that when these individuals choose — and it is their choice always — to endure voluntary amputations for their own personal benefit, society professes itself shocked and disapproving. Yet this same society respects the concept that any individual should risk total annihilation in war, subject to the judgement of any superior officer at all and for purposes ranging from a promotion for the lieutenant to higher profits for the bullet company. Hell, they don't just respect that idea, they flat expect it. And they'll shoot your ass if you don't go along with it.'

N.S.: If you could make it happen by snapping your fingers, wouldn't you want your whole family to be physical and mentally normal?

Oly: That's ridiculous! Each of us is unique. We are masterpieces. Why would I want us to change into assembly-line items? The only way you people can tell each other apart is by your clothes. (Miss Olympia begins to giggle and refuses to answer seriously to further questions.)

Zephir McGurk's love life took place in his safari car with the

khaki canvas shades pulled down all around. If surplus females
arrived on Arty's doorstep, or if one didn't appeal to Arty
(whose taste, when you come right down to it, was for standard
pneumatic types with commercial grooming products), he
would send her on to McGurk. Arty's line wasn't particularly
imaginative. He would give her the old 'If you would do *me* a
great service, console my trusted lieutenant in his spartan dedication' routine.

It evidently worked often enough to keep McGurk healthy
and even-tempered. McGurk was such a gent that nobody who
went tap-tapping at his windshield in the dark after the midway
was closed ever went screeching in fear or pain or shame
through the camp before dawn. There were occasional exits
like that from Arty's van, but the guards would catch them and
calm them and give them hush money.

McGurk's little trysts were always discreet. He was never
seen with female company and he was never late to work. We
figured he escorted them to the gates and kissed their hands
adieu before first light. Arty claimed that McGurk actually fed
them to Horst's cats, but that was Arty. McGurk was silent on
the subject and would not be baited.

Once, when I was in trouble and pacing the camp in the dark, I
did hear something. But I had maggot brains that night and
may have imagined half of it and misunderstood the rest.

I'd gone to cool my face on Grandpa's urn. I was lying on
the hood of the generator truck with my face against the silver
loving cup that held the old Binewski ashes and served as a
hood ornament. Whoever drove the generator truck would
always complain that the wind whistled through the urn's
handles like a siren at any speed past thirty-five. Al just said,
'Tough' and that was that.

On the hottest night Grandpa seemed to cool off before
anything else. Leaning a cheek or my forehead against the urn
felt like packing ice in my burning brain. So there I was,
finished blubbering but still half loony, leaning my face on the
urn, when I heard something. It came from McGurk's safari
car, parked just ahead of me. I could have spit on his bumper.

It was a rough, strangled sound and I figured it must be McGurk's climax song. But it kept going on. It scared me. I thought someone was dying. I remembered what Arty said about McGurk's feeding his women to the cats, and I thought he was strangling somebody. Then I heard a word in his own voice. 'Please,' he said. Then the ropy, gurgling sound started again. He was crying. For a minute there was another voice, softer and smooth — quick. I couldn't tell what she was saying. Then McGurk again, desperate, almost shouting. 'Don't you see? There'll be nothing left of you that I can get a grip on!' Then the soft woman's voice drifted monotonously among McGurk's ugly sobs. I got down and went away from there.

There were promotions scheduled for next morning. Four women were due to 'complete their liberation.' All had abandoned their legs entirely and were left with arms only from the elbow up. They were ready to shed their arms at the shoulder. These liberations were supposed to take place between 8 and 11 A.M. Dr. Phyllis would spend the afternoon whittling on fingers and toes.

I figured McGurk's lady had to be one of those who were doing arms. I thought about going to the line outside the infirmary early to try to figure out which one it might be. I decided against it. I didn't want to know.

McGurk seemed the same as usual that day and every day afterward. That's why I say I may have misunderstood or imagined the whole thing.

Up on the roof of the van, Arty flopped in exhaustion. 'Hey, oil me, Oly. Will you?'

It was scary to have him ask. I crouched over him, rubbing my fingertips into the knotted tension of his neck and shoulders.

'You're ugly, brother, and you've got rigor mortis from the nipples up.'

His eyes closed and his face relaxed slightly.

'Silence, anus,' he responded ritually. He took a long, slow breath and held it before he spoke again. 'I think Elly's coming back some, don't you?'

'She doesn't flop as much. Maybe not as limp as she was?'

'Yeah. I think she'll come back some. Not like before, though.'

'Maybe Iphy's just learning to handle her better. Balance and support.'

He shook his head against the mat, eyes clenched shut.

'No. She's coming back. Just takes time. She'll be able to help take care of the baby.'

'Maybe. You know, Chick could help you sleep nights. You look about three hundred years old.'

'Chick doesn't like me. I wouldn't want to tempt him.'

'He's still sore about Elly.'

'And other things. Another chore. He'll do it, though. And Papa's mad at me. He says we'll kill the whole outfit by hanging it all on one novelty act. That's what he's calling my show lately. A novelty act. He says my 'fans' will pass away when some new fad hits the air. Mama is mad too but she pretends not to be.'

'You're a creep, I guess.'

'Did you ever wish you were dead?'

'Not lately.'

'Guess it's you and the Pin Kid, hunh?'

I stopped kneading his spine and looked at his shadowed profile. He looked like a sleeping hieroglyph against the blanket. I forced my thumbs to rotate so he wouldn't notice.

Down the line I could see Mama outside the Chute. She was folding a dust cloth and talking to someone still inside the door of the Chute. It was Iphy, walking out huge and awkward. Elly's head tucked into Iphy's throat, the cloth billowing around the frail legs beneath them, the belly balanced in front of them.

'I can see Iphy. She looks like an old car.' Mama and Iphy tottered out of sight.

'The Pin Kid seems O.K. You could do worse. Do you reckon you'll leave?' His eyes were open now, his neck twisting to let the eyes touch me. His eyes were grey, very pale. I pinched his round, hard buttock, slapped his back sharp and loud.

'Trash! Stuff it, Arty.'

He closed his eyes again. 'I'm gonna cut down to three shows a week. Saturday, Sunday, Wednesday, eight P.M. Flat.'

'Papa will flip.'

'That'll give him his carnival back the rest of the time.'

'Mama will think you've fallen to the vilest depths of leisure.'

'Oly ... stick by me. How about it?'

His eyes were open again, looking straight at a fold of blanket in front of him. The big chain-link fence was below us on one side of the van. It stretched a long way and the Arturan camp sprawled out from it in a refugee confusion.

'I'm gonna stick a broom,' I muttered grimly, 'up your ass, brother, and peddle you as an all-day sucker.'

Massaging the twins on the sea-green carpet of their front room, crawling around on my knees to reach the peculiar juncture of the split spine, the small of their backs that was actually much wider, nearly two backs wide.

'Sorry I can't quite lie on my stomach.'

'It's O.K., Iphy. Does that hurt?'

'Hurts good.'

Elly stretched limply away from Iphy, folded oddly across Iphy's side.

'No wonder your back's bitching, getting pulled in different directions by Elly and the belly.'

Iphy's pale face softened in pleasure. 'Elly, belly, weak as jelly.'

'Arty thinks Elly's coming back some,' I said.

'Does it make him feel better?'

'Do you think she is?'

'Sometimes. For a second. No more. That's good. Now work on Elly.'

I inched slowly up Elly's arms and shoulders, probing, stretching, lifting, rotating but feeling how much of her muscle was gone into soupy flab like the dismal mush in her skull.

'Iphy?'

She blinked awake.

'Having that baby inside ...' I held Elly's neck in my fingers and felt the strong hammer of her blood. 'Is it bad or good?'

Iphy blinked again. 'Good. Inside me is good. The bad is outside.'

'Arty's not happy.'

'I know.' Her tone was peculiar. Something familiar made me look up. She was absolutely twinkling. She pulled her lips flat, widening her grin grotesquely. She tipped her head back, let her eyes droop to slits. The colored beads of her eyeballs slid from side to side and her voice rolled out in Arty's pompous, patronizing bell of power: 'Happiness! Happiness, I tell you! Are you listening? Happiness? You Poor Paralyzed and Constipated Dung Chutes! Happiness is Not the POINT!'

I fell down laughing and Iphy laughed and we rolled giggling and kicking on the thick softness of the carpet, tangling hilariously with the flopping, laughless Elly until I hurt all over from laughing and kind Iphy stretched away from her dragging belly trying to breathe but was caught by the laughter again and again.

'Whyever,' she gasped, hee-heeing. 'However,' she ha-ha'd, 'could we love??' which set her off again and me with her, chortling, 'love him!!' and screaming with the sunburst air of laughter and pounding our heels on the carpet and kicking our heels toward the ceiling until we both collapsed, exhausted, into feeble titters. Only Iphy had the strength at last to shout, 'He's such a SIMP!' which set us off again.

I went to tell the Pin Kid that he and I were washed up. Kaput. *Finito.* He was lounging on his bed of nails while he worked some new spots around his belly button with the needles. I hunkered beside him, watching him lift a flap of skin and shove the big pin through, then hold the flap in one hand, twiddling the knob at the needle head idly as he waited for the thin trickle of blood to dry up.

'Ya know, Vinnie,' I said, 'I decided to stay with my brother.' It was hard for me. A swallower girl was hanging freshly laundered curtains on the backdrop nearby. Some of the kids were throwing things into the air and not letting them hit the ground, juggling practice, with a scratchy tape blaring Mozart or something.

I watched the gem-sharp face of the Pin Kid absorbed in his own white skin. I looked hard to see if I'd hurt him. Maybe my whole life was set in that instant. I was a sixteen-year-old freak brat. If he'd said anything — a word might have been enough, 'Don't,' or a crease of the brow, a shadow of pain in his eyes could have seduced me. The pain I was looking for in him would have been my excuse, my motive, my escape tunnel to the world beyond the Binewskis.

But he half smiled in puzzlement. His eyes felt the pebbled gut of a fast creek, bright and open and empty but willing to be full.

'Well ... sure,' he said. As though he'd never imagined anything else for me.

'I mean,' I said, frowning until my glasses slipped and my bare pink eyes popped into the light at him, 'I mean always.' I stopped because he was rolling off the nails and he'd forgotten to pull the big needle from his belly skin and the thin red blood was spattering his cut-off jeans. When he turned away from me, reaching for a shirt, I could see the rash of tiny pockmarks from the nail points reddening his lovely arched back, his curving graceful hump with the brightness of blood barely restrained at the surface of his white skin.

'Well, Oly ... Well, sure ... Hey, Arturo, he needs you.' This Vinnie, the Pin Kid, was a nice boy. Even half-choked with disgust he tried not to hurt me.

That's when it clicked that the mechanics of my life were not going to run on the physics that ruled the twins or Mama in her day. If I bled it didn't mean what Iphy's blood meant. If I loved it wasn't the same as Iphy's love or the love of bouncy girls in the midway.

Arty had done his best to teach me this all along but I had seen him as a special case, not governed by the prosy gravity that held the rest of us. Vinnie, the Pin Kid, tried to keep me from knowing that he'd never thought of me the way I'd thought of him. His kindness scalded me awake.

My new eyes saw the old things. He'd felt the needle in his belly as he'd pulled the shirt over his head. Now his big hands, cleverly knuckled, slid out the needle, dropped it into a tall jar of alcohol, dabbed antiseptic on the two small holes above his belly button. He pulled the shirt down and tucked it into his red-spattered jeans.

'You're lucky, Oly,' looking gravely out from his deep

eyeholes. 'My ma cried a lot just looking at me. You're right to stick by your family.'

He stacked his props in his trunk and slid the nail bed out of the way. His legs were longer than me. His narrow shoulders nipped up near his tiny ears with the swirl of hump arching behind him. He moved as though he were all legs, a smooth bobbing in his gait that poured in through my eyes and settled in my right lung like a pool of ice. I got up while his back was turned and crept away.

From the journal of Norval Sanderson:

> *Went with Arty this P.M. to watch the Pin Act. It's one of his new days off and he showed up in disguise, dark green blanket up to his neck. Green stocking cap, dark glasses probably borrowed from Oly. The guard was in civvies and there wasn't a novice to be seen. He rolled up to my booth and nodded and it was a full minute before I realized it was the Worm. It delighted him to fool me.*
>
> *I'd been raving about the Pin-Cushion but it was the first time Arty had seen him. We stood in the back of the swallowers' tent and waited for the Pin.*
>
> *We were in time for the swallowers' finale. A blustering logger in front of us explained to his wife how the whole thing was collapsible swords and tricks.*
>
> *'They always think the real thing is phony and that the tricks are the McCoy. Never stops amazing me,' whispered Arty.*
>
> *I told him the guy got his money's worth feeling like he'd refused to be suckered. Feeling like he'd outwitted them. Showing off his worldly skepticism to his lady.*
>
> *The old swallower did his Ta-Da with five hilts coming out of his mouth in a glittering bouquet and the skinny son did his with the lit fluorescent tube going down his gullet as the lights dimmed and the whole tentful went 'aah' seeing that pale blue glow shimmering through the jagged shadows of his ribs.*
>
> *'Clever bastards, ain't they?' said the logger.*
>
> *When the Pin came on, nobody left. The logger looked a bit pale but stuck it out. Arty was fascinated. 'Nice timing, nice,' he*

murmured once while the young Pin latched a big chrome hook into the permanent hole through his tongue and did a little ragtime step with a twenty-five-pound weight dangling on a chain from his tongue. The Pin walked up the blade latter, danced on the bed of nails, then started with the pins and needles. Two of the kid swallowers were juggling fire steadily behind him and the Pin timed every move to build the heartbeat. He works with chrome knitting needles, ten and eighteen inches long. Impressive, through the thighs, through the skin of the chest. He's working on a new place on his belly, and the blood trickling out and running down his pale skin to the loincloth is effective. He was quite a sight by the time he started punching the needles through his cheeks and lips. We slipped out before the finale so Arty wouldn't get caught with his chair in the crowd.

'Not from a show family? Sure?' he asked as we picked our way back through the midway crowd.

'Just the apple farmers.'

'He could use a good talker to lead them through. That panto-mime stuff is O.K. but a good talker would add a lot.'

I didn't answer. He was thinking about Oly, young Olympia. I was surprised at the note of pain in his voice. As though he were afraid to lose her.

'I don't care. It doesn't do any good to care, so I won't.' Chick was as dry and flat as a cow pie. Arty flicked his eyes at him suspiciously and then looked at me. We three were in the Chute for our secret meeting. The guards stood outside in the night mist while, in the deepest room, in the soft yellow glow of the lit jars that held our dead brothers and sisters, Arty told us what we had to do.

Chick slumped against a glass case. I leaned against him, watching Arty shift slightly in his chair, thinking. I tried to read the clenching of Arty's jaws and the tilt of his gleaming head on his thick neck.

'I don't usually mind what you think, Chick,' purred Arty. His chin jutted at us, intent, 'As long as you do your job. But this time you've got to understand. It's just us three in the pinch. Mama and Papa can't deal with it. All the guards, all the simps, the Arturans, the show folks, even Horst — they could turn in a flash. They all have their own machines to ride.'

We listened. I could feel Chick's child bones vibrating against me, shaking to the tune of Arty's song. 'It's just us three now. The twins have other things to deal with.' Arty waited a beat to see if we'd react to that, complain or accuse. When we didn't he went on.

'You'll take three guards. I'll use the rest. By the time you're ready to start I'll be up there watching. O.K.?'

We nodded. Arty hit the start switch on his chair motor with a flange of his right shoulder fin. 'I need you bad, now. Don't fuck me over.'

Chick held my hand as we walked through the dark camp. The big men moved silently behind us. Arty and his crew of fifteen guards had gone through the gate into the Arturan camp.

When we came to Doc P.'s van we stopped at the door. My mouth was dry and my hands were wet. Chick's fingers gripped my palm hard. We stood staring at the white glow of the big van in the moonlight. I could just make out the twined snake emblem with the communication grid caught in the open mouths of the snakes.

Chick sighed. 'She's asleep,' he whispered. He moved to the door, tugging me along as he opened it and climbed into the dark stench of antiseptic. The light went on and I saw the inside of Doc P.'s van for the first time in the years she had traveled with us. White and stark. No cushions on the metal benches. Chrome on the outsize sink. A metal desk against the wall, the white doors of cabinets glaring in the hard white light.

Chick moved surely. He'd spent chunks of his life here. The bedroom took up the end and the sliding door opened as we soft-footed toward it.

'It's O.K.,' Chick said. 'Tell them to bring the stretcher.'

When I got back he was standing by her head, stroking her short grey-brown hair. I came close to look. Without her white wrappings and her glinting specs she looked soft and dissatisfied. Set grooves of disapproval curved down around her thin mouth. Her nose was shapeless, her skin thick.

'No wonder she wears a mask,' I whispered. Chick laid his hand on her cheek. I noticed that his hands were getting big and bony on his kid-spindly arms. He trailed a finger across her lips. 'She's always constipated,' he said. The guards set the stretcher down and I stepped back to make room. Her cot was narrow, not built in, and it had a thin pad instead of a mattress. I peeked into the white closet as they took her out. It was full of books. The shelves filled the closet from top to bottom and the books were each wrapped separately in a clear plastic bag. I used two fingers to flatten the plastic across a book spine so I could read the title. Some kind of surgical text. I checked a few more. All surgical texts. Chick looked in at me.

'That's what she taught me from. That's how she learned. The journals are in the cabinets up front.'

Chick showed me how to wash up while the guards moved her to the operating table.

'Are you gonna lose your dinner?' he was looking at me sharply.

I hung on to his eyes. They were as chilly and soothing as Grandpa's urn. I giggled greenly, nodding. His mouth twisted in dry exasperation.

'Jeez. Arty just wants you here to make sure I do it. You can't really help anyway. Go over there.'

He spun me with his mind and I knew it. I was moving into the latrine cubicle and falling to my knees. My stomach came all the way up and out, then snapped back like a frog's tongue. Then I was back at the sink with liquid soap covering my arms to the elbow and a white mask tying itself over my face and an itchy cap sliding down over my eyes. I giggled, watching Chick's hands under the rushing tap. 'This is why you never have dirty elbows, hunh?'

His eyes grinned at me over his mask but he didn't say anything.

'Mama thinks it's weird that your fingernails stay so clean and you never get a crust behind your ears.'

He was busy with the gloves. 'Just sit on that stool with the back. You won't feel a thing.'

But I was terrified. I thought she would wake up. I thought

she would rise off the table roaring and take us in her thick
hands and break us, and I thought Arty was sitting up above,
looking down through the mirror in the ceiling, and he would
watch Doc P. eat us and he would chuckle and come down and
make a deal with her because that was what he'd meant to
happen all along. I was hanging on to the seat of my stool with
both gloved hands, being scared that way, when suddenly I
started being scared that she wouldn't wake up and that this
other thing would actually happen. I opened my mouth to
speak. 'Arghi,' I said, and my little brother Chick looked up at
me, frowning between his mask and his cap, and I went to sleep.

'Why did I have to be there? All I did was get in the way and
have to be put to sleep and fall off onto the floor in the middle
of everything. I didn't help at all.'
　'Sure you did. You kept Chick from thinking too much.'
　'Why didn't you just put a clothespin on his nose?'
　'Trust me, Oly. You were useful.'

From the journal of Norval Sanderson:

> *'In the night, while they slept, he went among them and took
> their swords and shields and stacked them in a ditch by the road.
> He bound their hands and feet as they lay dreaming. They woke
> lying in rows on the death cart and their first sight was the body
> of their leader spread and bound on the great wheel before their
> eyes, his many wounds dripping in the dust. . . .'*
>
> Which is the way all coups and counter-coups should be
> accomplished — fast and quiet with only the guilty suffering. I
> have to hand it to young Arty. He might have made a grand
> South American general. He went fast and hard through the
> Arturan camp last night, checking off their names on his 'disaf-
> fected' list. Seventy people left the camp, escorted by the guards
> and handed a refund check for whatever they'd paid as an
> admission fee. Down the road they went, grumbling in their
> vans and station wagons. But, if they have any sense at all, they
> know they got off light and lucky.

If I hadn't been at the road myself to watch them go I might have speculated otherwise. There will certainly be rumors that Arty was less than fastidious in his techniques — that some were brutalized or even murdered. I might, I say, have considered the possiblity myself. But the angry frustration on those faces wasn't fear. Miz Z. handed out the refund envelopes at the gate, and Arty parked his chair by the Arturan Administration Office (the camper on the green Dodge pickup) to supervise — a guard beside him and others trotting up and away again for instructions or to report. Altogether an orderly and discreet process. When I wandered up to him he greeted me calmly. 'Just quelling this little revolt, Norval,' he said.

'What about the high priestess? Won't she fuss?' I asked. It seemed unlike the good doc to give up just because she'd lost her army. The primary weapon she held was her own surgical strike.

'Dr. Phyllis has been taken care of,' he told me. A guard ran up to say, 'That's the lot,' and Arty headed for the operating theater. I tagged along but he made me wait outside by his chair with the guard while he went up. I stood around listening to the surgery generator hum. Eddie, the guard, sat down in Arty's chair and dozed. I wandered home, composing imaginary coverage of Arty's repression of the Great Lobotomy Schism. I didn't discover Doc P.'s fate until this morning.

I took a tour of the Arturan camp early and watched the holes in the line close up. All the gaps left by the deserting schismatics — tent spaces, parking spots — that called attention to their emptiness like missing teeth have been sponged away. Miz Z. simply walked the lines and told everyone to move over and fill them. One fight broke out when a novice backed his scrofulous Volkswagen into one of the Harley sidecars, leaving a discernible dent. The other Arturans quickly subdued the irritated Harley owners and the rest of the morning proceeded in untrammeled harmony with much delighted gossiping: 'That Arturo! He's a pisser!' 'He showed 'em the road and told 'em they were welcome to it.' 'A relief, really. They were disruptive, arrogant. Definitely interfered with my P.I.P.' 'Them types wouldn't be happy anywhere.' 'They'll be causing trouble in some hallelujah bin next. . . .'

Miz Z. came clapping her hands down the line around noon saying there would be a special Aqua Man service at 1 P.M. They all scurried for clean bandages, barking at the novices to get ready.

It was a short service with only the Admitted admitted. Arty came in to a tape of 'The Ride of the Valkyries' and a roar of bubbles that subsided to reveal him floating in a hot-pink spotlight. He had a lot of gleam glunk on for the occasion and he made one of his more dynamic impressions. His talk was actually a chant — rhythmic: 'She served us — she served us all — now we serve her,' while an honor guard of one-fingered novices rolled out a wheeled cot with what remained of Doc P. ensconced in white satin. Chick tagged along behind. When the cot stopped in front of Arty's tank and the white spot hid it, Chick stepped up and peeled back the top sheet.

The crowd of amputees took a minute to catch on to who it was lying trussed like a leg of lamb. No mask. No cap. Only the spectacles glinting over her closed eyes were familiar. A short mop of grey hair spread around her face. She was still completely out. Those glasses were as useful to her as shoes, right then, but Arty, the clever little snot, knew the folks would need something to pin her identity on. Arty waited while the murmurs started and spread. Finally somebody down the front yelled, 'Doc P.!' and the joint went up like an ammo dump.

When the roar died down, the spectral voice of Arturo, from the glowing tank above the cot, introduced Doc P.'s replacement.

'The Apprentice — the Student — the Assistant. Now come into his own with his first act, this, the ultimate service to his teacher!'

Chick was charming — flushed pink and gold — his child body bobbing in an embarrassed bow to the storm of applause. Funny how all the Arturans adored him. They're delighted that he's now the surgeon.

24

Catching His Shrieks
in Cups of Gold

I'd expected Chick to fume endlessly about nipping Doc P. but he surprised me. In the act he was businesslike. Afterward he was gently nostalgic. He stood very close to her until the ambulance took her off. She was going to an Arturan rest home near Spokane. Chick also blossomed, as Mama would say, in his new fame as full-fledged surgeon. Arty claimed not to be surprised.

'That blush-and-shucks game of his was a dead giveaway. The kid always wanted an act of his own'

An act he had. The Arturans treasured him. On his eleventh birthday he was in the surgery for fifteen hours straight. He had a talk with the nurse on the day he was named successor. That cool and efficient personage became his dog and priestess on the spot. She'd never cared for Doc P.'s bullying. The Arturans pestered him constantly. I'd laugh, seeing some patriarch in a wheelchair rolling madly to catch up with the barefoot towhead kid in the dusty coveralls, or the two hard-bitten motorcycle vets sitting on a trailer hitch so this scrawny runt of a kid could peer into their big spongy ears or lift up an eyelid to examine the exploded blood map underneath.

'Well,' Chick confessed, 'I don't need to touch them or even look at them to tell what's wrong. But they like it, so I do it.'

They gave him no rest. Mama grumbled about his health and his lost childhood as she sewed baby clothes on her machine in the dining booth of the van.

'When does he climb trees? When does he sneak candy from the booths? Where are his friends to coax him into teasing the cats or giving Horst a hotfoot? They'll drive him into the ground. They'll suck him out of his natural growth. Look at his wrists and elbows! He's knobby!'

Arty was pleased in a guarded way. He kept an eye on Chick in case delusions of grandeur should beset him, but privately Arty was convinced that with Chick as 'The Knife' he was safe from revolutions. 'He's a loyal little insect,' Arty would grin. But Arty was intent on keeping the Arturan act solid. He toured the camp every day, supervised the office work, did his shows three times a week, conducted interviews, sent out advance men, advised Papa about the midway, and stayed away from Mama and Iphy.

Papa expected to assume Doc P.'s supervision of the twins' pregnancy but Arty slid Chick into the job. Papa sulked and spent more time drinking and playing checkers with Horst.

Iphy didn't bother to look up from her book when we came in. Chick sat on the floor and wiggled his toes in the carpet. I went my rounds with the dust cloth and made the bed and sorted the twins' laundry. Iphy read all the time. She liked mysteries. Every week's mailbag brought her a new lot of paperbacks. She took her daily walks and did her exercises grudgingly, wanting to get back to the book of the moment.

I came out of the bedroom with the laundry basket and looked at Chick. He hopped up and waved goodbye to Iphy as he opened the door for me.

'You're getting so used to doing things with your hands!' I said as we went down the ramp. He chirped, 'Elly is coming back some.' I felt myself swerving an inch above the ground giddy and happy.

'Put me down!' My feet touched and my stomach dropped into place. 'Are you sure?'

'Iphy knows but she's scared Arty will find out. Don't tell, Oly. Promise?'

'Are you doing it?'

We were near the laundry truck by then and Chick stopped

and looked at me, startled. His hair was hanging down around his ears, I noticed. Mama would be wrapping him in a towel soon, making him sit on a stool in front of the van, and stepping around him with scissors as she prattled and he squirmed.

'Are you doing it?' I repeated. He blinked and shook his head.

'I never thought of it. Do you think I could?'

'How do I know? I thought you could do anything.' I was impatient with him. It was one thing to be eleven years old when you were memorizing geography, but this was supposed to be the region of his gift, the terrain of his purpose.

'Well, I mainly take things apart. I can take anything apart,' he said. An amazed wideness settled on his eyes as he stared blankly at the door of the laundry truck.

Watching his possibilities dawn on Chick, I decided to ask the question that I'd been carrying for weeks. Ever since I'd realized how limited my own possibilities were.

'Chicky, listen. Remember how you used to pick pockets? Well, you know the sperm in Arty's balls?' I had his attention at least. 'Could you move that sperm — the wiggly little things — could you move them into me and get 'em into the egg thing in me so I could have a baby like Iphy?'

That, Miranda, was how I came to ask. Chick was hesitant, scared at first. He was afraid of botching the job. He insisted on trying it on the cats first.

The next week he managed to impregnate an elderly and irritable tigress whom Horst had never successfully mated. She had such a nasty attitude that she sliced up any male who propositioned her. Chick accomplished the miracle of Lilith, the tigress, early one morning while sitting on an overturned bucket in front of the cat wagon. I paced and fidgeted, ready to warn him if any of the Arturans should come along to distract him. He took what seemed like a long time. His hands clenched in a knot at his knees, his face flushed and beaded with sweat.

The male, at one end of the row of cages, slept through the process. Lilith, who had been named after Mama, paced and coughed and glared and switched her tail at the other end.

There was nothing to see. I was getting bored when he

finally let out a long cautious breath and looked at me. He rubbed his eyes with his fists. 'Wow,' he said, 'I think it worked.'

I went hopping and celebrating around, patting him on the shoulders and rumpling his hair. I was as happy as if it were my own stunt he'd just pulled.

Chick agreed to be ready to do it whenever my time came around if he could be sure of having both Arty and me still and in the same room, preferably for some time.

'Maybe I could do it without seeing you both, but something might go wrong. It's tricky.'

It happened one night in Arty's front room with Norval Sanderson there. Arty and Sanderson were talking their endless talk, Arty drawn up to his desk in the wheelchair and Sanderson stretched out in a soft chair with his legs ending in the loose sandals he wore to accommodate the bandages on his feet.

Chick was lolling on his belly on the carpet, pretending to read a big picture magazine about foreign lands. I was curled in the corner on a built-in bench, listening.

My pulse filled my head as though the heart had punched its way up my throat and was stuck beating between my ears. I couldn't take my eyes off Arty. He was in his wrangling mood. He loved to talk to Sanderson. He seemed to relax and enjoy the winding stalk of argument. Sanderson, the camouflaged hunter, pretended a casual indifference but secretly struggled to catch Arty unawares, skewer him on his own words.

Arty chuckled delightedly, 'Such a sadist! You go unarmed because you're sure you can make me turn my own weapons on myself! You don't want to dirty your delicate paws with my blood! You want me to rip out my own guts so you can tsk and sigh and write prize-winning features on the tragic flaw. The self-destructive vortex at the core of greatness! You do see greatness in me. Admit it!'

Sanderson, with his head tipped in cartoon contemplation, would tap his lip slowly with his thumb and question, always question: 'Is elephant gas great? Is it great in the pain that it causes the elephant? Or in the relief it affords when expressed? Or perhaps it is only great if it is ignited on farting and the resulting explosion is used to power a turbine? Is an elephant fart great in and of itself? Or only in its effect?'

'Ah! So now we're down to fart jokes! But you'll notice that I am sitting here with all I was born with, Norval, my lad, while you are being whittled away. How do you account for this?'

On and on they went, having such a good time. I loved Arty when he really laughed, and Sanderson made him roar. I watched, knowing this was my moment as Arty tipped back his smooth skull and rippled his belly in waves of pleasure that bounced out through his wide mouth and creased his grey eyes shut in the wild dance of his whole twitching, rocking body to the tune of the glitter inside his skull.

I sat very still. Chick had assured me that the thing in me was ripe and waiting.

There was Chick, on his belly with his bare feet kicking slowly in the air. His water-white hair hung in his eyes as he turned the pages slowly, revealing the mysteries of Tibet and the banner wall of the palace in Lhasa. His head turned slightly, one eye peeking at me. I grinned near convulsions. Do it. Do it now, while he's laughing, I thought. And Chick nodded slightly, turning back to his book as Arty said, 'Consider how protected our lives are. Never seen a movie, never set foot in a school.'

'But there's no reason for not seeing movies and whatnot,' protested Sanderson. The redheads have a portable set. It's sheer cantankerousness and barbarism,' he drawled.

'Early training!' barked Arty. 'Hatching habits!'

'Poor feller, try this ... ' and Sanderson pulled a flat steel bottle out of his tweed pocket and poured a golden dollop into a drained lemonade glass on Arty's desk. Sanderson pulled a long swig from the bottle, capped it, and sighed, 'Am-fucking-brosia!' while Arty cautiously nipped at his straw and made wry mouths at the taste.

'If that's your idea of pleasure, it's no wonder you need religion.'

Chick was flapping his magazine closed, pulling in his knees, getting to his feet with a stretch and a yawn, twisting to look at me. I stared anxiously at him. He winked.

'G'night,' he said to the room.

'You'll start on Miz Z. in the morning? I promised her,' said Arty.

Chick nodded and slid over next to the chair, looping an arm around Arty's neck, pulling his face close. Chick planted a kiss on Arty's bare, flat cheek and then went to the door and out. As he closed the door after him, my cap slid down my nose and then back up to its proper place again.

That was it. I didn't feel anything. But I believed it. And I didn't want to leave. I wanted to go on watching Arty at play, knowing he would talk for hours longer, until Sanderson's flask was empty and the black sky turned green and fleshy in the first seep of dawn. But I also needed to crawl back into my cupboard and feel miraculous. So I went home.

This, Miranda, is how you were conceived. Don't ever doubt that it was an act of love. Your father was as happy then as he was capable of being. Your uncle Chick, the dove, was delighted to do it, to be able to do it. And I was a seventeen-year-old dwarf, pink-cheeked, rosy-humped, scarlet-eyed. I was beside myself with glory. Understand, child, that my idea of you was as a gift to your father, a living love for Arturo. And that's not bad, Miranda, considered as a motive for your existence.

Eleven days later the twins gave birth to Mumpo. It was a long labor, twenty-six hours, and a difficult delivery. Chick did a lot but Mama and Papa helped. I wasn't allowed in the van. I sat with Arty all night and most of the day. He was sick with fear. I was sick myself. The Arturans were buzzing on the intercom constantly. I took messages and shunted them off. Miz Z. in her proud bandage (one little toe's worth) appeared at the door twice with a sheaf of papers, but I shooed her away. Arty wouldn't eat. He insisted on playing checkers, hour after hour, game after game. He beat me fifty times and he would have gone on forever except that I accidentally won a game and he threw the board off the desk in a fury. He rolled off to his bedroom and locked himself in.

When Papa finally came to the door with the news, Arty wheeled out of his room to hear. A boy. Twenty-six pounds, five ounces. The mothers were doing fine.

Papa looked young again, leaning in the doorway to shout the news; his mustache bristled with power and pride, which, he used to say, 'are the same except that pride leaves the lights on and power can do it in the dark.'

'Twenty-six pounds?'

'Thought it was twins, did you?' He chortled. 'Fat little! A natural! Twenty handsome inches long and twenty-six of the babiest pounds! What do you think, uncle? Cheeks like a politician! Ten chins right out of the oven! That Iphy! Took one look and says, 'Mumpo.' His name, see? Lily went to lay him on Iphy's breast and she like to die! Couldn't breathe, he's so heavy. Got to tell Horst; he's been sucking the bottle for two days worrying!' Then a sudden change, a confidentiality, a secret wondering, near whisper as he put one foot inside to keep it among us. 'That Chick, Great Christo, he's good. I would have popped it with a knife myself after so long. I was scared to death with the kid so big. Not Chick. He pumped in air somehow, don't ask me. That baby breathing easy for hours and still inside. That Chick, sweet lollyballs of the prophet!' And he was gone, thumping down the ramp, hailing people in the line, hollering, 'A boy ... Fine ... All fine ... A boy! Yes! By the bouncing melons of Mary! I'm a grandpa!'

Arty sat petrified in his chair, staring through the open door. Miz Z. appeared, heading for us, a clipboard in hand.

'Scare her off,' said Arty. He looked deflated and a little damp. 'Then go get the baby, will you?'

'What for?' I felt a fist of fear in my gut.

'I just want to see him!' He spun his chair away with a last look at my face. He disappeared into his room. I had hurt him. I tried to feel the little thing in my own belly. Nothing. But it was there. I'd make it up to him.

Mumpo changed people's names. Suddenly Iphy was Little

Mama to all the redheads and wheelmen, booth rats and *artistes*. Lily and Al were Gramma and Grampa. Even uncle and auntie jokes made the rounds along with Papa's licorice-marinated stogies and the bottomless keg on tap in Horst's van. But Mumpo himself lay like a big sagging pumpkin in the blankets. He was a bottomless craving and he was cunning. Arty saw it immediately. Iphy knew. I knew. Lily and Al refused to notice. Chick knew and didn't care. Chick loved the big glob.

That first day I poked my head through the twins' bedroom door and saw everything covered with white sheets and smelling of disinfectant. Lily hunched over the baby where he lay, naked and huge in soft, unmoving mounds on a wheeled metal table, as she sponged him, cooing. Chick was watching Iphy. He sat on the edge of the big bed and held her hand and Elly's pale useless hand, the arms overlapping so he could hold them both.

'How are they?' I whispered. He grinned the kid grin at me as though he'd walked on his hands or found a frog.

'Bushed. Pooped out. Beat.' They were asleep. Iphy as bloodless as a rain-drained worm. Elly with her mouth ajar and a thin trickle of saliva shining on her jaw.

'I could have made it quicker but Mama said it was important to labor. It didn't hurt them, though. I didn't let it hurt them. Did you see him?' His eyes glanced toward the flesh mound. I shook my head and moved over to where Mama could smile at me. She reached out an arm and hugged me. 'Isn't he amazing?' His eyes were open, filled with black. The eyes blinked and squinted suspiciously.

'Could you take him over to Arty? Arty is anxious to see him.'

Chick said it was O.K. and Lily chirruped and twittered excitedly, wrapping the baby to travel fifty feet, and exclaiming over his weight when she hoisted him across her chest.

In Arty's van she laid the big clump on Arty's desk and Mumpo's eyes went sharp and narrow, looking at Arty, and Arty glared at Mumpo and the two male things looked at each other with hate. Lily claimed that Mumpo couldn't focus his eyes yet but it was wonderful how he seemed to look right at you, though he's only an hour old and ought to be so tired he'd sleep, and she laughed at how excited Papa was thinking up 'Mumpo the Mountain' and other fat-man tags for Mumpo's show, though you couldn't be sure with a baby and for all we knew he'd be skinny by the time he was two.

Arty stared at the flesh that oozed from the blankets and finally broke in. 'O.K. Take him away. He needs to sleep.'

Lily took him out and that was the last time Arty ever looked at Mumpo.

The stick hit my ear and I yelled into the blanket as I woke up. My right arm jerked and the stick jabbed my elbow and the sting from my ear and my elbow pulled the plug on my nose and eyes so I looked wildly through the swimming murk of my watering sinuses as the white beam from a flashlight in the dark blinded my naked eyes and the stick whapped out of the blur again. 'Waa!' I yelled.

Then I heard the unmistakable rasp of Arty, angry, sputtering behind the stick, 'Cunt! ... Slimy! Twisted bitch!' as the stick wavered toward me and I curled in my cupboard with my arms shielding my eyes, yelling, 'Arty!' and the stick kept coming and I got a foot tangled in Mama's old white satin robe, which I used as a top blanket, and Arty's voice screeched in the light-smeared liquid blackness, 'I'll break you, you stinking ...' and the stick was on its way again and I grabbed for it snatched at the end as it passed my eyes and was amazed as the whole stick came loose in my hands with a slight tug and Arty wailed 'Shiiit!' and I saw the rubber bulb at the other end of the stick and felt a laugh trying to choke its way past my thumping heart because Arty was hitting me with a toilet plunger.

Then the lights went on and Papa was there, hairy-bellied in his pajama pants and Mama blinking and fuzzy behind him. I scrambled for my glasses and jammed them on so I could see Arty crying naked in his wheelchair with the blue veins pumping through the fine skin on his head and the flashlight on the seat beside him with its lens glowing a feeble yellow against the ceiling light.

'What the fuck?' Papa was gasping, and Mama fluttered and I stared through my safe green lenses at Arty, gibbering with frustration in his chair because he couldn't keep a grip on the stick with his flipper even though his belly rolled in crevices of muscle, though his chest was a plate of bronze, though his ribs jutted with the wings of muscle, though he could lift a hundred and fifty pounds with his neck, he still couldn't hold the stick to hurt me when he needed to.

'She's knocked fucking up!' howled Arty. Papa had his gentle hands on the smooth gold skin of the Aqua Boy, holding him against the back of the chair, saying, 'For Christ's bloody sake, son,' and wouldn't let go.

Mama brought a blanket to put around Arty. I crouched deep in my cupboard with the old white satin robe pulled up to my eyes because Arty knew. But he knew and was angry. The stomach thing happened, as though the baby, the tiny frog babe, Miranda, was trying to crawl out and escape by any route possible from his fury. I sat there holding in everything, clenching my ass and my cunt and my jaw and my eyes and praying the broadcast prayer of the godless, 'Please, please, no, please.'

Arty got his jaw back in order and resigned himself to draining his anger in words. He told them. 'Ask Chick. He told me. She's stuffed. Knocked up. The stupid traitor.'

Then I saw that Chick hadn't told him everything. Arty was leaning back in his chair and Papa sank down on the bench by the door trying to get it straight. 'Oly, what's he saying? Is this true?' I never opened my mouth but sat there, curled in amazement at Papa being Papa again for this one groggy moment. 'But that's no reason! There is no excuse,' rapped Papa , 'for attacking your sister physically!'

Arty rambled bitterly, 'That hunchback bastard redhead guy, the Pin Kid. Moving in on the shit-sucking show, knock up the boss's daughter ... work his way in ... get his claws on the money.'

I saw Arty shaking in his blanket, so hard that the wheels of his chair squeaked in minuscule quivers on the floor as he talked.

'He's drunk or stoned,' came Mama's voice.

'Drunk? Have you been hitting that stuff?' Papa wheeled Arty away through the door to his own van and I lay down and watched the door close and pulled the white robe up to my chin as Mama folded up on the floor beside my cupboard and looked in at me. Her soft face was crumpling with weakness and the loosening of her fiber, but her hands reached in and touched my face, long, cool fingers stroking my cheeks as she whispered, 'Did he hurt you dove?'

When I shook my head she took a deep breath and went on, 'Tell Mama now, are you pregnant?' and I nodded, staring at her through my green lenses, and she nodded seriously back at me. Her pale hair floated raggedly around her head. 'Are you glad, dream? Or is it something you don't want?' Her whole body smelt of cinnamon and vanilla as she leaned forward, asking.

'Glad,' I croaked, and she leaned in to lay her cheek on mine.

Papa came back and patted my head and took Mama back to bed. I lay in the dark listening but they kept their voices low and I couldn't make out what they were saying. It was probably my roaring blood that drowned them out. I was happy.

Arty was hurt. I imagined him clambering through the door alone in his chair with the flashlight and plunger to punish me. To hurt me for hurting him. I swelled with enormous love for him. See, I thought, how he has scared us all these years, and he can't even grip the plunger in that strong, awkward flipper. He needed to hurt me and couldn't.

He must love me, I thought, amazed. A faint whiff of nausea hit me at seeing pain as proof of love. But it seemed true. Unavoidable.

Afternoon. The midway music clanking faintly nearby. Everybody at work but me. I was alone in the van, sick in my cupboard. I was swamped hot and cold with the vicious swim of nausea. The cupboard doors hung open so I could see the gleaming linoleum. Orange brick pattern. I wanted the floor to be blue or grey so it would cool me. The white sunlight through the window hit the bricks with a terrible heat splash that burned through my dark glasses. If I closed my eyes, my head spun and my stomach did its tumbling act. If I rolled over to face the back wall, I smothered. I hugged my knees over my cramped belly and felt sorry for myself. I was almost dozing when I heard a step outside. Chick came in quietly.

'Should have told me, Oly.'

I grunted and stared at his bare, dusty feet kicking the bottoms of his ragged coverall legs. He pulled the curtains and the light greyed mercifully. 'You seen Arty?' I asked as his legs reappeared. He crouched on the floor beside me. He stuck out a grubby hand and touched my forehead. 'That's better.' I felt cool and quiet suddenly, as though I'd been floating motionless in a pond for hours.

'He's working. Still mad.' Chick looked down at me curiously.

I put a hand on my chest where mad Arty had left a ball of sick snakes knotted and jabbing each other poisonously. 'This too, please.' Chick frowned at me and the pain narrowed to a single vibrating spot like a bee sting. I tapped my fingers on the pained spot, impatient. 'Go on. Keep on. Do the rest, please.'

'I could put you to sleep. Want me to?'

'No. Did you tell him?'

'He didn't believe me. He thinks I'm just trying to smooth him down. And the Pin Kid is gone.'

I got up right away and went to the swallowers' stage, dragging Chick along. We poked our heads in through the rear flap and watched the scuttling shadows on the backdrop as the swallowers went through their act. Their chatter was marked by silences as the swords went down. The swallowers' oldest girl finished her turn and came rushing out, sweating. I snatched at her arm. 'Where'd the Pin Kid go?'

She shrugged, reaching to scratch under her sequined vest.

'Gee, Oly, I don't know. Daddy's mad at him. They were supposed to do a turn together. They've been rehearsing. But he was gone this morning when we got up. He took his knapsack and bedroll but left his trunk.' She rolled her eyes, perplexed. 'He'll have to come back for the trunk. And he knows we're breaking down tonight. Maybe he'll be back before we leave. Maybe he'll catch us in St. Joe?'

I could see the buckled trunk, drab in the dusty grass against the tent wall with swords and torches collapsing against it. The swallower's girl tossed her hair back and waved as she made off to the other side of the stage for her second entrance.

Chick was staring at the trunk. I could feel him thinking. The trunk looked abandoned, like letters in an attic, to and from the dead.

'We better go see Arty,' I muttered. Chick nodded, still looking at the trunk.

'Tell them to come back tomorrow.' It was Arty's voice seeping through the door crack. The bald novice who answered the bell left us waiting so he could see 'if the Master has a moment for you.' The shaved head appeared again, smirking consolingly. 'I'm afraid the Master ...' he started. But I jumped forward, shoving the door wider, hollering, 'Arty! You pig shit! Arty!,' bursting past the gasping novice with Chick behind me, trotting toward Arty's desk while I watched his face set in anger and his voice boom, 'Get her out! Out!' and the novice's three-fingered hands closed on my arms, but it was really Chick who lifted me. I knew by the softness, the easiness as I sailed back out through the door and landed on the deck. Chick leaned out and looked at me. 'I'll talk to him. Wait,' he said. Arty's door closed and I stood waiting. Angry myself, for a change. It was a relief from feeling sorry for myself.

As we moved that night in the dark toward St. Joe, Papa drove with Mama in his co-pilot's seat. Chick and I huddled in the dining booth and he told me.

'O.K. Now he really does believe me, kind of, because he talked to Horst about the tiger being pregnant and Horst told him it couldn't happen because she hadn't been with anybody. But he's still pretending he doesn't believe me. He won't admit anything. Besides, he's scared his juice isn't good. He's afraid he can't plant babies. But he says he's sick of the novices sliming around and he'll let you come back to work for him.'

'But what about the Pin Kid?'

I couldn't see Chick's face in the dark. He waited a few seconds before he answered. A dozen heartbeats.

'He just says, 'What Pin Kid?' and then won't listen. That's another thing. You're not to mention the Pin Kid or your baby or any of this to Arty. He wants you to act like always.'

I took Arty his breakfast in St. Joe. I cleaned and dusted and carried messages and shut the novices out of his van completely. I rode on the back of his golf cart to his show tent and waited behind the tank listening to the big St. Joe crowd roaring and sighing like the tide. I scrubbed Arty after the show and rubbed him down and painted him for the next show. I did all the usual things. He was sullen and moody at first but then he forgot and was just like always.

The Pin Kid never came back for his trunk. We never heard anything more about him. When I did think of him it was a pleasure — a fool's pleasure — that Arty had got rid of him, run him off, scared him away, for fear of losing me. I don't think Arty had him killed.

Elly was coming back. Iphy tried to hide the change but I sat for hours watching Mumpo twitch and Iphy crooning over him. I saw the differences. When Iphy used both hands to change Mumpo, or to turn him or wash him, Elly no longer collapsed like a spent balloon. She was holding herself upright without Iphy's arm supporting her. There were also moments when I could have sworn that Elly's eyes were focused, looking at Mumpo, looking at me, or following the movements of Iphy's hands. Elly's mouth stayed shut for longer periods. She drooled less. Once I saw her hand lift deliberately to her swollen, seeping breast.

'I use this little pump on Elly and put the milk into the bottle,' Iphy was explaining. Mumpo lay beside her on the bed sucking noisily at the rubber teat on the bottle. The pale blue milk sloshed and bubbled in the glass as the pull from his mouth drew the level down fast.

'He's so hungry all the time. It takes both of us to feed him but it's so awkward holding him *and* Elly so he can nurse straight from her titties . . .

Iphy stole a look to see if I believed that she still had to hold Elly. Elly's mouth opened and she said, 'Greedy, greedy, greedy.'

It was as clear as pizzicato. 'Ha ha,' said Iphy, staring at me intently. 'She's been making more sounds lately. Ha ha. Sometimes they're almost words.'

Perched at the foot of the bed with my feet over the edge so my shoes wouldn't dirty the sheets, I nodded and said nothing. The bottle ran dry and the deep voice of Mumpo rocked out an echoing belch. The lips of Elly closed primly and her eyes wandered again, soft, not looking while Iphy looked at us all so fast that her eyes must have ached with the whip of their nerve stalks.

Papa ordered signs painted for 'Mumpo, the World's Fattest Baby' and tried to talk Iphy into arranging a schedule so the baby could nap in a show booth and tickets could be sold. Iphy insisted on waiting until his first birthday. Papa was indignant. 'This is a working outfit! No moochers! No parasites! And what about yourself, young lady?' he demanded. 'How about a turn in the variety tent? You can work around Elly. There must be some way!'

Iphy bristled and reminded him of all the money she'd made for him the years she worked with Elly. She told him to wait. Papa left her alone. Iphy wasn't worried about it.

'Papa's just trying out old reflexes. He's not the boss anymore.'

My belly grew. It hung at an odd angle and gave me a lot of back pain. The veins in my legs threatened to rupture until Chick took care of them.

I spent time with Iphy and became convinced that Elly was almost all there, almost all the time.

'She's lying doggo, Iphy, don't lie to me.'

Elly's face was frozen on Iphy's shoulder but her arms were

coming back. Their dead flabbiness was turning to muscle again, and I could see it rolling thinly beneath the white skin, filling out the sleeves of her blouses.

'Elly? You've been exercising in secret, haven't you?' I'd ask, coming up close and staring into the unfocused eyes. She never reacted.

'Buzz off, Oly,' Iphy would snap, and I'd wander away, speculating about Iphy too, and how much more like Elly she was now. Stronger. Meaner. She never cried anymore. Never sang. She cleaned. She fed Mumpo, lying down beside him because she couldn't lift him. She gave up on bottles and turned so he could reach Elly's breast when he had flattened her own. She urged him toward solid food and he gobbled that, too, spilling nothing, sucking it all in, then demanding tit.

In Santa Rosa a Twins Fan Club came to the door. They were sixteen-year-old girls who had started dressing the 'Twin Way' when they were twelve or so and were still wrapping two waists in one big skirt like potato-sack racers. They dyed each other's California hair to the blue-black gloss of the twins.

I went to the door. The pair in front tried to look past me into the trailer. 'We just love them! Is it true they had a baby? We wanted to give them a present.'

The bouquet came in, passed from mock pair to mock pair and finally to me. I said Elly and Iphy were sleeping or maybe working. I took the green paper cone of flowers and thanked them and shut the door. Iphy watched through the curtains as the troop hobbled and giggled away, four pairs of twins with their arms around each other. Iphy absent-mindedly hugged Elly, who flopped from the squeezing.

'We used to have a lot of fans in this part of the country,' said Iphy. She put the flowers in a big jug of water and they sat on the table for days.

It was easy for me and it could have been much harder for the twins. We had a small world, peculiarly unalarmed by nature. We had no worries about food or shelter, the opinions of the family, or the hardships of lone child rearing. There were Mama and Papa and Chick. There was an inexhaustible reservoir of obliging redheads.

Part of being pregnant is that you think about it so much that you're seldom bored. Terrified often enough, but rarely bored. There was some disappointment in my mind occasionally. I'd sit in the sun next to Grandpa's urn on the generator truck and drift into lip-sucking melancholy.

Life for me was not like the songs the redheads played. It wasn't the electric clutch I had seen ten million times in the midway — the toreador girls pumping flags until those bulging-crotched tractor drivers were strung as tight as banjo wire, glinting in the sun. It wasn't for me, the stammering hilarity of Papa and Lil, or even the helpless, dribbling lust of the Bag Man rocked by the sight of the twins. I have certainly mourned for myself. I have wallowed in grief for the lonesome, deliberate seep of my love into the air like the smell of uneaten popcorn greening to rubbery staleness. In the end I would always pull up with a sense of glory, that loving is the strong side. It's feeble to be an object. What's the point of being loved in return, I'd ask myself. To warm my spine in the dark? To change the face in my mirror every morning? It was none of Arty's business that I loved him. It was my secret ace, like a bluebird tattooed under pubic hair or a ruby tucked up my ass.

Understand, daughter, that the only reason for your existing was as a tribute to your uncle-father. You were meant to love him. I planned to teach you how to serve him and adore him. You would be his monument and his fortress against mortality.

Forgive me. As soon as you arrived I realized that you were worth far more than that.

Lily collected Mumpo's castoffs and washed them and folded them into the drawers next to my cupboard. She moved the dish towels and the knives and forks and her plastic-bag collection and sewing scraps as well as Papa's junk tools. 'These will be your little hope chest,' she said.

Lily was delighted to have me swelling close to her, not cut off and strange as the twins had been. She would hug me distractedly in the kitchen or as we did the laundry together. 'Now hope hard!' she'd whisper, squeezing me, with her watery blue eyes blinking in filmed pleasure. An odd, warm scent of her favorite spray warmed by sweat and a faint bite of rot had begun to drift around her. I would lean against her, watching her hands, her crumpled-paper skin rustling as she stroked my face. 'You won't tell ... ' she whispered once, 'don't ever breathe it ... I don't like Mumpo ... I love him ... I'd tear my heart out for him ... but there's something about him I just can't like.'

Mumpo was eating the twins. 'Mama, he only shits once every three days and then not much. Is it O.K.?' Iphy fretted and Elly had frozen into an intelligent frown that bobbled perpetually against Iphy's shoulder. They grew frail and bony except for the four breasts that ballooned every three hours in time for Mumpo to wake. He bellowed before he even opened his eyes, roaring until the gap was crammed with raw tit. Then he vacuumed the bag until it draped flat over the protruding ribs of his mothers, and bellowed for the next tit until all four milk bags were drained and limp. He would sleep for three more hours before beginning again.

'Every baby is different,' Mama would say diplomatically. But later, in the home van, she'd shake her head at me and crackle, 'Greedy! Takes it in. Won't let it go. Keeps it!'

Mumpo grew, spreading around himself in looping, creased pools of pinkness that pulsated with his breathing.

Chick checked me over each morning before he ambled off to the Arturans for the day. He was ragged, growing out of his clothes. Mama was too distracted to notice. He missed Dr. Phyllis.

'It was easier when she was here,' he explained. 'I'm scared a lot now. Almost all the time.'

He came in for meals with his hands bloated like a drowned corpse's from the perpetual washing followed by the airtight gloves of surgery. He sank into a doze if he sat still for more than a few minutes. He worried about the ritual wrangling of Horst and Norval Sanderson.

'It's fair, isn't it?' he'd ask me. 'That's the way Doc P. set it up. Horst gets the legs and arms and Mr Sanderson gets the fingers, toes, and hands and feet. It's because the little bones are bad for the cats. That makes sense, doesn't it? Why does Mr. Sanderson keep trying to cheat? I had to ask a novice to guard the thighs in the refrigerator truck the other day because Mr. Sanderson kept sneaking them away in garbage bags. Horst threatened to let Lilith, the Bengal, loose in Mr. Sanderson's trailer some night if he doesn't stop. Horst is drinking all the time now. He might do it. And Papa goes over there to drink with him. They sit inside with the checkerboard and argue and drink and forget whose turn it is to move.'

Chick talked to me more all the time because he had no one else.

'Arty doesn't like the hometown surgeons getting in on the Arturans. He doesn't like the rest-home doctors setting up. But I do. I can't do it all. They can't all travel with us. Arty wants it all where he can see it but it's too big now. There are too many.'

Arty got a new folder of clippings every morning. The office novices would comb papers and magazines from all over the country for any mention of Arturism and for anything that might affect Arty. He subscribed to a broadcast-monitoring outfit that provided video or sound tapes of any news item, comment, discussion, or joke that mentioned Arturism on television or the radio.

'Here's another imitator in California, the Reverend Raunch! That's three in one state!' he snarled as I brought in his breakfast tray. 'And there's that brain-slice scam in Detroit, a takeoff on Doc P.'s trip. The silly cocksuckers are getting hauled in front of a grand jury. Ass lickers will screw us all!'

Arty didn't need to worry about the tadpole competition but he did. His tent was the biggest ever made on this continent, and it was always full, with a crowd as live as a hurricane wailing for him. But Arty sulked over every ten-cent Baptist, sneered at the plastic surgeons, turned green at ads for weight-loss clinics and alcoholism programs.

He'd gloat sometimes. 'I have the best tools. I talk to Doc P.'s keeper every week, you know. And my little brother did a much tidier job on Doc P. than Doc P. ever did in her life. Smartest thing I ever did was tuck Chick in her pocket.'

I didn't pay much attention. I was caught up in the amazing contents of my belly. Everything else was insignificant. As the time got close, though, I got scared. I wasn't afraid of dying. Chick wouldn't let me die. I wasn't afraid of the baby dying. Chick would make sure it stayed alive. Still, a sick grey fear sat in my chest, nameless. Chick kept offering to put me to sleep.

'Hey, it's good. Doc P. is happy. I'd like it myself. I'd put myself to sleep only there's nobody to do my job.'

When my labor started Mama gave me tea and Chick put me into one of the Arturan wheelchairs and took me to his surgery. It was late in the afternoon. The Ferris wheel lights were bright against the dusk and I could smell popcorn and hear the talkers hollering, 'Show the little lady what you're made of!'

It didn't hurt. I sat up against pillows and slept for a minute at a time between squeezes. There was no pain but it was exhausting work. I remember looking at Chick and Mama and trying to tell them why it was called 'labor.'

I remember seeing Miranda's head for the first time between my legs. She looked so silly, like a red turtle's head stretching on its spindly neck and turning, blinking, wobbling, I nearly laughed. And I remember Chick's smile as he reached for her. She slid out onto the white cloth he held for her, and he lifted her dripping, squirming little carcass and put it on my collapsing belly. 'I like this!' he said. This was his second delivery, of course, and he told me later that Miranda was easy compared to Mumpo, that he'd worked much harder to suppress the twins' pain.

Mama and I examined her amazing body and found only that ridiculous tail. My heart died. Arty would despise her. But

Mama told me to go on hoping. 'Go ahead and love her,' Mama said. I've wondered since whether those were Mama's last sane words, the final sizzle of her synapses.

Then the real fear began. With the baby outside me and vulnerable, I suddenly saw the world as hostile and dangerous. Anything, including my own ignorance, could hurt her, kill her, snatch her from me. I wanted to cram her back inside where she'd be safe. I was too weak to protect her. I needed the family. Arty had to care about her. Iphy had to help me. Papa had to be sober and brave, and Mama had to lay off the pills and be wise. But there was really only Chick, and I was terrified whenever he was out of sight. I scared him with my clinging but I couldn't trust the baby to anyone else.

She had Arty's face and I named her Miranda because Miranda's father loved her.

Arty did not love my baby. He never asked to see her. When I finally went to see him — took him his breakfast a few days after she was born — I left her with Chick. I was testing the water and I found it cold.

'How kind of you to call,' Arty sneered. 'Good of you to take the time. I suppose you won't be working anymore. Gone into retirement like Iphy.'

I felt my lungs ice over. I couldn't snap back at him. I went back and hid in the cupboard, holding Miranda, careful not to press her bottom the wrong way for fear her tail would be twisted or pinched.

I always slept curled around her in my cupboard. It made Mama nervous but there was no room for me to turn over so I thought there was no danger that I'd crush or smother her. I didn't dare put her in a box or drawer separate from me.

'He doesn't hate her,' Chick said. 'How could he?' Chick was holding Miranda in the sink as I bathed her. His arm looped behind her flat little back so she wouldn't topple over and crack her perfect skull. I was afraid to trust myself bathing her. Her five-month-old fingers grabbed at his moving lips and he kissed them, making slurpy noises. 'Mama and the redheads say you should be getting better now, Oly. Not so afraid.'

My arms disappeared below the elbows, covered by the warm grey water in the sink. Across the lot, Leona the Lizard Girl was floating, still and silent, in the green murk of her jar. Miranda could chortle and hurl a spoonful of pablum at the wall but she would be as helpless as Leona against Arty. I wanted Chick to believe me, to be frightened and watchful as I was.

'Baby's no threat to him.' Chick spoke as though he were answering my thoughts. A bubble of light swelled in me. He was right. That puny tail of hers was no threat to the Aqua Man.

'Besides,' Chick protested, 'he keeps after me to bring Elly back. He says it would be good if she could help with Mumpo. I've been working on it but it's tricky in there. In her head.'

My bubble fantasy sank into a chilly puddle. So that's why Chick was so sure of Arty's benevolence. 'Guilty,' I said.

Chick nodded agreeably, his shiny head bobbing on his scrawny neck above Miranda's unfathomable curls. 'He feels bad.'

I sponged her puffing cheeks and she opened her gums and clamped down on the sponge, squeezing it happily. 'I thought she was coming back.'

'It's slow,' he nodded. 'It was starting anyway. But I'm trying, a little bit every time. You should go over more. They're lonely, the twins. It helps if things are busy, exciting around them. Elly notices more.'

'I help Iphy with the cleaning.'

'You don't like Mumpo. You think he's bad, but he's not. Take Miranda to play with him.'

'He doesn't play. He just lies there and eats.'

Chick's golden face fell into a shadow of hurt. 'He's a wonderful baby. He's different from Miranda.' His face drooped down to rub against her damp hair. 'But he's wonderful.'

I reached for a towel. 'Let's get her out now.'

She rose, dripping, straight up from the water and swooped into my arms, crowing.

'She likes to fly.' I smiled up at Chick, ashamed of insulting his other child.

'I have to go to surgery now.' He wouldn't look at me. His face was flushed.

'We'll come with you.' I started dressing her quickly.

'No, Oly. Don't. It's hard for me to concentrate when I have to take care of you. I have hard things to do.' I watched him through the window as he walked away. The ragged straps of his coveralls rode his bare bony shoulders as though nobody loved him.

Miranda was just learning to walk. She traveled from Papa's big chair to the built-in sofa bench where Chick slept at night. Then she fell, face first, and split her lip. I was crying. She was bleeding and screaming. That was when Arty decided to come calling. It was the first time he had ever seen Miranda.

It is true that I'd been useless to him since she was born. She changed me. When I did work I was afraid to be close to him because I had something to lose.

After he wheeled out in disgust, I ran, with the baby still bleeding in my arms, and burst through the door of the surgery. The nurse grabbed my shoulders and hustled me into the waiting tent. Chick was severing a thigh. A critical procedure. She gave me a swab for Miranda's lip and went back to the surgery.

He came out in his green scrubs and I flung myself on him. He was thirteen years old. I was nineteen. Miranda was one. He looked at her and she stopped crying. Her lip stopped bleeding. She reached up to him and he lifted her. She sighed and let her head fall onto his shoulder.

'He called her a norm,' I stormed. 'He says he'll feed her to Mumpo! He wouldn't even look at her tail! Iphy will laugh all crazy and Mama will pop a pill and Al will swig on his bottle and nobody, nobody can help me but you!'

His child face rumpled in puzzlement. 'I don't understand,' he said.

At once a coolness swept over me. A woods-pond stillness filled me. 'No!' I shrieked. 'No! Don't!' But it was too late and the anger and pain were small and hard in me, not gone, but distant.

'Now explain, please,' Chick pleaded. And we walked calmly out through the tent flap and strolled up the grass behind the midway booths, and Miranda fell asleep in Chick's arms on the way.

I believe Chick tried. When he came out of Arty's van he looked a thousand years old. He was the one who had to tell me.

Dear daughter, I won't try to call my feeling for Arty love. Call it focus. My focus on Arty was an ailment, noncommunicable, and, even to me all these years later, incomprehensible. Now I despise myself. But even so I remember, in hot floods, the way he slept, still as death, with his face washed flat, stony as a carved tomb and exquisite. His weakness and his ravening bitter needs were terrible, and beautiful, and irresistible as an earthquake. He scalded or smothered anyone he needed, but his needing and the hurt that it caused me were the most life I have ever had. Remember what a poor thing I have always been and forgive me.

He saw no use for you and you interfered with his use of me. I sent you away to please him, to prove my dedication to him, and to prevent him from killing you.

The Arturan Administrative Office arranged everything. They located the convent school. They deposited a lump sum of money in a trust fund to be doled out to the nuns.

My job was to take you to that cross-cursed old woman — who, don't forget, had given up children for her God-love long before you or even I came along. I had to take you to her and come back without you.

My job was to come back directly, with nothing leaking from beneath my dark glasses, to give Arty his rubdown and then paint him for the next show, nodding cheerfully all the while, never showing anything but attentive care for his muscular wonderfulness. Because he could have killed you. He could have cut off the money that schooled and fed you. He could have erased you so entirely that I never would have had those letters and report cards and photos, or your crayon pictures, or the chance to spy on you, and to love you secretly when everything else was gone.

Arty could have done worse, but he chose not to.

25

All Fall Down

Hopalong McGurk smiles with pearly dentures because my perfect Binewski teeth went down the spout with everything else. Yet the day we lost it all was nothing special. Miranda had been gone a year or so. Late in the morning I was in Arty's dressing room as usual, coating him with grease as the tent filled and the ropy voice of the crowd came through the wall, thickening the air. Arty lay on his belly on the massage table while I painted him. He watched me in the big wall mirror.

'Thick in the creases, please. I want to shine.'

I pushed the rolled flesh at the back of his neck and slathered a handful of grease over the smooth skin. He put his forehead against the bench and arched to pull the rolls out flat. I smoothed and rubbed and the sheen came up onto the back of his skull and crept toward his ears.

'Do you want the tips on your flippers?'

'I like it. The whole crowd breathes in when I go like this ...' He spread his flippers and winked into the mirror.

I slid a hand under his chest and heaved. His back muscles rolled in cut slabs, every knob of his incredible spine visible as he bunched to help me. When he was balanced upright on his rear fins, I worked on his forehead and pulled the grease down onto his long eyelids and the flat cheekbones.

'I want a straight stroke of the white under each brow, down the nose, and under my lower lip. Not too blatant for the folks up close to the tank.'

I opened the jar of deli-white and spread his right fore-flipper. The pale glitter was already dry between his web creases. I painted brushfuls of soft gleam onto the fine fan of bones that were almost a hand sprouting from his shoulder. He flexed and spread and the light danced on the webbed flap.

The flippers on Arty's hips were graceful. Nearly flat, twisting at their short joints like swans' necks, smooth and powerful and extending with asymmetrical purpose. The little toelike thing that never had grime beneath its square nail could grip or scratch or turn a page. He twitched as I stroked on white, sending ripples through his whole body.

'Good. Go ahead and grease it now,' he said.

The undercoat caught the light in a subtle prism. When it was set, the final greasing had a sheen of its own and kept the white on even through the hour under water with Arty squirming his wildest. The white tipping and streaking were new touches. Arty examined himself in the mirror and his wide mouth wriggled from corner to corner.

'My, my. Won't they just lick my jizz today?'

The sky above Molalla was aching blue but I walked from Arty's tent to our van in the same air I'd sucked all my life. It was a Binewski blend of lube grease, dust, popcorn, and hot sugar. We made that air and we carried it with us. The Fabulon's light was the same in Arkansas as in Idaho — the patented electric dance step of the Binewskis. We made it. Like the mucoid nubbin that spins a shell called 'oyster,' we Binewskis wove a midway shelter called 'carnival.'

It was noon and the crowds were building. Arty was in his tank holding elevation services for the Admitted in the big tent. Sanderson was hawking maggots in his elegant kudzu grammar. The redheads threw daring looks from every ticket booth and candy stand. Two dozen simp twisters did their best to shake, shock, and dizzy the change out of all the local pockets. I strolled down the midway, ready for lunch. I thought Crystal Lil was brewing Scotch broth for all her children.

But then I saw Lily in front of the twins' van. She opened her long face and yelled, 'Chick!' just as Chick pelted past me, elbows and knees pumping toward her. His white hair lashed behind him and I began to run. 'It's Elly!' howled Lil.

The bedroom door was open. The pink bed was filled with thrashing. One bare leg bent, beating its hard heel into the limp thigh of its mate. A long arm arced out of the snarling hair and flesh and whipped downward, clenching scissors.

'No!' said Chick, but the glinting fist landed and the heel went on kicking its other leg. 'No!' Chick pounced on the bed and two frail arms jerked up out of the long black hair. The furious leg straightened and fell down on the sheets. Iphy's red-smeared face tipped up between the raised arms and she lay quietly down beside Elly. The bubble pumping red from Elly's breast flattened and then ceased. The two shining eyes of the scissor handles sat straight up in the shadowed socket of Elly's left eye.

'No.' Chick reached for Elly while Lily, on her knees beside the bed, moaned, 'Baaaby.'

'Elly?' said Chick.

I could see the thing on the floor in front of Lil, the bloody diapered heap of Mumpo.

'I can't find her!' The creak of fright in Chick's voice. A long thin tone whined from Lily's open mouth.

'I killed her,' said Iphy calmly. She looked up at the ceiling from between arms stuck to the sheets by Chick's mind.

'I can't fix her!' Chick was crying.

'She killed my little boy.' Iphy's voice was flat as Kansas.

'Mumpo,' said Chick and he lunged off the bed and saw the mess on the floor at Lily's knees.

'Oh no,' Chick whispered. 'I didn't feel him go. Mumpo.'

Lily keened. 'I did it,' sobbed Chick. 'I brought Elly back.'

'Arty,' said Iphigenia. Then she died.

Rooted to the carpet, I stood and watched her go.

Chick whirled to look at her, his tear-slimed face broke. He threw himself on her, his hands grabbing her face. He jammed his face against hers, screaming, 'No!'

Lil rocked on her knees beside the cooling pile of Mumpo. The high whine came and went with her breath. Chick's face and hands were buried in Iphy's dark mane. He said, 'Arty.'

I broke for the door. Arty, I thought. Tell Arty. I hit the ramp as Chick passed me, his blond body hurtling barefoot to the dirt. I chased him. He stopped when he hit the midway. He stamped his feet into the sawdust, gathering himself, staring up the line to where the big tent loomed fifty feet above the booths and rides. 'Arty,' he said, and I heard him through the wheezing music from the Mad Mouse as he stood, clenching his fists in the midway, stretching his neck with his eyes closed. No sign appeared around him. The air did not quiver. But silence came off him and the stretch of his neck cords made him old, and the veins blue and hard against his skin, and far down the line Arty's tent, full of Arty and his cripples, blew upward, incinerating.

The white rocking air hit us before the sound. I heard nothing, but raised my hands against the rushing air, and the fire came, toppling toward us in falling blocks like the wave in a child's dream, huge, though the torches were booths and tents no taller than a man could touch with his hand. It came billowing, scorching toward us, and the Chick, in his pain, could not hold himself but reached. I felt him rush through me like a current of love to my cross points, and then draw back. I, with my arms lifted, felt his eyes open into me, and felt their blue flicker of recognition. Then he drew back. He pulled out of my separate self and was gone. He turned away — and the fire came. The flames spouted from him — pale as light — bursting outward from his belly. He did not scream or move but he spread, and my world exploded with him, and I, watching, bit down and knew it — bit down with a sense of enormous relief, and ground my teeth to powdered shards — and stood singed and grinding at the stumps as they died — my roses — Arty and Al and Chick and the twins — gone dustward as the coals rid themselves of that terrible heat.

Many died. Many burned. Babes snuffed to grease smears in the blackened arms of their charcoaled mothers. Sudden switches, lean and brittle, had started as dancing children only seconds before. All the dark, gaping corpses, in their fire-frenzy ballet, flexed and tangled in the dreams of the finders. The fire-fighters and ambulance shriekers who had worked arson-struck tenements and the crashes of jumbo jets puked and retreated, or quit their jobs to grow lettuce, but still dreamed, after wading the ashes of Binewski's Carnival Fabulon.

For me there were only Arty and Al and Chick and the twins snatched into nothing — and I with them — grinding, for relief, my teeth into powder.

The cats were lost but Horst made it. He took care of business while I was in hospital. He brought me the papers to sign but he made the decisions. I didn't object. He sent what he could find of Zephir McGurk home to his sons. He cleaned and polished the Fly Roper's stork-shaped scissors before mailing them to the ex-wife in Nebraska. Horst was the one who identified Arty's boiled body, no longer beautiful, in the dark char left when the big tank vaporized. He gathered the torn, soggy jar kin from the remnants of their shattered jugs and ushered them, with the rest of the Binewski dead, through what he called 'decent' cremation.

The family living vans weren't touched by the firestorm. Horst took out everything personal and then sold the vans. Norval Sanderson died in the Transcendental Maggot booth near Arty's tent, but his van was safe. Horst was quick enough to get the papers, tapes, and journals out and away before the reporters got hold of them. He stored everything and rented a shabby room for himself near the hospital. He was occupied for months with the dismantling and bankruptcy of the Arturan rest homes. He visited me every day except Wednesdays, when he trekked down to the state mental hospital near Salem to visit Mama in her padded room.

He brought me from the hospital to a small rented room across a dark hall from his own.

'We might as well say here, in Portland,' he said. 'Every place is the same now.'

The Binewski name stank and drew flies. Horst gave my name as McGurk when he rented my room. 'Zephir was a good man,' Horst told me. McGurk loved Arty so I kept the name.

Horst was the one who found Crystal Lil after the firestorm. It was a year or more before he told me about it. By then I had a job recording books for the blind. I had begun building a small life in the strange, stuck world. Horst had met a woman with strong thighs and a Siamese cat. He was moving in with her. He took me to McLarnin's bar for our goodbye. Horst had a few extra jolts and then told me.

'I was looking for your papa. It was all over but the screaming. I came around the end of a van and saw him on the ground. He must have just stepped down from the generator truck when it blew. Your grandpa's silver urn was lying in the gravel beyond him, battered. There was blood on it. I think it was Al's.'

Horst couldn't look at me. He wound his thick fingers in his grey mustache and glared into his glass.

'I knew he was dead and I stayed back. I couldn't go up to him. I sat down in the gravel by the urn but I couldn't touch that, either. Then here comes your mama, calling 'Al' like it was suppertime. She was off her head. Out of it, you understand.

'She runs to where he's lying and rips off her blouse — pulls her skirt down — hikes her underpants tight against her crotch. She's saying, "Al ... broken ... just completely broken ... we'll have to start over." She crouches over Al's body, straddling his thighs, fumbling at his belt, opening his zipper, yanking those white jodhpurs down to his hips and talking softly. She settles herself over his limp penis and she rocks, rubbing her crotch against him, stroking his chest, not noticing the half of his face that isn't there anymore — not noticing the handless stump of his arm smoldering, but rubbing herself slowly like a cat against him and running her hands inside his shirt against his chest hair and saying, "Broken ... Al ... after all our work ... we'll start again ... Al ... you and me ... Al."'

Mumpo was not quite three years old when he died. And you, Miranda, were two, stringing beads and eating vanilla wafers in Sister Lucy's nursery. But you were nine years old before the doctors let me bring Crystal Lil home to the house on Kearney Street.

I was full-grown before I ever set foot in a house without wheels. Of course I had been in stores, offices, fuel stations, barns, and warehouses. But I never walked through the door of a place where people slept and ate and bathed and picked their noses, and, as the saying goes, 'lived,' unless that place was three times longer than it was wide and came equipped with road shocks and tires.

When I first stood in such a house I was struck by its terrible solidity. The thing had concrete tentacles sunk into the earth, and a sprawling inefficiency. Everything was bigger than it needed to be and there were so many shadowed, dusty corners empty and wasted that I thought I would get lost if I stepped away from the door. That building wasn't going anywhere despite an itchy sense that it was not entirely comfortable where it was.

That was when I first recognized a need to explain myself. That was the time when I realized that the peculiar look on people's faces when they saw me was not envy or hatred, but could be translated into one simple question: 'What the hell happened to you?' They needed to know so they could prevent it from happening to them.

My answer was simple, too. 'My father and mother designed me this way. They achieved greater originality in some of their other projects.'

For a while I told people this. I was proud of it. It was the truth. Only a few folks ever actually asked — little children, drunks, or people so old that they exempted themselves from the taboos of courtesy by pretending senile irresponsibility. I got interested. I'd throw the answer even when the question wasn't voiced but was only lightly etched in the flesh around the eyes. I'd smile calmly and announce it to the kid at the gas pump, or the garbage collector, or a lady with a shopping bag at a street light.

Some, particularly women, would turn away as though I hadn't spoken or they hadn't heard me. They thought I was crazy. They didn't want to encourage me. Next thing I'd be asking for money.

I worked on polishing my story and my delivery. To excuse them for wondering, to make them feel all right about it. I felt exhilarated by each explanation, but still they shut me out.

'Shit!' some would say. Or 'Do tell!' The best I could hope

for was 'Born that way eh?' Were they bored by it? Or embarrassed? Did they assume I was lying?

This mystery appeared when I first stood in a rooted house. I hadn't understood before that anything about me needed explaining. It's all very well to read about houses, and see houses from the road, and to tell yourself, That's where folks live. But it's another thing entirely to walk inside and stand there.

Al always laughed at the stuck houses. He hauled out his only bit of scripture to deal with houses. 'The birds of the air have their nests,' he would announce as though it were a nursery rhyme, 'the foxes of the ground have their holes.' And he would raise one finger and jut his eyebrows forward in his teaching way, 'But the son of man hath nowhere to rest his head.'

BOOK IV
Becoming the Dragon

26

NOTES FOR NOW
The Swimmers

I, the dwarf whose ears are separated only by an oozing hemorrhoid, am now being punished for sentimental collapse during my swimming lesson. It was the soft flab over Miss Lick's neck that broke me. The firm way she has of pushing her jaw down into the cushions of her multiple chins as she smiles at me in the water. I had set myself up with a splurge of vanity for my own malignant resolution. Then the mere sight of Miss Lick's neck tipped me off my perch. I blubbered all the way down and damned near gave the show away.

There I am, soaking in the green air above the water, keeping tabs on the lifeguard who is fluttering winsomely at a golden-brown boy wearing, apparently, three pounds of grapes stuffed down the front of his wet swim trunks. The room echoes flatly, and four little girls are huddled in the water on the other side of the pool, swearing to each other in whispers that they have seen me in the dressing room without my swim cap and my green-tinted goggles. They are assuring each other that I am as bald as a baby's ass and that my eyes are bright red.

With my eyes closed I can feel the children looking at me. They have stopped their games for a moment in the shallow end where they can watch me. I too am at the shallow end, sitting on the steps in water up to my nipples. Miss Lick is plowing up and down the pool in her ponderous and dutiful laps. The children's eyes are crawling on me. If I opened my eyes they would smile at me and wave. They are just old enough to be embarrassed at their normality in front of me.

Because I am Olympia Binewski and am accustomed to the feel of eyes moving on me, I turn slightly on my submerged seat and reach down as though examining my toes under water. This angle will allow the children a clear profile view of my hump. I have never claimed that my hump is extraordinary in size or conformation, but it is a classic of its kind, rising in a clean arc and pulling my shoulders up, pinching my chest out in a narrow wedge. The top of the hump, if I bend at a certain angle, is as high as the back of my head. Now I will bring both hands out of the water and remove my goggles. There is some splashing from the children. They are impressed at the size of my hands on the ends of my short, thin arms. I smile and open my eyes so they can tell in the dapple reflections on the water that my eyes are a deep rose pink rather than red.

But Miss Lick is standing in the shallow end, glowering down at the children. I can hear her harshness. 'Are you swimming laps or fooling around?' And four little creatures do not speak but kick off from the wall and chase each other down the far lane of the pool to escape.

The light is pale green and moves on Miss Lick's enormous shoulders and chest. She turns and nods at me — a quick twitch of tension at her mouth that stands for a smile. She is telling me that she has saved me from the stares of idiots and that I am safe with her to guard me. Then she plunges back into the water and moves forward, beating the surface with the sound of a hiccuping cannon.

The children turn and come back but they won't dare stop at this end again. Miss Lick doesn't like children. She hates beautiful female children. These four ten-year-olds are long and absurdly slim, with clean faces. They are frightened of Miss Lick but not of me.

Maybe it's because I am so old. They would worry if I was their age and they could imagine being me. They tell each other that I was 'born that way,' which is reassurance for them and comfort for me. Nothing could make me hurt them.

But they are wise to fear Miss Lick. She could lose control for an instant and grind them to paste.

* * *

Miss Lick is giving me a swimming lesson. She holds me in her arms and mutters, 'Tip your head back, arch your spine. Good. Now kick from the hip.'

Her face is big and serious, watching me carefully. Her arms and hands are warm beneath me. I lie on my back and squint up into her bulging face and know that she is the only friend I've ever had. We are in water that would be over my head if she let me go. I can hear the thrum of other swimmers beating the water around me. The light bounces off the walls and is broken by the water. Miss lick holds me up. 'Good, Oly,' she says, and she smiles at me.

Miss Lick is six feet two and a heavyweight athlete. She is not quite 40 years old and has 20-inch biceps. I have 7-inch biceps. I am 36 inches tall. I weigh 64 pounds and I am very old at 38. My arthritis is actually 110. But Miss lick is even older because she is closer to death. Miss Lick has her arm around the bomb that will kill her and she is dickering to buy it.

'Kick!' she barks, grinning down at me. Suddenly the sting of grief spurts from my sinuses to my belly. This is all Miranda's fault, I tell myself in rage. If my daughter weren't such a fly-brained slut I wouldn't be in this position. I could be a quiet, pleasant old dwarf, curling into a dry and sanitary death in my own blankets without ever having injured a soul. But here I am rocking in the arms of the creature I intend to slaughter. When I stop kicking and double up in pain, Miss Lick is worried.

'Water in your nose?' she asks, pumping her huge pillow hand gently against my hump. 'Did you swallow some?'

Looking up through my smeared green lenses I see a roll of fat covering the artery in Miss Lick's throat.

When I refuse to go to dinner at her house Miss Lick wants to carry me up to my apartment and tuck me into bed. 'God, I'm so thoughtless!' she groans as she wheels the big sedan through the dark streets. 'I act as though you're a goddamned mountain like me!'

'Not at all.' I squawk, with my fingers clutching the soft leather of the front seat. 'Not at all,' I repeat, grabbing with one hand at the dashboard and the other at the armrest to keep from hurtling into the dark well of legroom as Miss Lick stops for a light.

'You're sure you don't want me to come up with you? I could make you some soup. I know you don't eat.'

'Not at all,' I fiddle with the door handle, and the door eases open at last and a crack of cool air slips in, dulling the hot reek of her chlorine flesh in the car. 'I'm going to unplug the phone and crawl right into bed. I'm recording early tomorrow.'

Her big hand touches my hump as I slide toward the pavement. 'Let me give you a lift to the radio station in the morning,' she urged.

'Not at all.' I can barely think anymore. If I don't get away from her I will disintegrate and ruin everything.

'Thank you so much. I'll see you in the pool tomorrow evening,' and I grab the car door with both hands and slam it on her goodnight and turn away, steering at top speed for the lobby entrance because she never pulls away from the curb until she sees me safe inside.

This building is new and Miss Lick could put a fist through my front door as easy as belching, which she does glibly. Miss Lick can belch every syllable of the name 'Harry Houdini' on demand and enjoys being asked. Still, I lock the flimsy veneer behind me and then unplug the phone, I told her I was going to bed and I can't risk a busy signal if she rings to check on me.

It is garbage night for Crystal Lil. I have to go home. Taxis are expensive for moderately employed dwarfs who rent extra apartments, swim at private clubs, and fancy themselves as righteous assassins. I use the footstool to stare into the mirror over the sink in the all-new bathroom. Straightening my wig, adjusting my glasses, I smirk at myself because it serves me right for being such a flabby clot as to lose my nerve. Getting all choked up with sympathy for Miss L. A good two-mile walk in the dark and cold will teach my knees and ankles a little respect for discipline and self-control.

Fatigue makes me giddy. By the time I get to the alley behind Lily's house, my head is floating several feet above my

body and I have a bitter tendency to giggle. I can see myself
and the view is pathetic. I don't dare use the front door in case
Miss Lick is pursuing her surveillance hobby.

The old dwarf rolls up the cat-shit dark stairs of the decrepit
garage to get to the roof. Her feet hurt and her knees are
pleading for a transfer to Bermuda. 'Eeh,' grunts the frog-
faced albino. Her hip joints have gone past red-hot to a temper-
ature unfamiliar even to the flap-titted hunchback. 'Hunh,'
says the bald-headed mother of morons, as she stops to lean
against the open door to the roof.

The air is grey, lit by a street lamp at the end of the alley.
The garage roof is flat and attached at the rear to the tall wood
house. The rain pops and silvers on the slimed pool of water
that fills the center of the roof. The house fire escape sinks its
feet in the roof tar. Miss Oly, the third or fourth Binewski
child, depending on whether you count heads or asses, takes off
her blue-tinted spectacles and rubs the sweat from under her
bulging pink eyes and off the bridge of her wide, flat nose and
then hooks the glasses back over her ears and settles them in
place. Raising the entire flesh of her forehead and skull for lack
of eyebrows, Ms. Binewski proceeds, with anxious care, to roll
bowleggedly away from the cat stench of the stairway, around
the edges of the rain pool, making for the first length of the
cast-iron fire ladder. There she goes, humping up the damp,
sooty rungs. She stops climbing and hooks her chin over the
rung in front of her to rest for three breaths, thinking it may be
time to get a cane. Or maybe a pair of canes hefty enough to
help a burst toad of an elderly cretin up such flights of carpen-
terial fancy as those cat-slimed stairs in the garage without
having to reach out and touch each sodden step with a hand.

She, this Oly, has reached the first slat landing of the fire
escape and is hauling her thick carcass onto it with her spider
arms and resting again — or, more accurately, peering through
the dirt-fogged window of the room that looks out of this arse-
alley backside of the noble West Hills, and, if those are tears
puddling in the bottom of those wire-framed glasses she's
wearing, then this flabby old douche bag will be too blind to
stay on the platform and will drop and crack like a beetle on the
garage roof, next to the ornamental pool.

No, she claims she's not crying, though her sinuses are trying to squeeze out through her eyeballs. She is, however, feeling sorry for herself because this is 'her' window and the big dusty room on the other side is 'her' room and Oly misses it and would like to crawl in and shut the window and never leave it again, but she cannot because instead of a brain she has been blessed with a flame-purple hemorrhoid and she is in miserable, though voluntary, exile until her little project is finished.

There, is she crying again? Or is she only realizing that if she had washed that smog-clogged hunk of glass anytime in the last three years she might actually see her reading chair and her hotplate sitting on the cupboard and the cupboard doors that open into the blanket nest where she sleeps with the doors snugged shut and her knees tucked up to her chin. This failure in the service of transparency is disheartening to the delicate mucous linings of the amphibious Miss Oly. Picturing her cranky joints curled in her own warm nest causes further heat and discharge from her cherry-pink eyeballs.

Quietly she slips the lock, pushes the window upward, snakes through into the warm dark, and feels the cushion-thick carpet beneath her brogans. She smiles her frog smile and considers calling a taxi for the trip back since surely she has punished herself sufficiently for what was, after all, an understandable weakness. Next time, she muses, I'll simply stick my hand in boiling water.

I go downstairs and yell, 'Garbage!' three times at Lil's open door before she sits back from her magnifying-glass approach to the evening game show. Her white head moves, groping with ears and nose more than her sad, jellied remnants of eyes. Each time I look at her the white hair is paler and thinner, like spun glass above her mummy-grey scalp.

'Garbage?' she screams.

'Garbage!' I bellow.

She launches from her chair, leaping upward, neck extended, the tender underside of her jaw exposed in a flesh wedge aimed at heaven. Sailing the room, tacking from chair to table to cupboard, hand over hand, she locates her two wastebaskets and the tidy, plastic-wrapped bundle beneath the sink, clutches them to her breast, and turns toward the doorway, searching for me. I step in just far enough to grab the stuff. She opens her arms, letting it all go down to me. This is our Thursday ritual. To complete it, she will nod and turn away silently. I will lug the stuff to the junk closet at the end of the hall, where the big black bags of garbage from the roomers sit. Then I will drag all the bags out to the sidewalk, stacking them in the plastic barrels that sit there all week. That is all. We've done it this way for years. By the time I climb the stairs back to my room, Lil will be resubmerged in her struggle with the magnifying glass and the TV screen. Beyond the chant of 'Garbage' we never speak. But tonight she cracks the mold. She follows me to the door of her room, leans there, waiting as I drag the big sacks past her. As I open the big front door onto the wet night, she calls out, 'Thank you,' in a clear, unbroken voice.

I look back. She is poised, her milk-veiled eyes aimed in my general direction, her head tilted back, listening. 'You're welcome,' I say, and she goes back into her room.

I climb all the way up to Miranda's door and knock. Then I hear a soft male voice laughing inside and turn away. She opens. 'Miss McGurk!' smiling. 'You're sent by fate to try munching Gorgonzola and artichoke-heart salad while listening to ...'

As she tries to pull me in, I try to pull her out into the hall. 'Could I just speak to you for one moment?' She shrugs and steps out, folding her arms, looking down at me with her eyebrows pinched in concentration. 'Something is wrong with Lily.'

Her eyes spring open and she sets to move quickly, 'Is she hurt? Shall I call an ambulance?'

Gratified, I pat her arm, 'No, no. She's acting a little odd.'

Miranda hoots. 'How can you tell?'

'No. She's acting strangely. I can't be here for a bit. I have to work. Could you keep an eye on her? Tonight? Just stroll down and listen for her breathing. You can hear her in the night if you put your ear to her door. She has a heavy sigh in her sleep. And if you can't hear her, or if she sounds strange ...'

Miranda hoists her eyebrows at me in surprise. 'Sure. I'll check on her. I'm not working tonight. Don't worry.'

Nodding and waving, I retreat quickly. She stands looking after me. As I go down the stairs I hear the soft male voice call, 'Miranda?' and then her door shuts quietly.

I stay in my room for a few hours, arranging the papers in the big trunk. At around eleven I hear Miranda on the stairs. Her footsteps pass down to the ground floor and pause for a while at Lily's closed door. Then she goes back up. I find myself smiling as I listen.

I go down myself an hour later. The wheeze and bubble beyond Lil's door is regular and strong. I use the wall phone to call for a cab and wait for it on the front steps.

I sulk all the way back to the tinhorn apartment. I want my own moldy room with its pale stench and its frail, maniac noise. The new building seems lifeless, incapable of decay. Its halls are narrow and pharmaceutically bright. Each floor is the same as all the rest. The only sound is the faint hum of the elevator. The orange carpet from the hall spills under my door, flooding the whole apartment. The rooms are low and square and it feels rented because I refuse to actually live here. In my home the air reeks of dust and jumbled layers of life, and it is dim unless you are right next to a window.

Here the telephone is white and has its own table. Where I live the phone is an ancient black-and-chrome wall box with coin slots and numbers scratched into its paint. It rings often but few people ever use it to call out. It is too exposed there in the grease-brown entryway. Whenever it rings, Lily answers, though it is never for her.

27

NOTES FOR NOW
Getting to Know You
and Your .357 Magnum

What a bouncer she would have made! Shy as an egg, but so disguised. I can't help it. She charms me. To see her hunched over her plastic tray — chin shoved straight at the big screen, her paw pokes a fork in the air, and she laughs, 'Hu-hu-hu,' through her bulging cheeks.

'Smart little shit, I'm tellin' ya!' she says after cleaning her cheeks with a gulp. 'Lookit 'er drive that sucker!'

The young woman on the screen is bent over a complicated hunk of shiny machinery. The driving Miss Lick finds so admirable is a surefingered dial-twiddling and button-tapping.

Miss Lick scoots back in her chair and lunges for another flabby forkful of limp turkey from her compartmentalized supper.

She loves this — carrying our Lickety Split food trays back through the discreet door in the big bathroom to her home-movie theater, perching on straight chairs with the trays on our knees, watching the screen full of Miss Lick's girls. She adores the reruns, and nearly cries at the 'before' footage, angry grieving for the misery of their lives before she rescued them. She is hypnotized by the surgery or treatment flicks, chewing slowly, nudging me with an informative elbow and a nod when a particularly smooth bit of scissor or saw work is goring its way across the screen. Now that she allows me to see these segments, she is anxious to impress me. But her joy is in the work shots of the 'successes.'

'Look at that! Know what she's doing? Reading the rings of rat-assed Saturn! Can you imagine? Six years ago the only rings she knew were for slipping over limp cocks to make 'em rise!'

The young woman in the white coat reaches for the paper that is spewing from a printer. She turns toward us and the light to read. She smiles, a sudden grin of utterly cheerful mischief flashing out of her intense flesh.

I want to ask what it is that she hasn't got anymore. The lab coat hides her chest. Was it breasts? Two new figures appear — a plain woman and a spavined boy, twenty and twenty-one years old. They stand at attention in front of Miss Lick's girl as she speaks.

'Teaching 'em! See that? She's got these fuckers trailing after her!'

Miss Lick's big hand bunches and jabs my thigh sideways in hilarious friendship. 'Eh? Eh?'

My tray flips forward, spewing goo, and she's on her knees choking with apologies as she plucks up the gobs and wipes up the smears. 'Creeping Christ! I'm such a clod! Are you all right? Hey, I'll have a fresh new one for you in thirty seconds flat. Just sit. No, no, I'm going to.'

She tears me up. I sit here laughing at her. She is a galumphing dugong, an elvish ox, a sentimental rhino.

'They're like my kids, all of them.' She sniffs, her thick forehead creasing, anxious that I should understand and approve.

'Did you, no offense now, but did you ever wish you'd had kids? Not the man bit, but the kid bit? No? Well, your're right, I know it. You're right. But you want to make a difference. A person wants to feel as though they've accomplished something.'

She mooches around for my approval. She's a sullen buffalo with the world but she's a child to me. She is bigger than Papa. She could break me with two fingers. But she can be small around me. She can chatter to me though she sticks to brusque efficiency with everybody else. Oh, she is solicitous and protective with her girls, but never childlike. It's because I like her. Arty was right. She soaks it up like booze and it turns her to water, makes her defenseless.

Am I the first person who's ever liked her? It makes me sad. She's pretty lovable, after all. She knows how to enjoy things, and she's so decent it's scary.

There she sits, sprawled in a hard, straight chair, hour after hour. It never occurs to her to drag in a soft chair for herself. She thought about cushions for me, though. Draped my straight chair with towels from the bathroom because one day in the pool she saw red lines on my hump. I'd been leaning on a locker. She never forgot. She always makes sure I'm comfortable.

'So why don't you bring in an armchair for yourself?' I asked her.

'What? Too much trouble. I don't need it. I'm padded.'

She's wearing flannel pajamas and a floppy bathrobe. Her potato feet stick out, the soles jammed against the tile floor, propping her in the chair as she reaches, sorting through the film disks. Her chubby toes sprout, wiggling, from the main tuber.

'Got a new scout flick today.' Her approach to the scouting tapes of potential recruits is different, intense, questioning, critical, analytical, running them again, backing them up to replay a gesture, a frown, a smile.

'This slut tried a one-handed pigeon drop on me. As soon as she discovered this bag, brown paper bag, under her ass on the park bench, I smelled old tuna. She screeches "For heaven's sakes!" I sat there watching the real goddamn pigeons crapping on the lawn, listening to her go on about "Where could all that money have possibly come from?," and then finding a little brown envelope of snapshots. Twelve-year-old sucking a Doberman's dick, and she's miscarrying with righteous indignation and trying to get me to pay attention and all the time I'm thinking, "This is where I've got to at last. I'm looking like a gobbling pigeon, just like all the drooling biddies shuffling on the mall." It makes me bitter. I reached in my wallet and pulled out a hundred. "Now, honey," I says, and I hand it to her, watching her eyes freeze as she shuts up. "You take this so you don't get your ass kicked when you get back to the slimy pimp that runs you. Save us all trouble and time." She starts up protesting, waving this lunch bag of funny money at me. "Believe me, sweetheart," I says, "you're not cut out for this business." I went back to the office and crabbed at people all afternoon. Anyway, I saw her again in the Park Blocks while I had the equipment.'

The frail, colorless girl on the screen is far away and small on a park bench. She sits, twisting her shirttail edgily and looking nervously around. I can't make her face out clearly.

'What do you think?'

I squint through my glasses, trying to see the wispy features. 'Isn't she like an "after" already?'

Miss Lick slaps her knees. 'True enough!'

'I mean,' I try to see the outline of the girl's breasts under her shoddy shirt, 'she's got nothing to sell you.'

'Oly! What do you think I am?' Miss Lick is hurt. 'She could use some schooling and a decent job. Those skinny mice have got nothing. All they can do is latch onto some man or die.'

'I didn't mean . . .'

'Sure. Forget it. Here's the bang-tail filly again. I'll think about that con sharper. Maybe something can be done. The bang-tail has me flummoxed, though.'

I clench my teeth and telescope my head downward between my shoulders. The 'bang-tail' is Miranda. I've already spent hours watching replays of Miranda lounging on the steps of the art school, eating ice-cream as she walks down the street, waving her tail on a velvet-draped stage during one of the Glass House private showings. Here she is again, flirting with her Binewski eyes, stretching her wide Arturan mouth to loll a tongue suggestively around the ice-cream cone, alert to the effect she's having on the guy in the coveralls waiting beside her for the traffic light to change. It screws me up totally to see Miss Lick's films of Miranda.

'What's she about? Hopeless, you think?' Miss Lick is sensitive to my moods. 'Say it, Oly, is she useless?'

'No!' I snap and then wave my hand weakly, trying to soften it.

'I haven't heard a peep out of her in weeks. There's one

month left to her school year. She's supposed to go straight in to surgery the week after the semester ends. But you'd think she'd call. I have a bet with myself that she'll hit me up to double my cash offer. The hell of it is, I don't know if it's worth it. Art types. But I made the offer and I'll stick by my word. She'll do the tail and then we'll see. Thing is, she's made the tail erotic rather than a disfigurement. Maybe I'll stop with that. I'm soft but I'm not nuts. No use wasting money and time and energy on a stupid cow who can't benefit . . .'

'She's not stupid.' It slips out before I could stop it.

'Yeah, she is, but I can never resist . . .'

'Not stupid!' Miss Lick looks at me with her mouth poised for a word, her clever eyes calm on me, waiting. I feel everything slipping away from me, all the care and planning, and volunteer misery. 'I don't know! Don't mind me. I feel sorry for her.'

Miss Lick always melts at 'feeling sorry.' 'Hey, don't I know? Don't I just know precisely?'

'I mean,' I dig my fingertips into my knees for control, 'she's already in school. Where's the percentage?'

'The men like that tail. I could subtract that distraction for her as a start. That's what I had in mind.'

I take a taxi back to my alien apartment, crawl under the bed with two blankets, and huddle there on the orange carpet.

'So the nutso wants to sell me a nine-millimeter full-auto with a clip as long as an elephant's dong and he won't let up. He's revving his tonsils and I'm standing there staring at him, thinking what he'd look like with that clip rammed up his . . .'

Miss Lick is lolling on the fir-needle sponge beneath the trees. She stretches out on her belly, arms stuck out in front of her, hands clasped warmly around what looks like a small gun, just the tip of the barrel showing beyond her puffy knuckles. The thing blaps like a knife in the eye when she squeezes. A dark blotch appears on the sheet of typing paper tacked to the tree fifty feet away. She milks off four shots and then pushes up to her knees and breaks the pistol open, its barrel lifting at the root like a shotgun as she nips the casings out with a sturdy fingernail.

'Hot!' she winces. 'Want to look?'

By the time I reach the shredded target paper, she's reloaded and caught up with me, the ground snapping and hissing under her weight. She flicks the paper scraps away and fingers the yellow splinters that look as though somebody small and very rough had busted out of the old fir. 'Nice tight pattern.' She looks at me for praise.

I nod, though it's too high up for me to see inside the teacup-sized crater. I don't tell her for fear she'll lift me up to look.

'So I walked out,' she continues the tale. 'If the silly sucker had just sold me what I wanted he could have made his money and saved his breath.'

She sticks the gun into the holster under her left arm. I hear a small snap as she buckles the gun nest closed.

'Ready for work?' she claps and grins and reaches for the heavy machete leaning at the foot of the tree.

She gives me thick gloves and I follow her all afternoon as she chops at the saplings and brush and blackberry vines that clog the back acres of 'the homestead' as she calls it.

The big brick house with its turrets and diamond-paned windows sits close to the road, surrounded by civilized green and leased to the regional director of a major computer manufacturer. 'He always invites me to his sociable dos on the terrace, 'says Miss Lick, 'and his wife tries to maroon me in the library with one of the firm's middle-aged bachelors or get me drunk and show me pictures of starving babies to make me blubber before she tells me how much the firm contributes to famine relief. She's inventive, I have to admit. And he's subtle.'

The wooded acreage isn't included in the lease. 'I get my firewood here,' she explains. She just likes it out here. She wears boots and a wide tweed bag of a skirt with her hooded sweatshirt to wallop around in the woods. She calls it 'tending the park' or 'minding the homestead.'

She cuts brush and I drag it out and throw it on a heap that rises and spreads in the small clearing.

She's rambling on about guns. 'I used to carry my old man's .45 but the bastard was built for a hip holster. Barrel was too long to be discreet in a lady's suit. The poor broad that makes my clothes got old suddenly every time I walked through her door. So I got this little bitch of a COP. Stands for Compact Off-duty Police. Fires a .357 Magnum round. Has a rotary hammer like the old Sharps and Brownies. Guy, when I bought it, tried to sell me a little automatic. Told me a lady needed more than four shots. I says to him. Well, if I shoot some sonofabitch I'm not gonna miss, ya know. And he shuts up like a bank on Sunday. I think it's a cute gun. I like those four big barrels looking down on anybody who'd give me a hard time. Little gun, big bite. Always liked a .45 though. Cut my teeth on them because my dad always had them. He taught me to shoot.'

She talks and swings the heavy blade, tearing the cuttings away with her gloved left hand and pushing them behind her to where I plod.

Thomas R. Lick seems to have been the only man in her life. Her tongue is modeled on his. Without ever having known him or heard him speak, I know she mimics him. She moves like him. She looks like him. Her politics and prejudices and pride are almost certainly his. And I look like Arty.

I am thinking about Arty and throwing an armload of spider-and-scratch onto the heap when she hollers, 'Hey! Shit-for-brains!' in her jollying-the-help tone. 'Boss is gone! Break time!' She comes red-faced from the dark of the trees. I sit down, suddenly nauseated.

'Hey! Don't faint.' She is patting me clumsily, smoothing my hump, pressing my head down so my wig slides to my glasses. I start giggling helplessly and bat at her to get free. 'I'm all right.'

'You were pink and sweaty and then boom, your face was ...'

Laughing, I flop back on the heap so I can look up at her. 'I had a brother who used to call me shit-for-brains.'

She grabs at the ancient wheelbarrow that lugs the tools and drags it toward me. 'Brother? That's something. Is he dead? You never mention family. Kind of figured you for an orphan. Born of joy and mirth, like. Something like that.'

She's reaching under my arms to lift me like a child. I hate having her lift me. She does it too easily. She folds me up tidily in the wheelbarrow and I lean back, trying not to be angry. Her chin stretches like the prow of a Buick as she shakes her head. 'Hang on for the ride!' and she runs, trundling me and the barrow, the branches whipping the sky above her and her pink and blinking face grinning like the hilarious moon, all the way to her car.

'If I could think of a way to seal her asshole, I'd do it. And maybe stitch her mouth shut and feed her with a tube going in under her chin.' Miss Lick is half-joking in the elevator. Her hands are shoved flat into the pockets of her suit jacket and she rocks back on the thick heels of her crocodile shoes and rolls a chuckle at the mirror-bronze ceiling of the rising cubicle. 'You'll see what I mean. This little broad hasn't a hair left, bald as you are. A double mastectomy. And she's still got that sex thing. If I let her walk from her room to the can, three men would climb out of the light sockets on the way and find holes in her to cram their dicks into.'

The elevator stops and the door sighs open. Miss Lick lowers her voice and mutters down at me, 'I've been thinking testosterone. You'll see what I mean.' A silvery grandma-nurse passes us in the hall, nodding her little grey bun and her perky white cap and twinkling, 'Good afternoon, Miss Lick!' with only a slight hesitation in her smile for me.

We are visiting Miss Lick's latest, a nineteen-year-old gymnast with a bent for engineering and a yen to get into the space program. Miss Lick likes the idea of producing an astronaut but is hampered in her efforts by the requirements of the work. 'She's got to be physically functional all the way. It's a nuisance.'

Jessica H. is in Miss Lick's favorite nursing home, recuperating from the relatively minor surgery that closed her vagina and removed her clitoris. The girl has pushed her sheets off and is languidly stroking her firm, golden belly with one finger. The bandages look like a diaper. Her chest is blank and nippleless but the scars are almost invisible.

'Jessica!' booms Miss Lick from the doorway. The girl's smooth, oval head turns casually on the pillow and she looks at us with long, oval eyes, the lids as hairless as sea shells. Then her lush, wide mouth opens slightly in a smile and she is looking at me as Miss Lick bustles with the flowers and rumbles awkwardly, 'Want you to meet Miss McGurk. Olympia McGurk. A good pal of mine.'

The girl is smiling gently with cheekbones that could cut your throat and a nose and chin from some old painting that I can't quite remember. While this face is delicately smiling, the long throat and the flat muscular chest and the round shoulders begin to shake with laughter. With this laugh still going she says to me, 'How much did she pay you? A few million, I hope!'

28

NOTES FOR NOW
One for the Road

Miss Lick watches me surface and blow. She grins as I scrabble for the guttered side of the pool. 'It's amazing that you and I are so much alike, isn't it?' I kick off on my back, paddling away from her, grinning.

She's right. We each appear totally alone in our lives. I'm the shy, isolated dwarf creeping in and out of my shabby room, living only through my throat and my inherited work. She is the muscular monolith, cut off by brass, stalking around in her old man's ambition, too imposing in finance and physique for the regular commerce of talk and touch. We choose to seem barren, loveless orphans. We each have a secret family. Miss Lick has her darlings and I have mine. All we've really lacked is someone to tell. Now she tells me, and I tell all to these bland, indifferent sheets of paper. The only point where our narrow tracks converge is her bid to turn my darling into one of hers.

Does she lie to me? She keeps things from me. She wouldn't let me watch the surgery or treatment sections of her home movies for a long time. Does she keep more aside? Hide more of herself? Horrors she doesn't trust me with? Titillations she is ashamed of? I sail along thinking she is perfectly open. Her eyes are as wide as a child's when she talks to me. But maybe I'm the fool. Maybe lying so constantly has burnt my view. Believing that she is fooled, I consider her too simple to lie.

We are alone in the pool. The lifeguard has gone for the night, trusting Miss Lick to lock up. Miss Lick sits on the side, her huge legs drooping into the water. She shudders as I stop to breathe at her end.

'Do you ever,' her eyes circle the echoing green of the big room, 'do you ever get the feeling somebody's watching us?'

My head swivels, searching automatically, though I know that the watcher is me. 'You're just tired and spooky. You need your supper.'

She shrugs it off. Forgets. But does she really know? Is she playing me while I play her?

It rains every night now and the air is soft in the morning. Almost warm. A faint haze, not quite green, softens the iron branches of the trees. Miranda's anatomy drawings are finished. She has mounted them on cardboard and she stores them in a huge plastic binder.

'I want you to look at them.'

'I can't.'

'All this time you've never looked.'

'Just not at the ones of me. I don't want to see myself.'

'You look in mirrors. I'm better than any goddamned mirror.'

'It's not your work. I like your other drawings. This just scares me.'

'I take it personally. This is my best work. The best I've ever done. I don't see you as ugly. I see you as unique and wonderful.'

'It's hard dealing with you seeing me at all.'

'Miss-fucking-steerious! I'm handing the whole mess in tomorrow morning. The competition results will come out in two weeks, the day before I go into the hospital.'

'Hospital.'

'Or whatever. I don't know where Miss Lick has that work done.'

'I have to get back to work now.'

'The semester ends Friday.'

'Thank you so much for the tea.'

'I'm calling Miss Lick today to arrange things.'

'See you soon.'

'I may not come back here afterward.'

I trotted down the hall with her leaning out of her doorway to talk to my back.

'I'll be in a nursing home for a while and then I'll probably move away.'

I'm not even tempted to anger. Time is a rap on the ear with a brass knuckle. I've been letting it ride. Having my little cake — chummy with Miranda over tea, chummy with Miss Lick over home movies — snuggling down in a thick-headed fantasy that what little I was doing would make the difference, as if putting across the lie was success. All I had to do was accept mild discomfort in a strange room, sneak up the fire escape to visit Lily and Miranda, and this puny martyrdom would miraculously obliterate the problem.

The next morning I get to the club an hour before the lifeguard arrives and use the key Miss Lick has given me to get into the pool locker room. I lug two gallon jugs of concentrated ammonia in a shopping bag into the dressing room, stack the plastic bottles in my locker, and cover them with the bag.

The door from the locker room into the footbath is solid wood hung in a steel frame. The auger is an ancient handcrank from the landlord's tool kit in Lily's basement. On my knees on the cold tiles I open the door slightly to slide a single sheet of the *Oregonian* underneath. The door swings shut, leaving half the paper on each side to catch the wood dust. I drill the hole under the lowest hinge and within a quarter inch of the frame. The bigger bit enlarges the hole to a one-inch notch in the door's edge. I wrap the dust in the paper, ready to carry away with the auger.

The clear plastic tubing slides easily through the hole. On the footbath side of the door a few inches of tubing droop toward the chlorine reek of the blue surface. I bend to suck air through it. The tube is clear, not pinched by the door closing. With the tube gone the hole is in the dark below the hinge, hardly visible unless you are on your hands and knees.

I work the narrow end of the funnel into the end of the tube, coil the arrangement tidily, and tuck it under the bag in my locker. As I walk out through the big glass doors in the front lobby I see the glossy young lifeguard putting her bicycle into a stanchion.

Miss Olympia Binewski McGurk, the albino dwarf, takes two steps to the average one because her mystic breastbone has spent thirty-eight years trying to increase its distance from her agnostic spine. Those two steps carry our Miss Oly, the hunchback, into the tidal stench of corned beef and cabbage filling the dim cove of McLarnin's at ten o'clock on a Tuesday morning when Jimmy McL. himself is steaming the wherewithal for the famous eleven-to-four buffet. The bar is clean. The glasses wait, glittering in their racks.

Miss Oly hoists her twisted frame onto the least spinnable bar stool and nods encouragingly at Jimmy. The mirror is obscured by bottlenecks, leaving shards in which Miss Oly catches a flicker of her blue-tinted spectacles and goat-grey wig bobbing over the waxy wood. Her big, soft voice is deeper than the tenor McLarnin's.

'A shot of Jameson's please, Jimmy,' she says, and McL. sways toward her, wrapped in cabbage mist from the kettles and flapping a bar towel in front of his red knob nose to clear the view.

'Celebrating, are we?' gurgles Jimmy in sympathy with the tall, tipping bottle.

'You too?' asks Miss Oly, squinting her rose-pink eyes behind the sapphire lenses.

'Thank you,' McL. deliberately misunderstands. 'I'll stick with Murphy's though. I was weaned on it.'

'Is that so?' Miss Oly would like to know.

Jimmy gives a slow, thoughtful swipe at the bar with his towel and raises his crisp white eyebrows. 'True enough. I was colicky as a babe and my mother'd send me off to sleep with a rag-tit tied up in thread and soaked in Murphy to suck on. She swore by it for a whole night's rest.'

'I was thirty-eight years old,' muses Miss Oly, 'before I ever felt the burn of whiskey on my lip. But I knew it right away for what it was.'

'The virgin's arms,' nods Jimmy. 'God's breath.'

'I am amazed at all the years I spent without whiskey,' says Oly.

'Just as well. It takes a lady of a certain age to contain the stuff. Particularly the Irish. No offense but a bit of weathering and experience are required not to go right off the edge with it. I would hesitate to serve Irish to a green schoolgirl. Mixes and vodka are enough for them to go wrong on. I couldn't look at myself shaving if I poured Irish for the young.'

'Don't tell me you look?'

The diplomat McLarnin senses a delicacy about mirrors in Miss Oly, and deftly switches his bulk to block her exposure to the jolt of her own image reflected in shreds behind the bar bottles.

'You've a voice like mulled toddy, Miss O,' grins Jimmy. 'I cried like a busted banker at your story on the radio this morning.'

'Hush,' grunts Oly, ducking a peek into the empty darkness behind her. 'The Story Lady of Station KBNK isn't supposed to be boozing at ten A.M. Today's show was an old tape. I called in sick. Besides, McLarnin, I have the voice of a baritone kazoo and your real name is Nelson. You were born in Nebraska. Admit it.'

'You're bitter this morning, Miss O. And it leads you to grievous error. I was born up the street at Good Sam, fifty-six years ago, and I've lived in the sound of its sirens ever since. Not unlike yourself, I imagine.'

'I was born in a trailer. No idea where it was parked at the time. But I was conceived here.'

At 5:30 I am sitting on the windowsill of a deserted conference room on the fourth floor of the TAC Club, watching the circle drive inside the entrance gates. Miss Lick's sedan blows in on time and the lackey in the club uniform opens her door for her. He takes her keys and tools the car out to her private parking space as she heads for the entrance. I get down off the sill and settle into an armchair to watch the wall clock.

I can feel her in the building. With my eyes closed I can see her crossing the lobby, nodding to the woman at the reception desk, clumping down the carpeted corridor to the elevator. I know exactly how she will stare at the elevator door, waiting for it to open, with her big hands folded in front of her to prevent fidgeting.

Usually I am in the locker room when she walks in. Today her face — ready to smile as she pushes through the door — will lift in puzzlement. She will skin down and get into her tank suit wondering about me. I can almost hear her splashing into the footbath and feel the air move as the locker door hisses closed behind her. I can smell her heat mingling with the metallic green fumes of the chlorine in the unventilated cubicle.

There is no bulb in the ceiling fixture of the footbath. The only light is the grey murk that comes through the small diamond-shaped window in the door to the pool. She will be standing there, ankle-deep in chlorine water, peering through the thick, wire-reinforced glass. She will be searching the pool for me.

She stands, rotating her big shoulders, her elbows flapping like wings. She bends, hiking a foot out of the blue water, running her fingers between her toes, trading feet for the same ritual.

Planting both feet in the soup again she takes the plastic quart jar of chlorine from its niche in the tiled wall, opens it, and, ignoring the measuring scoop, sprinkles a goodly pinch of the sea-green crystals over the surface of the water.

The plan is simple. She is always the last one out of the pool. The lifeguard locks up and leaves as Miss Lick begins her second mile of laps. The respected Miss Lick has her own keys and can come in to swim at 3 A.M. if she wants to. She can certainly swim alone with her dwarf pal and lock up behind herself.

I, pale thing, always climb out before Miss Lick, and have showered and dressed before her pork palms slap the pool deck to hoist her out. Sitting on the bench in the locker room. I can always hear her sighing and swishing for long peaceful minutes in the footbath before she comes in to scour herself under the shower. Miss Lick never gets enough of that chlorine footbath.

There is plenty of time to empty the full chlorine jar into the water of the footbath. It's simple to close the footbath door to the locker room and turn its deadbolt, and then slip out to the corridor and down to the hall door opening onto the pool.

I stand, silent, behind the tall stack of paddleboards until Miss Lick emerges from the pool, cascading water, and stomps over to the footbath door. As the door wheezes closed behind her I am there to twist the deadbolt.

The monster is caught in the closet with her eyes stinging in the rising chlorine. She is pounding the sides of her fists on the door to the locker room as I scuttle for the hall, run the few silent yards to the other entrance, and gasp my way in with my heart screaming hide-and-seek in my ears.

Her pounding fills the room. I race to my locker, scatter it empty, an ammonia jug in each hand, dragging toward that little hole in the door.

'Oly!' she bellows beyond the wood slab. The name freezes my lungs. The skin all over my body rises in pimples of fear.

'Oly! Are you all right?'

Now she is pounding on the poolside door. The drum wave moves away from me as I shove the tip of the hose into the hole. The stink of chlorine is strong from the small hole and my eyes water from bending close to it.

'Ahoy!' she roars at the far door. The pounding wood is like the beat of fists on my spine. With the jug under one arm, I carefully pour ammonia down the mouth of the funnel, watch it sear downward through the clear plastic tubing and rush through the door, toward its mingling with the chlorine and a new toxic identity.

'Ahoy! Ahoy!' Mary Lick would never yell 'Help!'

A bubble of hysteria giggles up through me, rocking the jug tucked under my arm. A smack of ammonia fume hits my nose and the roof of my open mouth, burning. I turn my head, gasping. Almost spilling.

I hear splashes beyond the wood, and the pounding rips out again above my head. 'Oly! Oly! Oly!' she screams. Her voice is harsh and ragged now. The ammonia jug is nearly empty. It's taking too long. The pounding stops. In the silence I can hear the faint trickle of the last ammonia running out of the tube and into the chlorine water on the other side. A weight hits the door, inches away from me, and slides, squeaking downward. Silence. Then the whisper. 'What the fuck?' The words rush out of the funnel into my face with a strange sick breath that sets me coughing. She's found the tube. The funnel jerks from my hands, whips wildly through the air, smacks the wall, hops and twists on the floor. The funnel's open mouth shrieks, 'What the fuck?' in a whisper. The end of the tubing spurts out of the hole beneath the hinge. The tube and the funnel fall dead to the floor. The whisper comes from the hole, 'Daddy?' as I scramble away from the hole on my knees, coughing as the whisper comes again. I choke and hold my breath to hear as the hole says, 'Please ... Please.'

I know her locker combination. Scuttling for the lock I can hear the hiss of the whisper but I can't make out the words that press themselves through the hole. The dial sticks and clogs and I can hardly see through my tears. I miss and try again, with a high whine coming out of my own throat. The lock falls to the floor.

The holster is under her suit jacket, on the hook. I yank a bench close and climb to reach the gun. Jump back to the door on tiptoes with the fat gun heavy in one hand. I reach for the knob to twist open the deadbolt and dodge as the door gushes open against me. The gas comes out and I choke and fall to my knees with fire in my eyes and a rake in my nose and throat.

She is huge, lying across the doorway. Her breath sounds high and it bubbles. Her white arms have tumbled over her red bloated face. She moans, a small sound from the wet heap of her chest. I drop the gun and pull her long arm by its wrist, crying, 'Mary! Help me. Mary, move. Come on, Mary. Oh, Mary, I'm so sorry.' And I am sorry and I don't care if she wakes and kills me if only she will wake up and move. I never meant this. I never wanted to hurt her. I only needed for her to die. Not this pain. Not this fear.

'Mary!' I yell, yanking on the heavy arm. 'I didn't mean it like this.'

Miss Lick's eyes pop open, staring upside-down and furious. Her wrist flicks loose from my hands, swatting me, groping for me as I fall clattering against the forgotten gun on the floor. Her hand snaps onto my throat, hot and hard. A white light comes on behind my eyes as she lifts me above her with my right hand fluttering at her fingers on my throat and my left hand heavy with the gun. I am rising, until my ears explode and I begin a long, slow fall at the end of her arm, toward the tile floor, watching the sudden black hole where her right eye was, her big legs flopping in the footbath and the sputtering roll at the crotch of her tank suit as a dark liquid runs onto the tile. Her hand is still huge on my throat, but she's gone. I'm alone.

News article from the May 18 Portland *Oregonian*:

Two women whose bodies were found huddled in the footbath of the Thomas R. Lick indoor swimming pavilion of the Timber Athletic Club following a hazardous fume alarm this morning were apparently victims of murder and suicide. Portland Police Detective M.L. Zusman, directing the onsite investigation, told reporters that both women had apparently died of gunshot wounds and that a gun had been found at the scene. The exact cause of the deaths will not be confirmed until the completion of post-mortem examinations by the Multnomah County Medical Examiner.

Investigation at the scene was delayed by the presence of irritating fumes from an unidentified gas present in the pool and locker-room area. The gas is currently undergoing laboratory analysis for identification. Fumes were first noticed by a janitor who entered the pool area for regularly scheduled cleaning at 8 A.M. Firefighters who responded to the alarm discovered the two bodies.

'At first we didn't know who did what to who,' said Detective Zusman. 'But a note was found on the scene. Or rather a notebook which seems to give an account of the incident up to a certain point.' Contents of the note have not been revealed. The names of the victims are being withheld pending notification of their families. It is not known whether the victims were members of the prestigious private athletic and social club. TAC spokesmen refused to discuss the incident until more information is available. The Lick Pavilion will be closed until the police investigation is completed.

Earlier reports that one of the bodies was that of a handicapped child have since been contradicted. Police confirm that both victims were adults.

Delivered by regular mail, May 19:

My dear Miranda,

Since you were a year old you've been told you were an orphan. This was not true. Your father died when you were very young but I, your mother, have been watching over you until now. I am your mother, I, the dwarf in Room #21.

Your name is not Miranda Barker but Miranda Binewski. Barker was the ironic label chosen by the Reverend Mother Aurora when you were still in diapers and first entered the convent school.

You will have a lot of questions. Enclosed are two keys. The long key is to my room, #21. On the floor in the closet is a big leather trunk. The short key will open the trunk. The top tray inside is full of your school records, photographs, sixteen years' worth of letters from Reverend Mother Aurora and Sister Lucy. They're addressed to me and they report on you. That should be enough to convince you that I'm not imagining our relationship out of drugs or lunacy.

The big manila envelope in the top tray of the trunk contains the deed and tax records for the house and all my financial papers. The deed is in your name. You can withdraw from, or write checks on, the trust account. You will also find the papers for the vault where all the other Binewskis currently rest. Please note that cremation is a family tradition. Beneath the tray is all the record there is of my history and yours.

Please take care of Crystal Lil. Her medical records and prescriptions are in the white folder in the big envelope. The trash goes out on Thursday nights and her bills need to be paid on the fifth of each month. She is your grandmother.

After twenty careful years of not revealing myself to you, I find it hard to reverse the process. For all you lacked in a parent, I hope you can eventually forgive me. I can't be sure what the trunk will mean to you, or the news that you aren't alone, that you are one of us. Yet I hope that someday you'll come to collect us all from the shelves of the vault. Take down Arty and Chick and Papa and the twins, and all that's left of the Jar Kin, and, by then, Lily and me. Open our metal jars and pour all the Binewski dust together into that big battered loving cup that first held only Grandpa B. Bolt us to the hood of your traveling machine and take us on the road again.

                                    With love,
                                    Olympia Binewski
                                    (Known as McGurk)